ANOTHER CHANCE

Tales of South Philadelphia

ANOTHER CHANCE

A Novel

Dominic T. Biello

iUniverse, Inc.

New York Lincoln Shanghai

Another Chance
Tales of South Philadelphia

iUniverse books may be ordered through booksellers or by contacting:

iUniverse
2021 Pine Lake Road, Suite 100
Lincoln, NE 68512
www.iuniverse.com
1-800-Authors (1-800-288-4677)

credit cover graphic as follows: Joseph Sohm/Visions of America/Getty Images

This is a work of fiction. All of the characters, names, incidents, organizations, and dialogue in this novel are either the products of the author's imagination or are used fictitiously.

ISBN-13: 978-0-595-40612-8 (pbk)
ISBN-13: 978-0-595-84978-9 (ebk)
ISBN-10: 0-595-40612-2 (pbk)
ISBN-10: 0-595-84978-4 (ebk)

Printed in the United States of America

"A Turtle for Margaret"

ACKNOWLEDGEMENT

Without the loving support of my wife, Peggy, this creative endeavor would still be sitting in a box in my garage. Her belief in my ability and her input and editing has made this project a reality.

Special thanks are owed my friends Cal Burgart, Dan Ferris, Rit Yongchindarat, Dave Nyman and my Aunt Grace for their positive support and encouragement. I also want to thank Gunnar Loy for his insightful advice and for keeping me honest.

I especially appreciate my good friends Ralph Masci and George Berardinucci for staying in touch with me all these years. Your stories and insights were extremely valuable.

Finally, for my daughter Dominique I have these words—*follow your passion.* It's the foundation of life.

INTRODUCTION

Present day Philadelphia can trace its history back to the Swedish settlements established along the Delaware River in 1647. The Dutch seized the land eight years later only to have it taken away by the English in 1664. In 1681, on the land first settled by the Swedes, William Penn founded Philadelphia, "The City of Brotherly Love."

In 1762, Southwark, the oldest district in the county of Philadelphia was formed by an Act of the General Assembly from parts of the original Swedish settlements of Moyamensing and Wicaco. In later years the remaining portion of the Moyamensing tract plus a 1,000-acre parcel of land called Passyunk became townships. The north and south streets continued per Penn's original grid layout of the city while the east and west streets deviated according to already established trails.

Southwark, Moyamensing and Passyunk were consolidated into the city in 1854. The consolidation of these three areas came to be known as South Philadelphia.

During the ensuing years waves of Irish, Polish, Jewish and Italian immigrants seeking to start a new life began arriving at the port of entry on the Delaware River. Unfamiliar to the ways of this foreign land, they bound together in ethnic neighborhoods in order to keep alive the traditions and mores of their former lives. Eventually, the city grid, first imagined by William Penn, began resembling a multi-cultural patchwork.

This story is merely one of the thousands of threads interwoven throughout that patchwork of neighborhoods that sewn together makes up a cultural quilt known as South Philadelphia.

PROLOGUE

Friday, September 1, 1939

South Philadelphia was Little Joey Giampietro's home. The Italian Market on Ninth Street was his playground and grammar school. Everything that he would ever need to know about life, he learned here.

The dickering black-clad widows squawking in their regional Italian dialects, the loudmouthed hucksters hawking their produce, the gamy chicken pluckers, the bloodstained butchers and the squat old Italian men smoking their rancid stogies were Little Joey's muses glibly counseling him on the mundane world of the straight and narrow. The young scoundrels of the shadows, some gnarly street-wise hoodlums, a nimble-fingered pickpocket and a few ne'er-do-wells were his mentors luring him down the dark alluring alleys of vice.

These external influences paled in comparison to what emerged from his psyche today. On the threshold of adolescence, a mysterious power tantalized Little Joey's jumbled mind. Coursing through his veins like the venom from a snakebite, this enigmatic sensation forcefully emerged to mix with the poisonous ingredients of his suppressed emotions—his mother's sudden abandonment and his secret aversion to being placed in the Teti household. This emotional mixture melded into an insidious toxin. Its by-products, confusion, anger and distress subtly contaminated his vulnerable pubescent mind.

Whereas Sal Teti was the catalyst for this poisonous brew stewing in Little Joey's mind, his daughter Rose was the antidote. She filled the void of nurturing love that Little Joey desperately craved after the Teti family adopted him. Treating him like the brother that she never had, Little Joey misinterpreted this affection. His obsessive fixation on Rose blurred the lines delineating passion and sisterly love.

Occasionally, however, she reminded Little Joey of his mother. Rose's bouncy step and chestnut brown hair would inadvertently shift his focus to the transgression of his mother's affections. During these moments, he subconsciously blamed himself for her sudden, unexplainable abandonment. He always fought to repress this self-recriminating thought. A few times, he lost the battle. Slipping into a vertigo-like funk, feelings of shame and cowardice would swell up inside of him. Powerless in the face of its onslaught, these feelings paralyzed him. With labored breaths his eyes would loose their focus as his fuzzy mind tried to zero in on the one murky image of that life-shattering moment. Then, like smoke wisping from a chimney, it disappeared leaving the fetid odor of the loathsome Sal Teti lingering in his nostrils.

Instinctively, he muted his revulsion for Sal Teti because he secretly adored his daughter Rose. Unable to adequately control or even verbalize his escalating feelings, Little Joey took the voyeuristic approach following her whenever these emotional inclinations arose.

On this particular Friday from across Ninth Street amid the maze of street carts lining this bustling thoroughfare, he stalked Rose Teti with aching anticipation. Never losing sight of her, Little Joey fell into the rhythmic pace of the shuffling pedestrians—stopping, scrutinizing then scowlingly moving along. He observed Rose's every movement with tantalizing fascination until he could replay it in his mind at will.

Later that night, alone in his dank room above the Downtown Bar & Grill, Little Joey fantasized about the day's events. In the recesses of his mind, the omniscient ghost of his mother seduced him into her ethereal brothel offering him Rose Teti as a virtual surrogate. Once again, the puzzling sensation arose. Slowly coursing through his body, a nascent ache in his groins erupted. At that moment, the familiar creak of Rose's bedroom door broke the musty silence enshrouding him. Leaping from his bed to the door, he cracked it open to catch Rose's naked body dash into the only bathroom in the house.

Moments later she dashed out, and then abruptly stopped. "What's the matter with you?" Rose quizzed noticing Little Joey's puppy-like demeanor and searching stare.

In front of her bedroom door, Little Joey stood gawking with a full erection desperately seeking to escape from his pajamas. An uneasy moment ensued. Words formed on his dry lips, but he could only utter a faint hissing sound from his cottony mouth.

Rose recoiled as she looked down. Pointing at the protrusion, she was unable to contain her amusement. "What's that thing? A mouse?" The flimsy towel enveloping her slid down teasingly as Rose let out a whimsical gasp. "A little mouse, a Mickey Mouse," she boisterously chortled. The ensuing bursts of loud, uncontrollable, belittling laughter alerted her inebriated gangster of a father sequestered in a room down the hall.

Speechless and shaking with embarrassment, a misunderstood and impressionable Little Joey quickly tightened his body while squeezing his legs together in an attempt to hide the object of Rose's derisive laughter.

Pouring out of his room, Sal Teti immediately understood what was happening. His face contorted into an aura of viciousness. "You perverted little shit," he hellishly yelled, "the apple don't fall far from the tree." Teti spontaneously smacked Little Joey across his face, sending him crashing onto the floor with a loud thud. Kicking him wickedly, Teti whipped off his belt screaming, "Get into your goddamn room, you little pervert!" Teti booted Little Joey toward the door then followed him into the room wildly.

Tonight Little Joey's hatred of the Teti family would forever be branded on his soul.

1

Casually leaning back against a railing with his bent elbows resting on the weathered handrail, Joey "the Gimp" Giampietro surveyed the tired skyline of the deteriorating hotels lining the Boardwalk in Atlantic City. Once the "Queen of the Resorts," Atlantic City was desperately in need of salvation.

Gambling was coming to this town the Gimp thought insightfully. He could smell it in the cold salty air whipping in off the crashing waves of the Atlantic Ocean behind him. It had to. This town couldn't last much longer without it.

The Gimp, a fortyish capo in the Vecchio Crime Family of Philadelphia, deliberately allowed his prophetic speculations to dissipate into the cold night air. For the moment he sought a respite from the persistent struggle within his troublesome soul. Choosing to wallow in the serenity of the dark emptiness surrounding him, he found it womblike in a surrealistic way.

Dressed in a suit and tie under a full-length brown leather coat, the Gimp wore a matching brown felt fedora hat. Bending the lower part of his leg back, he rested the right heel of his soft brown-leathered Gucci shoe on the bottom rung of the railing. Without changing positions, the Gimp glanced at his wristwatch. He was early. Unmoved by any urgency, he continued enjoying the moment. A few lone board walkers shuffling to and fro fixated his attention. The smooth rhythm of their movement had a trancelike effect on him. It evoked good memories, or at least his version of them.

He had come a long way since his father and mother first introduced him to this place. The memories of that special day with his parents slowly flooded his mind. His first and only big adventure was driving down the White Horse Pike in an old black Ford Model T jalopy while slavishly lapping a chocolate ice cream cone. The country was in the midst of the Great Depression. Times were tough. Still, his father spared no expense.

The Gimp's chubby face became childishly animated. Without moving, he closed his dark brown eyes. Inhaling a large helping of cold salty air, he exhaled it slowly.

That day with his parents in the summer of 1934 was the only time that he could remember feeling truly loved. It was his fondest memory. His father playfully hoisting him onto his shoulders at the beach, his mother fussing over him all the way from Philadelphia succored him on many a cold wretched night in the prison cell of his youthful mind.

Her maternal intonations of guidance on that day replayed in his head randomly throughout the ensuing years. During those years the indirect power of her myopic message secretly grew while gradually masking its source. In this way she unknowingly became his personal oracle.

Then, unexpectedly, a man bundled in a tattered Navy Pea Coat laboriously pedaled an empty wicker-rolling chair past him. Its clanging chain and squeaking pedals broke the spell leaving his fragile psyche momentarily vulnerable. Surreptitiously, the other memories, dark, foreboding memories of his youth, seeped into his mind. Without warning, his animated smile flat-lined. The emotional angst of the gruesome front-page newspaper photos of his father, the disdainful newspaper articles and his mother's bewildering desertion tightened the muscles in his throat making it hard for him to swallow. Out of the blue, the floodgates burst open. Surging through his mind, this tsunami of onerous memories drenched him with its unfettered emotional ferocity forcing him to come face to face with the one traumatic moment of truth that forever haunted him. Clenching his teeth and eyes tightly, the Gimp's sweat-beaded face became contorted in agonizing resistance to this repugnant memory when luckily a familiar voice, a vibrant voice from his recent past, broke the unholy grip on his calamitous mental meanderings.

"Joey? Joey? You okay?" The voice materialized into Johnny "Gaga" Bellino, a capo from the New York Mafia crime family of Tony Manfredi and a former associate of the Gimp.

Bellino, a larger than life character, possessed a legendary volatile personality. His ambitions were boundless. Unsatisfied with his place on the evolutionary scale of criminality, he desperately wanted to move up—and fast. Both men had cemented their places in their respective organizations during the sixties while working as a team for their respective bosses. Their nefarious deeds cemented a personal relationship that a conspiratorial meeting like this one necessitated.

The Gimp's corrugated facial muscles relaxed. Hastily opening his eyes, he produced a white linen handkerchief to pat dry the beads of sweat on his furrowed forehead. To the Gimp's dismay these agonizing episodes were occurring more frequently in recent weeks. "I'm fine Johnny. I'm fine. How ya doin'?" the Gimp inquired trying to deflect the subject of his agony.

"Things could always be better." A long pause ensued. Oblivious to the noise of creaking wooden planks caused by the jittery motion of his feet, Bellino eyed the Gimp appraisingly with a sideward glance. Tugging the collar of his dark blue overcoat up around his neck, he put his hands into his coat's pockets. "Boy, it's cold here." Although he was known to be rash and impetuous, even crazy at times, Bellino was having difficulty broaching the reason for their meeting.

"This meet was your call," the Gimp groused still warm from his heightened emotional state.

The gusty wind was unable to displace a single strand from the heavily greased mane of Bellino's pitch-black hair. "Know why I asked you here?" Bellino asked shivering.

"Nah. Enlighten me," the Gimp replied in a tone tinged with sarcasm.

"Gambling, Joey. It's gotta come to this place. Look around. The people of this god-forsaken town want it. Every fuckin' gambler up and down the East Coast wants it. And the state of New Jersey needs it." Bellino skipped a beat to catch his breath. "There's a fortune to be made here in the coming years for guys like you and me, Joey. But we're gettin' shafted up the ying yang. People like you and me are only gonna get the crumbs. Know what I mean?" Bellino said expressively with hand and head motions accentuating keywords while his suspicious beady eyes darted in and out of the shadows of the darkened buildings along the Boardwalk.

"Is dat what you brought me down here to say?" an irritated Gimp asked making a quizzical facial expression before continuing in a forceful tone. "Big fish eat little fish. Dat's our business, Johnny. Capisce?"

"I don't know 'bout you Joey, but I'm tired of being a little fish. I want to be that big fish. Get my drift?" Taking a deep breath to release his anxiety, a cagey Bellino continued, "This is the deal. You and me, we take care of business. Watch each other's backs and share the profits." Pointedly shaking his index finger downward, he emphatically continued, "The time is now, Joey. Next year maybe it'll be too late. We gotta move on this now!"

Bobbing his head in vacillation, the Gimp pursed his lips then responded, "What about Manfredi and the Old Man?"

With a wry snort of derision Bellino answered. "Ain't you been listenin'? That's what I been talkin' about." Thrusting in front of the Gimp the makeshift image of a gun using his outstretched thumb and index finger, Bellino continued, "You gotta do what you gotta do. We both line up support. You take care of your boy. I'll take care of mine."

Rubbing his chin with a judicious look, the Gimp remained quiet for a long moment. The Old Man, Giuseppe Vecchio, had treated him like a son. It was true that he could be a little more generous, maybe a lot more generous.

Bellino sensed some hesitancy in the Gimp's face. He had laid his cards on the table. There was no turning back. The Gimp should know that, Bellino thought as he watched him suspiciously.

The Gimp eyed Bellino with a measured glance while weighing his options. There wasn't any compunction on his part about completing his end of the arrangement. He viewed it as an inevitable part of criminal evolution. It was the timetable that bothered him. Since that was only a minor inconvenience, the Gimp nodded his head agreeably. "Okay."

When he uttered that single word the Gimp's eyes rolled slightly in his head, as the elusive voice echoing in his head lately seemed to whisper a vague warning, *"Be careful Joey. Don't let other boys get you into trouble."*

Unnoticed by Bellino, the Gimp slightly shook his head with a befuddling glance trying to dispel the reverberating voice. Finally succeeding, he continued cautiously, "I'm wit you all the way Johnny, but what about the other Dons?"

"Don't worry, one guy's already in the bag. The others are all fat and happy. They won't give us any trouble. Manfredi and Vecchio go back to before Luciano. They're the last of the self-righteous mustache Petes. I don't know how they lasted this long. Nobody gives a fuck whether they live or die. These days it's all about the money." After a reflective moment, Bellino's hyperactive eyes looked around like he was about to impart a secret and continued, "They got three measures coming up for a vote in the New Jersey Assembly this year. We need to get crackin'. You're key to this Joey. I can't pull this off alone." Bellino made a point of his last statement with burrowing eyes and a tightly clenched fist with the index finger pointing unwaveringly at the Gimp.

Making his final pitch with a clear and commanding gaze, Bellino spoke compellingly. "They're old farts Joey. They're past their prime." Oscillating his outstretched hand between them, he made his closing pitch, "Guys like you and me are the future."

The Gimp seemed oddly distracted, but nodded in agreement. "Okay, okay, I'm in. But here's the thing. I need to clean up some shit. Get all my ducks in a row before I do this dirty deed. Give me till after Easter, six maybe seven weeks. Deal?"

Bellino looked the Gimp in the eye searching for signs of duplicity. What he saw instead confused him. The Gimp's eyes were like a hollow void with glossy wraithlike pupils dancing around. There was no treachery in them. They were cold and empty. He could not see the simmering vengeance roiling the Gimp's sedimentary soul. Bellino extended his hand with a smug conspiratorial smile.

The two capos shook hands firmly and passionately like men forming a conspiracy often do. Then they went their separate ways disappearing into the languishing silhouettes of the decrepit buildings along the Boardwalk.

In the flickering shadows of a fifth story fire escape in nearby Haddon Hall an impeccably dressed bald-headed man in a full-length cashmere topcoat lowered a pair of binoculars. A slightly faded, black ashen thumbprint was still prominent in the middle of his forehead from his attendance at Mass that morning. Today was Ash Wednesday, the beginning of Lent, a season of penance and reflection culminating with redemption for Catholics and Christians around the world.

The man had intently observed the meeting of the two crime family capos in the cold of the night. One was returning to South Philadelphia, the other to New York. This meeting between these two capos could only be a harbinger of trouble ahead for the Manfredi and Vecchio Families he would report.

Lighting a long H.Upmann Cuban cigar, he momentarily savored the pungent aroma of the tobacco. Clenching the cigar tightly in the corner of his mouth, a reflective smile expanded across his striated face. They're a bunch of amateurs, he thought ruefully. One was crazier than the other. The next generation of mobsters would be the last, he silently concluded. What the hell, he thought, shrugging his thick-shoulders indifferently. Turning away, he descended the fire escape to the bar in the hotel lobby to enjoy a bedtime brandy.

2

It was past noon and a woozy Gimp awoke from a fitful sleep drenched in sweat. Sitting on the edge of the couch, he rested his sweaty, pallid face in the indentation made by his two cupped hands. His elusive dreams elicited an ominous foreboding.

Dragging himself to his feet, he wobbled up the staircase to the second floor bathroom of his home in the upscale section of South Philadelphia called Girard Estate. "Marie," he shouted in a hoarse voice. There was no answer from his wife of over twenty years. "Anna," he called in a lower, less demanding voice. His twenty-year-old daughter was not at home either. Entering the bathroom he grabbed a towel. After turning on the faucets, he splashed the cold water on his face and head several times before turning the faucet to a hotter setting. Perking up, he enshrouded his balding head with the towel and vigorously dried what little hair remained. Five weeks had passed since his meeting with Johnny Bellino in Atlantic City and the Gimp was still no further along in *cleaning up his shit.* Looking into the mirror he promised himself that today he would focus on the business discussed with Bellino. He remained unaware that his procrastination and vacillation was merely a mask concealing the core reason for his burgeoning psychosis. Like other despicable memories, he suppressed it vehemently, but its lingering effect continually haunted him in the darkness of his soul.

While soaking a fresh white hand towel in the hot water, the Gimp sank slowly into a psychotic funk. The steam emanating from the hot water filled the room summoning the unpleasant memories from his adolescent years. Gaining intensity, they scalded his mind until collectively they cried out for revenge. Applying a warm wet towel to his face momentarily dampened the insidious effect of these memories. The more he fought them, however, the stronger they became. Slowly, these imperceptible scars on the ravaged landscape of his mind melded into a formidable force. Together, they were wearing him down. He became afraid to face them. They were consuming him. As this recurrent regurgitation of his past became more pronounced, the Gimp hoped vengeance was the balm for his troubled soul. It was vengeance he swore long ago. It was vengeance he craved. Unable to wait for a propitious moment to extract his pound of flesh, he let a contrived expediency guide him. Never contemplating the rippling effect this action could have on his life.

Removing the towel he began the shaving process, the old fashion way. Taking a shaving brush, he ran it under hot water for a couple of seconds. Then using a circular motion, he ran the badger-hair shaving brush along the glycerin-based shaving cream creating a nice lather. Beginning slowly, the circular motion gained in intensity as the Gimp's thoughts again regurgitated the past. His face contorted. He clenched his teeth tightly. His body shook to the point of a fever pitch. All of a sudden, the soap popped out of his tightened hand, breaking this hypnotic spell. Breathing deeply, his dull eyes stared aimlessly into the cloudy mirror. After a moment, he wiped away some condensation on the mirror with his towel and began applying the soap to his face in a lethargic circular motion. To mitigate this escalating unpleasantness, he forced himself to think of his daughter Anna.

The Gimp knew whom she was dating. Soon, he would learn more about this Johnny character and his intentions. Lately, however, he sensed Anna chafing against his parental prerogatives. Protecting her and her mother from the destructive vagaries of the world was his duty. Neither of them understood or shared his concerns. There were times he felt that neither cared. With Anna's twenty-first birthday fast approaching, he feared that she would revolt outright. Finishing that thought, he began shaving with his straight razor in the direction of the stubble on his face. As the stroke of the razor cleared a path on his face and neck, Sal Teti popped into the Gimp's mind. His face soured and his left eye began twitching uncontrollably. He promptly stopped shaving for fear of nicking himself with the razor.

Sal Teti, Giuseppe Vecchio's long time friend and capo, escaped his vengeful wrath by dying naturally. The Gimp felt cheated—deeply cheated. He needed closure badly. His soul demanded it. Somehow, it had eluded him. As the Gimp's expanding psychotic vein of vindictiveness grew, Rose Teti came to mind. Her humiliating laughter, echoing in his head for over thirty years, qualified her as a candidate for his budding retributive rampage. But she was under the protection of Sid Greenberg and the Old Man—an untouchable.

Breathing heavily, vengeance oozed from every pore of the Gimp's body. Someone had to pay for the sins of the Teti's. Someone had to be the scapegoat. For some time now, he innately sensed who that someone ought to be. It was an easy selection—a perfect sacrificial offering. With his partially lathered face framed by the steamy mirror, the Gimp snorted unwaveringly with flaring nostrils, "That scumbag pool hustler Cisco is gonna pay." The ensuing moment turned silently livid as the Gimp imagined Rose and Cisco having a good belly laugh at his expense over ice cream floats at a soda fountain. Flushing that thought out of his mind swiftly, the Gimp was determined to have the last laugh before squashing that scumbag like a cockroach. He knew that his top enforcer, Carlucci, would see to the details. Like the Gimp, he too had a personal score to settle with this contemptuous character. Slowly grinding his teeth, the Gimp's vindictive thoughts hopscotched across his mind. Moments later, the crescendo of grinding teeth abruptly stopped. Cisco could never satisfy his avowed thirst for revenge, the Gimp realized. There would be no closure unless he could destroy all evidence of Teti's family including Rose's *dipshit* son, Americo.

Releasing a heavy sigh he couldn't wait any longer. The venomous emotions of his youth ruthlessly intensified to a fever pitch. He needed to send a message right now. He needed to strike fear into the hearts of those who would belittle him. Steeling himself for the night ahead, he angrily pounded the counter top with his beefy fist toppling his toiletries. Tonight was only the beginning. He would have his pound of flesh.

3

It had been raining off and on all day Saturday. By later that evening, Johnny Cerone was betting that he could make it from his parent's house on the eighteen hundred block of Ritner Street to the Diner before it started raining again. He lost. Again.

Unable to pick up his girlfriend, Anna Giampietro, for their usual Saturday night date because of car problems, Johnny decided to meet her in a public location. He didn't want her cozying up to his parents. That type of familiarity led inevitably to a conundrum called marriage. Johnny's life was already in a downward spiral for the last year. Any talk of marriage would only hasten the descent. Still, the topic skulked there in the miniscule crevices of his mind like the juvenile angst of a monster in the closet or under the bed. That topic, however, was a problem for another day, he decided. Today he had more pressing issues—the lack of money.

Tiny rivulets of rain slowly pelted Johnny's face as he dashed up Seventeenth Street towards Jackson. Luckily, he had worn a trench coat. With a derisive smirk he laughed and mumbled to himself lowly, "Luck? What Luck?" March Madness had totally consumed Johnny this year. So, did the gambling bug. Usually, he looked forward to this annual college basketball event as a harbinger of spring, one of the more pleasant times in the Delaware Valley. Mild weather and refreshingly clean air highlighted this time of year. People shook off their moody wintry attitudes and began to smile. This year Johnny would enjoy neither season. How could UCLA win six consecutive NCAA Men's Basketball Titles, he brooded. "Six," he shouted in frustration to no one in particular. Flapping his arms like a madman he silently continued his cynical self-flagellating discourse. Nobody's that good. Wooden was lucky. Damn lucky! But the man is not invincible. Besides, anything could've happened. For Christ sakes, Keith Wilkes could've gotten sick or Bill Walton injured. After all, didn't Walton have knee problems Johnny propounded mutely?

Walking along briskly, Johnny stopped thinking for a moment. Perhaps, he hoped, some insightful reason would emerge to explain going against conventional wisdom and taking Florida State and four and a half points. None materialized. It was that damn half point that was his undoing he silently rationalized. In his heart, however, he knew that he was only kidding himself. He did that a lot lately, hoping to exorcise the cynicism that slowly was strangling his spirit. His brother's death affected him in more ways than he knew or would often admit.

Desperately sidestepping any personal introspection into that topic, Johnny instinctively turned right then left through a narrow labyrinth of brick row houses that lined these South Philadelphia streets. Tranquility suddenly overtook him. The endless rows of houses gave Johnny an illusionary sense of security, a feeling of stability and permanence. When walking, Johnny liked to take the side streets. He grew up running up and down these streets. They grounded him in the reality of a pleasant childhood.

Tonight, however, he could not escape the reality of the moment. He needed cash. With his hands deep in his coat's pockets and his collar up, he anonymously passed these endless rows of red brick houses lining the poorly lit streets. The momentary calming effect he enjoyed was punctuated by a raucous marital dispute echoing from another cavernous street nearby. Following that noisy disruption, an irate neighbor leaned on his car horn in the distance hoping to evoke a response from someone to move his or her double-parked car. These ambient disturbances were common occurrences downtown and woven into its social fabric. Rhythmically zigzagging his way between the tightly packed cars, tonight these everyday sounds amplified Johnny's exasperation with his entire life. Unable to hold back the floodgates of introspection any longer, he sagaciously realized there were many different routes for him to take, but only a few destinations. This thought was an allegory of life for many of the denizens of South Philadelphia.

Diagonally crossing Snyder Avenue, he was unable to pacify his anxiety. Gingerly, he tap-danced his way around a series of puddles. The sound of a car splashing along broke the strange silence permeating the empty streets. Not even that disturbance combined with his diversionary mental games could hide the truth. "Damn it," he bemoaned in a hushed voice to himself. Then finally in a moment of total exasperation he thoughtlessly screamed at the top of his lungs, "Fuck!"

If anyone had heard his scream they would have thought it obscene for a split second then shrugged it off. This was South Philadelphia. People here were known for their emotionally invective outbursts. For Johnny it was a cry for help. For the next few seconds the truth gushed out, torrentially drowning him in a deep moroseness. He missed the influence of his older brother's clarity of vision and strength of character. Those traits instilled stability into his life, a freedom from worry. Since his death he floundered in a sea of uncertainty. Seeking a diversion from his grief he began gambling. Now he owed money to his parents and bookie, often borrowing from Peter to pay Paul. There was only one alternative.

In order to make last month's payment on his car and get it out of the repair shop, he would have to borrow money from Anna. Again. Johnny knew that Anna loved his intermittent anguish over money especially when it involved his car. It aroused her sexually in a perverse sort of way. Coyly, she would make him squirm in her immitigable style. In the end, she would downright make him beg. It was demeaning for a man who knew better.

Right now, however, it appeared the only option available to him. No matter how hard he fought the siren song of Anna's easy money, he always succumbed to its alluring enticement. It scared him. He was getting use to it.

4

Looking out over the intersection of Passyunk and Snyder Avenues from the second floor window of Chickie's Poolroom, the Gimp intently surveyed the wide triangular intersection like an animal on the prowl. Instinctively, his cruel brown eyes narrowed when a silhouetted figure suddenly darted out of the darkness. For a moment he thought that he recognized the scurrying creature of the night, but his mind drew a blank. His wide neck stretched forward to watch the shadowy individual step widely around a puddle of water then make a brisk diagonal dash across Snyder Avenue and disappear.

Relaxing his posture the Gimp's barrel chest suddenly puffed out with pride. Something about the glistening wet asphalt of the streets below triggered a narcissistic retrospection of his criminal career. The turning point, his now legendary encounter with Carmine Tucci, was always the highlight of this sort of reflection. Tonight that remembrance stiffened his resolve to begin the process of eliminating the self-conscious blight on his dignity. This brought a wicked smile of contentment to his face. The Gimp was finally committed to a course of action, allowing him to bypass any introspection into the real motivations that secretly gnawed at him for all of these years.

Attentively, he watched his prey behind him through the reflection in the window. Tonight, like always, the Gimp fancifully edited the chapters of his life to suit his frame of mind. Unaware of the full story of his own life, the Gimp never realized that it was directly tied to the ascendance of what would eventually become known as the Vecchio Crime Family.

5

Joey Giampietro was truly a product of his environment. His birth on October 25, 1929, *Black Friday* on Wall Street, was a harbinger of his future and initially received with polite indifference by both of his parents. His mother Grace, a flapper, openly fraternized with the local criminal element to the consternation of her husband, Angelo. A womanizer himself, Angelo overlooked his wife's dalliances as long as she didn't bring them home with her. Eventually, she became pregnant with her son, Joseph.

Idle speculation among the fast crowd of the small community of South Philadelphia abounded regarding the responsible party to this blessed event. Only Grace knew the real father's identity. Not wanting to put a damper on her eye-popping life style, she kept that bit of information to herself hoping to exploit it at a later time. Her naiveté in that regard would be her eventual undoing. For now though, Angelo would do just fine.

Aside from that fact, the event did put a serious crimp in her lifestyle. Angelo, however, didn't mind the babysitting chores. He actually enjoyed it. In many ways the child resembled him. So, he brushed off the innuendos floating around. The true bane of his relationship with Grace revolved around money. It took money to raise a child and continue looking good for her nights out on the town. Verbal tirades ensued until in a moment of dire frustration she physically lashed out on her now out of work husband. Soon after that confrontation, Angelo received the lucrative job offer of driving a truck on the weekly beer run from Canada for Salvatore Teti. It was like manna from heaven.

Salvatore "Solly" Teti ran a string of speakeasies downtown with his partner, Giuseppe "the Old Man" Vecchio. This was a reward from Sal Sabella, the local mafia chieftain for their services during the Castellamarese War in New York during 1929.

Times were changing, however. Charley "Lucky" Luciano initiated his grand scheme of organizing crime into a business like enterprise. Sal Sabella, once a supporter of a Luciano enemy, saw the handwriting on the wall. Quickly retiring, he turned over the South Philadelphia operation to his second in command, Lou Arena. Even during these turbulent times Teti and Vecchio continued to prosper due in part to the friendships and alliances they had fostered during their time in New York. As the New York crime families began to coalesce under predominantly Italian auspices, the diverse Philadelphia crime organizations maintained separate spheres of influence delineated by ethnicity.

Bootlegging, a thriving industry in those days fell under the control of the Jewish mob run by Sidney Greenberg. Sid had the corner on the Philadelphia market due to the support of Luciano's partner, Meyer Lansky. Like true businessmen, new spheres of influence were negotiated. A deal was struck and Lou Arena gave organizational responsibilities for delivery and distribution to Teti. Logistically, he was a natural at it. Teti and Greenberg hit it off right away. When the occasion arose, the astute Vecchio suggested Greenberg as the godfather for Teti's expected child.

A Jewish godfather was unheard of in the Catholic Church, but Vecchio attended to that delicate matter. Unbeknownst to Greenberg, Vecchio appeared on church documents as the official godfather. This was accomplished through financial persuasion allowing Sid to stand in attendance during the brief ceremony for Teti's only child, Rose. The Baptism cemented the business relationship between the two families. Everyone prospered.

Vecchio's personal family was the model Italian-American family. Always extremely discreet, respectability was his mainstay. Raised in the ways of the old world, he took honor and self-respect seriously. A straight arrow type, he gave in to the temptations of the flesh only once. Married upon his return from New York, he wrote his momentary indiscretion off to youthful folly steeling himself against the luring distraction that such temptations constantly presented.

Teti, however, was a womanizer. On several occasions he playfully chided Vecchio about his timid demeanor with women and dubbed him, *the Old Man*.

Actually vecchio meant old man in Italian. Taking his title in stride, Vecchio turned its utterance into a pronouncement of respect.

Prohibition ended on December 5, 1933. Again, Angelo Giampietro prospered. His loyalty and natural affinity with vehicles was noticed. As a result of this ability, he graduated from driving a beer truck for Teti to personally chauffeuring the new boss, Lou Arena. This moment of prosperity, however, was fleeting.

The upstart Leonetti brothers were threatening to cause havoc within the newly defined criminal order of Philadelphia. Still smarting from a previous attempt on Gino Leonetti ten years earlier, the brothers decided to now take their revenge in one swift stroke.

On a crisp fall day in 1934, Angelo Giampietro pulled up at the corner of Washington and Passyunk Avenues to pick up Lou Arena from a visit with his ailing mother. Phil and Tony Leonetti made their move. They were awkward and poorly timed, but extremely deadly.

Lurking in a doorway, Phil Leonetti removed his gun from his waistband. By chance Angelo noticed this action. Widened in horror, his eyes and frightened face telegraphed its ominous message. Lou Arena immediately saw the look and deflected Tony Leonetti's aim at the last moment.

What ensued is part of the mythology of South Philadelphia. Phil shot Angelo twice in the head as he haphazardly tried to exit the car. Lou Arena managed to wound Tony in a running gun battle, but had the bad luck of leaving himself vulnerable as he turned to face Phil. Tony came up from behind and emptied his .38 into the soft midriff of the slightly corpulent boss. Not satisfied, Phil also managed to get in two shots to Lou Arena's hunched back before slowly walking away.

Funeral parlors were a growing business along the South Broad Street corridor. The Italian community placed special emphasis on a proper interment. The Broad Street Funeral Company addressed those concerns and consequently had the lion's share of the business. The layout of the building could accommodate six funerals simultaneously or it's respectfully demur viewing rooms could be reconfigured into one massive ballroom of mourning replete with professional mourners.

Such was the configuration for mob boss Lou Arena. The smell of carnations permeated the funeral parlor. The floral designs of these pungent flowers depicted the subtle theme surrounding the death of each individual. This night, amid the mourning multitude of maudlin matrons dressed in black, the theme was blood. Red carnations and red roses ruled. They formed clocks showing the exact time of Lou Arena's death. There were several different designs of Italy all with a red rose strategically placed in the approximate location of Arena's hometown. A massive spray of pure white roses seemed magically suspended over the open casket. People filed past the casket. A specially designed large floral container stood strategically nearby to hold the hundreds of Mass cards sold by the Catholic Church for just such an occasion. Each one an individual petition to God for the salvation of Arena's nefarious soul. A few left envelopes of money owed to him lest he return from the wretched depths of hell to collect the debt. Such superstitious speculations were prevalent though not often voiced openly. Some bowed their heads respectfully and quickly shuffled passed. Others knelt and said a prayer. Many more waited in a line that snaked around the perimeter of the room overflowing out onto South Broad Street. This extravagant display of remorse showed respect for a man who would pay widow's utility bills to help keep them warm in winter or find a job for a prideful husband on the verge of despair. This was the way of the mafia in South Philadelphia—make money from their human foibles and parse it back sparingly. The crime lords had become a stabilizing influence and the Leonetti's had willfully disrupted this balance during these financially troubling times.

The Old Man astutely watched the entire funerary affair with the eye of a businessman. He became aware of these social machinations from his involvement in his family's real estate business and its sponsorship of immigrants known as the *padrone* system. Capitalizing on his established connections, he built his own base of support. His willingness to assist poor immigrants ignorant of the laws and mores of their newfound homeland perpetuated the *Robin Hood* myth among the legions of ordinary people. These were the very people who played the numbers daily and bought *hot* items from the peddlers of ill-gotten goods. Eventually avenging the hit on Lou Arena would be the Old Man's personal crusade. Its success would guarantee his eventual ascension to the ultimate title of respect—Don. In the meantime he would let someone else be the red herring. He would wait patiently for the Leonetti's to show their hand. Unsurprisingly, Grace Giampietro showed her hand first.

6

Angelo Giampietro's funeral was uneventful even though pictures of his bloodied body were splashed across the front pages of every local newspaper. It occurred the day after Lou Arena's burial in Holy Cross Cemetery. Totally distraught, his wife Grace subtly threatened suicide. After a while, however, with a few glasses of champagne running through her veins she began reminiscing about the good old days. Trying to put herself back into the spotlight, Grace chattered endlessly about the speakeasies, all night parties, Little Joey and Angelo's former job. It made her feel important again. Regaining her courage, she resurrected a plan.

Grace's plan was simple—blackmail. She went to Teti seeking money in return for her silence about her son's true father. "Teti dearie," was Grace's subtle way of signaling her shakedown gambit. "Gracie needs a big favor that only Little Joey's dad can provide," was the second part of her spiel. It had worked before when her husband needed a job. Teti kept that incident as their little secret, never mentioning it to the Old Man. Therefore, Grace had no reason to believe that it wouldn't work again. Grace only saw the playful side of these libidinous gangsters indulging on occasion in flights of whimsical fantasy. Deluding herself with the notion that these men only killed one another, she never considered that they would harm a defenseless woman, even a blackmailing one. She was wrong.

It was a reckless gamble on her part. She never saw the big picture. Teti wanted to dispose of this pretentious harlot along with her little snot-nosed boy before the entire affair got out of hand and disrupted the natural order of business. He also didn't want it to become a bone of contention with his wife. So, he offered Grace some money to move away.

"Pshaw! I ain't leaving my friends. You can stick your money where the sun don't shine," she boldly replied to Teti's offer. The hard economic times had dispersed her family around the country. Out of touch with them, she had nowhere to go especially with a young boy in tow. That complicated matters for everyone, especially Teti.

Teti was not a ruthless murderer. He was supposed to have made his bones during the Castellamarese War, but the actual details were sketchy. Only the Old Man knew the truth. Without lying, he stepped up and vouched for Teti and the subject was never revisited. Vecchio was a loyal friend even in the raucous heydays of the "Roaring Twenties." No words about what transpired were ever spoken between the friends. No subtle acknowledgement of a debt—nothing. Still, the debt was on the books sequestered in the in the back of both men's minds. It was a burdensome debt. Teti obligingly paid its price with unwavering loyalty to the Old Man. However, the intestinal fortitude to commit murder eluded him. He didn't have it then and he certainly didn't have it now. Accustomed to his free wheeling lifestyle, Teti saw no alternative and informed the Old Man of Grace Giampietro's threats.

Vecchio viewed murder in terms of business. It was either good or bad for business. Murdering a child, especially one so young was bad for business. Killing manipulative women who even slightly disrupted his future plans was another matter. The woman had knowledge of criminal dealings that could be troublesome at worst. Her blackmailing ways were a personal affront to his honor. This convinced him that she posed an imminent threat to the organization and thus his future plans. Still, killing the young boy's mother weighed heavy on the Old Man's heart though he would never admit it even to himself until years later. Of course, he was capable of the insidious crime. The woman had no honor or respect in the community. Necessity dictated his course of action. Agonizing over his decision and not willing to condemn Little Joey to an orphanage, the Old Man approached Teti one night at the bar after closing. "Solly, we need to talk," he solemnly intoned.

Grabbing a bottle of grappa from underneath the bar and two short-stemmed glasses, Teti motioned for the Old Man to take a seat at a table. He had no forewarning of the life-changing request that was about to be made. Sitting down across from the Old Man, Teti said in a cavalier tone. "Shoot."

The Old Man smiled coyly at the word and replied, "If only I could. If only I could." He looked deep into Teti's eyes then continued, "I need a personal favor Sal. A big favor."

Teti became serious. The Old Man never used his god-given name unless it was important. "Go on," he tersely replied after a reflective moment.

The Old Man swallowed hard and said without quite asking, "I would like you to adopt Little Joey Giampietro when all this unpleasant business is over." It was the only time that the Old Man would ask Teti for a personal favor.

Teti was taken aback for a moment. Breaking eye contact with the Old Man, he sunk his head down toward his chest. Words, any words eluded him. He remained speechless for the longest time. Hours later after finishing the bottle of grappa, Teti begrudgingly relented and tepidly agreed to raise Little Joey. Teti never revealed the gist of their unholy agreement that day to anyone bearing the emotional brunt of the unsavory arrangement in silence. Only on his deathbed did he confess the truth to his daughter Rose—a truth she could never reveal.

With every angle now covered the Old Man personally dispatched Grace to the Tinicum Marshes just south of Philadelphia on the way to Chester. It was an unfortunate event that was dictated by her naïveté in understanding the business rules of these men. Actually, Teti had sent the wrong signal by offering her money. His show of weakness only emboldened her. Thinking she could get her way with verbal tirades, she treated these men as if they were like her husband Angelo and paid with her life. So, on a drizzly evening in late Fall, Grace Giampietro, a woman whose only ambition in life was to have fun was quietly strangled in a remote area outside of Philadelphia. Her ironic sense of humor squeezed dry by a thin cord known as a garrote.

Before burying her in a shallow grave ten feet off a weed-infested road in the Tinicum Marshes just south of Philadelphia, the Old Man removed a gold chain bearing a gold cornicelli as a remembrance for her son. It was the only sentimental act the Old Man ever committed and one of the few times that he truly felt any remorse.

In later years the Gimp would use the same area for similar pernicious deeds. During one such occasion the voice first revealed itself to the Gimp. Digging furiously, he stopped when the howling wind chilled the hair on the back of his neck causing an uncomfortable prickly feeling. This moment of uneasiness lasted several seconds. The Gimp paled. Beads of sweat formed on his ashen-forehead. Grasping the gold pepper dangling from his neck, he superstitiously believed it would ward off evil spirits. He thought that he heard a mumbling voice in the distance. Looking around with eyes flickering restlessly, he called out, "Hello?" There was still no answer after repeating the greeting several times. Shrugging this incident off to nature's chicanery, he never recognized the voice as the silent wailing of his mother's tormented soul warning him of a similar fate.

In those same ensuing years the Old Man personally engineered the brutal retributory slaying of William Leonetti. This act sent an ominous message to the Leonetti Family who quickly fled the Delaware Valley. His power base grew proportionally. Ten years later, Giuseppe Vecchio was the undisputed Don. His reign would be the *Pax Romana* of the South Philadelphia underworld for over the next two decades until all hell eventually broke loose.

Of course during that time there were always disputes. Egos would expand. Set boundaries were violated. For the Old Man mediating these disputes was always a ponderously delicate matter requiring tact. Most were settled reasonably. Occasionally, one would confound the Old Man.

Such was the case of Carmine Tucci versus the Gimp.

7

A new parenthesis began in the Gimp's life during the summer of 1950 with his marriage to Marie Croce. The Old Man had made the traditional introduction on the Gimp's behalf that spring. Marie's father could think of nothing to impede introducing the two and accepted. Marie felt betrayed by her father for making such a decision for her without her consent. Blatantly resisting this old world style of courtship at first, she finally deferred to their wishes. A short time later she married Joseph Giampietro. The following April their daughter Anna was born.

Ecstatic with the recent birth of his daughter, the Gimp had just been found innocent of the murder of a local construction union agent on grounds of self-defense. It was a major coup that garnered him the respect of the Old Man's peers outside of the small territorial confines of the Vecchio Crime Family. With murder added to his criminal resume, he now had the credentials to become a bona fide capo. The acquittal only enhanced his position. Soon, he thought, Marie and he would move out of their small house on Manton Street to a larger more fitting abode. For the moment though, he relished the memory of his triumph.

The Gimp faced his moment of truth during a shoot-out with Carmine Tucci, a local trade union boss, on an unusually pleasant summer afternoon in 1950. Tucci had ties to the corrupt New York trade unions, but was considered a maverick. Known for his stubbornness, he walked a fine line that all men walk who serve two masters.

This lucrative source of revenue caught the Gimp's eye. Looking to make a name for himself, the Gimp saw this business as a perfect revenue enhancer for his own ambitions. Tucci was the perfect target.

The irascible Tucci resented the Gimp's interference in union business—his business. Tucci complained to Teti who just shrugged and casually said, "Take it up with the Old Man." Teti didn't stand to gain personally and wanted no part of this trouble. These days he deflected anything involving the Gimp to the Old Man.

"But you always took care of this kind of bullshit," Tucci shot back questioningly.

Teti pursed his lips while trying to remove a renegade piece of chicken from between his teeth with his tongue. This offensive habit was his idiosyncratic way of getting rid of people. Tucci looked on in disgust as Teti spoke. "That's all changed. It's outta my hands." Teti quickly turned away signaling an end to the conversation.

Feeling irate and isolated, Tucci's suspicions of duplicity were confirmed by his meeting with Teti. He was being slowly squeezed out. Tucci was not one to back down from a fight.

Neither was the Gimp. Subconsciously, the Gimp never liked Tucci. Acting like they were long lost buddies, he secretly resented the man. There was an air of arrogance that swirled around Tucci that stuck in the Gimp's craw like a tough piece of braciola. "*Here was a gigolo, a sex-craved scumbag, who thought he was the cat's meow,*" the Gimp would repeatedly obsess during his usually sleepless nights. This obsession accelerated in his mind then escalated into action. Quietly, the Gimp began courting the rank and file union members to vote out the womanizing son-of-a-bitch. The union members gave the Gimp the obligatory lip service, but still knew where their bread was buttered. Tucci still decided when and if they worked. Wired into the contractors, they appreciated his low-keyed approach to touchy labor issues. This frustrated the Gimp immeasurably, but he understood the implications. It was business—strictly business. Percolating several levels below the surface was the real reason that the Gimp detested this cocky union business agent. Tucci's muscular physique, chiseled facial features and thick black curly hair contrasted starkly with the Gimp's balding leonine like features. His suave manner always checkmated the Gimp's brusqueness. Women swooned over Tucci. He aroused their femininity in ways that the Gimp only fantasized about alone in his room. The Gimp felt silly and inadequate in his presence though he would never admit it. Subconsciously, he was insecure about his awkwardness with women.

Tucci noticed his uneasiness and leveraged it at every opportune moment. He regarded the Gimp as unremarkable—a braggadocio. Unable to have him eliminated in the literal sense because of his ties to the Old Man, Tucci languished. Eventually, Tucci's inability to separate business and personal matters would be his undoing.

The Old Man favored the Gimp. He also knew him well enough to sense where this confrontation would eventually lead. Trying to keep the peace he agreed to meet Tucci. Arriving separately at Independence Hall in the historic section of Philadelphia, Tucci and the Old Man strolled around the grounds and discussed their business. The gray, cold winter day kept the tourists to a minimum.

Tucci represented the embodiment of the Teti affair that personally gnawed at the Old Man. A womanizer like Teti, Tucci's loyalty was questionable. He would not fall on his sword for the greater good of the organization the Old Man surmised. Better to let fate take its course, he concluded. Obviously, this confrontation evoked on some subconscious level the demons of the Old Man's past. Yet, like the Gimp, he would never explore the subtle influences of such thoughts for fear of what he may uncover. Rationalizing his motivations and never confrontational, the Old Man took the circuitous route hoping Tucci would bow out quietly. After hearing Tucci's pleadings, the Old Man knew otherwise. Coyly, he asked in a low accented voice, "What would you have me do Carmine?"

"It's my turf. Tell him to back off," Tucci demanded already sensing an unsatisfactory conclusion to this meeting.

"Maybe if you paid more attention to business and not your other affairs, this wouldn't be happening," the Old Man said making his innuendo obvious.

"My personal life is my business. If that fat bastard were your blood relative it'd be different. I don't understand why you're taking sides with this idiot," Tucci said spontaneously out of frustration.

The off-handed comment sealed his fate. The Old Man's icy silence and slit eyes was all the response Tucci needed. He totally understood the implications. In the end, he and the Gimp would have to settle their differences like duelists, once and for all. Tucci nodded his head politely toward the Old Man and quickly disappeared into a crowd of tourists. Killing the Gimp would solve all of his problems. Still, he vacillated.

The union hall on East Passyunk Avenue was a dingy smoke-filled edifice that had all the trappings of a flophouse. Tucci sat with his feet propped up on the desk. Lost in thought, his mind swiveled between personal and business matters. Lately, his personal matters revolved around a woman. This wasn't just any woman. They were soul mates. Tucci was in love just like Frank Sinatra and Ava

Gardner except that his picture wasn't splashed all over the tabloids. Intermittently, he would snap back into focus and realize that he needed to take action. Otherwise, his supporters wouldn't just vote him out of office they would laugh him out. The rank and file members already noticed the far off look in his eyes when talking business with him. His grip on the union purse strings was tenuous. It only took one contractor to break rank. All this combined with a pressing development in his personal life drove him toward a pernicious end game. He knew that he had to kill the Gimp. He wanted to do it. He needed to do it. However, his thinking was continually blurred at this crucial juncture in his life. His mental acuity was dulled by his fanciful preoccupation with his lover who held his attention in bondage.

Something else was going on here, he quizzed silently to himself. It made no sense he concluded, but he couldn't quite put his finger on the reason. With his ruminations eluding any logical conclusions, a sudden sense of purpose enveloped him sharpening his resolve. Yanking open the top drawer of his desk, he grabbed an old snub-nosed .38. With the snap of his wrist he flipped open the chamber. Making sure that the gun was loaded, he slid the weapon into his coat pocket. The Gimp was already two steps ahead of him.

Instinctively, the Gimp sensed the coming battle and never let his guard down. Looking over his shoulder was ingrained in him during his youth and it always served him well. The Gimp always said, "Do unto others before they do unto you." He thought that he was paraphrasing a quote from Julius Caesar. He was mistaken. Still, it was his favorite saying—the mantra of his life.

A four-month cat and mouse game ensued, ending on a fateful June afternoon just before the Fourth of July. Surreptitiously tailing Tucci to find the right place to confront him proved daunting. In need of help he enlisted the assistance of another brash street urchin, Anthony "Mad Dog" Carlucci. Together they managed to triangulate on the wily and extremely suspicious Tucci. A high-water mark in the Gimp's life, he would never again exhibit such patience. This time it paid off.

Unlike the Gimp who was awkward with women, Tucci had a natural affinity with them. His mellifluous compliments would send the blood rushing through the veins of the coldest ice queen. Definitely a lady's man, he kept a small apartment in Queens Village for an occasional afternoon tryst even though he was married with a baby boy and another on the way.

One such affair started out as a one-night stand. It lasted over a year. Beautiful, independent and loving, she embodied everything he sought in a woman. The connectivity between them, a raw tingling passion, was electrifying. He enjoyed their time alone even when they weren't making love. She was special in so many ways that he lost count. Unwilling to break up his family, she refused to talk about marriage even though she was single. A strict Catholic in appearance, she circumvented the topic of adultery counterbalancing this sin with her unbridled love for Carmine Tucci. So, they went to great lengths to keep the affair secret. No one ever caught wind of it—not even the Old Man.

Feeling like a man in a vise, Tucci finally decided to solve his problem once and for all. It was too late. The Gimp had already preempted Tucci. Still, even with all of the Gimp's planning, luck would be the deciding factor this day.

After making love this fine afternoon Tucci left his apartment. Glancing up to the apartment window, he was about to wave goodbye to the love of his life. Instead of a smile on her creamy face, he saw fear.

Immediately, Tucci turned around to see the Gimp quickly approaching him from down the street. Instinctively, he drew his gun. To this day witnesses disagree about who fired the first shot. As the gun battle progressed down a side street, Tucci adroitly maneuvered the Gimp into a corner. Caught off guard, the Gimp faced Tucci like two duelists. The Gimp looked helplessly down the barrel of Tucci's snub-nosed .38. Arrogant even in the face of death, the Gimp's soulless eyes dared him to shoot. Obligingly, Tucci triggered the gun, but it was now empty. A wicked smile spread insidiously across the Gimp's face. Without thinking of whether he had any bullets left, the Gimp gleefully aimed his gun pointblank at Tucci's chest and fired. At that moment a legend was born. It didn't matter that he was a psychopath; the Gimp had looked death in the face and won. Since that fateful day this one moment of truth continued to give meaning to the Gimp's life.

The Gimp always liked to anchor himself with the memory of that brief moment on a sunny afternoon. All of his fantasies came true that day. He always remembered that moment when faced with a challenge and challenges always lurked in his mind's eye.

8

Completing his brisk diagonal dash across Sixteenth Street at the intersection of Passyunk and Snyder Avenues, Johnny hugged the wall to avoid the rain before continuing to the Diner. Unthinkingly, his crossing was just seconds ahead of a lumbering oversized car that resembled a barge floating along the canal adjacent to the upper Delaware River.

Arriving at the door of this stainless steel landmark to a foregone era of simplicity, he shook his head and arms like a wet dog before entering. Once inside, he immediately removed his trench coat and sat down at the horseshoe-like counter grabbing a handful of napkins to wipe the wetness from his ruddy face.

A neatly pressed waitress immediately appeared and intoned her rote, impromptu greeting in a shrill voice, "Cawfee, Dearie?"

Still wiping his face, Johnny responded, "Two creams!"

The waitress squatted down to retrieve the small measured containers of cream from a refrigerator under the counter and Johnny's eyes immediately connected with a half dozen pair of soulless eyes glaring at him in *Goyaesque* fashion. For these stoic-faced customers Saturday night meant sitting at the counter nursing undersized cups of coffee. Several of them habitually took a drag on an unfiltered cigarette. They appeared like characters only Rod Serling could have created for *The Twilight Zone*. Night after night here they sat zombie-like.

Johnny knew the nicknames of these craggy-faced characters and their jaded stories. Scalper Al, Bobby Blues, Joe Cadillac and Frankie Juice sat at the counter stoically. Their real names didn't matter. It told you nothing of the true nature of these individuals. However, their nicknames gave one an insight into their character. Tonight, Johnny was not in the mood to hear them reiterate their ailments or missed opportunities. Their stories were aberrations to the soul at best, but were essentially mind numbing recounts of a quintessential episode in the life of an otherwise boring individual.

Acknowledging them all with a subtle nod of his head, he quickly diverted his eyes to the overhead clock on his right to truncate their unholy ocular grip. Feeling comfortable now that he had plenty of time to regain his composure, he welcomed the arrival of his own undersized cup of coffee. The steam from the coffee in front of him mesmerized him as it rose in Rorschachian designs inducing an introspective moment.

At twenty-three he was a computer programmer sitting in a cubicle in the basement of a cold gray building. Boring at best, the job fulfilled his basic needs. Still, he made a good salary, but was still dead broke. His life seemed at a standstill. A complacency replaced the spontaneity in his life that he suspected—no knew—was already ingrained in the people that surrounded him at the counter. Morosely, he wondered if his destiny mirrored their ungodly stares. Evading that depressing rumination, Anna, his nemesis of love, popped into his mind. She seductively teased and taunted him. His friends had begun calling him *Wimpy* after the character in a popular cartoon. At first he didn't catch the subtlety of the nickname. He thought they were referring to his borrowing habits.

When they realized that he wasn't getting the message his friend, Tommy Dee, took him aside and spelled it out plain and simple. Anna was bad news. Warning him not to get involved, Johnny just shrugged it off to jealousy. Now he was in deep, very deep. He shuddered at the thought of the alternatives. "Stupid, stupid, stupid," he mumbled to himself.

The waitress caught the gist of his mumbling and reacted defensively toward Johnny. "You got a problem?"

Catching him off balance momentarily, he suddenly realized what he had said. "No, no, no problem. I lost some money on the game tonight. It was stupid. Totally stupid! Know what I mean," he responded in an escalating anxiety-ridden tone of voice.

The waitress shrugged indifferently. Use to this type of unusual behavior, she moved away to serve another more amiable customer.

This interruption allowed more mundane concerns to wheedle their way into his consciousness. His first and most pressing concern was his alter ego—a mustard-colored 1970 MGB roadster. In the repair shop for over a week, Armando, the mechanic, finally found the root cause of all the problems. Maybe. He hoped. At least it was running. The two-year old car had been in the shop for repairs at least a half-dozen times. At one point Armando refused to repair the car anymore because of Johnny's tardy payment habits. Johnny was in a panic. The balky Armando relented, provided Johnny paid cash on delivery. This strained Johnny's finances. It was a constant sore point in his relationship with Anna. Her bankroll kept the car rolling and his head barely above water. Each time it broke down he swore to get rid of it. Once repaired, however, he immediately took back his vow. He loved the car. From somewhere deep within his being he felt a sense of freedom when he drove it. Johnny didn't know why he felt that way. He just did.

Anna on the other hand hated the car. She felt threatened by it and was astute enough to know why. It definitely wasn't the money or other women ogling Johnny when he drove the splashy car. Infidelity she could handle. Independence was another matter. Oblivious to her machinations, Johnny thought she was merely jealous about the other women. Sometimes in a playful mood, he would even tease Anna by referring to the car in the female tense. She took the teasing in stride, but was secretly delighted every time the car gave Johnny problems forcing him to depend on her for transportation and money.

He looked at the clock again. Anna would be here soon. The notoriety that he received as a result of his relationship with Anna was enticing. Her voluptuous figure continually seduced him to the point of foolish carnal indulgence. Luckily, thus far he was able to control the wellspring of desire that sent him home some nights with aching groins. He never overstepped his bounds. Johnny knew that the Gimp was as unstable as nitroglycerin and a powerful force in the South Philadelphia underworld. He only met the guy in passing—a polite introduction that evolved into an occasional "Howyadoin." Johnny had heard all the stories and rumors. A simple misspoken word could set the guy off let alone a sexual dalliance with his only daughter.

Johnny drained his cup of coffee in one gulp and motioned to the waitress for another. His anxiety surfaced for a moment. Time was running out for him. He cursed himself for getting into this predicament. If he couldn't muster the intestinal fortitude to be frank with her, he would have to craft a deviously delicate solution.

"But, but those luscious lips, those gorgeous eyes…" he pined inwardly as his mind drifted into the realm of fantasy momentarily. Snapping back to reality he looked at the clock again. Anna was running late. He relapsed into his perpetual subconscious state of anxiety.

As the waitress refilled his cup, Johnny looked at the clock again like a man praying for a sign from heaven.

9

The Gimp pursed his lips tightly as his fanciful mental meanderings fizzled out. Refocusing his attention, he attentively watched the activity to his rear like a stalking lion through the reflection in the window. This exercise was intentional. The subliminal voice inside his shiny pate whispered enigmatically, *"Joey! Don't play with your food. Just eat it."* A quizzical look slowly crossed his face. He tried to discern the meaning of this utterance, but failed. Continuing to toy with his prey, he hoped that his dawdling would unnerve him. He was wrong.

Armand "Cisco" Francesco was shuffling the deck of cards. A cigarette dangled from his mouth that he would occasionally roll across his lips. Shuffling the cards devoutly, his small powerful build coupled with his thick gray-tinged black hair cut evenly around his head gave him the appearance of a monk from a religious order. It was a deception of innocence that he often used to his advantage. Tonight it wouldn't work. This tough audience knew better.

Cisco would continue shuffling the cards until the Gimp either sat down or lost his patience. It was his way of challenging the Gimp and it didn't go unnoticed. He thought that he was in this untenable position because of his cheating ways. It never occurred to Cisco that cheating was a ploy. A good ploy, but it still was a ploy. So, he bought into that notion without giving it a second thought.

A known card shark, thief and all around rapscallion, it went without saying that Cisco was suspected of cheating the Gimp. Actually, Cisco didn't need to cheat. The Gimp was a terrible card player. With this in mind Cisco decided not to let the Gimp *lose large*. The Gimp didn't care. He knew that he was a poor card player. It was just a pastime to him. However, all this was a perfect ruse for a much more complicated gambit swirling in the Gimp's mind.

Cisco knew that he would have to face this day inevitably as long as he remained in South Philadelphia. He wasn't a stupid man. Kowtowing to a nut case wasn't desirable either. There were other reasons why he remained in town, personal reasons.

The poolroom door flung open widely and Louie "Snake" Biscione entered. He hesitated momentarily. His steely coal black eyes searched the poolroom and ominously lingered on Cisco momentarily where they silently imparted a greeting. People who knew Louie dismissed the obvious physical similarites between him and the slithering reptile. Instead, they chose to accept his nickname as a representation of the serpent's deadly characteristics. Louie was used to the nickname by now. Although in his youth he would take umbrage to the monicker, he quickly saw the intimidating value it afforded him in his chosen profession. A strong-arm man by trade, Louie was not a pyschotic killer. Appreciating his style and manner, Sal Teti used him to collect his loans. Teti took care of him in his youth, but those days were behind him now. These days he served a new master. After a moment Louie the Snake strode over to the Gimp.

"Where's Antny?" the Gimp curtly inquired followed by a sinister grin flickering across his face.

"I dunno," Louie tersely replied.

"Is that business with that Nicky Sox taken care of?"

"I dunno. I don't think so."

"What the fuck *do* you know?" The Gimp slams the heel of his hand down on the table in a fit of rage sending the cards flying all over the place. "Go get that little weasel Nicky and bring 'em here. Don't come back without 'em. I'll take care of this myself."

Louie, adept at restraining his contempt, slithered out of the poolroom. Cisco quietly watched this one act play in amusement. He knew the drill. There was no comprehensible subtext to the machinations of the Gimp. What you saw is what you got. Tonight was different.

Cisco underestimated the Gimp. Thinking that he needed to manipulate the cards in favor of the Gimp, he was unaware that the Gimp had already made that arrangement. The cards were marked. Trying to contain his loses to acceptable levels while pacifying the Neanderthal on the other side of the table would be trickier than Cisco imagined. The hardest part of the evening would be to keep the contemptuous smirk from his face.

Cisco was acutely aware of this personal shortcoming. He also knew that this was nearly impossible to accomplish since he was contemptuous by nature. Either you accepted him as he was or you hated him. There was no in between. The number of people that he truly cared about or merely respected could be counted on one hand. Two of those people made it difficult for him to leave this town.

Just as that thought crossed his mind the poolroom door opened again and Cisco smiled inwardly. One of those people had just entered the room.

10

Americo Teti entered the poolroom nonchalantly. His dark boyish good looks and lustrous wavy black hair exuded the qualities of an actor rather than a henchman. He was one, but not the other. His casual manner annoyed the Gimp. Too cavalier for his taste, it almost bordered on presumptuous. Teti sensed the Gimp's irritation by the lividness in his darting eyes and quickly readjusted his attitude. A minor deference to a major ego, he amusingly thought. Neither proud nor ambitious, Teti simply liked the respect people downtown paid him for playing the role of a made-man. Only the Gimp knew the truth behind the facade. Since the Old Man was Teti's godfather, he let the myth perpetuate. Working around this impediment, the Gimp found satisfaction by humiliating Teti at every opportunity.

Someone else also knew that Teti's reputation, as a made-man was bogus. Lurking in the shadows that night, Cisco witnessed the entire affair. Neither Teti nor the Gimp knew of his presence. Teti's mother did because she sent him.

Rose Teti was just as wayward as her son. The proprietress of the Downtown Bar & Grill located at the busiest intersection on East Passyunk Avenue, she inherited the place from her father, Salvatore Teti. A popular watering hole for those downtown denizens seeking the excitement of rubbing elbows with the local criminal element. The food was good and the customers loyal. With pre World War Two fixtures, the establishment approached the threshold of historic consideration. All of these factors fostered its popularity in recent years outside the small enclave of South Philadelphia. Still, the business languished. Its profitability teetered from month to month unlike the days of her father's lively management.

Sal Teti laundered his ill-gotten gains through the business before his untimely death. The cause of his death is still subject to debate and occasionally comes up whenever someone drinks too much and starts reminiscing. The coroner's autopsy listed it as an abdominal aneurysm. This formal description seemed like Greek in the intransient world of South Philadelphia. Someone, unfamiliar with anatomical terms, immediately conjured up an image of someone plugging Teti. Though untrue the story spread throughout the city. Nonetheless, people still believed what they wanted to believe.

This event was still many years away when Teti's daughter Rose discovered that she was pregnant out of wedlock. Blaming the Gimp at first, Teti reveled in the thought of honestly *making his bones* on this misbegotten scum. Strongly discounting this theory, his daughter assured him otherwise. Since Rose had recently been dating several young men, she coyly played a shell game with her father. A stalemate ensued.

Facing the stigma attached to her plight did not concern Rose. Keeping the name of the child's father from her own father took precedence in her mind. Afraid of her father's response if he knew the truth, she turned to the Old Man for help.

Through his influence in the corridors of City Hall the Old Man managed to keep the name of the father of Rose's child off the record. His response was meant as a *quid pro quo* for the Teti's family suffering due to the Giampietro affair. In the end this elaborate ruse proved unnecessary. Her father had a strong suspicion of his grandchild's parentage and decided to leave well enough alone. He loved his daughter dearly. So, he succumbed to her wishes. Considering Rose a harlot, the Gimp never gave it a second thought.

Inevitably, after Sal Teti's death young Americo assumed his grandfather's persona. People even began calling the young boy Teti in deference to his grandfather. On the surface the young boy had none of his grandfather's criminal tendencies. In his heart, however, they were simpatico. The young Teti did nothing to stop it. He liked the special treatment he received. Never considering the potential ramifications of this deception, Teti myopically continued down this seductive path oblivious to the consequences.

Being raised by the young Teti's grandfather, the Gimp became a surrogate uncle of sorts. Secretly, he harbored a bitter resentment against him. To ease his evolving inner demons the little boy served as a surrogate for the Gimp's simmering ire toward America's grandfather and mother.

From the first time the Gimp met Rose Teti, he had a crush on her. He had no clue that his feelings were Oedipal in nature. In the 1930's no one understood or even cared about the libidinal feelings of young boys. You were just told to deal with it.

Born and raised on a farm in rural Pennsylvania, the Gimp's mother had no family nearby to leave the boy with during her frequent escapades. So, she would leave little Joey with a neighbor. Deeming the young Joey an irksome imposition, she left him to his own devices. Consequently, his social interactions were minimal. Alone for long periods, he became isolated from other children. Unfortunately, for Little Joey, testosterone does not take this into account when it begins flowing in the blood of young boys. In the Gimp's case this hormone began its eruptive cycle earlier than usual.

The Giampietro family had just returned from a fun filled day in Atlantic City. Feeling particularly frisky one evening from being in the sun all day his mother sought a release from her licentious urges. Unfortunately, his father was summoned to chauffeur Lou Arena and would be out for most of the night. Unable to contain her desires any longer, Grace phoned an obliging character. Asleep in an adjoining room, Little Joey heard moaning from the parlor. Quietly, he cracked open the door and found his mother and another man engaged in feverish sex. Instinctively, he became jealous of the man thrusting wildly into his mother. Her moans made him cringe in fear for her life. Since it wasn't his father it disturbed him deeply. He interpreted her actions as a betrayal of his affection. Instinctively, he wanted to strike out at this vile interloper violating his mother. Instead, he froze. Afraid and ashamed, he tried to cry out, but his mouth was so dry that he became speechless. In his younger years the Gimp viewed the incident as a bad dream. Still, the sweaty, washed out face of the man obsessed him. This surreal episode would feed his psychosis for his entire life. Yet, amid all of this emotional confusion, something else stirred within him.

In later years that emotional stirring returned with unabashed ferocity the first time he saw Rose naked. An erection noticeably emerged in his shorts. The Gimp's lack of social acumen could be tracked from that moment. Rose disparaging laughter, plus Sal Teti's explosion of loathing, short-circuited the little boy's psyche forever. The date, September 1, 1939, was forever etched in the Gimp's mind. Little Joey earned his nickname that day. Teti whipped the boy so savagely that it left him limping for weeks. It wasn't a far stretch for the other street toughs to taunt him by shortening his name.

After that unfortunate event Teti went to great lengths to keep his little girl away from this perverted fiend. Obviously, he thought, this snot-nosed kid was just like his mother. The incident exacerbated Teti's wrath toward the boy. Corporeal punishment for Little Joey began forthwith. Unable to comprehend Teti's motivation, he internalized his feelings. What really bothered the Gimp was his perceived rejection by Rose. His dark side erupted during those days gradually gaining momentum over the years.

Sizing up the young Teti right away when he came of age years later, the Gimp didn't want young Teti claiming his grandfather's mantle of capo. It rightfully belonged to him, the Gimp quietly concluded. He had earned it by sustaining Sal Teti's brutalizing treatment.

The thought of taking up where his grandfather left off never crossed Teti's mind. He had no designs on being a leader of a platoon of half-witted thugs. Thus the Gimp never felt threatened. For Teti this was a blessing in disguise. Still, Teti needed to *make his bones*. So, the Gimp gave Teti a *job*. It would be Teti's opportunity to be a bona fide member of the crew. Teti couldn't refuse unless he was ready to move out of town into obscurity or worse. He wasn't a dumb man, just someone out of his element. Instinctively, the Gimp capitalized on the young man's dilemma.

Rose found out about it by chance. A few awkward questions from her son and Rose put two and two together. After a gut wrenching night of lost sleep she decided to act. She asked Cisco to intercede.

Armand "Cisco" Francesco, a handsome young man with dark magnetic eyes, a thick mane of black hair and an innately suave way about him grew up in his father's poolroom. His accidental encounter with Rose Teti changed the course of both their lives in ways they could never have imagined.

One day in 1943 Rose entered the poolroom. Avant-garde behavior for a young lady during this era, she never gave it a second thought. As a member of a Home Front Mobilization team collecting used newspaper for the war effort she deemed her effort patriotic. The poolroom was empty. Practicing nine-ball as he often did, Cisco also watched the place for his dad on occasion. Rose's silky, long chestnut brown hair, svelte figure, dark, creamy skin and sultry presence combined with her spunky personality to arouse Cisco's interest immediately. Life's foibles had not cast their imprint on this young man yet. Carefree and open, his smile was expressive and revealing. "Hello gorgeous," rolled off his lips mellifluously.

Rose gulped as she unsuccessfully tried to regain her composure. Men had made passes at her before, but this struck her differently. "Ah, well, you see I collect war to help the paper effort," she uttered in a staccato-disjointed response.

Cisco arched an eyebrow realizing the impression that he had just made. "You mean you collect paper for the war effort," was his unflappable reply.

Rose didn't hear a word he had said. Almost on cue, Glenn Miller's rendition of *Moonlight Serenade* softly emanated from the radio in the back of the room. Its romantic effect immediately cast a spell on the two of them. During the ensuing year they engaged in an on again, off again type relationship. Cisco always shied away when Rose sought to take their relationship further. In his gut Cisco knew her protective father would disapprove of their relationship. There was also bad blood between the families. Regardless of those discordant obstacles, Cisco and Rose were in love. So, they gingerly worked around these annoying obstructions.

Sal Teti finally saw the look in their eyes and knew he had to put a stop to it. Under the deceptive shell of a hardened Mafioso beat the heart of a compassionate man. The bravado and anger he exhibited was often self-directed, but made for good theatre. Like most fathers he loved and cherished his daughter. Once his daughter evolved into a lovely young lady, he began fantasizing that she would meet some dashingly handsome officer returning home from the war—move to the suburbs and raise a family. Seeing his daughter fall in love with a petty hustler like Cisco broke his heart. So, when Teti finally caught Rose and Cisco in a lover's embrace, he made it clear in no uncertain terms that Rose was not the girl for him. Seeing the perfect opportunity, he strongly suggested that Cisco take his *hustling* on the road and not return. Ever.

Cisco like everyone else downtown did not see through the façade of Teti's blustering bravado. If he would've stood his ground, life may have dealt him a different hand. Cisco pouted for days after the warning, grappling desperately between self-preservation and his feelings for Rose. To compound matters, the police unexpectedly began sniffing around his father's poolroom concerning several petty burglaries in the neighborhood that indirectly involved Cisco. The mounting pressure seemed oppressive. The two detectives were on the Old Man's payroll. Cisco saw the handwriting on the wall and its message was clear—hit the road.

In his youth Cisco still had a faint touch of the romantic in him. Meeting Rose for one last amorous rendezvous, the intensity of their passion was unleashed. It would always remain the highlight of both of their lives. He left the next day.

Teti sensed his daughter's unhappiness. He too was unhappy. Teti toyed with the idea of finding Cisco and sending the both of them to Florida to live. But Cisco had gotten under his skin and Teti had taken to drinking more heavily. Then something wonderful happened. She discovered that she was pregnant.

Teti and Rose spoke very little during her pregnancy. However, with a baby in the house the ensuing years brought them back together as a family. The topic of the baby's father was gingerly circumvented in order to maintain the status quo. Yet, Cisco remained an invisible barrier between them. If Teti did have second thoughts about Cisco, it died with him on that lonely night while pondering the measure of his life.

Unaware of Teti's death, Cisco had hustled a small town sheriff's brother in a pool game and found himself incarcerated in a South Carolina jail awaiting trial on some trumped up charges. The South in the 50's was an inhospitable place. Their treatment of Blacks and Northerners harkened back to the days of the Carpetbaggers. Astutely aware of the Sheriff's interest in his new Cadillac, Cisco bided his time for the right opportunity to approach him. The Sheriff, being a Southern Baptist, wasn't so easily corrupted. Like his Northern brethren in law enforcement he needed to save face. A sixty-day sentence plus the forfeiture of the Cadillac seemed appropriate.

By the time Cisco managed to straighten out his situation the Old Man had settled Rose's affairs. He had come to terms with his emotions long before he heard through a contact about Rose and her father. The child was his son, he knew, but it would never be the same for the both of them. He would return to South Philly eventually. Contrary to his image as a low life renegade, Cisco harbored a soft spot deep in his heart for her. Stubborn to a fault, he would never admit to Rose that he loved her or was proud of his son. But it was apparent in his eyes and demeanor when the two were mentioned or in his company.

Young Teti was never told about Cisco. Although in later years he suspected it by the way Cisco would watch him. Once, when Rose was in a particularly good mood Teti asked about his father. Rose just smiled broadly and said, "I loved him. That's all you need to know."

The night ordained by the Gimp for the young Teti to make his bones was damp and moonless. The *job*, a Young Turk much like Cisco in his youth, conducted his business indiscreetly. His transgression seemed vague and elusive. Only the Gimp knew for sure. Maybe. It was indicative of the Gimp's imitable style. Teti knew the fellow and was having trepidations. The Gimp suspected as much and followed him.

Meanwhile, lurking in the shadows Cisco followed the both of them. Cisco always had a small .25 caliber automatic tucked away on his person. This night he opted for an untraceable .32 snub-nosed in case things got dicey.

The whole scenario was reminiscent of slapstick comedy if it wasn't for the final outcome. Teti found the Young Turk at a popular club called The Underground on Locust between Broad and Thirteenth Streets. They exchanged friendly greetings and Teti moved to the end of the bar and nursed a drink. He exited shortly after and waited. The long wait raised Teti's anxiety level. His prey finally appeared and headed toward his car. Quietly, Teti slid up behind the man. Teti hesitated. At that moment Teti knew that he couldn't do it. The man turned around sensing danger and went for his pocket. Lunging at him, Teti slipped on the pavement. Just then a shot rang out and the man fell on top of Teti. Immediately rolling out from under the dead body, Teti came face to face with the Gimp. The gun was pointed at Teti.

"Get outta here," the Gimp said in a disgustingly vile tone.

Not far away with his revolver at the ready, Cisco witnessed the entire episode. He could have easily unloaded the .32 into the Gimp. Hesitating for a second, he lost the moment just like his son. The Gimp quickly escaped into the darkened silhouette of the adjoining buildings. Regrettably, that one moment in time replayed in his mind more often than he cared to admit. No amount of personal supplication could expunge it.

Tonight as Cisco shuffled the cards he wondered again. Would he pull the trigger if he were given another chance? *If, if, if* he kept thinking to himself. "If frogs had wings they'd be birds," he finally muttered unthinkingly.

"What bullshit's that?" the Gimp retorted as he sat down.

"Gimme those cards," the Gimp said with contemptuous delight as he grabbed them from Cisco's hand and tossed them across the room helter-skelter. "Pops! Gimme two fresh decks," he demanded. The Gimp's eyes narrowed as he pointed a finger at Cisco. "I got a feelin' you ain't gonna be so lucky tonight, hustler. And I ain't never wrong." The Gimp turned his head and scowled as he flung a twenty-dollar bill in the air, "Hey Teti, make yourself useful and go get me and the guys some cawfee from the Diner, willya. You know how I like mine."

The Gimp just answered Cisco's question.

11

Anna Giampietro was late. Tardiness, her trademark characteristic, defined her persona. A trifling annoyance, everyone accepted it as a fact of life. Trying to change her behavior would be an exercise in futility. Already set in her ways at twenty, the two skills she would ever need in life—manipulation and seduction—were already mastered. Anna naturally assumed the world revolved around her point of view. Her father agreed—to a point.

Joey Giampietro had fast-tracked his way to the exalted position of capo in the South Philadelphia underworld. It was an ascension lacking all the diplomatic finesse of his boss, Giuseppe Vecchio. His inimical style was crude but effective, keeping his criminal cronies constantly second guessing his moods. Consequently, these people, plus those sycophants seeking to be included in the Gimp's inner circle, treated Anna like royalty. Adjusting her mien appropriately, she began acting the part. The Gimp too indulged his only daughter's whims with one exception. Only families—blood relatives—were allowed in the Gimp's house.

The house, a large semidetached model across from the park in Girard Estate, differed significantly from the less spacious two and three-story row homes typically found in South Philadelphia. Instead of the hustle and bustle of the surrounding mean streets, his house was nestled away in an urban setting reminiscent of a tranquil suburban community. This discreet location satisfied the Gimp's pet peeve of privacy while psychologically providing him a womb-like environment. It was this latter reason that drove the Gimp's exclusionary directive regarding visitations to his house. Harkening back to his mythical memory of his parents, he considered this house a sacred receptacle not to be tainted by outsiders. Sequestered within its massive stonewalls, this secluded nurturing environment provided him an emotional fortress—his personal safe haven. So, to avoid explaining to Anna the unexplainable, he encouraged her to meet friends at other locations. Johnny was no exception.

It wasn't until Anna was older that she gave his compulsive behavior any thought. When Anna became a teenager, a confrontation became inevitable. Sensing Anna's growing indignation, the Gimp felt he owed her an explanation. So, he made one up on the fly.

"In my business, treachery is a way of life. People ain't always what they seem to be," the Gimp explained to her once, "wouldya just please try an see it my way this once?"

In truth it was a perfectly logical motivation. It just wasn't his motivation. He said it in such a demure manner that Anna was taken aback. She would always remember it as one of the few times that she actually heard her father say, "Please." Anna acquiesced to her father on this matter, but constantly bickered with him on other matters, as she grew older. Her choice of men was always a volatile topic. Sometimes they would both be brutally direct. His vitriolic criticism would eventual touch a personal nerve in Anna. The result would be long periods of silence between them until Marie Giampietro, the Gimp's wife and Anna's mother, pointed out how silly the both of them were being.

"The two of you are as stubborn as mules," she said to them on one occasion, "and just as stupid."

Once during a particularly heated exchange with his daughter, the Gimp started braying like a mule. The sheer spontaneity of his response startled Anna into wide-eyed silence. This unusual sound even lured Marie into the room piquing her curiosity. Outrageously out of character for the Gimp, they all broke into laughter. In her twenty-one years of marriage to the Gimp it remained one of the few moments that Marie remembered warmly. He never again let his guard down and the rest of their time together was deeply rooted in respectful toleration and conjugal frigidity.

In a perverse way Marie was glad that he reverted to his usual paranoid behavior after that incident. Slowly empathizing with this complex man, she had begun putting the pieces of his life's puzzle in place. After awhile, she began seeing the similarities to her own life. Of course, there were missing sections to both puzzles.

If he had continued to accept the reality of his human foibles, it would have disarmed her. Instead, she steeled her resolve to emotionally punish him for the emptiness in her own heart.

In the early days of her marriage this emptiness morphed into a heartbreaking nightmare that haunted her in the middle of the night. A denizen of the night, the Gimp never suspected her anguish. Eventually, it encumbered her waking thoughts, but pills eased her pain. The nightmare subsided and a perpetual morass filled her life. As her parents grew older she kept busy working the family business.

Marie's father owned a modest business on Ninth Street in the Italian Market section just below Washington Avenue. It initially was a haberdashery that catered to the unique styles of the Italian immigrants. This included the somber black dresses of the perpetual widows. Later he expanded the business to include utensils designed to ease the preparation of Italian meals. Her mother was the first cousin to the Old Man. Both parents were familiar with the petulant Joseph Giampietro and his popularity with their cousin. Although her parents were somewhat Americanized, they still maintained the basic traditional mores of their Italian heritage through the years. Thus, when the Old Man formally asked her father on behalf of the Gimp for permission to date Marie, he acceded. Marie was noticeably distraught. "How could you do this to me without asking?" she railed.

"The Old Man vouched for him. Besides, I'm not asking you to marry the man," the father intoned pleadingly.

Marie resisted. She wanted to make her own choices. Several weeks later her destiny would surface to change the course of her entire life. She often thought of the irony of it all.

Tonight Marie looked lovingly upon Anna. Something was different about her. She had become a woman right before her very eyes. Marie felt that she had blinked and missed the joys and pain of her daughter's adolescence because of her growing disdain for the Gimp and what he represented. Marie gently stroked Anna's silky jet-black hair. Like the Gimp, she was overly protective of her daughter and kept a discreet eye on her through several good friends.

"Bring this boy around the store sometime. I'd like to meet him," Marie said softly.

"Which one?" Anna said with a toying look in her eye.

A hint of a crooked smile crept across Marie's normally stoic face. Anna responded with a smile and gave her mother a warm hug then left.

Although the Gimp appeared uninterested in Anna's boyfriends, he wasn't above having her followed. Anna suspected her father's protective contrivances. Even if untrue, she didn't like the shadow of his presence always swirling around her. It was stifling. Many guys wouldn't give her a second look because of her father even though she was an attractive woman in the classical Italian style.

Anna's skin was exquisitely dark and creamy like her mother's. Her dark black eyes were oval-shaped, as were the bones of her face and the contour of her brow. Sensuality exuded from every curve of her body. She learned quickly how to use this to her advantage. The Gimp, well aware of her machinations, constantly thwarted her insipid dreams of indiscretion. This adolescent revolt against parental authority would only come back to haunt her in later years, he would rationalize. So, as any devoted parent would do, the Gimp decided to save her from herself and quietly intervene when appropriate.

Anna knew how her father thought on these matters. After considering her options she decided that the only way to break away from his interference in her life was to get married. Since love between her parents was absent in her family life, it never became a consideration. A show of affection took the form of presents. Denied nothing, she could have whatever her heart desired. Total independence was another matter. Consequently, in any marriage she needed to be the hammer. Therefore, she sought a potential husband who could be a nail. Johnny Cerone fit the profile perfectly. Tall and handsome, he hailed from a second-generation American family of Italian descent. His sculptured physique, sensually obscene when his shirt was off, appealed to the baser sexual instincts of women. Although the physical aspect of a partner enticed Anna, his impression-able personality became the deciding factor. Johnny thought of himself as a free spirit, open to all possibilities. Anna saw him as a piece of clay on the pottery wheel of life, a man who didn't know exactly what he wanted. She would mold him into an object that she could possess and if she wished, discard like other objects in her life that no longer served her purpose.

All these thoughts and more crossed Anna's mind as she drove her car through the crowded rain soaked streets of South Philadelphia this Saturday evening. Intent on manipulating Johnny, Anna didn't notice the black Impala convertible following her.

12

With eyes flickering to and fro Johnny waited anxiously in the glass-enclosed entrance to the Diner for Anna to drive up. He knew that if she parked her car and came in it would be an hour before they would leave. This way he would jump into her car and they could leave without the usual fanfare. Instead, he thought that they could have a serious conversation before Anna got him all hot and bothered. It wasn't that he didn't want to make love to her because he surely did. He just didn't want to marry her. Obsessing over this thought already tonight, he tried to rationalize it away. Besides, the timing was all wrong he mused.

"*Money, money, money,*" the word reverberated in his head like an iron ball of a pinball machine bouncing wildly. There were few alternatives to ingratiating himself to Anna. Of course, there was always a loan shark. That thought, with its desperate overtones, lingered in his mind until he realized its implications. What's the matter with me, he thought dourly. I'm on a treadmill to nowhere that's about to spin out of control.

Just then Anna's champagne colored 1972 Camaro Super Sport pulled up and Johnny's anxiety temporarily dissipated. Her long eyelashes accentuating her oval face with a warm lustful smile melted all of Johnny's fears into a puddle of desire. With his trench coat slung over his arm Johnny broke free from his imaginary treadmill and bolted from the entrance of the Diner like a schoolboy running in the rain. Anna indicated with sensually expressive eyes that she would drive and Johnny responded like a well-trained dog sliding quickly into the passenger seat. "You look gorgeous," Johnny said eagerly.

Anna smiled with an amusing glint in her eyes as the nipples on her full breasts hardened. She loved it when she was the sole focus of attention. It always made her feel in control.

"Did Armando get your car fixed yet?" she said in a restrained manner.

"Yeah," he said tersely.

Toying with him now, Anna knew Johnny was hard-pressed to ask her for money again. She knew that he needed money. He always needed money. That's why he was a perfect choice for her little plan. So, she let him hang in the wind for a moment.

"You want to go to Jersey for a drink," Johnny asked.

"I thought we'd drive around for awhile," Anna's eyes were averted for effect as she replied. "I like drivin' in the rain. It makes you feel clean."

Johnny just nodded docilely.

Anna glanced at Johnny in an enticing way. "You need money to get the car out?"

Johnny bit his lip trying not to look overly anxious then replied slowly with measured words, "Yeah, it would help 'til I get paid next Friday, if that's okay?" The scent of her perfume kept him from being morose allowing him to endure the unendurable.

Anna kept her eyes on the road while trying not to be sarcastic. "How much this time?"

Johnny pursed his lips then spoke in a low tone. "Two hundred ought ta cover it." Actually, he only needed a hundred. The other hundred was a groveling tax so he would have some money to pay the bookie.

Anna had Johnny where she wanted him. It had nothing to do with money. It was Johnny's total deference to her tonight that excited her. She could afford to be magnanimous. Grabbing the steering wheel with her left hand Anna flitted through her purse with her other hand until she produced, as if by magic, two crisp one-hundred dollar bills. Handing them to Johnny she smiled sensually. "Let's go uptown and have a drink."

Johnny hesitated thoughtfully before he took the money from her. Anna smiled seductively at Johnny. Her perfume had already titillated Johnny's sexual appetite. Johnny looked out the window at the rain then looked at Anna with enticing eyes, "Maybe we should take a spin by the lakes. Only the ducks will be out tonight."

Abutting the Philadelphia Naval Yard, Roosevelt (FDR) Park or as the locals call it, "The Lakes" is situated at the southwestern corner of Broad Street across the street from JFK Stadium. Originally called Municipal Stadium, it was the home of the Army-Navy football game and the annual Police Officers and Firefighters Hero Scholarship Show. "The Thrill Show," as it became known, was created in 1954 when an explosion killed ten firefighters. The proceeds from the show benefited the education of the children of Police Officers and Firefighters killed or severely disabled in the line of duty.

The Gimp was a major contributor to this event. He knew that each precinct and firehouse had a quota to make and made sure that the local precinct and firehouse in his neighborhood made their quota handily. Of course this prompted jealousy among the other precincts and firehouses. So, in a variety of devious ways they managed to extract additional contributions from the Gimp's rank and file to make up the difference. Everyone understood the rules. No one complained. After all, it was for charity.

Both the stadium and the park were part of the Sesquicentennial Exposition in 1926. While the stadium was built expressly for the Exposition, "The Lakes" was designed in the early 1900's and modified for the Exposition in 1926. Occupying a 348-acre area at the confluence of the Schuylkill and Delaware Rivers it became a favorite spot over the years for a quick romantic interlude for those lovers who didn't want to make the trip over the Walt Whitman Bridge to New Jersey and the scores of cheap motels that line Route 130.

Discreetly, the black Impala convertible followed Anna's '72 Camaro Super Sport south on Broad Street. Once they passed the on ramp to the Walt Whitman Bridge, the driver backed off considerably, allowing the two tempestuous lovers a head start. There was only one possible destination on a night like this one. Finding them wouldn't be a problem.

A short time later inside Anna's car, Johnny and Anna were hungrily groping at each another. Their heavy breathing steamed the windows while raindrops resonated on the surface of the car in rhythmic fashion. Without breaking the kiss, Johnny let his carnal appetite rule as he unbuttoned Anna's blouse and attempted to unsnap her bra.

"Be gentle," Anna said languidly. She tried to fantasize what it would be like if Johnny took complete control, but the thought had a dulling effect. Instead, she fantasized a faceless powerfully built man ravaging her despite her pleadings. This thought excited her beyond belief. The thought of subjugation excited her immensely on this level of intimacy, but scared her on every other level. Reminding herself that the Gimp's daughter should not be submissive, the mere thought of the animal magnetism of her imaginary lover was a powerful aphrodisiac.

She pulled away, breathing rapidly. Gently stroking her hair he kissed her again hungrily. His hands caressed her warm silky skin. Slowly, he pulled away and bent his head moving his mouth over her bare skin until he reached her exposed breasts. A muffled groan emanated from her succulent lips as she writhed in pleasure. He loved it when Anna was captive to her primordial instincts. She flinched when suddenly the thought of Johnny dominating her crept back into her mind.

"What is it?" he asked.

She saw a look of disappointment on his face. Remembering her original reasons for seducing Johnny she said alluringly, "Do you love me Johnny?"

Off guard and at a disadvantage, Johnny tried to obscure an affirmative response with a deep guttural sound while attempting to recapture the moment.

Anna's pleasure, however, turned to one of domination. If she could not bear the thought of Johnny possessing her then she would possess him. It was that simple. She released the deep moan of a woman enthralled, but still pressed him for an answer. "Johnny, do you love me?"

"Of course," he mumbled almost inaudibly. Realizing that the moment was lost, he snapped back to reality thankful that he didn't cross the line.

Without warning two bright headlights pierced the condensation on the rear window bathing the two lovers in an eerie yellow light. Anna haphazardly scrambled to cover herself just as someone knocked on the passenger window. Cautiously, Johnny inched opened the car window. Noticing a police emblem just above the brim of a hat, Johnny squinted his eyes as the flooding glare of a flashlight blinded him. The policeman quickly focused the flashlight on Anna who had at least managed to cover herself with her blouse.

"What's going on here?" he quizzed as a smirk transformed his normally stolid face curling the ends of his mouth upward.

Johnny bumbled his response, "Nothin, nothin at all. She, she just ah, spilled somethin. That's all. Yeah, just, ya know, spilled somethin."

"Yeah, I can see the drool marks. Let me see some ID," the policeman retorted sarcastically.

Anna extended her arm across Johnny's chest to hand the policeman her identification. Reacting like a contortionist, Johnny quickly fished through his pockets for his wallet dropping the two one-hundred dollar bills on the floor in the confusion. The policeman immediately noticed the money.

"You dropped something, Sir," The policeman coyly remarked arching his calculating eyes.

Gathering the loose one-hundred dollar bills after handing the policeman his driver's license, Johnny suddenly realized the policeman's avaricious intent.

The policeman looked at the licenses smiling broadly and said, "Joey Giampietro's daughter?"

Anna bit the inside of her cheek and nodded humbly.

Johnny quickly interceded. "We don't need to get him involved, do we officer?"

The policeman hesitated for a moment in thought with tight, protruding lips. Sheltering the licenses from the rain, he asked, "You get your Thrill Show tickets yet Mister Cerone?"

"No," Johnny replied tersely.

The policeman gave Johnny an icy stare then answered tersely in a cold and inimical voice. "Well it's your lucky day. I got some right here."

Johnny hesitantly handed the policeman a single one-hundred dollar bill.

"How 'bout your friends?"

Johnny brooded before extending the other one-hundred dollar bill to the policeman. The licenses were quickly returned. While rhythmically fanning the bundle of tickets the policeman momentarily considered keeping the tickets for himself in the hope of netting another unlucky sucker. Not wanting to tempt fate, he tossed the bundle onto Johnny's lap.

"Next time take this shit over the bridge to a motel will ya," the officer declared sternly. "I don't take kindly to being the bearer of this kind of news to Mister Giampietro. You get my drift?"

Johnny nodded obsequiously amid the pitter-patter of the raindrops.

"Now get dressed and get outta here!" The policeman turned and stomped off in a series of splashes back to the police van.

From deep within the bowels of the black Impala convertible the foreboding silhouette of the driver was momentarily illuminated when he struck a match. He lit another cigarette and gleefully blew a funnel of cigarette smoke from the slightly cracked window.

13

Directly north of "The Lakes," a mere twenty city blocks away, another realization was gradually unfolding. This one wasn't unpredictable. It was suppose to be manageable. In hindsight it was inevitable.

Cisco knew that he would have to lose to the Gimp on this dank evening. He accepted this preordination. No one would stand up to the Gimp on his behalf. Accepting his fate, he hoped to lessen the pain as much as possible. His trademark contemptuous smirk was even absent this evening. Of course another important variable was the amount that he was going to lose tonight. Cisco thought that he could control this variable through guile and slight of hand. This little contrivance would allow the Gimp to save face. He was wrong. The Gimp's winnings were mounting fast as the cards and events turned against him. There was nothing that he could do about it. At this moment fate wasn't looking kindly on Cisco. Then it got worse.

Anthony "Mad Dog" Carlucci entered the poolroom and immediately pulled up a chair beside Cisco. The Gimp smiled wickedly. Motioning for Pops, the houseman, to bring two fresh decks of cards, the Gimp then turned to his trusted henchman with a reproachful glance. "Did you take care of that twerp, Nicky?" he croaked.

"Nah. He ain't goin' no where." Only Mad Dog Anthony could get away with a reply like that to the Gimp without him going into a ballistic rage.

"Well you can furgetabout it cause I sent the Snake to bring that little asshole here. We'll talk about this later," the Gimp said with finality.

Anthony Carlucci surreptitiously known as Mad Dog Anthony was a small unshaven bulldog of a man with ill-groomed, shaggy brown hair and a personality to match. His heavy garlic-laced breath mixed with the poolroom's consumptive cigarette smoke to create a potent toxic effluence that seemed specifically directed toward Cisco. It wasn't. He just didn't brush his teeth. Carlucci's nonstop idle chatter and Teti mulling about, distracted Cisco from noticing the markings on the newly entered decks of cards. Loosing his concentration, Cisco reminisced about a time long ago.

Cisco and Anthony knew each other long before each had acquired their individual reputations and unique sobriquets. Actually it was Anthony who began calling Armand "Cisco." It was a play on his last name and the radio show *The Cisco Kid*. The name stuck to Armand to the degree that almost no one remembered his real name. Anthony's nickname, however, was based on an actual grizzly event that would happen after the two went their separate ways. The name served Anthony well. It was a constant reminder of the vicious nature of the man.

In their preteen youth Armand and Anthony often hung out together. Armand, always impish, liked to play tricks on his friends that sometimes got out of hand. One such occurrence would unknowingly pit Anthony against Armand for the rest of their lives. Armand never gave the incident a second thought, forgetting about his childhood foolishness. Anthony never forgot. The incident sliced at the root of his manhood. He let it fester unchecked until it totally consumed him. After that incident their relationship devolved into an adversarial mixture of artificially infused hubris. It was actually Anthony's only way of suppressing his deeply wounded psyche. Never understanding Anthony's evolving resentment toward him, Armand considered Anthony a mean spirited thug with a chip on his shoulder. A confrontation was inevitable.

Both grew into street toughs and the idle chatter of their friends often revolved around who was the tougher of the two. Armand's contemptible scowl became the stuff of street corner legends. In the future, Marlon Brando and James Dean would refine the facial feature for the movies, but for now Armand had the patent. A rumor circulated that he was born with it on his face. There were a few who didn't believe it. So, for whatever reason they set out to remove it. Although he never looked for trouble, Armand never ran away either. Always a hustler more than a brawler, idle talk had a way of a materializing.

Anthony on the other hand was inclined to settle any disagreements with his fists first. This method of communication began quite innocently. Since his formal education was not worth mentioning, he reverted to the common practice of using his hands expressively in conjunction with his limited vocabulary. Combined with his volatile personality, it eventually evolved into his only method of expression. What one said or how they said it always presented a dicey proposition in Anthony's presence. Instinctually, he was a predator. Intellectually, his IQ bordered on moronity.

Impatience was another trait that molded Anthony's persona. The blending of all of these traits converged into a dangerous mixture. In his youth it was partially contained. However, when he heard the speculation floating around the streets about Armand's physical prowess versus his own, he immediately sought out a confrontation to silence the idle talk once and for all.

This happened in front of the poolroom owned by Armand's father on East Passyunk Avenue in 1944. Armand initially downplayed all the talk even conceding that Anthony was the tougher of the two. The contemptuous smirk on Armand's face as he conceded to Anthony only fueled his ire more.

What happened next is a matter of conjecture. The final outcome was not. Though no one would actually step up and say it, everyone there saw Anthony throw the first punch. A fight ensued that resembled a wrestling match more than a boxing match. Anthony, brawnier than Armand, should have dominated, but Armand was quicker and more flexible. In the end Armand somehow prevailed pinning Anthony underneath him to the cold-jagged concrete sidewalk. In those days Anthony still retained a modicum of restraint. Armand relented in a gracious manner. Anthony didn't know the meaning of gracious.

"You know I'm gonna have ta kill ya some day," Anthony chortled after Armand helped him to his feet.

Instantly, Armand responded with a silly smirk, "Over my dead body."

Anthony's forehead creased in incomprehension. His first thought was that this guy was screwing with him. Then as if struck by some esoteric prod to his brain he realized the levity of the response. He broke into a voluminous belly laugh and punched Armand's bicep with an amicable poke. "That's the way I see it too."

Armand instinctually knew that Anthony was serious—dead serious.

Replaying this adolescent event in his mind, Cisco unwittingly threw out a Queen of Spades.

"Gin." The Gimp ferociously intoned as he quickly laid down his cards on top of it. He was ecstatic. This was going just as he had planned, he thought to himself. Unable to mask his inner gloating, the Gimp's face beamed with delight.

Broodingly, Cisco's eye caught the malefic stare of the black Queen. At first he thought that it was an ominous warning of things to come. Not a superstitious person, Cisco quickly dismissed any sinister implications. Personally, he wanted to tell the Gimp what an idiot he was for saving Queens this late in the hand. No. He wanted to shout it in his face. He should have played to bury the son of a bitch from the get-go instead of pussyfooting around, he thought self-reproachfully. Despite these thoughts, Cisco kept his face impassive.

The Gimp scooped the cards from under Cisco's nose while making a snorting noise.

"It don't seem to be yer night tonight, hustler."

"I've had worse."

The Gimp makes a jerking motion with his head then sardonically replied, "It ain't over yet."

14

Embarrassment oozed from every pour of Anna's body. She winced as Johnny unconsciously yanked at her bra straps in an expeditious effort to reconnect the hooks on the two supple pieces of silky material.

"You're pulling too hard for Christ sakes," Anna said scoldingly.

After a distressing moment Johnny finally succeeded, exhaling heavily as he slumped back into his seat. "We better get out of here before that cop comes around again," he muttered.

Anna finished buttoning her blouse then squiggled around in the driver's seat until she finally felt fairly comfortable. Her seething emotions were dangerously pulsing through her veins. The synapses of her mind were arcing between pleasure and anger. She bit down on the inside of her tightly pursed lips. Starting the engine Anna darted Johnny a fiery stare that would melt iron. Then it happened. Banging on the steering wheel with the palms of her hand she screamed wildly, "I've never been so embarrassed in my entire fuckin' life! Never!"

Johnny cowered reflexively. Sensing that any response would only escalate the situation into a shouting match, he constrained his natural instinct to respond and decided to let her continue to vent.

Exasperated by Johnny's calm mien, Anna jammed the car into gear and slammed down on the gas pedal, fishtailing the Camaro onto the slippery road and almost crashing into a tree. Consciously losing control startled Anna like a stinging slap to the face. It was sheer ecstasy. For one brief moment she felt incredibly light and joyous. Her overwrought imagination wondered whether Johnny could ever make her feel this way. Somewhere in her brain a little voice answered her quizzing directly. "*No, you need a man of strength. Someone to be your equal.*" Sighing, she put these thoughts out of her head. They scared her because she knew her inner voice was true. Besides, moments like this could be addictive. With that in mind she simultaneously regained control of the car.

At that moment the exhilarating emotional roller coaster ride came to a screeching halt. But her volatile emotions still roiled beneath the surface of her voluptuous countenance. Temporarily suppressed for now, Anna initially believed that she could control her craving. In the ensuing weeks she would realize the fallacy of that notion.

Unlike Anna's feeling of exhilaration, Johnny became downright scared. Tonight he had witnessed a catharsis. He sensed the change in her demeanor. This instantaneous change scared him. Her wily ways had previously been predictable and more easily sidestepped. Now, he was unsure of what she was capable of doing. Tonight he entered uncharted territory, he thought with a guilty reproach. The splattering rain on the windshield suddenly broke his train of thought.

"I need that drink now," Anna said briskly while simultaneously turning on the windshield wipers. The hypnotic movement of the wipers further diffused her surging emotions allowing her a moment of clarity.

"A drink sounds good to me right now too," Johnny retorted. He noticed her helpless little-girl lost glance that she used so convincingly. Then it happened.

"My father wants to meet you," she said matter-of-factly. That simple declaration resounded ominously throughout Johnny's entire body.

Wriggling in the passenger seat, Johnny appeared stunned and visibly distraught. "Really?"

"I knew it would make you nervous," Anna said, "so I kept waiting for the right moment but it never came."

Uncharacteristically maintaining the speed limit, Anna turned north onto Broad Street toward Center City. The constant drone of the engine mixed with the hypnotic movement of the windshield wipers to produce a meditative effect on a distraught Johnny.

"So why does he all of sudden want to meet me?" Johnny paused momentarily, "Is there somethin' goin' on that I don't know about?"

"I guess he figures it's time. After all, we've been seein' each other for almost a year and I guess he figures we're serious."

"Serious?" Johnny shot back quizzically.

"Aren't we serious, Johnny? Tell me! Tell me right now. Because if you're not, I'm goin' to have some explainin' to do to my father," Anna replied in a subtly threatening way.

"Serious like what?" Johnny quizzically pressed.

"Like what are your intentions, or is it just slam-bam thank you ma'am?" Anna blurted out indignantly.

Caught off guard by her vehemence, Johnny silently pondered the situation a moment too long.

Anna seized the initiative. "Then that's it, you just want to use me. All that talk of love tonight was just to get into my pants," Anna said in a conclusive voice.

"Don't be putting words in my mouth," Johnny responded defensively.

"Then you meant it?"

"We need time to explore this."

The fright in Johnny's voice gave Anna a disproportionate amount of pleasure.

Fending off total submission Johnny still felt numbed and isolated. "Listen, I'm really attracted to you Anna. Really. But we need to talk about this sensibly, ya know. We don't want to rush in to somethin' that might not work out no matter how we feel."

"The rush is over, Johnny. We've been together a whole year. Either you know how you feel about me or you don't. My father's not stupid, just old fashioned when it comes to sex. So, what do I tell my father?"

Johnny frowned in concentration searching for a noncommittal response. None came immediately to mind. There was no weaseling out of this one, he thought. Sighing heavily he decided to play for time. With that thought he suddenly realized his whole life was nothing more than perpetual procrastination. He shook his head in disbelief. The moment that he feared most had arrived. Virtually in another place, Johnny grinned broadly losing track of the conversation at hand. Mimicking an actor in a romantic scene, he intoned in a cavalier burst of spontaneity, "Tell him that it would be my pleasure to meet with him at his convenience to discuss my intentions towards his lovely daughter Anna."

Johnny's offhanded sarcasm was misinterpreted. The joke was about to be on him. At that moment Anna stopped for a red light at Washington Avenue. Anna, who never was one for sentimental fiddle-faddle, blew Johnny a kiss. Her florid face beamed with delight. "Good answer. Great Answer! You and my father will get along famously. He's really a reasonable guy," Anna said with a tinge of facetiousness.

Impulsively, Anna leaned over toward Johnny giving him a smothering kiss. Taken aback momentarily, Johnny responded hungrily. His passion got the best of him as their little cat and mouse game titillated both of their carnal instincts. Passionately embraced, Anna and Johnny were oblivious to their surroundings as the stoplight turned green.

Stopped directly behind Anna's Camaro, the exhaust of the black Impala convertible enveloped the idling car like a teakettle approaching the boiling point. The driver viewed the silhouetted figures before him like a romantic scene in a silent movie. He flitted his cigarette out the window angrily and then laid on the car horn until Anna responded by driving away. The occupant had seen enough. With squealing tires the black Impala convertible turned right onto Washington Avenue heading east, its chrome wheels and the 456-Super Sport emblem glistened noticeably under the street lights. It continued to rain. Heavy drops thumped the canvas roof of the black Impala convertible as it came to an abrupt stop on Carpenter Street near Tenth astride an opening in a seeming endless chain of vehicles.

At this time of night parking was at a premium in South Philadelphia. The driver reverently engaged the reverse gear adroitly maneuvering the car into the opening in one swift movement. Coming within inches of the abutting cars the black Impala convertible grew silent. Drivers in South Philadelphia may not know the geometric theorems governing the parking of vehicles, but they knew the practical applications. Tight spots were a way of life downtown.

At that moment a dark curly haired figure emerged from the car. Cosmo Tucci, the son of Carmine Tucci, chugged on a cigarette defiantly. His hair matched his wardrobe. Both were entirely black. Rarely did he dress in any other color. If he would have stayed in high school longer, he may have learned that his preference for black was allegorical for his perspective on life. But his destiny was sealed long ago and higher education was not part of it. Tonight, as he walked the cold damp streets back to his apartment, the streetlights glistened off his short black leather jacket heightening his pernicious demeanor. His long suppressed obsessive behavior had become more noticeable lately.

Teti had mentioned it in passing one recent afternoon. Tucci didn't see it that way. Jabbing a finger at his head, Tucci replied to Teti, "You don't know what goes on in my fuckin' world. So don't act like you do."

Teti never mentioned it again.

The Gimp had given Teti the responsibility of keeping the young Tucci a.k.a. "Cuzz" busy. "Cuzz" as Tucci was also known downtown, was a sobriquet bestowed on him derived from his god given name of Cosmo. Actually, it was part of the common South Philly vernacular used to address someone in a friendly way. It became especially handy when someone didn't know the other person's name. Besides, family relations abounded downtown. Subsequently, the odds were good that the other person was your cousin. Thus the phrase "Hey Cuzz" entered the unique lexicon of South Philly.

Cuzz preferred to be known by his last name like Teti. Teti liked it because it honored his grandfather. Tucci did it to keep the memory of his father alive. He also knew that it aggravated the Gimp. There would be a day of reckoning for these two when the Old Man passed. Both men knew this was inevitable.

The Old Man had made it a point of honor for the Gimp to take care of the young Tucci. So, he was bound to keep it—for the time being. Of course the Old Man wasn't dumb or entirely caught up in all the honor bullshit. He used it to serve his purpose and his purpose was to keep the Gimp off balance and looking over his shoulder. This had the further effect of checkmating the Gimp. Therefore, the Gimp bided his time and gave Teti the responsibility for keeping Tucci busy and in line. Keeping the belligerent asshole out of the Gimp's face was Teti's first task. Consequently, Tucci was given the unglamorous task of babysitting Anna. The Gimp knew nothing of her lifelong infatuation for him.

Tucci spent so much time following Anna that it bordered on voyeurism. Eventually, he found himself fantasizing about her. Spitefully violent at first, Tucci's thoughts slowly softened towards Anna every time that he saw her. Lately, however, something had changed.

Tonight, as he returned to his apartment, he grappled desperately with strange feelings and emotions coursing their way through his body. When Anna leaned over at the red light and spontaneously kissed Johnny, the young Tucci's blood boiled. At first he shrugged it off to fatigue. Then he reminisced about her infatuation with him when they were kids. He was her first crush. When she began avoiding him, he took it personal. That the little bitch may be teasing him finally crossed his mind. Dismissing that thought, he called it a night.

Flipping the stub of his cigarette into a puddle of water in the middle of Tenth Street, he turned to unlock the door to the stairway that led to his apartment above Perricone's Bakery. Suddenly, Tucci felt an ache in the pit of his stomach. The splat of the rain on his black leather coat made him stop. A random breeze sprayed the cold mist across his face before he entered the stairwell. As he turned to close the door behind him, a bone chilling realization struck him. His gut instinct told him that his life teetered on a dangerous precipice. Unsure of the outcome, he would continue walking along its rocky ledge he thought. Tantamount to a game of chicken, he refused to yield. He had nothing to lose.

15

Half an hour later the rain subsided. Snake pulled up outside the Downtown Bar & Grill in a 1967 Silver Buick Riviera Grand Sport with a black vinyl top. He turned off the powerful 430 cubic inch, 360 horsepower engine and methodically surveyed the surrounding streets with his beady eyes. The Downtown Bar & Grill had been his favorite haunt in his younger days. It rekindled fond memories of better times.

"If Solly could only see this place now," Snake grumbled to himself disapprovingly. Any other night he might wait for his mark to come outside in deference to the memory of his old boss, Sal Teti. Tonight, however, business seemed slow and the Gimp was impatient. Sighing heavily, he removed a .38 Special from a hidden side panel on the driver's door and exited the car. Snake never underestimated anyone especially this little publicity seeker. His kind had no common sense.

Nicky "Sox" Socci was sitting alone at the nearly deserted bar nursing a beer. Slight of build, his elbow propped his lurching head on the heel of the palm of his hand while watching the Johnny Carson Show. With a cigarette scissored between his fingers, he took a final swig on a bottle of Schmidt's. Tapping the bottle on the bar top, he motioned for another cold one. "Ralph! Another Schmidt's," he bellowed then belched loudly.

Nicky acquired his nom de plume because of his last name and his insistence on betting every year that the Boston Red Sox would win the World Series at the beginning of baseball season. Almost a sure thing, the bookies lined up to take the bet. In the end it didn't amount to a lot of money, but Nicky craved the attention. Perception meant everything to Nicky.

This obsession with perception also spilled over into other areas of his life. When he heard of the legendary tipping habits of Frank Sinatra, Nicky began to emulate him. After all, Frank was the man and Nicky's skinny, lithe body build resembled the fabled crooner in his earlier years. Since he always paid with the flourish of a celebrity, Nicky had running tabs at all the right bars in South Philly. A likeable guy, most people saw through his little masquerade and they let him pretend. Commenting on Nicky was always worth a few minutes of lighthearted conversation at the local bars when there was nothing else to talk about.

Lately, however, Nicky became the main topic of conversation for all the wrong reasons—his luck was running out. If this trend continued, his new nickname would be Poor Nicky.

It started with the large bet that he laid down on Muhammad Ali against the hometown favorite Joe Fraser. Greed got the best of him on that day in 1971 and he never recovered. On a downhill slide ever since, the wily Nicky Sox resorted to shopping around town looking for a chink in the point spread on all the games. When he found at least a point and a half gap, he would bet both sides hoping for the game to fall in the middle. He went on this way for a year winning a few bucks, but never catching a break. Then one day the game fell perfect for him. Thinking his luck had changed, he rushed to collect his winnings. Unluckily, the several bookies he bet with stiffed him. Since he didn't collect his winnings, he couldn't pay his loses. This caused a chain reaction that eventually led to his present predicament.

Ralph put up with the fanciful bravado of cheap drunks like Nicky Sox. Usually, they kept throwing money onto the bar like big shots and never counted it. Actually, they were so drunk most of the time that they couldn't count it. Ralph liked those nights. Usually two deep at the bar, he would never go home with less than a C-note.

Tonight's behavior portended Nicky's dire straights. With his exaggerated conduct under wraps, Ralph wouldn't be surprised if this guy paid his bar tab with loose change from his pocket. Holding an unopened bottle of beer in his hand, Ralph looked dourly at Nicky Sox. Nicky got the message. It was cash up front. Word had spread that Nicky Sox was down on his luck—a stiff. It got worse.

Nicky owed money to a loan shark who recently fell under the Gimp's protection. Borrowing the money some time before this transpired, he never knew about it. As far as Nicky knew, the loan shark was fair game. Hearing the bad news from a frustrated free-lance bookie that he stiffed rattled him. Already becoming a pariah downtown, Nicky was now looking at some serious physical consequences. Even amid his new dire circumstances, Nicky still craved the attention. So, instead of lying low until he could at least pay the *vig* on the loan, he shows up at one of the most visible places downtown.

When Ralph the bartender first saw him enter the bar his jaw dropped. This guy must be a total idiot he thought. Nicky's perspective was decidedly different. In order to change his luck he needed to tempt it. He devised this superstitious concept on the fly with no basis in reality.

Superstition was a part of the culture downtown. Mothers and daughters would light candles to their favorite saints hoping for some type of miraculous intervention for their loved ones. Men would wear gold cornicelli better known as golden peppers to ward off the evil eye. If this didn't work they would blame anyone, but themselves when the cards would turn against them. Grasping at straws, their minds would sometimes scheme to rationalize their troubles away as Nicky had done.

So, there he sat sipping a beer and passing the time. As the night grew older he thought that his luck might just change. Then Louie the Snake entered the bar and Nicky's capricious thoughts were squashed like a fly under a swatter. His stomach turned sour. Beads of sweat formed on his forehead. Slowly, Louie approached him with his trademark slithering swagger.

"Nicky, Nicky, Nicky did ya think yer were gonna get a free pass?" Louie hissed in a mocking singsong tone.

"Come on Snake, really I'm good for the dough," Nicky mumbled.

Louie half-heartedly smacked Nicky across the face with the back of his hand. "You ain't good for shit." Louie smacked Nicky a little harder across the face a second time. "At least ya could a made up something. Anything. Ya ain't even tryin. Don't insult me like that. You'll make me turn you into a bloody pulp before the Gimp has his fun with you. I'm in a bad mood Sox and I'm itchin' to take it out on somebody. And it might as well be you."

Squirming on the barstool, Nicky pleaded, "I ain't gotta beef with you Snake. But I'll try. I'll try. Really I'll try."

"Good, 'cause when you see the Gimp tonight he ain't gonna be in any mood for your half cocked answers. He'll be insulted that you didn't even care to make up a good lie for him. So you got til we get back to the poolroom to make up something. Try not to grovel or beg either. That shit's irritating." Snake gave Nicky a toothy smile that turned deadly serious as he pushed his hand slowly out from his side to reveal his piece. "And don't be totally stupid. You're in it now so take your shit like a man. Capisce?"

Nicky managed a muted, but frightened nod. His normally straight shoulders slumped as he pondered his fate.

Tonight was a night that all gamblers dreaded. Throwing good money after bad, the stupid ones thought they could turn their luck. The smart ones cut their loses and ran. Nicky was now going to pay the price for his stupidity. Taking his medicine like a man was another matter.

16

Deciding to walk home, Johnny Cerone kissed Anna goodnight in front of her house. He lived only a few blocks away and the rain had stopped. The walk home would help clear his mind, he thought desperately. Without turning back to watch Anna enter her house, Johnny started his march home with his hands in his pockets and his head hung low. Anna didn't notice nor did she care. Skipping up the steps to her house, she acted like a schoolgirl winning the big prize at the annual church carnival.

As Johnny walked amid the shadows of the sycamore trees lining Shunk Street, he tried to reconstruct the evening's events into some semblance of order. Nervously, he fanned the stack of Thrill Show tickets in his pocket with his thumb. The rhythm of his mood silently pulsated like the ebb and flow of his silhouette on the houses and fences along his path. Realizing his options were nil, he might as well suck it in and face the consequences like a man, he dolefully thought. Unexpectedly, a jerking car with squealing tires and loud music abruptly stopped blocking his path at the intersection of Twentieth and Shunk Streets. Startled by the suddenness of the moment, Johnny froze like a deer looking into the headlights of an oncoming car.

"Yo Johnny," croaked Tommy "Dee" DiRienzo as the staccato rumbling of his 1965 Pontiac GTO created an audible beat. "Hey, it's me Tommy Dee. Snap out of it," lambasted Tommy whose swarthy countenance and robust head of reddish brown curly hair glistened under the street lamps dull glow as his head protruded out of the car window.

An arched smile replaced Johnny's dour looking face. Shaking his head incredulously he chortled, "Only an asshole like you would pull a stunt like that." Johnny was eager to bear his soul to someone—anyone—but not Tommy Dee. Still, Tommy was one of his oldest friends. Looking for a distraction, Johnny jumped into the car. Barely seated, Tommy let out the clutch and raced away in his usual hot-rod fashion. As they cruised along the car-infested streets, Tommy caught the reflection of Johnny's sullen eyes in the car window. Not one for quiet reflection, Tommy felt compelled to speak.

"Where's yer cousin Joey been these days? Haven't seen 'em around," Tommy said matter-of-factly.

Johnny shot Tommy a look of askance. "What are you talkin' about? You don't give two shits about Joey," Johnny said flippantly.

Momentarily taken aback by Johnny's vehemence, Tommy replied in a staunch tone of voice, "No I don't. I was jus tryin' ta, ya know, break the ice, make conversation. That's what people do. Say something. Anything. Just stop sulkin'. Yer makin' me nuts."

Acknowledging Tommy's sincerity, Johnny bobbed his head approvingly while turning the annoying radio off in one swift motion. "Let's go get somethin' ta eat. I'm starved. How bout Ninth Street for a steak?" Johnny quizzed hoping food would relieve his anxiety.

"You buyin'?"

An incredulous look overcame Johnny's face. "You always were a frickin' mooch," he said with bluntness. Squirming in his seat, Johnny blindly searched his pockets and produced a ten-dollar bill. "Ten dollars worth," he said sarcastically. A long pause ensued then Johnny continued, "Now can ya just drive quietly and not talk for a while? Okay? Can you do that for me?"

"Okay. But you don't got to get so personal bout it," Tommy said curtly.

Driving up East Passyunk Avenue Tommy made a left onto Wharton Street and rumbled to a stop across the street from the birthplace of the *South Philly Cheese Steak*. The late hour and the dampness in the air did not deter a bevy of voracious customers from gobbling down their cheese steaks and fries. Most of these people were eating hunched over a stainless steel counter bordering the curb in order to avoid the oily cheese drippings from finding their mark on the consumer's shirt or pants. Meanwhile, the vendors' shadowy barren carts and stands in front of darkened shops lined Ninth Street in the distance.

In a few hours the gruff vendors would be returning from the food distribution center at Front and Pattison Avenue with fresh produce and fish. Their smoldering fifty-five gallon drums reignited to keep them warm on cold damp mornings as they stocked their carts and stands at the crack of dawn. For the moment in the predawn hours, Ninth Street belonged to a ghostly netherworld of the departed immigrant shoppers. Amid the gradient-colored shadows, the wispy fragrance of their hopes and dreams still gave this thoroughfare its rich cultural tradition.

Tommy stepped up to the order window. "Steak wit. Grill the onions," he rattled off.

The cashier silently rubbed his thumb over the top joint of his index finger in a rasping motion indicating the required payment. Tommy took note. With his right hand in a fist and thumb extended, he lithely motioned toward Johnny who stood behind him. Johnny ponied up a ten-dollar bill and the cashier shouted in a raspy voice tinged with attitude, "Steak wit. Make sure ya grill the onions for this scooch."

Johnny quickly added, "The same."

"Ditto," shouted the cashier quickly handing Johnny his change in one seamless motion. By the time Johnny put his money in his pocket the cheese steaks were served up and the two boyhood friends found a niche at the stainless steel counter. While ravenously appeasing their appetites, they began a conversation between chewing their sandwiches.

Tommy made annoying movements with his tongue including a sucking sound in an effort to get every morsel from between his teeth.

"You're fuckin' annoying Tommy. No wonder you can't get any girls. They probably leave you sittin' at the table you do that kind of shit."

"Hey, big shot. Don't pick on me cause Anna's givin' you a hard time. I warned you bout that broad. She's psycho like her old man."

"Yeah and he wants to meet me," Johnny blurted out without thinking only to clench his teeth in regret. The two friends were like brothers, but Tommy was still a blabbermouth. Secrets were anathema to his personality. This went back to the seventh grade at Saint Monica's grade school.

Tommy was always a little awkward around girls. They would often find him somewhat amusing, but otherwise undesirable. This rejection developed into a complex that he attempted to overcome by loquacious techniques. So under the guise of helping his friend, Tommy would always preempt Johnny's designs on the girls trying to impress them with his concern for his best friend. His unbridled chatty style usually doomed his schemes and no one got the girl. This personality flaw branded him as untrustworthy. It only became worse as he got older. Still, Johnny remained loyal to his friend. Besides, he couldn't keep a secret either. His excuse centered on his astrological birth sign Gemini, signifying a natural communicator—information in, information out.

The two friends always got into abusive verbal scuffles as a result of one petty indiscretion or another. Eventually, they would joke about it by teasing each other. The Gimp, however, was not a joking matter. Tonight's indiscretion did not fall into the petty category. It could be downright fatal Johnny thought soberly. Immediately, he clammed up.

Tommy sensed something amiss with his friend of fifteen years. His mind told him to mind his own business, but his mouth would not obey. "No shit?"

Downplaying his slip of the tongue, Johnny curled the ends of his lips downward while shrugging his shoulders, "No big deal. I been expecting it."

Tommy makes a fist moving it back and forth in an almost theatrical stabbing motion, "You been bangin' Anna?"

"None of your fuckin' business!"

"You want my advice…"

"No!" Johnny responded before Tommy could say another word.

"Be that way. I hope he cuts your balls off," Tommy outrageously replied.

Johnny's mind fast-forwarded to a scene in the *Valachi Papers* inferring the savage severing of a gangster's penis for screwing his boss's girlfriend. He knew that the Gimp was perfectly capable of such a heinous act. Just the mere thought of emasculation sent a shudder up his spine. The scene looped several times in his mind rendering Johnny momentarily speechless. Hoping to dispel this thought, Johnny bit down tightly on the inside of his lips. Meanwhile, several blocks away Nicky Sox grappled desperately with his own images of the Gimp's retributive behavior.

17

Louie the Snake's Silver Buick Riviera proceeded south past the church of The Annunciation on Tenth Street like a hearse on the way to Holy Cross Cemetery. At that same moment Nicky Sox found religion and quickly made the sign of the cross. Catching this display of desperation from the corner of his eye, Snake made a wry snort of derision. "Lookin' for a miracle Sox?"

Trying to contain his escalating state of anxiety, Nicky Sox replied languidly through his parched lips, "I'm all out of miracles. It's jus a habit I grew up with. Thought it would bring me good luck. That's all."

"Yeah, well, yer lucky I came and got ya instead of Antny. Else ya be pissin' yer pants right now," Snake remarked with a tinge of pity in his voice that Nicky immediately grasped.

"Listen Snake maybe we…"

Snake cut him short immediately. "Maybe nothin'. Ya fucked up, Nicky. Take yer medicine. You had a good run. Let the Gimp have his fun then go lick yer wounds wherever you go to do that sort a shit and live to enjoy another day." After a short pause he added, "And fer God's sake don't piss yer pants."

Nicky Sox had the illustrious distinction of being a bed wetter long after the fifth grade. It became common knowledge when one of his friends overheard Nicky's mom fiercely berating him for the infantile behavior. Eventually the teasing banter of his friends subsided, but he remained stained by the subtle implications of it well into his teens. A few people like Snake still judged his youthful distress as current. In their eyes he would never be able to live it down.

Tonight, Nicky secretly wondered if it would recur in front of the Gimp. That was the real reason he blessed himself as they passed the church. Unable to voice his private thoughts, he managed a muted nod in response to Snake's rebuke. After stopping for a red light, they continued their procession silently along the bleak corridor of houses that lined Tenth Street until they turned right onto Snyder Avenue. Along the way Nicky slowly sank into the Riviera's bucket seat and wished he had used the restroom at the bar.

As the Silver Buick Riviera crawled westward along Snyder Avenue behind an electric bus, Cisco silently calculated his loses this evening. So was everyone else in the poolroom except for the Gimp. He was having too much fun. Cisco nervously rolled a lighted cigarette around in his mouth. This uncharacteristic behavior didn't go unnoticed. The Gimp's effrontery grew as the night progressed. "Yer panties in a bunch there hustler," the Gimp chortled on more than one occasion as the Gimp picked one of Cisco's discards.

Although never reaching the appropriate educational level in school, Cisco had a natural affinity for instantly evaluating the chances surrounding each *Roll of the Dice*. Tonight was different. No matter how hard he tried, he couldn't manipulate the outcome using the various skill sets acquired during his lifetime of nefarious pursuits. Losing didn't bother him. The man sitting across the table from him did. If it were just the money, Cisco would shrug it off to bad luck. This gnawing aversion was something deeper. Not willing to label it hatred, Cisco never remembered feeling any other way. Some people just deserved killing, Cisco silently concluded. For the second time this evening he lamented not acting on that thought.

Misperception was symptomatic of the Gimp's skewed thought processes. It evolved unnoticed from the protective mechanism that cloaked his fragile psyche. Unlike Cisco, mitigating risk never appeared on the radar screen of the Gimp's life. Blustering forward was all the Gimp knew. His psychotic brazenness soon would be reenacted for Cisco's benefit.

A loud knocking on the poolroom door accompanied the Gimp's clumsy card shuffling. Startled by the suddenness, the cards spewed haphazardly across the felt-covered table. With an irritated scowl on his face the Gimp motioned for Pops to let the visitor enter. "Probably Snake with the dead-beat," the Gimp said briskly while gathering the random cards with a wide sweeping motion of his stubby arms.

"Yo! It's Snake. Open up," Snake howled demandingly while simultaneously pounding the door with his fist.

Pops sluggishly shuffled across the floor and unbolted the two locks securing the heavy wooden door. As quick as Snake and Nicky Sox enter the poolroom, Pops bolted the door again.

Smiling broadly, the Gimp facetiously welcomed Nicky Sox like an old friend. "Nicky, Nicky, you never write; you never call. What am I supposed to think?"

Nicky Sox is taken aback then after a moment pleaded feebly, "I'm good for the dough. I didn't know he and youse was connected."

"We're all connected Nicky. Everyone downtown is wired in. We're all each other's customers. Right Antny?"

Carlucci looked askance then managed a muted nod startling Nicky Sox as he suddenly stood up. Nicky's eyes widened registering fear. He stepped backward and bumped into Louie the Snake. Bewildered, Nicky's movements resembled a pinball hitting the bumpers in the nearby pinball machine. Regaining a semblance of control, Nicky spun around searching for a sign of sympathy from the few onlookers. He found none. "I'm good for it. Honest. I'll pay the vig. I jus' need more time. A little more time," Nicky pleaded desperately through parched lips in a voice filled with panic.

The Gimp extended his left-hand quickly out from his side to a disoriented Nicky who reflexively clasped it. Locked in the Gimp's iron grip, Nicky trembled. Goosebumps raised the hair on his arms and traveled quickly throughout his entire body prompting an immediate urge to urinate. Clasping the joined hands with his right hand, the Gimp began speaking in a maleficent voice as a broad grin trundled across his face. "And what do I tell the butcher?"

Nicky Sox now was totally confused. "What butcher?"

Getting more serious the Gimp spoke firmly with escalating anger in his voice. "You know. The butcher, I'm his customer. Capisce? If I can't pay the butcher do you think he wants to hear that you owe me money. Of course not. Cause he owes the slaughterhouse some dough. And they owe the ranchers and the ranchers owe the feed grain people. We're all connected Nicky. It's a vicious, vicious circle. And it's getting all fucked up cause of you!"

Nicky is cringing as the Gimp noticeably squeezed his hand tighter and spoke without thinking. "Gimp I'm sorry. I'm sorry. You're hurting my hand. Please."

Usually, uttering the forbidden word *Gimp* would immediately send him into a murderous frenzy. The word forced him to connect with memories, bad memories. Instead, tonight the nervous tick above his left eye became pronounced as he moved his upper jaw to and fro in a disjointed motion. No one ever called him that to his face and got away unscathed. Somehow restraining his natural inclination to rip Nicky's arm from its socket he managed a few words. "You left-handed or right-handed Sox?"

Before he could answer, a wet spot appeared at Nicky's crotch that quickly spread until it became a puddle. This enraged the Gimp who immediately snapped Nicky's left arm then forced him to the floor to writhe in his own excrement. Red-faced with anger, the Gimp screamed at the top of his lungs, "Get me my money you disgusting little shit! I don't care who, what, where or how! Just get the fuckin' money! Or the next time I'll drown ya in yer own piss!"

Swiveling around to face a seated Cisco, the Gimp slammed his fist into the middle of the table sending the cards and tally sheet asunder. His voice crackled noticeably over Nicky Sox's moaning pleas for help. "This little game is over!" Turning to Teti, he demanded, "Teti, how much does this dipshit owe me?"

Teti took his time picking up the tally sheet and reviewing it, "Thirty-five hundred and change."

The redness drained from the Gimp's face. His voice scratchy from the screaming, he faced Cisco and said staunchly with a pointed finger, "I'm a sport, hustler. The next time I see ya I want the whole thirty-five hundred. Give Pops here the chump change."

Nicky's moaning became louder annoying the Gimp who turned around and started kicking Nicky across the floor. "You want to moan, I'll make you moan, you little faggot!" With his voice now suddenly shaky and his face turned haggard, he again turned to face Cisco and warned, "Don't make me have to do this to you. I might like it."

Motionless except for his eyes, Cisco calculated whether he would be able to kill the Gimp before Carlucci or Snake could react. It would be worth his own death he ruminated if he could strangle this son-of-a-bitch with his bare hands right now. But he waited a moment too long. Carlucci and Snake innately sensed danger. Both had seen that look countless times over the years. One welcomed the opportunity with a daring smirk on his face while the other's eyes begged Cisco off. A silent Cisco again missed his window of opportunity.

Breaking eye contact with Cisco, the Gimp turned immediately to Teti. "Teti, get this moaning sack of shit over to Saint Agnes." The acrid smell of urine rose from the carpet to overtake the normally stale tobacco laced air of the poolroom. Making a sniffing sound while crinkling his nose, the Gimp commented in a hoarse voice, "This place smells like piss. Let's get the fuck outta here before I lose my appetite." The Gimp and his entourage of Carlucci and Snake quickly exited without any fanfare, leaving Teti to clean up after them.

Glad to see the crew leave, Teti breathed a sigh of relief. Standing over Nicky, Teti was feeling sorry for his old schoolmate. Then Cisco stepped up across from him. "Grab him under the armpit and we'll get 'em up at the same time." Together they lifted the ashen-faced Nicky up. Teti wrapped Nicky's good arm around his shoulder and shifted him slightly to balance him as they exited the poolroom and descended the stairs.

Pops surveyed the mess left by the Gimp with a disgusting look of disbelief. He shuffled around the room picking up the cards. Cisco watched the old-time number writer a moment with his hands in his pockets. An image of pathos for a split-second, Pops had been dapper in his day and sharp as a tack, Cisco quietly remembered. Trying to avoid any comparisons to himself, he quickly turned away to exit. He stopped a moment pulling from his pocket a slim bankroll. At first glance with his head lowered he peeled off three twenty-dollar bills in what could be construed as an act of pseudo-reverence. Partially turning, he handed the money to Pops as he passed nearby. "Here Pops."

Pops accepted the money with an arcane smile on his face and gave Cisco some generic advice. "You be careful Cisco. I ain't seen 'em this mean in a long time. You watch yer back. There's somethin' eating at that man's soul." Pops pursed his lips and continued straightening up without looking back to conceal the look of sadness in his eyes. Over the years he had witnessed this genre of drama acted out once or twice. It always ended tragically.

18

Palm Sunday, March 26, 1972

Marie Giampietro tapped lightly on her daughter's bedroom door several times. "Anna. It's seven-thirty. Let's go. We're going to be late," she said softly. Tapping again more rapidly, Marie exclaimed, "Anna!"

A disheveled Anna cracked open the door peering out through puffy eyes that seemed to be in a permanent squint. "Do I really have to go, Mom," she whined. "Really?"

"Your grandfather expects you. Show a little respect once in awhile, please."

"Awright, awright. I'll be ready by eight-thirty. Okay?" Anna replied in a disgruntled tone slowly closing the door on her mother.

Retreating to the privacy of her bedroom to wait for her daughter, Marie forgave herself for her little white lie. Anna's attendance at Mass this morning was for her own edification and not her father's. Each year on Palm Sunday, a special day of remembrance for her, Marie wanted to unburden her soul to her daughter. This year was no different than past years. The words that would have been so easily spoken long ago became more difficult to utter as the years slipped away. Time had taken its toll. Now Marie only found spiritual comfort in her daughter and the tradition that she had established unwittingly.

Usually at this time of the morning the Gimp lied supinely downstairs on the couch. She never checked because she really didn't care. His late hours and sleepless nights exiled him to the couch indefinitely long ago. This began innocently enough when the Gimp started coming home in the wee hours of the morning and awakened Marie. After several days of lost sleep, Marie gave the Gimp an ultimatum—either get home earlier, take pills for his sleeplessness or stay on the couch until she left for the store.

Unwilling to accede to her demands, the Gimp chose the couch. This wasn't a big deal for him since he came home near daybreak anyway just as Marie was leaving to tend to the store. Like two ships passing in the night, they barely spoke to one another. An acceptable arrangement for both, it became the norm rather than the exception. It only became awkward on special occasions like Palm Sunday.

Normally, Marie would just stay in her room, but occasionally they would engage in polite conversation. Obtuse during these exchanges, the Gimp's awkwardness became progressively worse over the years though he never became mean or violent. On rare occasions Marie would be gracious, even compassionate and give the Gimp a kiss on the cheek or forehead. She did this to remind herself that even the Gimp was a human being and deserving of forgiveness. In her heart, however, Marie knew that she was incapable of forgiving this murderer of men.

As Marie and Anna descended the stairs quietly, the Gimp lounged peacefully on the couch with his eyes closed in a silk dressing gown that covered his clothes. Wearing the silk gown calmed him. Subconsciously, it reminded him of his mother's womb although he would never accept that as the reason or would he wear it without clothing underneath. Nakedness was abhorrent to the Gimp even though he had his avaricious claws in the emerging pornography business of Center City. Becoming aware of Marie and Anna's presence, he immediately sat up.

"We didn't mean to disturb you dad," Anna said lovingly stepping around a coffee table to give him a kiss.

"I was just resting my eyes," the Gimp lied lifting up into a slouched position to accept a kiss on the cheek. Tiredly slipping back onto the couch he quizzed, "Where you two goin' so early?"

Marie replied succinctly, "Church."

Saint Rita di Cascia Church, located at Broad and Ellsworth Streets, was named in honor of the beloved saint of Italian-Americans. Born in Umbria, Italy, Saint Rita is best known as the patron of desperate, seemingly impossible causes. This patronage stems from her tumultuous life as an abused wife and mother of twins.

After her husband's murder and her children's death at an early age, Rita entered the monastery of Saint Mary Magdalene in Cascia and devoted herself to the passion of Christ for the rest of her life.

As Marie knelt in this sixty-five year old church, she reflected on Saint Rita's life and its similarity to her own. Although the Gimp had never physically abused her, his violent nature outside of their home scared Marie. The overwhelming thought of those events would send her into a depressive state for weeks. Witnessing his *Doctor Jekyll and Mister Hyde* personality first hand had definitely traumatized Marie. It was the most horrific type of abuse—always living in fear. Never knowing if a word or simple facial expression would ignite the volatile fluids flowing through her husband's veins, sent shivers up her spine. Suppressing her thoughts only made her anxiety worse. So, she decided to allow herself to remember and reflect on her life with the Gimp one day a year—today, Palm Sunday. After the ushers passed out the traditional palm fronds, Marie began weaving one into a cross.

Reflecting further, Marie had wished that her daughter would be a little more inquisitive about the past, but came to accept her indifference and never pushed the issue. Someday she'll ask, Marie hoped. When that day came she prayed that she would be up to telling her the truth.

Anna sat between her mother and grandmother with folded arms and a humdrum look on her face. She didn't understand her mother's fascination with this church nor did she care. If she had ever thought to ask her mother the significance of this yearly tradition she may have been surprised, very surprised. Contorting her face to contain a yawn, the tedium of the morning dulled Anna's senses as it did every year. So, Marie's secret remained ensconced in a world of dark motives. Using the tip of her frond of palm to get her mother's attention, Anna reverently whispered, "Can I leave now Mom. The Mass is almost over."

"You have to take your grandparents home," Marie replied distantly while finishing her weaving. "I have somewhere to go."

"Take them with you. I'm sure they won't mind."

"Anna. It won't hurt you to be a little considerate one day a year. Consider it your penance."

On that note the Mass ended and Marie quickly left for her yearly pilgrimage to Holy Cross Cemetery.

19

Celebrities didn't frequent Gaetano's Restaurant in the heart of the University of Pennsylvania campus for the ambiance. They came for the original home style cooking. So did Johnny Cerone. It was one of the few eateries that he enjoyed outside of South Philadelphia. Only a block away from where he worked, Johnny became a regular, but not on a par with Dean Martin or the Eagles Football team who also frequented the restaurant.

After ordering lunch, Karen Bridges, Johnny's attractive co-worker, excused herself from the table and found her way to the ladies room. In the meantime Johnny watched two college freshmen gorge themselves on an extra large pizza.

Karen was Johnny's only female friend. This meant that he could talk to her truthfully. She made him feel secure and at ease when discussing his personal life with her. Free of the judgmental fears that accompany such discussion, he relished their lunchtime chats. In this regard she was unique. His male friends would taunt him endlessly if he confessed his misgivings or personal observations with them. Even so, Johnny circumvented certain topics with Karen. Ribaldry of any kind was absolutely out of the question. Sexual topics were gingerly approached in a mature manner. This personal respect for each other strengthened the foundation of their friendship. Although, Johnny had virtual fantasies occasionally about the persnickety little blond with a cute build and dark blue eyes, he never considered making an advance nor dreamed of a romantic involvement. His fantasies merely released his testosterone.

This may have been true for Johnny. For Karen, it wasn't so cut-and-dry even within the parameters of her methodical thought processes. Secretly, she desired what every woman wanted—to be loved—but on her terms. Therefore, over a period of time she subtly took the Systems Analyst approach to flow-charting the thought processes that produced the results known as Johnny Cerone. It was her method of approaching a serious relationship with this rascal. However, she did not take into account Johnny's unruly approach to life. If Johnny had thought about it or just paid proper attention, he would have noticed the warning signs from someone with an analytical mind.

Karen had a plan for her life. Her five-year goal segued into her ten-year plan. Once all her objectives were attained there would be a general review and a new projection set. This analytical approach to life fit perfectly with her Systems Analyst's skill set. Lately, however, Johnny's roller-coaster life began to disrupt her cubbyhole methodology. Her fastidiousness seemed less apparent at work. At lunch they talked less and less about work and more and more about lighthearted subjects. Their conversations devolved into non-linear trains of thought. Slowly, she let her guard down. Her questions and comments became more random and spontaneous. She even broached the sex taboo and asked Johnny several personal questions. Here was a man, she ruminated, who could program a computer using logic yet totally discard it in his everyday decisions. The rationale he used for making decisions astounded her. It only added to her fascination with his chaotic life. Not knowing from one moment to the next which way your life would take you was tantamount to living a hallucinogenic fantasy to her. It tickled her imagination to such an extent that sometimes she fantasized herself as *Alice in Wonderland*. This went on for a while until she felt silly one day when she realized that she physically resembled the Robert Louis Stevenson character. At that moment she also realized that she could easily fall in love with this rapscallion. This was upsetting. Her ten-year plan had no contingencies for this type of love. Immediately, she steeled herself from this wayward thought. She was only kidding herself she concluded. Still, she looked forward to her lunches with Johnny. Savvy enough to comprehend that such a life was not meant for her, she still teetered on its dangerous precipice.

Today, unlike other days, she sensed something disheartening brewing in his life. While in the ladies room intuition told her to beg off and not do anything foolish, but she mistook it for logic. Her defense mechanisms were askew. At this point she was ready to do something totally illogical.

It was lucky for both Johnny and Karen that the *L* word never came up. Johnny would have strung her along simply because he didn't know how to say no. Besides, a romantic relationship between them would never have worked out. She just wasn't his type—too brainy and obsessive for him. Her classical beauty accented by her understated stylish attire attracted him. Still, Karen had a cold edge about her. Taking the imaginary challenge he felt sure that he could warm her up, he thought giddily, whereas there was no taming Anna. His mind often wandered in this way comparing the two women physically. Otherwise, there was no comparison. At this moment, however, he didn't need any more entanglements, he mused as reality slowly depressed his libido. Thoughtlessly putting his hand into his jacket pocket, he felt the wad of Thrill Show tickets. Karen was an untapped resource, he brooded. Wincing at that thought, Karen startled him as she quietly sat down at the table.

"I didn't mean to startle you," she said in a sweet voice tingling with a twitch of nervousness.

"Jus daydreamin'," he shot back.

"So. What's the status of your car?"

"Status quo. Same car. Same mechanic. Different problem. More money."

"Didn't Armando fix it right the last time," she quizzed as the waitress delivered their order.

The waitress interrupted, "Get you anything else?"

"No, thank you," replied Karen in a genuinely polite manner as she cut her piece of pizza with a fork and knife.

The waitress quickly fanned through several checks. Finding their check, she slid it towards Johnny. No reaction was forthcoming and the waitress swiveled around to serve another customer.

"So, what about the car?" Karen asked in a tone of bewilderment. Her question caught Johnny stretching his neck while biting a folded piece of pizza in midair. He gulped his mouthful of pizza down then responded as he swallowed, "Electrical this time. Some short in the wiring harness."

Karen quickly interjected. "It's none of my business, Johnny, but if I were you I'd get rid of that car."

Johnny interrupted her before she could say another word. "I know all the arguments Karen. I agree that it makes no sense—to you. But I see it an entirely different way." Using his hands expressively to make a point, Johnny spoke passionately, "You see cars are an extension of some people's psyche, visible expressions of who they are on the inside. If you drive a plain white sedan, you seriously need to consider getting a life."

"I don't drive a plain white sedan."

"I know you don't."

"You're an enigma Johnny Cerone. That's what I love about you," she blurted out with a restrained giggle without even realizing what she had said.

There it was—the dreaded *L*-word. Johnny evoked a look of uneasiness as he tried to decipher her intent. The thought came to mind of Anna coercing him on Saturday night into an undesirable response. Was the same thing happening here, he silently asked himself? Slightly squirming in his chair he adroitly expanded on her first question without any other commentary. "To me my car is analogous to freedom. Going through the gears up by boathouse row along the Schuylkill with the top down on a sunny spring day—you get the picture."

"Sounds wonderful. Maybe we should do that for lunch sometime. It's not that far away. Besides, it would get us out of the basement with all of those machines humming in our ears. We could have a picnic."

There was the answer to his question. No further explanation was needed from Karen. Johnny innately understood the comfortable relationship paradigm that he enjoyed with this woman was changing right before his eyes. Unlike the beguiling Anna, Johnny assumed he could be straightforward with Karen. Inwardly brooding, he wondered for an instant whether men could have a simple platonic relationship with a woman. Wouldn't it be nice if he could meet someone with Anna's innate sensuality and Karen's clarity of vision, he capriciously thought? However, this train of thought elicited a feeling of self-disdain and embarrassment for his lack of intestinal fortitude with Anna. Fearful and speechless to Anna's machinations, Johnny resolved himself at that moment against ever cowering again.

Karen didn't see the trepidation in Johnny's eyes. Intently focused, she spoke in a practiced manner. Simultaneously removing an envelope from her purse she slid it toward Johnny. "Here, I know you would never ask me for it."

Oblivious to Karen at this most inauspicious moment, Johnny impulsively blurted out in a cold detached manner, "You and me. It ain't gonna happen. It would never work." His frankness momentarily fell on deaf ears and was temporarily relegated to the no-man's land of miscommunication—out of sync with what was physically happening. Johnny suddenly looked down at the envelope languidly as he simultaneously finished his spiel. When he looked up he caught the discomposure in Karen's wide-eyed stare.

"Whatever gave you that impression?" Karen said shrilly. With her feelings now exposed, she immediately blushed. This irretrievable moment of embarrassment forever etched in her mind's eye.

Johnny was mute. With his mind verbally barren, he sat there expressionless.

Totally surprised by his nonchalance, Karen took it personally. Friend's should be understanding, compassionate even, she thought. Johnny thoughtlessly crushed her fantasy, shattering it like a mirror emitting hundreds of glass shards piercing her heart. There was a time when misunderstandings could be discussed. Affairs of the heart never reached that level. Karen knew that she changed the rules unilaterally and was upset because she had not factored into the equation the emotional consequences of being spurned.

After spreading some money on top of the check, Karen stood up slowly. Speaking in an emotionally suppressed tone tinged with embarrassment, she said nearly in a whisper, "You can pay me back when you get it. No hurry. I'll see you back at work." Turning quickly, she stopped a moment to regain her pride then walked away without looking back.

Johnny slid his right index finger under the envelope lifting it while clamping it with his middle finger. Looking up he caught the eyes of the two nerdy freshmen staring at him. Their agape mouths caked with pizza sauce at the corners. The scowl on Johnny's face was enough to turn their inquisitive looks away.

Tapping the envelope on the table in a reflexive cadence, he tried to focus on the event that had just transpired. Reverberating in his mind the tapping transposed his thoughts into the religious training of his youth.

In Christian churches throughout the world, he thought, the theme of this week was redemption. In the pulpits of these churches, the priests gave sermons then performed rituals reinforcing the theme like a medieval morality play being played in the villages and towns of Old Europe. Johnny knew the message well. It was part of his psyche after fifteen and a half years of parochial education.

Guilt oozed from every pore of his body right then. There was plenty to go around. He couldn't contain it any longer. Karen was the only sanity in his life and now that was gone, he brooded. He was at the nadir of his existence. At this juncture of his life he hoped that the priests and nuns were right. Self-flagellation was no longer an option. It was Easter, redemption was at hand, he concluded. It had to be. Swallowing hard, Johnny made several penitential facial expressions before folding the envelope neatly. He stopped for a reflective moment tucking the envelope securely in his shirt pocket. He never thought that like Christ, his greatest tribulation laid ahead.

20

At the same time that Johnny Cerone was contemplating the course of his life, Cisco was reevaluating his own life. The weekend rain had washed away the grime from the sidewalks that accumulated under the winter snow. In the process it also cleared the air making way for spring. Somehow, the air swirling around Cisco remained stagnant and murky.

Casually leaning against the front fender of a faded and rusting '64 Chevrolet Bel-Air outside the Downtown Bar & Grill, Cisco watched people scurrying around. Taking a thoughtful drag on his Marlboro cigarette, he tried to imagine the trials and tribulations of their lives. His responses were always the same singular answers regardless of the angle of his perspective. Family, money, pride and sickness paraded before his mind's eye with purposeful steps. It seemed to him that life was nothing more than a vicious circle. Yet, at the center of that circle was the nucleus around which everything else revolved. For Cisco it was Rose Teti.

If Rose had flat out told Cisco that she liked having him around, he would have been decisive. For some obtuse reason she couldn't. So, Cisco was left to divination. To him it was always a good sign that Rose accommodated him with a small studio size apartment in the rear of the building. She even fed him. Lately, this modified carrot and stick approach was no longer enough to pacify Cisco. He needed more to make South Philadelphia his permanent home.

She too needed more, wanted more, and desired more. Every time that he appeared at her doorstep she became hopeful of rekindling their relationship. Somehow, however, the past resurfaced and dashed her hopes every time. Eventually, she gave up and accepted the reality of the situation putting on a strong façade for Cisco's sake. Rose would never understand the complex entanglement of mindless feuds, vindictive snits nor her involvement in any of it. The dangerous cat and mouse game the Gimp played with Cisco perplexed her. Somehow, the Old Man must be involved, she concluded. Otherwise, he would have made a concerted effort to dispose of the wily card and pool hustler a long time ago.

At one point Rose considered divulging a secret to Cisco that her father confessed shortly before his death. Everyone in the mob had a secret. Some were more secret than others. Letting that genie out of the bottle, she feared, was unpredictable. Revealing this one would only create more problems than it could solve for the two forlorn lovers. Therefore, it remained a dusty skeleton in her closet never to be viewed.

Cisco scooted up onto the fender as he lit another cigarette. He preferred to lie in bed and ruminate about his predicament while smoking, but Rose wouldn't tolerate smoking in the room. This life style preference seemed either eccentric or hypocritical to those people unfamiliar with Rose's personal life. It made perfect sense to her family and closest friends.

Philomena Teti died of lung cancer at a young age. Although her husband Sal was a two-timer of the first degree, her death affected him deeply. Tears welled in his eyes at the funeral. It was rumored that the Old Man had to take Teti aside to console him. Rose on the other hand began reading anything she could find on the subject of cancer.

The stories relating smoking to cancer in the early nineteen sixties piqued Rose's curiosity, but it was the Surgeon General Report on Smoking and Health by Doctor Luther L. Terry in January nineteen sixty four that prompted Rose to begin her crusade against smoking. The regulars at the bar knew her feelings and curtailed their nervous indulgence of the cancer sticks as best as they could.

Then one day without warning Rose totally banned smoking in the bar after reading an article on second hand smoke. After a revolt by the regular patrons and the threat of a walk out by the bartenders she was dissuaded from that course of action. A compromise was reached and smoking was confined to the area near the front door. The truce became routine. Everyone was able to live with her rule, but Rose would not abide smoking in her personal life.

Cisco bowed to her wishes. He had an inkling of her propensity for eccentric behavior when they were on more intimate terms. Her sexual preferences were ahead of the times and a harbinger of things to come. That was in the past. His focus today was at the other end of the human spectrum. It involved survival.

Rose saw Cisco brooding through the sign cluttered window of the bar. Sighing deeply, she quickly finished stocking the refrigerator with bottles of Schmidt's beer then went outside to join him.

Cisco dropped his cigarette and crushed it with his shoe when he noticed Rose exit the side door to the bar.

"What's up," she said as she approached him.

Cisco remained seated on the front fender of the parked Bel-Air. "The stars. The sky," he coyly replied.

It was an unusually beautiful day, bright, sunny and full of hope. A few customers entered the front of the bar for lunch. Rose didn't notice. Cisco did. He was always aware of his surroundings. It was part of who he was. Rose shook her head and replied with a perky smile, "Always ready with a repartee."

"Oh, sitting on the toilet with the dictionary again, are we," Cisco responded playfully.

Rose punched his arm. "Don't go spreading that around. That's personal."

Pinching his index finger and thumb together he quickly ran them across his pursed lips. "My lips are sealed." Then Cisco took a deep breath and turned serious.

She hesitated then continued, "How much money you need to take care of this?"

"Thirty-five large ones."

Rose whistled lowly through her tight lips.

"It ain't about money. Something's different this time," Cisco said with a look of perplexity on his face.

"It's always about the money."

"I don't think so. The twitch over his eye was pulsating. I never saw 'em so out of control," Cisco explained. Changing his tone of voice he continued in a mildly sarcastic tone, "You gonna make your customers wait? That ain't like you."

"Ralph's behind the bar. He can handle it," Rose responded in a low, confident tone deflecting Cisco's attempt at changing the subject. Then seeking to mitigate Cisco's predicament she suggested, "I can talk to the Old Man?"

Cisco responded with an icy stare, "That'd be like sending me before Pontius Pilate. No thank you. I'll work something out."

"Like what?"

"Like you don't want to know."

Rose pouted in disbelief. Cisco's eyes were incapable of hiding anything from Rose. They gave credibility to what she was about to say. "You think you can just take him out. Is that what you're thinking?"

Cisco was always amazed that Rose could see right through him. "Why not? Then Anthony can have his shot at me too." His melancholic eyes counterbalanced his forced smile. He was tired, tired of the bullshit, tired of his false bravado.

"Now you're talking stupid. It's not like you. Not like you at all," she said annoyingly. "God knows the man needs killing, but even if you managed to pull it off they'd have to kill you. You know that," Rose pleaded.

"Better than me being dead and them being alive."

After a reflective moment, Rose's face brightened as an idea came to her. "Why don't you go see Sid?"

Cisco's one eye arched with pursed lips as he entertained the idea momentarily. "What can Sid Greenberg do for me? He went legit years ago. Besides why would he go to bat for me?"

Rose didn't want to mention that he would do what he could for her. It would hurt Cisco's fragile pride at this moment. Cisco realized that point by her sudden pause. He was grateful that she was so considerate. It was a small part of his deep affection for this woman.

"He'd do it because he never liked the Gimp either. He still carries some weight in this town. Besides, I wouldn't call Las Vegas legit." With a pleading look on her face she rationalized, "You go see him. He always liked you. It can't hurt. Even if he says he can't do anything. I'll let him know you're coming."

Cisco was quiet. His demeanor signaled his acceptance of Rose's idea. It was an entirely plausible option, Cisco thought hopefully. It was definitely worth exploring.

They looked at each other caringly. Each had so much that they wanted to say to each other but couldn't. There was a time when there were no obstacles. That time had passed. Once there was an unencumbered avenue of emotional exchange. Now a self-imposed barrier existed that expanded each year making it harder and harder to express their emotions. Her father, the Gimp and their son had always been part of that barrier.

These thoughts flashed through each of their minds instantaneously, but neither acted on them. Cisco's smile appeared cautiously hopeful. Maybe there was still a chance, he thought expanding his smile broadly across his face while winking at Rose. At that moment she was thinking the same thing.

21

The aroma of fresh baked Italian bread overcame the smell of stale tobacco. It snaked its way up through the crevices in the floorboards of this hundred-year-old building like a siren's song to the hungry. Gently filling his nostrils the sumptuous bouquet coaxed the young Tucci from his disquieting slumber.

Rolling over underneath his disheveled blanket he peeked at the alarm clock on the cluttered table next to his bed. It was half past twelve in the afternoon. Burrowing his face into the pillow he lied perfectly still for a moment trying to summon his wits. Finally, he threw off the blanket and sat on the side of his bed resting his head in his hands. He had lied awake for hours staring at the ceiling before finally going to sleep around 3 A.M. Even then he was restless. Reaching over to the cluttered table by the bed he grasped a pack of Camel cigarettes. It was empty. Crumbling the pack up, he flung it across the room toward an overflowing trash basket. He missed. Standing slowly and peeking between the blinds, his eyes appeared to be in a permanent squint. He watched people scurrying in and out of the bakery. His slotted eyes widened when he spied Marie Giampietro exit with a bag of bakery goods. As he watched her disappear across the street, he nodded his shaggy head approvingly. Thank God, he thought, that Anna looked like her mother and not her father. He remembered the bawdy barroom advice of balding, overweight men to their young impressionable counterparts. "Look at the mother," one of them once said, "that's your girlfriend in twenty years." With tight arched lips and chin held high Tucci again nodded his head. "Not bad," he whispered, "Not bad at all."

While Tucci was secretly ogling the Gimp's wife, Teti was chomping down a tripe sandwich from Vinnie's Roast Pork on Ninth & Christian St. Not as well known, but like the all-night steak shops five blocks away, Vinnie's served his food standing up. It was one of the few food stands that served the Italian delicacy on a roll.

As Teti picked at his teeth with a toothpick, he recounted the events of the previous night. He had just come from the hospital. Nicky Sox was hurting, but okay. Both had graduated South Philadelphia High School at Broad Street and Snyder Avenue in 1963 after being asked to leave Bishop Neumann High School in their freshman year. Their expulsions had occurred separately, but it was a tenable foundation for a friendship. Loyalty always ranked high among Teti's positive traits. Consequently, he loaned the tightly bandaged, black-and-blue Nicky Sox some money to keep Carlucci and Louie the Snake off his back until he could make another arrangement. Nicky was overly appreciative.

This was also Teti's way of rebelling against the oppressive techniques of the Gimp. He sighed sadly. Trying to live up to his grandfather's reputation was becoming more difficult as the years rolled by he brooded. It was getting to the point where he couldn't remember why he had gotten involved in this criminal subculture in the first place. Now there was no way out except feet first. He had taken the oath and he knew too much, he silently lamented.

Trying to suppress the debacle of making his bones was futile. That moment was relived constantly when in the presence of the Gimp whose disrespectful treatment toward him was a constant dagger of remembrance in his side. His deference to the Gimp's wishes was akin to being an indentured servant. Often, he wondered if he could pull the trigger the next time around. The answer never materialized. Instead, it hovered above him like a massive andiron about to fall. Luckily, his partner Tucci did the strong-arm work or this lifestyle would be totally unbearable. He had moved out of the apartment above the bar to a small walk up in Queens Village in order to give his mother some breathing room and exert his independence. That was the way he told the story. Actually, his mother couldn't stand the rancid smell of cigarette smoke on his clothing. Her constant admonishment about the multiple dangers of smoking finally prompted him to move out. Still, he stopped by the bar everyday to check in with her. There were a few women in his life, but no one serious. That was the way he liked it—simple with no entanglements. His plan of action today was to lay low. It was the mantra of his life.

Walking south on Ninth Street through the heart of the Italian Market, he watched people moving from one fruit stand to another like busy ants before abruptly turning onto Hall Street heading toward Tenth Street. Theirs was a meager existence, shuffling in and out of stores looking for bargains. Realizing that he was one of them, he put the thought out of his mind. This past week was depressing enough especially since seeing the much-heralded movie about a New York mob family at a matinee the previous Tuesday. Hearing people's comments as they exited the theatre after the movie was incredulous. A myth was being weaved like an Arthurian Tale from the Middle Ages. There was no honor among thieves. Nor was there any respect. Maybe in a parallel universe, he thought, but surely not in this one.

Teti knew this first hand because his grandfather had told him so. It was the last bit of advice that Sal Teti gave to his grandson before he died. Perhaps if he had heeded his grandfather's counsel, his life would have been set on a different course. Instead, he was kowtowing to the Gimp and his psychotic whims. If only he had the balls to kill the son-of-a-bitch, he wishfully fantasized. It was a wispy thought that occasionally entered his consciousness. The mere thought of one day actually performing the ignominious deed kept him going for the time being.

Arriving at the side door to Tucci's apartment he suddenly realized in a moment of clarity that there may be someone else who felt the same way that he did. Raising his eyes toward the second floor, Teti knew his hotheaded partner felt the same way. Taking a deep breath, he momentarily contemplated a plausible scenario to introduce the topic. It could happen he thought hopefully. The odds were in his favor. So, he kept the thought filed away for an opportune moment. Treachery among thieves would be more apropos. Now that part of the movie was believable he chuckled to himself as he hammered on the door to Tucci's apartment.

Tucci was in the shower working out plausible scenarios for an entirely different reason than Teti. Oblivious to the banging on his door, he was singing off-key a chorus of a Frank Sinatra classic ballad *Witchcraft* humming through the parts where the words eluded him. This behavior offset his usually volatile demeanor by channeling his obsessions into a more pleasant outlet. If he had stopped for a moment to think about it, his choice of songs would have given him an insight into what troubled his heart. Never bothering with such reflective behavior, he just accepted the soothing melody's effect on his soul. As he turned off the shower, he heard the banging on the door. Quickly wrapping a towel around himself, he exited the bathroom and threw open the window to the street below.

Teti began banging harder. Abruptly, the window above flew open and Tucci stuck half his naked torso out of the window. "Yo Teti! I'll be down in a minute," Tucci yelled loudly.

"Hurry up will ya I ain't got all day," Teti countered in an equally loud voice. Strolling over to the corner he waited pensively. An occasional neighbor ventured a side-glance of recognition toward him in passing. Trying to avoid any unnecessary conversations, he would nod ever so slightly. There was another matter on his mind. Unable to avoid it any longer, he now felt compelled to take it up with Tucci again.

Tucci's obsession with the Gimp's daughter had been noticed. It wasn't just the snooping that was noticed. It was the pictures. One night while carousing with someone he thought he could trust Tucci let it slip that he had taken several provocative shots of Anna. If the Gimp caught wind of it, Teti thought, there'd be hell to pay. By the same token he also didn't want to alienate this Young Turk. Tucci could be extremely helpful if Teti hatched a feasible plan to dispatch the Gimp to his eternal damnation.

This way it kept his dream alive. These thoughts and more scrambled about in Teti's head. Nervously, he kept shifting his weight from one foot to the other as he tried to devise a subtle approach to these volatile topics. Talking to Tucci was never easy. His attitude toward the Gimp was to be expected even though it was never discussed. It was just assumed. Teti had spent quite a bit of time with this young hothead and wasn't totally convinced that his animosity was entirely due to the murder of his father so many years ago. After all, Tucci's father had the drop on the Gimp and ran out luck and bullets at the most inopportune moment. No, there was something else eating at this young man. Something more complicated than the obvious. A sauntering young woman of exceptional physical proportions temporarily interrupted Teti's thoughts. The rhythmic swaying of this young woman's hips, however, could not derail Teti's train of thought from continuing its inquisitive journey. "Who knows the real reasons why people hate each other? It's all so arbitrary at times. Arbitrary to those on the outside looking in, but deadly serious to the one holding the grudge no matter how silly it may appear to be." Teti was amazed at the depth of his thoughts. Obviously this topic had some personal implications that needed further examination. With that thought Teti turned and noticed Tucci exiting his apartment thus shifting Teti's profound ruminations back to the more mundane matters at hand. For a second he thought he caught a glint in Tucci's eyes and buoyancy to his step. The moment passed, but not before raising another suspicion in Teti's mind.

Tucci shook a cigarette loose from a pack of cigarettes catching it with his mouth. Cupping his hands around a struck match, he stopped suddenly and turned his back to the wind to light it. Then blowing a steady stream of smoke from the corner of his mouth, he approached Teti while speaking. "Where ya parked?"

"Tenth an Fitzwater," Teti said.

"We'll take mine. It's jus around the corner."

Walking side by side they silently approached Tenth and Carpenter. Teti continued across Carpenter Street past the boarded up Community Hospital. Tucci stopped. Pointing down Carpenter Street with the cigarette scissored between his fingers he yelled, "Yo! Teti. The car's down here."

Stopping abruptly Teti motioned with a jerk of his head toward the steps of Christ's Presbyterian Church. "Let's sit here a minute," he said curtly.

Tucci took a long drag on his cigarette and suspiciously approached the nooks and crannies of the immediate area before sitting on top of the steps. Teti calmly sat down next to him looking straight ahead down Kimball Street to avoid looking into Tucci's eyes and thus making what he had to say seem personal.

"There's been some talk. About some pictures," Teti whispered in a quizzical tone.

Tucci crunched his lips making a light smacking sound before taking another drag on his cigarette. "I'm gonna punch that asshole's lights out when I see 'em!"

"You know the Gimp..." At that point Tucci cut short Teti's attempt at a warning.

"Yea, Yea. Fuck the Gimp!" Tucci said angrily in a muted voice. After taking another drag on his cigarette he flipped the butt into the street. "It was just a back up in case he didn't like what we told him."

"There ain't nothin' to tell him. Is there?"

"Depends on what he wants to know?" Tucci lit up another cigarette. "Besides, this is bullshit following her around. It's startin' to get on my nerves. He's doin' this to break my balls."

"Our balls," Teti aptly reminded him. Turning to face Tucci, he spontaneously blurted out, "You gotta thing for his daughter, Cuzz?"

His face lined by uninterruptible emotions, Tucci swallowed hard then leapt off the steps. In one pirouetting motion he turned to face the seated Teti speaking sternly with violence in his eyes. "None of your fuckin' business! Now let's get outta here." Tucci stomped away heading west on Carpenter Street.

Teti was momentarily furious with himself for being so tactless. Realizing that he and Tucci still needed to make their customary collection rounds he took a deep breath and hastily followed Tucci down Carpenter Street.

Arriving ahead of Teti, Tucci looked down at the front of his car completely dumbfounded. A rusted and faded 1958 Buick Roadmaster's bumper was resting on top of Tucci's Impala's bumper with obvious damage to the grill. Still seething with anger from his conversation with Teti, Tucci stomped about seeking something, anything to use as an instrument of revenge. Finding a wooden milk crate with metal corners, he raised it above his head like a Herculean figure, hurling the heavy crate at the Buick's windshield. The crate found its mark immediately with a loud thud. Protruding from the car like a surrealistic painting depicting anger, Tucci just stared at his handiwork, still unable to quell the anger in his soul. Coming upon this scene of angry retribution Teti grabbed Tucci's arm attempting to restrain him from further destruction.

Still in the throes of anger, Tucci yanked his arm away from Teti's grasp. In one final act of mindless rage he kicked in the side of the car door. Breathing deeply through his nose, Tucci's threshold of anger began slowly closing. The two men's eyes met in silent communication. Tucci was no longer in denial. His emotions were no longer capable of being masked. "Fuckin' faggot mother fucker," he croaked under his breath with a pounding heart while trying to make some sense of his roiling emotions. But that was not to be. He grappled with this thought as he reined in his emotions. So, here he was full of anger in a beaker of testosterone with no outlet in sight. It was a volatile solution running through his veins seeking a catalyst.

Teti surveyed the damage while expelling air from the pit of his stomach through his puffed cheeks. Giving Tucci a sidelong glance he worked his lips silently. "Let's get movin'."

Some neighbors peeked out through the slots of their blinds and the folds of their drapes. One sweeping glare from Tucci as he circled the black Chevy to open the door was enough to blunt their curiosity. One by one, they quickly closed their blinds and drapes. No one wanted to incur the wrath of these men for the brazen stupidity of another.

Peeling away with tires squealing defiantly, Teti and Tucci remained silent. Tucci ran the red light at Eleventh and Carpenter Streets squealing the tires again as he turned left heading south. Teti sat aimlessly staring out of the passenger window with a stricken look on his face. He made a concerted effort to stave off any further interaction with this brash young man. There was nothing further to discuss. Tucci's action had answered his tactless question and the answer spelled nothing but trouble.

22

At the same time Tucci was hotfooting it down Eleventh Street the Gimp was standing alone outside The Pasticceria on Christian Street pressing his intertwined fingers back toward his chest to crack them. He was trying to be unobtrusive. He was not.

Dressed in his signature full-length brown leather coat with matching felt fedora, the Gimp stood out like a sore thumb. Even though there was a cool breeze funneling its way down Christian Street, small beads of sweat were forming on his forehead. The voice in his head had multiplied. Desperately, he shook his leonine-head in an effort to dispel the squeaking voices resounding in his head. The message was a garbled mix of nonsensical words. "*Little boys imagine toys will bring them joy.*" It mesmerized him for what seemed like an eternity, but was only a few seconds.

In the past there was only one distinctive far-off voice speaking to him. Now there was a cacophony of voices speaking to him simultaneously. Fighting to be the spokesperson of the collective will, all repeated the same message in modulating intensity. Lately, they began encroaching on his few precious hours of sleep. Their chatter began slowly then quickly escalated to a fever pitch. Just as quickly, it dissipated leaving him with a feeling of apprehension. The Gimp's sweaty face went through several changes of expression before he began to relax.

A passerby gave him a quick sidelong glance. Oblivious to the stare, the Gimp wiped his brow with a newly pressed white handkerchief while slowly regaining his composure. Relieved at overcoming his demons once again, he sighed deeply. Pivoting on his left heel he continued into The Pasticceria and ordered one dozen ricotta cannolis. Pointing his finger at the display case, he said hungrily, "Give me three of those rum cake square too."

After paying his bill he exited the bakery. Hesitating for a brief reflective interlude, he thought of walking over to Ninth Street and surprising Marie. She loved their rum cake. However, that old feeling of awkwardness resurfaced and the Gimp dismissed the thought immediately. Besides, he didn't feel like smiling and making small talk with the old wrinkly silver-haired widows dressed in black that frequented the store. Instead, he got into one of his non-descript American made cars parked in front of a fire hydrant and pulled away slowly.

No one ever saw the Gimp drive the same car for more than a couple of days. Confounding his enemies was one of his idiosyncratic habits. This trait was born of the paranoia that grew out of the circumstances surrounding his father's death so many years ago. Choosing an everyday American car fit into his scheme. On the other hand he was downright cheap, hating to pay the outrageous price of a foreign import especially the German models. Once after a few drinks he confided to Carlucci, "It ain't that I can't afford the damn thing," pointing his finger wildly for emphasis he continued, "and I ain't cheap. You know dat. It's jus that I feel like those Germans are makin' a jerk-off out of me by charging all that money."

These thoughts, however, were far from the Gimp's mind today. The clock was ticking on the Bellino proposal. Remembering the meeting he still decided to focus his energy today on his daughter Anna's future. This sudden rush to marry blindsided him. He needed to think it through. Unknowingly, another matter would take precedence.

Tommy DiRienzo was waiting for an order of mussels at the Downtown Bar & Grill. Unlike his friend Johnny Cerone, Tommy relished walking the razors edge of the criminal netherworld. Going out of his way to frequent the haunts of the criminally minded, he yearned to be taken seriously among the clannish ranks of this criminal subculture. Watching jealously from the periphery of this subculture, he concocted various scenarios of criminal derring-do that would highlight him as a valuable asset—a sort of go to guy.

A Johnny and Anna marriage would definitely help, he mused. It would be the perfect opportunity to introduce him to the top tier of the downtown mob. A smile slowly passed over Tommy's face. Being best man would definitely be a good thing, he chuckled resolving at that moment to posture himself with Johnny for the honor. Impatiently, he looked at his watch. It was the tail end of the lunchtime rush and he was hungry. Nervously strumming his fingers next to his empty bottle of beer, he continued fantasizing.

Ralph the bartender noticed the empty bottle of Rolling Rock beer in front of Tommy. Catching Tommy's attention, Ralph, a man of few words, motioned with his hand toward the bottle with a questioning gesture followed by an inquisitive look.

"Sure," sputtered Tommy, pushing himself away from the bar then heading for the men's room. As he entered the men's room locking the door behind him, Tommy heard the faint ringing of a phone on the other side of an adjoining wall. Always interested in everyone else's business, he put his ear to the wall. Listening attentively, Rose's voice modulated between apprehension and appreciation as she spoke on the telephone.

"Hi Sid. Thanks for returning my call. (Pause) I'm doing well. Well, actually I need a favor. (Pause) I can't believe you already heard. (Pause) He won't take any money from me. I wouldn't even offer. You know how he is. But he might take it from you."

Someone banged on the men's room door. Tommy's interest was piqued now and he shouted out, "Hold your horses. Just give me another minute, will ya. I'm taking a dump." He returned to a listening position.

"I see. I'll pay you the money. (Pause) No I insist. (Pause) Good. Thanks Sid. I'll tell 'em you're expecting him. Bye."

Tommy took a quick whiz in the urinal, as the bang on the door became one of desperation. Quickly exiting the men's room the disgruntled patron mumbled some indiscernible expletive at him. Tommy was oblivious to the man's incoherent rambling. His mind was focused on deciphering what he had just overheard.

The news of Cisco's losses to the Gimp spread like wildfire. Now, he surmised that he had the inside scoop on the next move in this dangerous board game of life. Hopping up onto the bar stool, he didn't know who to tell first. Thinking twice about telling anyone, Tommy sketched out in his mind several possible ways that he might personally take advantage of this information. Suddenly aware of the order of mussels in front of him, he began dipping the fresh Italian bread into the juice of the pot of mussels while his eyes darted around the bar.

A short time later, Carlucci entered the establishment standing solidly in the doorway. Casually, he scanned the bar with a chilling intensity. The sunlight from outside blasted around him framing his menacing physique in the doorway like a *Goyaesque* painting.

Nearly choking with excitement, Tommy felt his heartbeat quicken. Forgetting his silent promise to keep the information to himself, he hopped off the stool. Blabbing his little secret to this man would get him instant gratification. He could still execute his other little plan. Tommy was on the threshold of the big leagues without fully realizing the rules of the game.

Concluding an afternoon of threats and coercion, Tucci and Teti headed toward Tenth and Annin Streets. The Gimp maintained an unremarkable social club in a converted corner store. Identified only by a small ragged sign in the obscure corner of the window as the Downtown Social Club, it served as a hangout for those pernicious patrons of criminal essence. Most of its members came from various local street gangs—Tenth & Annin being one of them. The furnishings included a pool table, makeshift card table with a worn out felt covering and a desk devoid of any accouterments except for a phone. A pot of coffee was usually brewing on a stand-alone table next to a small refrigerator. The desk was strategically situated in the far corner of the room with a commanding view of the entrance and windows. A door to the hallway linking the upstairs apartment of Carlucci and the Annin Street entrance was to the right of the desk. It was dead bolted from the inside.

Most days the card table with its low wattage circular light dangling over the center was busy accommodating a game of pinochle or hearts. Today the Gimp sat patiently behind the desk alone eating a cannoli and sipping a cup of freshly brewed coffee. The aroma of the coffee enveloped him. For a moment the malevolent energy usually emanating from his eyes ceased and he seemed genuinely at peace. Abruptly, an angry rapping on the hallway door broke his serenity. The foreboding rhythm of the forceful sound punctured the door energizing the room with a stream of negative energy. The Gimp responded cautiously with a single syllable guttural tone, "Yo?"

"It's me," snapped the familiar voice. "Anthony."

Looking through the peephole in the door the Gimp flipped the deadbolt lock open then moved to the side as he instinctively moved further away from the door.

Carlucci blew into the room like a ghoulish dervish. A day's shadow of dark beard grew sporadically from his cheeks to his irregular jaw line. The Gimp immediately relocked the door after him.

Anthony looked around questioningly, "Where's everybody at?"

The Gimp ignored the question and returned to the desk. He pushed the box of cannolis toward Carlucci. "Here, have one."

Carlucci pulled up a straight back chair and straddled it, resting his arms in a crossed position on top of the backrest. "Later. I just had lunch," he croaked.

Licking the powdered sugar from around his lips, the Gimp sensed something afoot. His puzzlement showed on his face while his eyes riveted on him. "Whatcha ya got?"

"The hustler's got a bead on the money."

"From Rose?" The Gimp prodded in a toneless voice.

Anthony answered quickly, "From Greenberg."

Contorting his face like an ogre, the Gimp stood up and moved around pensively. The tick above his left eye began to flutter and he shouted, "Fuck Greenberg. Fuck the money. I want this over an done with!"

"My pleasure," Carlucci stood up slowly emphasizing his eagerness to perform the task at hand on behalf of the Gimp.

Quickly rethinking his pronouncement the Gimp's temples throbbed with frustration. Berating himself silently for overlooking a possible Greenberg involvement in his little play, he felt his pulse quickening. The voice in his head screamed *caution* forcing him to blurt out, "Wait. Jus wait a minute." A silent moment ensued. Then with a furtive demeanor the Gimp's eyes narrowed, "I don't want this thing coming back on us jus yet. Maybe we should wait a couple of weeks," the Gimp offered thinking that he could somehow work this payback into the Bellino conspiracy. In this way he could assure Carlucci's loyalty in his grand scheme.

"I'm tired of waitin'," Carlucci countered impatiently.

Going against his better judgment, the Gimp relented. "Then we gotta figure something out. I know you're eager, but I don't want any grief from the Old Man. Him and Sid go way back. I want it taken care of, but I don't want it back on our doorstep." It rankled the Gimp to no end that he had to plan this way. Perhaps throwing Carlucci this bone would work out in a round about way he figured.

"I wanta do this guy personally," Carlucci said with an innate resolve in his voice. Obsessed with revenge he missed the words between the lines of the Gimp's machinations.

Then the Gimp cautioned, "For the time being we need an excuse to clip this arrogant son-of-a-bitch."

Carlucci's mouth split into a grin. "I'm way ahead of ya. That is if you don't care about the money?"

With an icy glare in his eyes the Gimp punctuated the air with his finger as he spoke doggedly. "No one from our crew, unnerstand?"

Anthony was silent for a moment then answered in a serious tone, "Unnerstood. Yer gonna like this plan Big Guy. I guarantee it."

The Gimp and Carlucci smiled at one another knowingly. Slapping Carlucci on the arm in a friendly gesture, the Gimp chortled, "Have a cannoli."

Carlucci was tempted. A persistent rapping at the front door changed his mind.

23

Traffic heading to South Jersey over the Walt Whitman Bridge was relatively light this time of the afternoon. Anna glanced at her watch. It was 2 P.M. Acclimating her father to the potential changes afoot took longer than she expected. It required delicate finessing and special handling. So, she was late as usual. Her friend and confidante expected nothing less.

Gloria Mc Clearey was Anna's best friend for as long as she could remember. Like bona fide sisters they grew up together attending the same schools and bearing their innermost secrets to one another. It was a friendship that defied logic. Their relationship grew stronger over the years in spite of the sheer animosity between their families. Gloria's maiden name was Tucci. She was the younger sister of Cosmo Tucci.

Both girls were born after the highly publicized shootout between their fathers. As the years passed, their girlish curiosity focused on different subjects. Since the Gimp never allowed any one into his house, Anna would spend her free time at Gloria's maternal grandmother's home.

Gloria's mother, Marianna, was still an attractive woman after bearing two children. Two years after the infamous incident the swirl of publicity surrounding it faded away. A plethora of witnesses, a high-powered attorney and a dab of congenial newspaper coverage combined to produce a sympathetic jury to the Gimp's plea of self-defense. After careful deliberation the Gimp was found not guilty. Of course this was aided in the background by the dexterous string pulling of the Old Man.

A monthly stipend was established for Marianna's family and the discourse in the streets returned to the mundane. It was during this time that Marianna met a young Army officer. Fresh and dashing, he came from an honest hardworking South Philadelphia family. Immediately, he swept her off her feet. Instead of the self-pity of a young widow relegated to a banal existence, he filled her future with hope and promise. When he received his orders to go overseas he asked Marianna to marry him. Desperate to get away from a community that she could scarcely tolerate, she agonized over his proposal. Vacillating from one moment to the next, she felt guilty about the instability of dragging her young children around the world.

Finally, Marianna's mother, Sophia, herself a widow, couldn't bear it any longer. She wanted her daughter to be happy. No, she deserved to be happy the progressive thinking woman mused. The old ways of long-suffering were in flux. Therefore, out of compassion for her daughter, Sophia relented and offered to take care of her grandchildren until Marianna returned to the States. She never realized the exigencies of the Army.

By the time Marianna returned her children were use to their grandmother. She felt a tinge of remorse for missing the formative years of their childhood. In her heart she knew that she could not have raised them much better. At least she accepted that rationalization. She also knew that leaving South Philadelphia behind was her salvation. Her husband was now a career Army officer and offered to take Gloria and Cosmo with him on his next posting. However, they were comfortable with their surroundings and had made friends. Their grandmother had nurtured them as only a grandmother could. Besides, Marianna was more like a benevolent aunt who sent presents for holidays, birthdays and other special events. So there they stayed.

Cosmo was old enough to remember his father and resented the Gimp vehemently. He was already on course for hoodlumism, daring all takers to try and knock the chip off his shoulder. He had many takers. Sophia was troubled by Cosmo's growing belligerence and sought the advice of the Old Man.

The Old Man owed the Tucci family nothing. Carmine Tucci burned the candle of life at both ends and in the process got burnt—fatally. His son was on the same road to perdition. In his heart the Old Man had a magnanimous edge to his otherwise Machiavellian demeanor. Relenting, he decided to explain to the Young Turk the *Facts of Life* as they applied to the mean streets of South Philadelphia.

On an unusually icy and cold January day Cosmo Tucci was summoned to the Old Man's office in the rear of Vecchio Real Estate on the corner of Eighth & Christian Streets. The normally busy office was ominously quiet today. Any other day the silence would be punctuated with the hustle and bustle of ringing telephones and a steady stream of customers paying their mortgages and rents. The Old Man had expanded the traditional role of the Italian *padrones* during the Great Depression and gave these people an alternative. He carried their mortgages and made small investments for them. It was their money that often funded his illegal operations such as bootlegging, gambling and loan sharking. Receiving a little more than banks had to offer, these people never made the connection. Instead, they sang his praise counseling others to only trust their own kind in such delicate dealings. In this way Vecchio made a comfortable living that seemed entirely legitimate on the surface.

Today, however, the Old Man decided to dispense with any pretense of civility and put the fear of God into this unruly boy. If this did not work he would wash his hands like Pontius Pilate did to Jesus nearly two thousand years ago and leave the young boy to an uncertain fate.

Cosmo Tucci arrogantly strode up to the office door as if he were part of the Mummer's Parade strutting up South Broad Street two weeks before. This all changed when he entered the realty office and came face to face with the Old Man. The expression on his face underwent a subtle yet profound change.

The Old Man had this effect on people. Not wanting to discuss what was on his mind in the office, the Old Man spoke in a toneless voice as he donned his overcoat. "Let's go for a walk." Walking the streets was the only milieu where the Old Man could truly speak his mind.

Tucci felt a strange hesitancy. He suddenly wasn't sure if he had heard correctly. "It's freezing out there."

"I know." With a slow, purposeful step the Old Man moved toward the door. Looking over his shoulder he spoke in a low commanding voice. "Let's go."

Tucci nodded begrudgingly with his eyes, and then followed dutifully. Nearly slipping on a patch of ice as they crossed Eighth Street, Tucci finally managed to stay abreast of the Old Man. Slowly, they walked toward St Mary Magdalena, the former Southeast Catholic High School, at Seventh and Christian Streets.

Looking straight ahead and speaking with a choppy mellifluous inflection associated with Italy, the Old Man quizzed Tucci. "Know why we're walking?"

"Nah."

"I didn't think so. The Feds, they use wiretaps and taping devices." The Old Man stopped dead in his tracks to face Tucci. "And I want you to understand perfectly what I'm going tell you." His dark piercing eyes emphasized that he was not trifling. He meant what he was about to say.

Tucci nodded slowly, deliberately as he tried to conceal the tingling sensation emanating from his bladder. The timbre of the Old Man's voice spoke volumes without uttering another word. Tucci acutely understood the implications of this meeting. At that moment it became an epiphany that marked his transition into manhood.

They continued walking slowly. The Old Man talked and Tucci listened. Speaking in measured sentences, the Old Man made it crystal clear in no uncertain terms that Tucci was close to being another occupant of the family burial plot. Tucci listened attentively to each word the Old Man uttered. Still eager for another chance, he temporarily vanquished the demons trying to breach the ramparts of his soul.

Gloria on the other hand acclimated to the South Philly way of life and easily made friends. Sophia and Marie Giampietro's parents were *paisans* from the same village outside of Naples. They also felt a measure of responsibility for Sophia's situation and would offer to watch Gloria whenever they could for the grand-mother. It was in this way that Gloria and Anna became friends.

While the Gimp and Tucci usually chafed in each other's presence, Gloria and Anna formed a sisterly bond. They went everywhere and did everything together. They even shared their clothes and make up. The only exception was boys.

Gloria's brother intrigued Anna in an existential way. She also found him sexy. When the unbridled giggling of young girls piqued Marie's curiosity one day, she eavesdropped on their conversation. At first the conversation was innocent enough until Anna voiced her desire to experience her first sexual encounter with Gloria's brother. Marie bristled at this notion and stomped angrily into their midst. Her demeanor required no explanation and the girls cowered under her indignant stare. Later that evening, Marie made it perfectly clear that Cosmo Tucci was not the man for her, ever. Marie's resolve in this matter was etched in Anna's memory until this day and the topic was never broached again.

Anna thought about that incident so long ago as she paid her toll and headed for Route 130 and the Cherry Hill Mall. She never remembered her mother ever being as stern as she was that day. Like a movie trailer, her mother's forceful diatribe vividly replayed for a fleeting moment in her mind's eye sending a quiver up and down her spine. Regardless, the thought of Gloria's brother, Cosmo, always had a mitigating effect on that memory. She still found him sexy and often wondered how he would be in bed. With a yearning in her heart she lingered on that thought until it was played out.

Refocusing her mind on more current news, a sense of self-satisfaction sent a warm sensation snaking its way through her body. It was the sort of news that had to be shared in person with her best friend. Yet, the thought of her friend's brother continued to surreptitiously slip in and out of her thoughts distracting her for long periods. She resolved to do something about it. Although today wedding dresses took precedence even if someone like Cosmo Tucci wasn't the groom.

24

Outside the Downtown Social Club Teti and Tucci silently mulled over the previous events of the day. Teti leaned against the fender of the Gimp's car with his arms crossed while Tucci paced in front of him darting an impatient glance between the front entrance and his watch. "What's takin' him so long?"

"You got a plane to catch or somethin'? Just settle down," Teti said casually. The less he saw of the Gimp the better Teti secretly thought.

Tired of waiting Tucci leaped the step to the front door and pounded it with the heel of his fist.

Teti watched Tucci stoically. He had learned that the Gimp reacted negatively to such displays of impatience against him. This time, however, he was surprised when the Gimp opened the door with quiet indifference. Teti lurched forward with measured suspicion sensing something afoot. Tucci immediately entered this den of inequity. Hesitantly, Teti followed him. Once inside the mood was relaxed, the Gimp being unusually amiable in his tone and manner. "Grab a cannoli, I'll be right out."

The Gimp disappeared into the makeshift restroom while Tucci picked up a pool stick and started banging the ivory balls around the green felt covered pool table. Still suspicious, Teti looked around the room for signs of some treacherous plot. None were visible. Carlucci had exited the side door to his upstairs apartment unnoticed after quietly explaining his duplicitous plan to the Gimp. It was just the three of them now. Turning the wooden chair around to its proper position Teti helped himself to a cannoli as the sound of gushing water followed by the vigorous scrubbing of hands emanated from the restroom. The Gimp exited with a dour look on his face vigorously drying his hands with a paper towel. Discarding the towel he points his finger at Teti authoritatively. "They're the best."

Teti nodded dully in mid bite.

"Awright. Whataya got for me, Cuzz. Teti's busy feedin' his face here," the Gimp intoned as he sat behind the desk.

At that moment Tucci caromed the cue ball and managed to sink the eight and nine balls in opposite pockets at the end of the pool table. With a hint of a swagger he pulled up a chair in front of the Gimp.

The Gimp was not amused as evident by his tightly pursed lips and wide nostrils. "You done screwin' around'? Now what gives with this Johnny what's his face?"

"Cerone. Johnny Cerone. Straight shooter. Bad luck though. Lost some dough on the UCLA game the other night. Been on a losin' streak. Drives some tinny mustard colored sports car. Right now it's in the shop." Tucci stops to think for a minute, "Oh, he works with computers for Penn down the street from Gaetano's. A regular workin' stiff."

With narrowing eyes riveted on Tucci, the Gimp acted as if he hadn't heard a word of Tucci's brief report. He finally spoke in a low hiss, "Is he bangin' Anna?"

The utter directness of the question caught Tucci off guard. Swallowing hard he brushed a dangling tendril of hair away from his face with the back of his index and middle fingers. This allowed him a split second to evaluate the Gimp's question. Coyly, he responded with a half-truth, "I ain't ever followed 'em over the bridge to a motel. But that don't mean he ain't."

Teti shifted in his chair watching carefully for some kind of facial response to Tucci's answer. The answer seemed to mollify the Gimp temporarily. But his stolid face with unblinking eyes was unresponsive for what seemed like an eternity. Teti had experienced the Gimp's volatility when he emerged from these trancelike moments. That moment never came. Surprisingly, Teti witnessed the Gimp slowly nod his head in resignation. "This stiff wants to marry her."

The swagger drained from Tucci's surprised face. Unconsciously, he tried to mask his feelings by leaning his chair on its back legs and nervously seesawing to and fro.

The Gimp was oblivious to Tucci's reaction and continued speaking. "But he ain't asked me yet. So, I guess I gotta talk to him. Set it up." Then he snorted contemptuously, "Probably shittin' his pants." Suddenly noticing Tucci's nervous seesawing motion, he quizzed, "Whataya got? Ants in yer pants?"

Tucci nearly fell over backwards, but Teti managed a steadying hand. Regaining his balance, Tucci sensed a strange vertigo-like dynamics swirling around him.

"Awright, enough of this bullshit. Let's get down to business," the Gimp demanded in a resolute but uncharacteristically businesslike manner while shifting his eyes toward Teti. "Whataya got for me?"

Throwing a large wad of money held together by rubber bands onto the desk, Teti explains, "All the accounts are current. Everybody paid up. The words must be out about Nicky Sox."

"It pays to advertise," the Gimp chortled in a mocking tone with an impish smile on his face.

"Speaking of which, Sox coughed up a couple hundred as a show of good faith," Teti explained in a matter-of-fact tone masking his delight.

The Gimp studiously grabbed the wad of money and started to roll it around the fingers of his right hand with nervous energy. "What'd he do, rob a gas station over the weekend?"

Teti bristled. "I dunno you'd have to ask him."

"That's Antny's job," the Gimp replied tersely exhibiting a strange hesitancy. Looking up at Teti there was a wicked smile in his eyes as he tried to sound unconcerned. "Leave Nicky to Antny from now on. I want him to handle that little snot." The Gimp peeled off a one-hundred dollar bill from the wad of money in his hand and flipped it to Teti. "Take your boy there," craning his neck toward Tucci, "and go and have dinner on me. The Cucina di Italia makes a great asparagus and ziti dish this time of year."

Teti caught the money with a look of intrigue imprinted on his face. The Gimp's usual abrasive demeanor was noticeably missing from their verbal exchanges this afternoon. Such moments were rare. He was actually pleasant, a perplexed Teti mused, entirely too pleasant.

Armando Tarentino operated a foreign car repair shop on Seventh and Reed Streets. It was situated in an old garage dating from the nineteen thirties replete with a circular wooden gangway leading to the upper floors that was perfectly suited to accommodate foreign sports cars but not the larger American made sedans.

Johnny was referred to Armando by the MGB dealership after they admitted that they didn't have a clue regarding a carburetor problem that Johnny's car was experiencing. Seeing Johnny's car for the first time, Armando shook his head despairingly. "English pieces of shit," he yelled in his bombastic inflection of the

South Philadelphia accent tinged with his Southern Italian dialect. His customers mimicked his pontifications on the shortcomings of the English sports car compared to their Italian counterparts constantly. After a few choice expletives directed toward the car's shortcomings, Armando would go about repairing the car in his elfin like way. This freewheeling style instantly ingratiated him to Johnny and a friendship was struck.

The repartee today was no different except that Armando had already repaired the car and was closing up shop when Johnny entered. A few compatriots of Armando mulled around the shop. All were waiting for what amounted to an Italian style *Happy Hour.* Finally breaking out the oily provolone cheese and fresh Italian bread they uncorked the homemade Italian wine. There were also bottles of Strega, Grappe, Amaretto and homemade Anisette. These liquors were not for the faint of heart and stomach.

Cleaning his hands with degreaser Armando quipped in a jovial manner, "Only ninety dollars today, Johnny. Cheap, no?"

Johnny had the money ready. Armando stuffed the cash into his pocket without counting it. "Aren't you going to count it?" Johnny quizzed.

"I make it up next time if it short," Armando quickly retorted. "You'll be back with that English piece of crap." He finished wiping his hands and signaled the others to start cutting the cheese and pouring the wine.

Johnny always curious about the Italian liquors, but ashamed to admit he knew nothing about them finally decided to take the plunge and poured the yellowish Strega into a slim shot-like glass. The others watched curiously raising their wine glasses as Johnny raised his glass of Strega. "Salut!" They all toasted. Johnny slugged the yellow fluid down in one gulp. The eighty-proof, odd tasting mixture of mint, fennel and saffron sluiced its way down Johnny's throat as the others sipped their wine and looked askance. All waited expectantly for his reaction. Suppressing the churning in his belly Johnny released a muffled cough.

Armando slapped him on the back good-naturedly. "Strega. The witches' love potion. You doomed now Johnny."

Unaware of Johnny's predicament everyone laughed heartily except him.

Breaking off a piece of Italian bread, Armando stuffed it with a crumbling portion of pungent oily provolone. "You still with that same girl, Johnny," he probed while chewing rapaciously.

Johnny gulped his bread and cheese down and hesitated a moment before answering. "Yeah. Well, actually we're talking about getting married."

Armando and the others' faces became animated in various configurations of surprise and dread just as Tucci's black '65 Impala slowly came to a stop perpendicular to the driveway.

"Too bad," Armando said in a straightforward manner while his illusively sarcastic face said otherwise. Bouncing his eyes back and forth between Johnny and the car Armando knew that something was afoot. Adroitly, he slid over and faced his other friends.

As Teti calmly exited the car's passenger door and proceeded into the garage, Tucci's scowl-imprinted face glared from the driver's seat in the background. Realizing that both Tucci's fate and his own were somehow linked, Teti had decided to deliver the Gimp's message himself. The Young Turk's recklessness was unpredictable. Besides, it didn't take a genius to predict the outcome of letting the two men meet face to face, Teti brooded.

Johnny watched Teti approach with mixed apprehension while Armando and the others continued their idle kibitzing. When Teti pushed his right hand slowly out from his side Johnny's eyed widened momentarily, but quickly receded upon registering the sudden movement as a sign of introduction.

"You must be Johnny? I'm Teti," he said in a friendly tone while still extending his hand.

Johnny quickly pumped Teti's hand and replied, "Yeah. Nice meetin' ya."

"Congratulations. I hear that you and the Gimp's daughter are tyin' the knot," Teti continued as he released Johnny's hand. Pushing his own hand back into his coat pocket, Teti motioned to Johnny with a slight bob of his head to move away from the others. Teti led him casually out of earshot of their conversation. He was no judge of character, but Teti knew the look of a dispirited soul. The Gimp's going to have this one for dinner, he thought empathetically.

"Thanks. I didn't know it was general knowledge," Johnny replied quizzically.

"There's a lot you don't know. Anyways, I'm here to tell you…no invite you to lunch at DeLuca's bout noon on Wednesday. Seems Mister Giampietro wants to get to know you better and tell you all those things that you don't know."

"I'm working that day," Johnny quickly retorted.

Teti immediately shot Johnny an incredulous look and blurted, "Is that what you really want me to tell him?"

Johnny focused on Teti's facial expression and comprehended the implications quickly. "No, no, I guess not. I'll be there. DeLuca's, noon Wednesday."

"You got it." Teti started to move away then quickly pivoted on his heels and turned back to face Johnny. "If you don't want to tick 'em off, ask for his daughter's hand in marriage. Then shut up and let him do the talkin' an you should survive the afternoon," Teti paused sensing Johnny's heightened skittishness. Then smiling impishly for effect he added, "Maybe."

25

Tony's Roast Beef on Twentieth Street was about as far west of Broad Street that Nicky Sox cared to venture. It was an ideal place to hang out while he regrouped. Just far enough from the usual haunts of the Gimp, it was a destination spot where he could still enjoy good food and a schooner of Rolling Rock beer in quiet anonymity. Or so he thought.

There was a reversal of fortune for Nicky Sox late that Monday evening when Carlucci entered Tony's Roast Beef. With his aching right arm in a cast he was in the process of awkwardly sloshing down his third schooner of Rolling Rock with his left hand. Nicky was trying desperately to forget the traumatic experience of two nights ago. Three schooners of beer were barely enough.

"Beef combo overboard with outs. And a Schmidt's," Carlucci barked.

When he heard Carlucci's distinctive voice bellow out, Nicky Sox slowly lowered the oversized mug. The pain in his arm intensified. Looking down from the end of the bar, Nicky recognized Carlucci's toothy smile staring him devilishly in the face. Slightly nodding with clenched lips, he took a measured sip from his schooner of beer. He had thought that Teti had bought him some time to figure a way out of his dire financial predicament but the appearance of Carlucci signaled otherwise.

Nicky riveted his eyes on the television above the bar incomprehensibly. His bladder reacted to the perceived threatening situation. Smiling tightly at Carlucci, he made a beeline to the Men's Room. As he hurriedly relieved himself, he shivered uncontrollably contemplating the worst possible scenario. Finally gaining control of his bodily functions, Nicky mustered the intestinal fortitude to return to the bar and face whatever consequences awaited him. There were no other options.

In the meantime Carlucci had secured the seat next to Nicky. Upon returning Nicky squeamishly smiled and sat down. "What's goin' on?"

"Funny seeing you here Nicky. This ain't one of your usual haunts," Carlucci observed.

"Had a yen for a combo and a beer. Ain't nothing like this place on the eastside."

Carlucci bobbed his head as he gulped his beer. Wiping his mouth downward between his left thumb and forefinger, he replied, "Let's get a table in the back."

Tightly grasping the handle of his schooner of beer Nicky acceded to this request. Unsteadily, he staggered toward the farthest table in the rear of the bar. Carlucci threw up a twenty-dollar bill onto the bar. "Bring us another round when you get a chance."

Nicky sat down facing the wall knowing that Carlucci would want the seat across from him in order to watch the comings and goings of the bar. It was a sign of deference to him that didn't go unnoticed.

The bartender brought the round of drinks and Carlucci's sandwich to the table just as he was sitting down. Nodding appreciatively, Carlucci took a bite of the juicy roast beef sandwich on an Italian roll with a slice of provolone added. Nicky watched apprehensively as he slowly masticated the concoction draining the remaining beer from his first schooner then quickly starting the second one.

Carlucci was toying with him now. He took a short sip of beer to wash down the sandwich then looked him straight in the eye. "How ya doin'?"

Nicky nervously waited for the other shoe to drop and simply responded, "Okay so far. The beer helps."

"Good," Carlucci responded punctuating the air with his index finger, "cause yer gonna feel even better."

Nicky eyed Carlucci suspiciously wondering if this was some perverse psycho-pathic game. "How so?"

"You want to get outta the jam yer in, right?"

"Yeah. That would be nice," Nicky coyly responded trying not to sound sarcastic.

"Well, I've got a sweet deal for ya."

Nicky slid back in his chair warily. What he thought he heard was uncharacteristic for Carlucci, he thought. Was this a ploy to lure him into a false sense of security or was this an honest offer. For a few seconds Nicky weighed his options. It seemed like an hour. Deciding that he had no other options, he prodded, "Go on."

Carlucci took another bite of his sandwich and chewed slowly. With a mesmerizing stare he looked at Nicky. Carefully, he evaluated his wording of this pernicious proposal. After washing down the remnants of his sandwich he spoke slowly and deliberately, "I'm going to propose a way for you to clear your debt and make thirty-five hundred to boot."

Skeptically, Nicky pushed forward in his chair and whispered, "I'm sorry but you and the Gimp are not exactly the benevolent type. You get my drift. So, who do I have to kill?"

Anthony chuckled lowly while wagging his finger at Nicky. "I told Joey you weren't such a swish." Wiping the smile from his face Carlucci proceeded to explain his plan, "You ain't got to kill nobody. You just gotta, you gotta relieve someone of their bankroll. Thirty five hundred cash and you get a ticket outta jail. A sweet deal."

Nicky wasn't the sort for murder, but he wasn't above larceny to get himself out of a mess. He liked what he was hearing so far. "And the mark?" he quizzed.

"The hustler, Cisco."

"No Way Jose! He knows me! If you don't kill me he will," Nicky responded excitedly.

"He don't know your brother does he?" Carlucci retorted enticingly.

A birdlike expression crossed Nicky's face as he contemplated the possibility. He'd be back in action. His brother would make a score and his slate would be clean, he quickly thought. Something else gnawed at his innards. "This ain't like you Antony. What's to stop you from doin' me after the fact?"

"What's to stop me now?"

"I don't know."

Carlucci leaned over the table menacingly. "Yes you do. Cause I laid out the plan. Now you're in my friend whether you like it or not. Jus don't cross me. Unnerstand?"

Nicky sank in his seat. Unwittingly he made a deal with the devil just by the simple exercise of listening. His only hope now was to make this thing happen and hope for the best. In a dismayed voice he responded, "Yeah."

"Good." Carlucci reached into his pocket and peeled off a couple one-hundred dollar bills from a small wad of money. He tossed it to an unsuspecting Nicky who flinched. "This is a show of good faith. You can pay back whoever fronted you the money or keep it. Either way you keep your mouth shut and you live to enjoy another day."

Nicky wondered momentarily if Carlucci knew that Teti fronted him the money. It was a fleeting thought and didn't matter at this point. All that mattered now was how he was going to convince his brother to save his precious ass. Before Carlucci laid out the specifics of the plan, Nicky excused himself for another trip to the Men's Room. It was at this moment that he realized how pathetic he truly was. Lamenting his hubris for thinking he could beat the system, Nicky knew that he was trapped. People like him were expendable pawns in the chess game of life. Life had become far too complicated. Nothing ever worked out, as it should, he thought. One day at a time, he silently repeated as he relieved himself yet again hoping to flush away the insidious memory of what he had become.

26

Wednesday, March 29, 1972

Jeweler's Row on Sansom Street between Seventh and Eighth Streets was strictly a Jewish principality amid the White Anglo Saxon Protestant fiefdom surrounding it. Diamonds, precious stones, metals and collectibles were its currency and Sid Greenberg was its reigning monarch.

Low keyed and humble, Sid held court in a basement frontage on the south side of the block almost directly in the center. It was classic Sid—humility and balance outside, tight-fisted control inside. It was akin to the Old Man's style to a tee. This mutual understanding of one another's management style allowed both men to prosper over the years. It also spoke volumes of their respect for one another and allowed them to peacefully reign over their respective spheres of influence.

Sid's distinction as a bona fide godfather also cemented the relationship between the Italian and Jewish criminal communities of Philadelphia. It was a conundrum to those outside the inner circle of the mafia in the roaring days of the twenties. A good friend to Sal 'Solly' Teti, Sid was also godfather to Teti's daughter. Since Sid had only a son and no daughter of his own to spoil, he relished the responsibility.

Sid Greenberg was also a shrewd observer of men. He had to be to have survived as long as he did in his line of work. Although a hustler of the first sort, Cisco had shown his mettle on several occasions. For that reason and the fact that he was also the paramour of his godchild Rose, Sid liked him and agreed to the meeting.

When Rose and Cisco fell in love it was Sid who was the first to know. Never intervening in the affair, he always respected his friend Solly's wishes. When his friend passed away, Sid became Rose's quasi protector of sorts helping her manage the convoluted financial mess that her father left behind. He would have gladly met with Cisco if he had asked, but knew the man was too proud to do so. It was characteristics like that, which endeared Cisco to this Jewish Godfather.

The possibility of an outstanding warrant for his errant deeds down South lingered in the recesses of Cisco's mind since his run in with that small town sheriff. So, he decided to forego purchasing an automobile until he felt reasonably secure that that episode of his life was well behind him. The reason for this, he confided to Rose one day, was the fact that many law enforcement agencies used their motor vehicle departments to track down people with outstanding warrants. It was Cisco's way of staying under the radar. Too bad he couldn't get lower on the Gimp's radar screen and avoid the son-of-a-bitch, he ruminated. It was a fleeting thought as he quietly sought the divination of his next move in the solitude of the small room behind the bar.

Accepting the inconveniences of his decision, Cisco still managed to get around the city even though he didn't own a car. Sometimes he walked. This allowed him to smoke as he gathered his thoughts. Of course Rose's car was always at his disposal. This morning he chose to use her car. Parking it in a two hour parking zone at Eighth and Spruce Streets, he walked the remaining three blocks up to Sansom Street.

Punctual as usual and uncharacteristically upbeat, Cisco danced down the steps this morning to Sid's lair and pressed the buzzer. He was quickly buzzed through the door since Sid had observed him on his newly installed closed circuit television camera. It was a gift from his son Benjamin who managed several Las Vegas Strip Casinos for various associates of his father. The bulletproof glass was also a gift though not widely known. Sid liked it that way.

Cisco and Sid cordially shook hands exchanging the appropriate personal inquiries associated with friends out of touch with one another for extended periods of time. Removing his loupe from his forehead Sid sat down in an oversized billowy chair and leaned back motioning with a benevolent gesture of his hand for Cisco to do the same. "Sit, relax. This is not a business transaction," Sid said in a soft fatherly tone.

Cisco readily complied and found the tension in his body release as he sunk into the comfortable chair. "This chair's great," he said in a surprised voice.

"It'll add years to your life," Sid said in a patronizing way that quickly turned serious. "Now what's this business with the Gimp or should I say Mister Giampietro."

"I owe 'em thirty-five hundred. It's that simple."

Cisco's matter-of-fact response produced a withering look on Sid's pale face. "Armand, we both know that's a lot of crock," Sid said firmly. "Nothing is that simple with that fellow. What's really going on here? What did you do to ruffle his feathers," Sid prodded staunchly.

"You know how the guy is."

"I know, I know. I've heard all the stories."

"It could've been anything. I could've looked at him crooked." After a contemplative pause, Cisco blurted out in frustration, "For Christ sakes, what's the Old Man see in that guy."

Biting the inside of his lower lip, Sid lurched forward in his chair consumed by secret thoughts. One night at his home in the tony section of Lower Merion Township the wine was flowing and the mood relaxed. That night Sal Teti had intimated to him of a dark secret that burdened him. No matter how subtly Sid probed for the answer, Teti would only say that it involved the Old Man and the Gimp. Sid rocked his upper body slightly until the thoughts that Cisco's verbal musing evoked had passed. Continuing to probe Cisco for an answer he uttered a single word, "Think."

While Cisco sought an answer, a thought came to Sid like a bolt of lightning. He slouched back in his chair contemplatively. A grimace transformed his composed face from the roiling of a long forgotten memory.

Cisco astutely noticed the change in Sid's demeanor. "What?"

The grimace transformed into a forced smile on Sid's face. "It may just be that you're the whipping boy for the Teti family because of Rose," Sid offered in measured phrases.

Both men were enshrouded by an eerie silence. As the implications of this statement gradually took hold, Sid objectified his previous musing, "Or he's just pissed at himself. Maybe both. Solly told me a story once about Rose and Little Joey. That's what they use to call him then." Sid formed a steeple with the fingers of his hand as he elaborated, "One of those innocent types of tales that all parents remember, but their kids forget. Only thing is that it upset Solly to the point of obsession. Not only did he embarrass the kid, but he continued physically berating him long after." Sid bent forward lowering his head as if in sorrow and looked at Cisco from eyes rolled toward the top of his head. His mood became somber as he spoke esoterically, "I'm being kind using such a ten dollar word. You know what I mean."

Cisco understood Sid Greenberg implicitly. His own father physically berated him once or twice. Cisco winced as he shifted in his seat, "So what do I do about it?"

Sid pushed himself from the chair without a quiver. Standing erect his posture was straight for a man of seventy-five. He captured Cisco's eyes and with a slight benevolent jerk pointed his right finger at him, "There's nothing you can do, or will do." He turned and walked behind a screen to a wall safe. Spinning the dial on the safe, Sid proclaimed, "Rose told me everything. She left nothing out. Nothing." Opening the safe Sid fanned some money as he continued, "If you do something stupid, I won't be able to help you." He tossed a bundle of money onto the table next to a bewildered Cisco. "Consider it a future wedding present for you and Rose."

Cisco started to refuse. Sid shot the palm of his right hand forward like a traffic cop halting an impatient motorist. Cisco pleaded anyway, "I can't take this. That's not why I'm here."

"That's the only reason you're here. And I'm going to go one better." Sid walked over to the glass counter with diamond rings and other precious stones reflecting light outwardly in an array akin to the aurora borealis. After scribbling something on the back of a business card, he turned and handed the card to Cisco.

Cisco looked at the writing then looked at Sid questioningly. "You want me to go see your son Ben in Vegas?"

"There is always a place in Las Vegas for someone with your talents my friend," Sid assured him.

"But I got a record."

"Ben knows the ins and outs of the business. He'll advise you. Trust me." Sid continued in a paternal tone of voice, "Pay the Gimp what you owe him quickly. Then leave South Philly quicker. You've got another chance here my friend. Take it."

"What about Rose and the boy?"

"First things first. You need to go quickly. I'll do what I can to expedite the rest."

"But."

"No Buts. Rose is like my own daughter. I promise you nothing will happen to her."

"The boy?"

"Teti will have to make his own way in life. But I'll see what I can do. No promises."

Cisco stuffed the thirty-five hundred dollars into his pocket then placed the business card in his wallet. Cisco grasped Sid's hand then placed his left hand on top of the clasped hands in a rare show of gratitude and respect.

Sid held back the emotions swelling in his chest. "Life is very complicated for the proud of heart."

27

Johnny Cerone was disassembling the top of his MGB convertible. Once the top and its framework were neatly stored in the compact trunk, he clipped on the car's tonneau cover. The canvas tonneau cover made the car look and feel like a true sports car. Johnny would have it no other way.

Making a right turn onto Twentieth Street from Ritner Johnny decided to tempt fate and stay the course to the Benjamin Franklin Parkway. As he shifted through the gears, Johnny was oblivious to the changing façades of abandoned buildings and trash-strewn streets. His thoughts were focused on his lunchtime meeting with the Gimp. Uncomfortable with asking the Gimp for his daughter's hand in marriage, he practiced several different ways of expressing himself in an attempt to smoothly work the topic into their conversation. Between shifting gears he used his right hand like an orchestra maestro alluringly beckoning a section of instruments into the proper musical tempo with his wand. Although his movements were mellifluous, his delivery was choppy and obtuse. Frustrated by his pretentious attempts to appear sincere, he temporarily deviated from his meeting with the Gimp to his relationship with his daughter Anna. This telesthetic transition of focus occurred as he passed the Franklin Institute at Race Street and turned left onto the Parkway just west of Logan Circle.

The Benjamin Franklin Parkway, a majestic tree-lined boulevard, connected Center City Philadelphia to Fairmount Park, the home of the 1876 Centennial Exposition. The Art Museum of Philadelphia rose above the Parkway like a Greek temple on Mount Olympus. Mesmerized by the Museum, Johnny drove toward it like an ancient Greek hurriedly seeking the wisdom of a great oracle. He passed the massive Free Library building first. Continuing pass these vanguards of a civil society, Johnny then wheeled by the Rodin Museum with the statue of the Thinker prominently displayed for all to see.

As the road coursed right around the Washington Monument, Johnny continued on to the East River Drive. He loved to drive along this road especially on a beautiful, sunny weekday morning after the congestive traffic subsided.

The Schuylkill River, Dutch for hidden river, flowed gently between the East and West River Drives. Actually, it was more like a fresh water lake due to the water works dam constructed in 1822 that altered the river. Landscaping surrounded the five acres of the water works and thus began Fairmount Park. Consequently, this length of the river was still relatively pristine. It was ideal for rowing.

This morning a crew of scullers was rowing in metronomic precision using the American Conibear style stroke in preparation for a regatta. Meanwhile, another crew adjusted the swivel oarlocks of their keel less boat and glided almost effortlessly toward the Ornamental Victorian style Boathouse bearing the seal of the University of Pennsylvania.

Johnny pulled into a parking area along the river south of Boathouse Row. Turning off the car engine, he relaxed and watched the remaining crew go through their paces along the river. Observing the rhythmic stroking of the oarsmen calmed Johnny's convoluted thought process. Slowly, his mental acumen returned allowing him the opportunity to ruminate over the events of the past few days. An honest introspective review of his life was in order at this moment, he thought. No longer could he deny the consumptive folly of his misspent youth.

Glancing at his watch, he suddenly realized that his moment of truth was fast approaching. A little more than two hours from now my life will be set on an irreversible course, he silently lamented. His procrastinating ways were over. Exploring his emotions was no longer an option, he finally acknowledged. His searching eyes quickly devolved into dark bitter pills of dismay.

Johnny exited the car to stretch his legs momentarily. Crossing his arms in thought he leaned on the fender of the MGB. Thoughts about Anna's domineering ways, her tardiness, her occasional manipulative demeanor and her father crowded his mind. "Ah," he exhaled sighing deeply. It always came back to Anna's father, he secretly realized. The specter of the Gimp hung ominously over his head like an anvil. It was too late now to do anything about it.

The rowing team had disappeared from view and the lucidity of his mind gave way to a murky cloud of inevitability. Johnny was at a mental impasse sinking slowly into a morass of diffidence. With his eyes out of focus and his head nodding involuntarily the words replayed in his mind. *"It's time to pay the piper."* Like the cataract on the Schuylkill River, Johnny was about to plunge into the mainstream of a life out of control.

Not wanting to brood any longer, he leaped into the driver seat of his car. Speeding off in a cloud of dust up the East River Drive he hung a left just before Ridge Avenue. He raced through the MGB's gears as he sped through a winding greenbelt. Downshifting to make a sharp right turn, Johnny headed south on the West River Drive on a collision course with his destiny.

28

DeLuca's Il Culmine Restaurant on Tenth Street, a short walk from the heart of the Italian Market district, was one of the few places the Gimp frequented. Serving fine Italian food since the early part of the twentieth century, it was also the final destination for many Italian immigrants. Fresh off the trans-Atlantic ships docked at the foot of Washington Avenue, they laboriously made the mile trek carrying all their worldly possessions with them to this boarding house and restaurant. It served as a thin lifeline connecting the old world to the new one.

The migration began slowly at first. The immigrants, *trapiantati* or transplanted ones wrote to their struggling families in Italy of the bountiful opportunities in this rich land called America. Jobs abounded for those willing to work hard. All that one needed was a champion to help the unwitting through the legal morass of this new land. Thus the dreams and inspirations fueling this continuous migration, took root. Soon immigrants began arriving in waves with restaurants and boarding house names pinned to their coats and shawls seeking a *padrone*. Like DeLuca's, these other restaurants and boarding houses were willing to assist these immigrants negotiate the laws and customs of their newly adopted homes. For this service there was a customary fee. Many other *padrones,* however, preyed on these unwitting people, duping them at every opportunity.

The Vecchio family had made a living being *padrones*. They were landlords and middlemen receiving commissions from large companies seeking *bracciante* or workers. They were not the worst example of the *padrone* system neither were they altruistic. The grateful immigrants would seek their counsel and do their bidding, always to the advantage of the Vecchio's. As the fortune of the Vecchio family grew, the budding criminal element from Second Street took note.

Threatening assassination or kidnapping, Giuseppe Vecchio's father caved in and began paying protection money to these unorganized Irish thugs. The young Vecchio was livid. He concocted different ways of dealing with these parasites as he called them. His father would have none of it. Then a chance meeting changed forever the course of Giuseppe Vecchio's life.

The year was 1913. Salvatore Sabella had just arrived in Philadelphia to organize the criminal activities of the Italians in South Philadelphia under the protection of a New York Mafioso named Joe Masseria. Giuseppe Vecchio was dining alone at DeLuca's when Sal Sabella entered seeking a table. The restaurant was full. Sabella was demanding. Vecchio overheard the conversation and offered to share his table. The conversation during this cordial unplanned meeting uncovered some areas of mutual interest. Eventually, after the discreet inquires of both men a friendship developed.

Shortly after that momentous dinner, the two thugs who were strong-arming the local merchants mysteriously disappeared. When the local merchants learned through the grapevine that Sal Sabella was responsible for their deliverance from the two loathsome *Amerigans* they gratefully paid Sabella instead. After all, they already had incorporated the cost of the shakedown into their prices. For them it was always good to have a man of respect looking out for their best interests.

The manner in which Sabella handled the matter impressed the twenty-year-old Vecchio. He liked the man's style in dealing with adversity and duly noted the response of the merchants. As repayment for Vecchio's friendship, Sabella dispensed with the Vecchio tithe. Not wanting the other merchants to know his complicity in Sabella's business, Vecchio collected the money from his father pocketing it for himself. It was only a matter of redistributing the family wealth, he rationalized. Melding style and his own business acumen in the *padrone* business, Vecchio set himself on a course to become the Old Man, Don Vecchio.

The Gimp had heard this story so many times that he bristled at the mere suggestion of it except when the Old Man was doing the telling. Today, however, he toyed with the idea of telling the tale himself as he hungrily looked over the menu. After all, he thought, the restaurant was one of the last vestiges to the memory of the thousands of Italian immigrants who immigrated to the City of

Brotherly Love. Scanning the room's memorabilia he realized that he would eventually be part of the story too—a modern day *padrone*.

Johnny entered DeLuca's five minutes early. As the hostess led him to the Gimp's table it appeared that the Gimp was deep in thought. Actually, the Gimp was fantasizing how his story would fit into the myth and lore surrounding him. It was a rare moment of mental solace that was shattered like a ball breaking a window by Johnny's appearance.

Johnny extended his hand. "Mister Giampietro, I'm Johnny Cerone."

The Gimp sized Johnny up for a second. Raising himself slightly out of his chair, the Gimp clasped Johnny's extended hand with a limp grasp signaling his indifference. "Sit," he tersely ordered.

A waiter quickly appeared dressed in black apron, black pants and a black bow tie on a heavily starched white shirt with his hair fastidiously barbered. His appearance exuded old world charm that was the mainstay of the restaurant. "Good Afternoon," he said in a polite tone. "Can I get you gentlemen something to drink?"

"Bring us a bottle of Ruffino Chianti. The good stuff," the Gimp commanded in a peppery tone. "And some fresh hot bread. Hot!"

"Of course Mister Giampietro," the waiter said obligingly wanting the Gimp to know that he was recognized. This also served in a subtle way to put the Gimp on notice that an appropriate tip would be expected. The Gimp was oblivious of such petty machinations and did as he pleased expecting personalized service wherever he dined.

Lurching forward in his chair the Gimp assumed a menacing posture. "So, Johnny. They call you Johnny right?"

Johnny nodded with obeisant eyes. His shoulders slumped as his facial expression now registered bewildered anticipation of the course of the conversation.

"What's goin on between you and my daughter?" the Gimp demanded in his usual gruff manner, a deep frown creasing his forehead. His dark eyes turned sinister and seemed to penetrate Johnny's soft doe-like ones.

Johnny was intimidated by the Gimp's pointed directness. He expected to engage in some perfunctory small talk before he launched into his practiced discourse. Instead, his train of thought became disjointed and his delivery choppy. "Your daughter, uh, I mean, well, I would like to ask you, Mister Giampietro, for your daughter's hand in marriage," he said sighing heavily once the request was completed. There he said it, he thought uneasily. On some level of consciousness, however, he hoped the Gimp would reject his request. Tell him his daughter was too good for him. Banish him from ever seeing her again. All of the above, his mind pleaded in abject silence for a deliverance from his mental anguish. He expected a miracle. None would appear.

"You would, wouldya," the Gimp replied coyly as the tips of his pursed mouth turned downward momentarily followed by several changes of facial expressions.

Frozen in his chair, Johnny's eyes busily scanned the Gimp's changing facial expressions for some sign, any sign of what he was thinking. Adroitly avoiding any direct contact with his cold steely eyes, the ebb and flow of anticipation coursed through Johnny's veins causing his heart to beat faster. Despite these feelings he was able to keep his face impassive. Then like a bolt of lightning from out of the blue the answer came.

"You have my permission," the Gimp said in an even-tempered tone couched by an evasive smile. It was an impulsive answer without any basis. The Gimp's thought processes were entirely instinctive except for several rare occasions. Johnny had no inkling to the inner workings of the Gimp's mind at this stage of the game. That would come soon enough.

At that moment the waiter returned with steaming bread and a bottle of Ruffino Classico. Johnny breathed deeply through his nose. Silently, he appreciated the momentary respite before engaging the Gimp in conversation again.

The Gimp gestured for the waiter to pour the wine. He disliked participating in the ritual wine tasting that accompanied a fine dining experience. "Just pour it. If it ain't any good I'll be sure an let you know," The Gimp said with a dismissive glance.

The waiter was non-plus and decided to perform the customary routine less the wine tasting. After all fine dining is an experience and should not be rushed, the waiter smugly thought with a patronizing grin. If this boorish lout was in a hurry he should have gone to some hoagie shop. "Are we ready to order?" the waiter asked in a professional tone devoid of how he truly felt.

"Veal chops for me," the Gimp hungrily replied.

"Very good, sir. Our specialty I might add." Twisting his neck slightly to face Johnny, he inquired, "And for you sir?"

"Osso bucco. Thanks."

Not wanting to repeat himself the waiter quickly wrote the order and stepped away quietly to service another table of more sophisticated diners.

Motioning with his eyes for Johnny to raise his glass of wine in a toast, the Gimp clinked the glasses together and blurted, "Salut!"

Johnny managed a muted nod with a forced smile then took a sip of wine.

Taking a gulp of wine then refilling his glass the Gimp began conversing in a composed manner, "So I hear that you're some kind of computer person."

"Programmer."

"What's that?"

"I write short programs that return information for different uses. Kind of like talking to a machine," Johnny said proudly.

Punctuating the air with his finger, the Gimp added, "A pretty smart cookie, I'll bet." The wine had made him more affable and hungry. He buttered a piece of hot Italian bread. It was at moments like this that people misjudged the Gimp and often regretted it. His patronizing demeanor viscerally beckoned one to bare their soul. It was like a hunter luring his prey from the safety of their lair.

Somehow Johnny sensed the trap and instinctively kept his replies terse and to the point. "I studied hard in school."

"College?" the Gimp asked.

"I dropped out after junior year to go to computer school," Johnny replied nervously.

"Got ya a good job, right?"

"Right."

The Gimp smiled broadly at Johnny's response while chewing the bread. This gave the Gimp a reflective moment. The boy was respectful yet closed-mouthed he thought, impressed by Johnny's response. This interview was off to a good start. Perhaps Anna had chosen well, he mused priding himself on raising an astute daughter. "You gamble?" the Gimp probed watching for Johnny's response as he took a gulp of wine to wash down the bread.

"Everyday. You know, life's a gamble," Johnny evasively responded knowing full well what the Gimp was driving at. His anxiety turned sanguine as he began enjoying this mental repartee. If he truly thought about it or even ventured a glance into the cold steely eyes of the Gimp he would have engaged the conversation on an entirely different level. Johnny had no way of knowing how his responses were being perceived by the Gimp. He personally thought that he was being a disrespectful wise ass unworthy of the Princess Anna. Instead, by gingerly parrying the Gimp's verbal thrusts he was endearing himself to the man.

In one continuous smooth motion from the kitchen the waiter appeared at their table, tray and stand delicately balanced at an angle reminiscent of the leaning Tower of Pisa. Serving their orders in an equally elegant fashion, he completed his task by filling their wine glasses. "Will there be anything else? More wine perhaps?"

"Another bottle would hit the spot," the Gimp replied in a mellow tone of voice.

Attributing the Gimp's change of manner to the wine, the waiter smiled approvingly and replied, "Very good sir." Retracting the foldable stand the waiter slid away to garner another bottle of wine.

The haunting voice resurfaced as a faint echo in the recesses of the Gimp's head while masticating his veal chop. He shrugged it off temporarily by a swift reflexive shake of his head.

It was returning more frequently in recent months. The Gimp thus far was able to resist the siren allure of the lilting voice. However, something was different today. A familiar voice spoke to him, a voice from his past. When he attempted to identify the vocal inflection, his mind drew a blank. Yet, he trusted it and for the first time felt compelled to listen to its persuasive advice. The Gimp's hands slightly trembled. Beads of anxiety driven sweat formed on his forehead. He was a man not use to doing other peoples bidding let alone an unseen voice. At first he resisted but the haranguing voice persisted. *"People will laugh behind your back, Joey. They think they're better than you."*

Johnny looked up from his plate of veal shinbones and smiled perplexingly. All in all, he thought confidently, the meeting went much better than he had originally anticipated. The next minutes would change that assessment.

Returning with another bottle of wine, the waiter noticed the beads of sweat on the Gimp's forehead. Silently offering him a fresh linen napkin, the Gimp's eyes widened and his nostrils flared.

"Did I ask for that?" the Gimp bellowed.

Looking askance the waiter bent slightly and whispered, "For your forehead sir."

The Gimp's face glowed red with anger. Irately he yanked the linen napkin from the hand of the waiter. Unable to contain the high pitch modulation of his voice he scurrilously retorted, "Next time mind your own fuckin' business."

The voice had counseled him on the waiter's presumptuous attitude and the Gimp silently concurred reverting to his gruff style. Sighing deeply he rotated his neck slowly trying to stretch out the sudden accumulation of stress.

Acutely aware of the Gimp's persona the waiter humbly apologized. Slithering away from the table the waiter made a mental note to let another waiter serve this menacing man. A mere twenty-five percent tip was not worth rousing the ire of such an unbalanced individual.

Johnny had witnessed this type of erratic behavior with the rise of the drug culture of the sixties and the growing use of methamphetamine. He knew *Meth Heads* personally who exhibited such psychotic behavior. Unpredictable and dangerous, he avoided them like the plague. Whether the Gimp was a *Meth Head* or not didn't matter. The man was teetering on the precipice of derangement. Johnny realized at this moment that he had just experienced an epiphany right before his eyes. It was an urgent call to action.

29

Perched above a storefront at the crossroads of Sixteenth Street with Snyder and Passyunk Avenues, Chickie's Poolroom had a strategic view of the flow of traffic on the streets below. It was one of many hangouts for the youth of South Philadelphia seeking to walk on the wild side or tempt the fates. Some survived others paid the price.

Card games were always brewing. Pool hustlers, like the sharks that they were, came and went seeking fresh *blood*. Cisco fit into both categories. Methodically, he practiced a double bank shot over and over again on the main pool table. Dividing his attention between making the shot and the entrance door, he had trouble duplicating it this evening. His interest this evening was not seeking a game of nine-ball with some hot shot willing to lose his money. Instead, he was hoping to run into anyone from the Gimp's crew except Teti.

Engrossed in another form of gambling, Tony "Bags" Bagnotta was playing a mechanical pinball type machine akin to tic-tac-toe except that diagonal lines did not win. The pay out was based on a schedule of games won that was posted on the wall next to the machine. The actual monetary pay out was general knowledge. Everyone knew that the pay out was a dollar per game, twenty game minimum pay out. This was not openly posted so that the proprietor could disclaim any knowledge of gambling. Like any game of chance the odds were always in favor of the house. Tony Bags was just casually passing the time. Like the two other swarthy looking characters suspiciously mulling around the pool table, he was waiting for a fourth to play hearts. No one would ask Cisco. His reputation preceded him in this world of dark motives.

The action was slow for a Wednesday night. Swearing under his breath that Pops had rigged the damn thing, Tony had already lost twenty dollars worth of dimes in the machine. Quelling his frustration he took a long drag on the cigarette dangling precipitously on the side of the machine. Looking at Cisco, Tony's face registered his intent to seriously ask Cisco to play. The other two caught his eyes and countermanded his thought with a slight swivel of their heads. Tony just wanted the action. The other two wanted to win.

The entrance door to the stairway creaked open and Johnny entered. Instantly becoming the center of attention, the air in the room now crackled with anticipation.

Thinking of the *fresh meat* that had just entered a smile erupted on Tony Bags' face. Tony remembered Johnny as a first class novice at cards. Figuring to win the twenty back that the machine just sucked up, he bided his time. The other two perked up and moved away from the pool table like sharks circling for the kill.

Cisco was uninterested. He had seen Johnny at the slightly upscale poolroom on Oregon Avenue and figured that Johnny was a broker, someone with little cash and even less card sense. So, he returned his focus to nine-ball.

Racking up the balls in a diamond shape configuration with the one ball at the top of the diamond and on the foot spot, he gingerly exchanged the eight ball in the center for the nine ball. Placing the cue behind the head string, Cisco broke the rack of balls squarely with one smooth, swift stroke of the cue ball. The six ball rolled into the corner pocket. Cisco immediately began triangulating on the one ball looking at it from several different perspectives.

Johnny had hung out at Chickie's a few times with Tommy Dee, but didn't have the cutthroat instinct that was necessary to survive in this type of environment. Tonight however, he wanted to avoid Anna and her usual friends. In the meantime he would gather his thoughts and decide how to break the bad news to her.

Tony Bags banged on the machine trying to sway an errant pinball into the appropriate slot. He cursed vehemently to no avail.

Behind the nearby counter Pops looked up indifferently through coke bottle-thick glasses. Holding the racing form close to his face, he adjusted it to the proper magnification of his glasses. A wrinkly smile slowly emanated across his face. He liked what he saw.

During his lifetime Pops had won and lost small fortunes betting on the ponies. At this point in his life he wasn't about to give up betting on them even if it meant going hungry for a few days. Catching Cisco's eye he beckoned him to the counter. Confidently, Pops pointed to one of the entries running at Aqueduct the next day. "Bet the bricks on this one," he whispered lowly in a harsh, rasping voice aged from over sixty years of smoking unfiltered cigarettes like Camels and Lucky Strikes.

Cisco dexterously flipped a cigarette from a nearby pack. Not caring who left them there he lit it quickly taking a long and reflective drag on its toxic content. "Ain't got any bricks, Pops," Cisco replied.

"Too bad. This one would solve all your problems," Pops croaked.

"Ain't got any of them either," Cisco said coyly.

Pops cranked his head up with a look of askance stamped on his face like a piece of coinage. "You're fuckin' with me now," Pops replied indignantly.

Cisco slapped Pops on his shoulder in a friendly manner. "I got it covered."

"Always bein' a wise ass got you in trouble. You got that covered?"

"In spades," he replied tersely returning to the main pool table and studiously examining his next shot while chalking his house cue stick.

Cisco loved to use the house cue sticks. He felt it made him less pretentious ergo less threatening. While on the road it always got him better odds in the beginning. Better to be ahead of the game than behind the curve he always espoused. Most of the time this ploy worked and his opponents underestimated him. It didn't work in South Philly where his reputation was well known.

Even so, he still had young hotshots gunning for him and he obligingly took their money. It was how he made his living. Being a barkeep or poolroom attendant just didn't seem to cut it for him. He occasionally contemplated his future and inevitably drew a blank. Cisco lived in the moment. The past and future were inconsequential. The present was the governing factor and at the present moment he was the master of his fate—at least for the time being.

This philosophy of life was the sticking point in his relationship with Rose. She needed security. Cisco was a free spirit and never the twain shall meet. However, Sid's proposal intrigued Cisco. Perhaps a compromise with Rose could be reached, he thought as he double banked the three-ball into the side pocket.

Tony Bags was hot for action, any action. It didn't matter if the fourth player didn't know a heart from a spade. He just wanted to play cards. "Yo kid," he called out to Johnny. "What are ya gonna do, be a stiff. Let's get something goin'."

Johnny was out of his element. Although he had played hearts on several previous occasions, he wasn't fond of the game. He bet on athletic games. Card games were a different arena—poker maybe, hearts, definitely not. Besides, he was broke except for some loose change in his pocket. He was a stiff. Realizing this point he hated himself for being in such a poor state of affairs. Tightly pursing his lips until the cheeks of his face nearly touched his eyes he said, "Not interested. Maybe another time."

Tony Bags was about to make a derogatory retort when Cisco for no logical reason decided to save this naïve young man the embarrassment. "I'm in if you need a fourth," he interjected while continuing his solo game of nine-ball.

Rolling his tongue on the inside of his tightly closed mouth, Tony Bags realized that he was checkmated. What the hell, he thought. Trying to act non-chalant he looked eagerly toward the other two potential players. They appeared noncommittal as they whispered to each other. Suddenly, Tony Bags realized that maybe he was being set up—double-teamed by these two guys. They had been hanging around recently. Played some cards, but he really didn't know them. He decided to cut his loses and opt out. Glancing at the clock behind the counter, he acted surprised and grumbled, "It's getting late. Where's the frickin' time go." Stabbing the air above his head with his finger, he mumbled, "I gotta go. Maybe next time." He slowly exited. Looking over his shoulder at the two shady looking characters, he made a mental note to find out exactly who they were the next time they showed up.

Cisco stopped momentarily and looked directly at the same two suspicious characters wanting to play cards. Sizing up one and then the other, Cisco smiled toothily and probed, "Didn't catch youse guys' names?"

The taller one maintained Cisco's stare momentarily then broke eye contact knowing that the ruse was over. "We got to go too. Later." Both exited in short order and the room was suddenly enveloped in an eerie silence.

Johnny looked bemusedly at Cisco. "What's with those guys?"

"Half-ass hustlers," Cisco said, intrigued by Johnny's wide-eyed naïveté about what had just transpired. Watching Johnny drop his pocket change into the machine, Cisco imagined the young man becoming jaded with life downtown then moving to South Jersey to work nine to five until he retired. Maybe, he went on, if gambling ever came to Atlantic City, the young man would make a yearly pilgrimage to see the Miss America Pageant or the Ice Capades. Eventually go on to lose a few bucks in the slots, Cisco disparagingly thought. Then for some unknown reason the thought of Rose at the beach in a one-piece swimsuit accentuating her sensuous long legs crossed his mind. He fell into a melancholic snit.

Cisco's curiosity was momentarily piqued. Out of the corner of his eye he caught Johnny pick up a lone dime from under the machine and insert it hopefully into the machine. Turning his focus back to the pool table Cisco slammed the cue ball with deflected English sinking the five-ball in the opposite corner pocket. The clicking machine caught Cisco's attention.

The lone dime from under the machine began paying off handsomely for Johnny. First he won five games. Then he bet it all and won twenty games. It was at this point that Johnny thought about cashing out, but he felt lucky tonight. He felt Cisco watching him, but didn't blink or turn. Betting the maximum five games he pulled the plunger releasing each ball separately. At the end of this exercise he had placed all the balls across the top of a red-banded row of circular receptacles and the machine began clicking away echoing throughout the empty poolroom.

The noise caught Pops attention. Johnny had hit the jackpot and Pops cursed under his breath. This payout would curtail his bet on the following day's race at Aqueduct.

"I'm cashing out, Pops," Johnny exclaimed enthusiastically.

"You don't have to be so fuckin' happy," Pops responded in a dour tone. "How many games?"

"Ninety-five."

Handing Johnny a fresh one-hundred dollar bill Pops ordered, "You owe me five."

Johnny's eyes showed definite distress. He needed the money, but was embarrassed to admit that he didn't have five dollars. Pops wasn't about to let him owe it since he only had a few dollars left after the payout.

Cisco uncharacteristically interceded. "I'll break the hundred," Cisco said. Pulling out a large roll of money, he broke the large denomination bill with twenty and five dollar bills. "I'm glad to see that someone beat this frickin' machine."

Pops went to hand Cisco the one-hundred dollar bill. Shunning the money by waving two of his fingers from his left hand, an impish smile floated across Cisco's dark face.

"Bet it on that horse at Aqueduct, what's its name?"

"Another Chance," Pops replied eagerly.

"I like it. If it wins we'll split it. If this guy could beat the house with a dime maybe there's still some luck goin' around," Cisco said hopefully.

Pops smiled broadly poking his index finger on the countertop. "Be here Friday. You'll see. You'll see. I might be fuckin' blind but I know my horses."

Turning to Johnny he handed him the money and quizzed, "What's you name kid?"

"Johnny."

Simultaneously extending their hands they grasp one another's and shook. "Cisco."

Johnny remarked mentally the firmness of his grasp. On some level he trusted this man. "Nice meeting you."

Cisco reassessed his previous thoughts about Johnny. Sometimes his imagination was off the mark.

30

Looking out the large glass window in the back booth of a diner on Broad Street, Tucci sat impatiently waiting for his sister Gloria to arrive. Nursing a second cup of coffee, he stared sardonically at the subway entrance on the corner across the street from the diner. After all these years it still remained as a physical reminder of a moment in his life he would like to forget.

Skipping over that memory, he returned to wondering what his sister had on her mind. The fact that she offered to drive in from Cherry Hill, New Jersey made it even more intriguing. Turning back to the cup of coffee in front of him, he stirred it slowly with a spoon and thought about the differences between them. Although Cosmo and Gloria were raised as brother and sister under the guidance of their grandmother they were as different as night and day.

Gloria bore no ill will against the Giampietro family. She could care less about Anna's father who always seemed jolly, accommodating and extremely attentive to both her and Anna. For no particular reason other than to see them giggle, he would buy presents for the two girls. To Gloria the stories and gossip about the two men seemed almost fictional.

This was in stark contrast to her mother, Marianna Tucci, who remembered the uncertainty of the years following her husband's death. Gloria missed her mother especially as she approached adolescence. She needed her mother to prepare and coddle her as she entered the unsettling gateway to womanhood. However, her grandmother more than compensated for her daughter Marianna's absence and Gloria grew up without the trauma and turmoil associated with parentless children.

Cosmo was another story. He was moody and belligerent and at one point in grade school confided to a teacher that he felt cheated because he had no father. The teacher was untrained to handle such a revelation. Yet he did his best to ease the young boy's pain. Befriending the young Tucci, the teacher would take him to Phillies' games at Connie Mack Stadium at Twenty-Second Street and Lehigh Avenue in North Philadelphia with the permission of the boy's grandmother. However, all was not what it seemed to be on the surface.

The first warning sign was when the teacher put his arm around the young boy. It was innocent enough at first, but then he started kissing Tucci on the forehead before he would drop him off at his grandmother's home. Tucci felt uncomfortable, but shrugged it off to weirdness. He enjoyed baseball and his grandmother was not able to fill that need. Even as a young boy Tucci had street smarts. So, when the teacher approached him in a remote restroom of the stadium on one particular summer outing Tucci knew the score. This guy was totally weird. Tucci had the good sense to know it. Quickly invoking the Gimp's name, the teacher stopped his threatening forward movement. Tucci loathed using the name of his father's murderer. Still, he heard others invoke the name in less dire situations. The results never failed to make the listener stop to consider the consequences of their action.

It had the desired effect. The teacher's face turned ashen white. Grimacing, torturous images quickly triggered through his mind. Everyone in South Philadelphia had heard of the Gimp. The teacher refrained from speaking. His mood turned somber and darker. His thoughts bounced around inside his head like a twenty-two-caliber slug would if this incident was taken seriously. It would be. There were others.

The entire ride home on the subway that day was one of silent contemplation. During that time the teacher weighed the pros and cons of his various malefic ruminations amid the squealing and rattling of the subway train. He was at an impasse. As the subway train continued racing along, alternately emerging from one dark tunnel into the dim yellow glow of the subterranean platform lights of the next stop, no alternatives presented themselves. Standing erect before reaching his destination the teacher brooded. Living in South Philadelphia would no longer be an option if Cosmo told anyone. He peeked a look at Cosmo. Sitting innocently looking at the dark walls of the tunnel, he wondered what the boy was thinking. Cursing himself under his breath for his deviant behavior, the teacher knew that he could not change. Perhaps he should encourage the boy to tell the murderous thug of what transpired—including the others. That would solve everything, he thought despairingly. He turned back to face the subway doors. The rattling of the train subsided. Suddenly, the swooshing sound of the train's doors opening signaled the end of the line for his procrastination. A decision had to be made and made quickly.

The dim muted glow of a nearby light bathed him in its cowardly yellow light as he stepped onto the platform. Cosmo followed at a guarded distance then bolted up the stairs to the street above. Finally, emerging from the underworld of the subway at the Ellsworth-Federal Station the teacher suddenly stopped on the corner of Broad and Ellsworth. Cosmo was standing there with a confounded look on his face. Searching each other's eyes for some hint of what the other was thinking, they parted company after a long silent moment never to see each other again.

The following year the teacher did not return to school. No one noticed his absence except Tucci. His trust in the altruism of his fellow man forever shattered that summer afternoon. In a perverse way the Gimp had saved him.

After glancing at his watch Tucci slowly cranked his head across his entire field of vision impatiently seeking his sister. It was after one o'clock and she was late. That wasn't like her. She was usually an early bird, he remembered faintly. After a moment his eyes settled on the constant throng of worshippers streaming through the ornate wooden doors of Saint Rita di Cascia's Church across the street to the left of the subway entrance.

It was Holy Thursday Tucci remembered from some long forgotten catechism class. While his sister went to a parochial school, he attended a public school. It was less embarrassing for his grandmother considering his unruly behavior. She insisted that he be confirmed and also make his First Holy Communion. Tucci relented to the stubborn insistence of his grandmother.

Watching the people slavishly adhere to a ritual imprinted on them in their youth, the theme of redemption crept into his consciousness. He didn't know if he believed in redemption or for that matter a God. The cynical lessons of his youth left little room for a Savior dying for the sins of the world in his mind. Let the suckers of the world make that bet, he chuckled inwardly. Faith, hope and charity were unfamiliar words in his lexicon of life at the moment. That was moments away from changing.

Abruptly, his cynical mental ramblings dissipated when he heard familiar giggling. Springing his head around, his eyes met Gloria and Anna standing over him. A thin smile cracked his lip through the permanent frown that seemed tattooed on his face. Anna was glowing in a white cashmere sweater that accentuated the contours of her voluptuous body. Gloria was equally attractive with more delicate features and smaller bosoms. Both gracefully slid into the booth across from Tucci.

"Surprise," Gloria said in a bubbling voice while ushering Anna into the booth across from Tucci.

"I'll say," Tucci said astonishingly all the time keeping his eyes on Anna. "It's been a long time. You look great."

"What about me," Gloria said in pouting tone that was meant to tease.

Tucci smiled broadly. "Of course you look great. We both come from the same blood."

They all laughed happily. Tucci's somber reflections turned sanguine. His blanket skepticism was put on hold.

"Same old Cuzz," Anna said using a term of endearment that harkened back to their youth.

"It's Tucci. Just like my dad," he corrected her.

An icy stillness enveloped the threesome for what seemed like minutes. In reality it was only a few seconds. The reference to his father hit a sour note on an otherwise happy encounter. If the mood continued, it would devolve into acrimony.

It was Gloria who quickly resuscitated the conversation before it had a chance to derail completely. "Anna and I are going to Saint Rita's for the Stations of the Cross and then we thought we'd all go to dinner. Just like old times," Gloria knew her brother would need some initial coaxing, but was sure he would succumb.

"I dunno," Tucci said hesitantly.

"Come on. We're adults. Besides, I'm getting married," Anna argued in a lilting tone looking coyly at Tucci. She thought that this would evoke a look of jealous surprise or at the very least a simple head jerk. Instead, his sulking demeanor caught her by surprise. It gave him a depth of character, a vulnerability that served to heighten his sensuality in her probing eyes. She felt a warm tingle run up her neck, bringing a red flush to her face. The less obvious effect was a moistness seeking to engulf the very essence of this sexy young man across from her. At that moment she wanted to make love to Tucci in the worst way.

Tucci sensed the change in Anna. The attraction was mutual, but fraught with danger. Suppressing his urge, his face reverted to its normal frown mode. After sighing deeply he spoke almost in a whisper, "Congratulations. I already heard."

Gloria looked back and forth between the two incredulously. The air around them snapped with the electricity of their unspoken words. She was jealous that her own life lacked the same power of attraction. Then she thought about Romeo and Juliet and spontaneously snapped her fingers in front of both of their faces, "Snap out of it! Get a grip you two. It's only dinner."

Anna took a deep breath twisting her torso slightly. She knew her mother's feelings on this topic. Marie's vehement disapproval confounded her. Without her mother's approval any paternal machinations, manipulations or implorations would be for naught. Actually her father never knew the entire story. Marie sanitized Anna's youthful fantasies twisting the story to avoid shedding any light on her true motivation.

"You'll be late for your penance. How 'bout we meet at Rocco's on Tenth Street around five," Tucci proposed looking from Gloria to Anna with bright inviting eyes now alive with possibilities.

Anna nodded sheepishly attempting to quell any further electrifying reaction between the two.

Gloria agreed, "Sounds like a plan. We have to go. We'll see you at five."

Gloria stood up allowing Anna to scoot out of the booth. Anna's scent swirled around Tucci, its essence stirring pleasant memories from the past. Removing a pack of cigarettes from the pocket of his black leather jacket, he was about to light one up, but decided against it. Instead, he tried to suppress his burgeoning emotions as he watched her saunter away.

31

The eighteen hundred block of Ritner Street was a parking nightmare. Built circa 1910 before the car craze overtook the American psyche, twenty-five solid brick row homes lined each side of the street without any consideration for the accommodation of automobiles. This was an endemic problem in South Philadelphia since the vast majority of the structures were built during that era to accommodate the growing population of immigrants.

Johnny Cerone's 1970 MGB was perfectly suited for this environment due to it compact size. He was able to find parking spots where most American automobiles would be unable to fit. Once, some thoughtless person blocked Johnny's car and was unresponsive to the persistent blaring of the MGB's horn. Johnny jumped the curb at an angle managing to escape the blockade by driving down the sidewalk to the corner. Tonight, he reversed that anarchistic action to the consternation of a few neighbors peeking from behind their drapes by hijacking a parking spot being saved by another more unscrupulous neighbor.

Taking the steps of his parent's home two at a time he knew that he was late for dinner. He knew that his mother wouldn't care, but wasn't sure about his father.

Michael Cerone was a cagey fellow ever since his eldest son's death in Vietnam in 1968. He was prone to bouts of depression that he shrugged off as commonplace events for people of advancing years. This rationalization fooled no one.

Michael Junior graduated from Bishop Neumann High School in 1965 and immediately enlisted in the Army volunteering for the 101st Airborne Division at his first opportunity. Like his dad, a World War Two veteran of the 101st Airborne, he wanted to prove his mettle. Instead of fighting in the streets, he would fight in a war like his dad did at Normandy and Bastogne.

Michael Senior felt differently. He went to war because he had to. Volunteering for airborne duty was a matter of financial incentive. It was considered hazardous duty and he was paid a princely sum for that time, of fifty dollars a month more. His heroism was not for God or country or even to live up to his own father's ideals. It was to save his friends' lives, good friends, and good people. For this he was awarded the Silver Star.

World War Two was wrought by evil men intent on evil deeds, he would tell his sons. All the conflicts since then have been tainted by ideological ambiguities for political gain. There is no glory in dying for an ambiguous ideal. Today's heroes seek to mitigate conflict by logically resolving their indifference, the father would rail. Johnny would listen to his father's words while Michael Junior would look at the pictures and the medals.

In the early hours of the morning before going to work at the Philadelphia Naval Shipyard, Johnny's father would sit alone in the kitchen with a cigarette cocked between his fingers brooding. Sometimes he thought of the friends that he lost while fighting in Europe. Most of the time, however, it was over his oldest son's death in a jungle at a place called Bien Hoa during the early spring of 1968. He always wondered if his son's comrades in arms tried to save his life or just let him die alone.

Johnny would see his father occasionally in this dark reflective mood when he would roll in from a night of carousing at the crack of dawn. His father was always in the same existential pose yet appeared like a character from a *Norman Rockwell* painting. He suspected the self-recrimination that his father was feeling when he noticed that his wartime photos and medals were no longer on display. Succumbing to his own failure in convincing his eldest son of the ills of war, it was his solitary way of protest.

This became more apparent when Johnny's father passionately counseled him to go to college upon graduating high school. His father continually reiterated his musings on his haunting war experiences from World War Two. Johnny surmised that a deferment from the draft was on his father's mind by this obtuse behavior and his insistence that Johnny attend college. Eventually, his mother confirmed his suspicion one morning when his father was out of the house.

Assunta Cerone, a matronly woman, missed her eldest son dearly. This time of year she thought of him incessantly. It was only the fourth anniversary of his death. The memory of his bright sunny face and raucous belly laugh were still integral parts of her daily life. So, the pain of his absence was still sharp and biting.

For all of these reasons, Johnny tried to have dinner with his parents on a regular basis. Even though there was little conversation, he knew his presence was comforting to them on some level. That's why he was reticent about informing them of his on again off again marriage plans and the dire implications of his present decision.

After Johnny's revelatory episode yesterday at lunch with the Gimp, he became painfully aware of his shortcomings. His indecisiveness was a smoke screen for his own pain surrounding his brother's death. He always knew that saying yes or no eliminated too many other variables. Yesterday's revelation brought home the stark reality of the consequences of such folly. His ambivalent attitude had placed him on the most dangerous precipice of his life. The pressures of the last several days were about to boil over.

Occasionally picking at a side plate of pasta, Johnny wasn't really hungry. During this silent meal he reaffirmed his decision to retract his marriage proposal to Anna. "Better my life be discombobulated for the moment rather than one of hellish anguish if I became part of the Giampietro family," he moaned to himself in a mumbled whisper.

His father stopped eating and peaked an eyebrow in askance. "What's this about hellish anguish? Spit it out if you have a problem with your mother or me," his father responded in a confrontational tone.

Johnny backpedaled quickly. "It's nothing. Just some work stuff, dad. Nothin' to concern yourself with."

"Well if you've got problems with me I want to know about it," his father persisted.

"It's nothing. Besides, it's none of your business," Johnny's voice got louder, the pitch higher and the mood uglier.

"If it's in this house, its damn well right my business," his father's voice now matching Johnny's in intensity.

"Mike," Assunta said pleadingly.

"Screw you," Johnny screamed at his father.

Sliding back from the table and standing in one quick motion, Michael Senior was still an imposing figure for a man of fifty.

Johnny stood staunchly to meet him face to face. An inevitable confrontation that was four years in the making was about to explode. Picking up his small plate of pasta Johnny slammed it against the kitchen wall. Four years of frustration, guilt and suppressed pain dripped down the wall in droplets of red tomato sauce like blood from a mortal wound. Johnny stormed toward the front door in the living room.

"Mike! Please," yelled Johnny's mother in a pleading tone. "Leave the boy be."

Michael Cerone no less in pain sought to expunge four years of self-recrimination in one violent uncontrollable outburst.

Johnny entered the vestibule fumbling with the front door lock. His father came up angrily from behind with a balled fist. "You ain't got balls like your brother. Go ahead and run you coward!"

Johnny turned to face his father and found him slamming the vestibule door in his face. Kicking the closing door Johnny shattered the glass insert sending glass flying all over the house. Then he abruptly turned and exited.

Michael Cerone stood looking at the mess dumbfounded. His face, ashen and pale, was drained of it natural ruddy color.

Standing behind him, Assunta wept in staccato bursts trying to hold back her tears. Unable to contain her emotions any longer she opened the floodgates of her heart letting her feeling gush forth like the rampaging waters of a springtime river overflowing its banks.

The three minutes that this familial confrontation took to unfold produced a long awaited catharsis. Assunta and Michael's mournful lives were finally resurrected from the pit of despair by this violent outburst. They embraced tenderly as only a husband and wife could.

Johnny's catharsis was incomplete. He still had the specters of Anna and her father dangling over his head precariously. Getting hurriedly into his MGB, he found himself blocked by double-parked automobiles. Pushing into his horn his face reflected the welled up anger that he kept suppressed for so long. Anyone crossing his path this night ran the risk of incurring its violent effluence. Not able to rouse anyone to action, Johnny jumped the curb and drove without caution down the sidewalk. Luckily, a few astute pedestrians managed to disperse in time to allow the car's passage without incident. Once on Ritner Street, Johnny drove westward like a man possessed, to the Schuylkill Expressway interchange just beyond Twenty-Fifth and Passyunk Avenue. Making a squealing right hand turn onto the freeway Johnny torqued his engine to dangerously high RPM levels as he wound through the gears. Taking the hairpin curve abutting the Atlantic Richfield refinery, he continued northbound bobbing in and out of slow moving traffic until he exited at Spring Garden Street heading for the Art Museum and a rendezvous with its calming façade.

Entering from the rear entrance of the museum, the MGB circled around the driveway into an available parking spot. Exiting the car after his hairy escapade up the Schuylkill Expressway, Johnny breathed deeply and regained control of his volatile emotional state. As he walked around the terrace he began to notice details of the architecture that he never noticed previously. The people mulling about in various locations on the veranda were more vibrant. Their movements more animated. Some still sported multicolored tie-dyed tee shirts harkening back to the tumultuous days of the Sixties. Examining the intricate patterns on the tee shirts, Johnny's eyes lingered excessively on two interesting designs. This caused several questioning stares, but he just smiled, eliciting a similar response from the questioning onlookers. Suddenly, he felt alive. As darkness closed in quickly he strolled to the top of the tiered steps and reflected on the illuminated City Hall with its statue of William Penn benevolently looking down upon the city. He sat down on the top step to enjoy this encapsulated view. It was picture perfect, like a matted backdrop used in a film scene. Other cities had there own signature picturesque vantage points, he thought. Never having traveled further than the Philadelphia, New York and South Jersey corridor, he couldn't attest to their authenticity. Were people the same across the country, he wondered or were they unique like the different city skylines he saw in magazines. A smile welled up from somewhere inside of him. His muscles relaxed and he promised himself right then and there that he would personally find the answer to that question. Soon. First, he had a pressing issue that needed closure. Suddenly, a steely determination reinvigorated him. Tomorrow he would tell Anna that he could no longer go through with the marriage.

32

For once Anna and Johnny were simpatico. At the same moment Johnny was preparing himself to tell Anna that he couldn't go through with the marriage, Anna came to the same conclusion through a very different train of thought.

Anna was in love with Cosmo Tucci. Dormant for nearly ten years, their affection for each other was rejuvenated tonight over dinner. Each word that they spoke to one another pulsated with unbridled lust. Tucci barely ate. Anna picked at her cannelloni. Luckily, Gloria was there to chaperone this encounter until cooler heads prevailed.

Anna proposed this dinner on Monday when the two went window-shopping at the Cherry Hill Mall for bridal gowns. It was suppose to be the reestablishment of a brother and sister relationship. Gloria knew Anna well enough to know that ulterior motives lurked behind her innocent looking eyes. Still, she went along with it and contacted her brother. Love conquers all she thought hopefully, but knew the odds against this relationship as well as anyone.

Sitting across from her brother, Gloria succumbed to the inevitability of the situation when she caught the sparkle in his eyes. The last time they were together she remembered his eyes as dull and hollow, practically devoid of any emotions. Tonight those eyes were vibrant and passionate tantalizing orbs. She was hard pressed to put a damper on them.

Looking at Anna, Gloria knew her friend was genuinely happy. She sighed deeply. Neither her brother nor her friend noticed. She brooded. Unlike Romeo and Juliet there weren't two families vehemently opposed to the union of these two lovers, just one—the Giampietro family.

Tonight, well, it was magic Gloria silently conceded. She would have gladly taken a cab home and let these two have at it, she thought. Then what? For now Gloria sensibly concluded, her brother needed to contain himself and be quiet. Anna needed to convince her mother of her love. Only then could they deal with Anna's father. "Gawd," Gloria blurted out as she thought about the Gimp.

"Something the matter?" Anna inquired in a sincere tone.

"Actually, yes."

Pinching his eyebrows together Tucci's eyes narrowed registering total incomprehension, "What?"

"Are you two crazy? Do you think anything is different than it was ten years ago?"

Anna pursed her lips, angry that her friend had broken the electrifying mood of the evening. "You're being a downer Gloria. I'm twenty-one. I can do what I like."

"Really?"

Tucci slumped back in his chair dejectedly. Looking at Anna pensively he had been down this road ten years ago and didn't plan on traveling it again.

Neither did Anna. Nor was she about to let him go again without letting him fill the wellspring of her desire. This was no one-night stand, she admitted to herself. It was the real thing. Momentarily flustered, Anna knew that without her mother's support they would be relegated to sneaking around like illicit lovers slinking in and out of some fleabag motel on the other side of the river. That just wouldn't do. A rapt smile and determined look in her eyes supplanted the fleeting distraught expression on her face. Reaching across the table she gestured for Tucci to take her hand.

Touching Anna's velvety hands changed his feeling of chagrin to one of desire rekindling the fire in his loins.

"I'll make this happen. I promise," she intoned in a sincere cadence. No one needed to speak her thoughts. Her whole body was communicating to anyone witnessing this exchange. It could be simply expressed in one word—Love.

33

Jimmy Socci, Nicky Sox's brother, was an unfamiliar face in South Philadelphia. The Socci family lived near Sixth and Fitzwater Streets in South Philadelphia. In high school Jimmy befriended a gang of *Two Streeters* who lived several city blocks from his family's home. Second Street was the Irish and Polish longshoreman's turf and was inhospitable to Italians. Jimmy the Wop, as he was known, found kindred spirits in the ruff and tumble beer-drinking crowd of Second Street. Nicky, on the other hand, was more of a conniver. Consequently, the two brothers grew up in different worlds, with different friends. Yet, they still remained close. Their parents were honest hardworking people. But the allure of the streets enticed both boys at an early age.

Eventually, Jimmy got a job driving a truck through his Irish contacts with the Teamsters Union. When a few errant drivers from a nonunion trucking company balked at joining the union, Jimmy was given the task of persuading them. Actually, it was considered his initiation dues. He not only convinced the two balking drivers to sign up, but also was instrumental in bringing the drivers' company into the Teamster fold. His rumored-method of persuasion was never questioned. Thus, Jimmy prospered. Moving to the small community of Bellmawr, New Jersey, he supplemented his income with an occasional *side* job.

Strong-arm was Jimmy's specialty—not murder. His contacts could mitigate an armed robbery or assault charge. If a murder occurred, he was on his own.

Nicky made a desperate pitch to his older brother to help him out of his predicament. Jimmy immediately dismissed the entire idea. The machinations of the Italian mob were too Machiavellian for Jimmy's taste. Knowing the stubbornness of his brother, Nicky pleaded with Jimmy. Finally, he begged him. Eventually, Jimmy came around when he couldn't find a downside except for the possibility of a set up. After careful consideration, Jimmy concluded that Carlucci's involvement meant that a set up was not in the cards. Still, he preferred the meat and potato approach of the Irish—plain and simple. The prey, however, was not so obliging. Careful to a fault, Cisco's feline movements kept Jimmy off balance. Earning his money was not going to be the cakewalk his brother had promised.

Tonight had to be the night. The Gimp's crew had avoided Cisco for two days and was getting impatient. If Cisco managed to pay off the Gimp, it would look bad for Jimmy and worse for his brother. So, Jimmy had stalked Cisco all day and was ready.

A state of escalating apprehension had gnawed at Cisco ever since the previous evening. The Gimp's usual haunts were eerily devoid of any activity. Even the club at Tenth and Annin was uninhabited. No one seemed to know the whereabouts of the Gimp, Carlucci or even Louie the Snake. Perhaps he should stay put, Cisco thought seriously. He discounted that idea. Although patience was his forte, he could no longer wait. Besides, he didn't want to conduct this business in front of Rose. Her involvement would only complicate matters especially if Teti showed up. And he knew Teti would show up if he forced the Gimp's hand, he brooded.

Reluctantly, he decided to make the usual rounds one more time. Putting the thirty five hundred dollars in a money belt he strapped it to his midriff. After buttoning up his freshly pressed shirt, he tucked his shirttails neatly into his pants. Donning his jacket he exited the bar without telling anyone where he was going.

A cold wind kept the memory of a harsh winter fresh in the minds of those who roamed the streets after dark. Waiting in the shadows Jimmy zipped up his jacket. He tugged on the ski mask rolled up around his head. Once he was satisfied that it was ready to be pulled quickly down over his face, he went on to his next task. Emptying one chamber of his .38 caliber revolver he rotated the chamber until he was sure that the first chamber would fire dry. It was a safety precaution. If by some odd chance Cisco got the upper hand by disarming him, he could rush him at an opportune moment. It would save his life and perpetuate his reputation. In any case he did not want the gun going off by accident. Noticing Cisco exit, he gave him some leeway. He knew his destination this time and had timed the walk within seconds.

Cisco had parked Rose's car near an alleyway on Wharton Street. The alley way was actually a dead end street called Warnock Street. The streets of South Philadelphia were imprinted on Cisco's mind, although he never paid attention to all the street names. As he approached the vehicle he unobtrusively slid the car keys from his pocket extending the door key between the index finger and middle finger of his right hand. It was an instinctive habit that would be futile as a weapon. Performing this little exercise, however, kept Cisco focused on potential danger. These days' druggies and *Meth heads* were lurching in the shadows looking for an unsuspecting patron to provide them with their next fix. These zombies of the night were the most dangerous. They killed people for totally inane reasons, sometimes for no particular reason at all. Cisco didn't want to be a statistic on the police blotter around the corner on Eleventh Street. Darting his eyes around like a sniper seeking his mark Cisco looked over his shoulder sensing something amiss. Seeing nothing unusual he swiveled his head around to open the car. To his surprise he was looking down the barrel of a nervously vibrating 9mm automatic pistol.

Tommy Dee had finally found the balls to execute his plan. Barely. Wearing a Halloween mask as a disguise, it would be downright hilarious if he weren't anxiously holding a fully loaded weapon in Cisco's face. Cisco was cool and collected in the face of the wavering pistol. He had been in a situation like this before and felt that the perpetrator wouldn't pull the trigger intentionally. Staying as calm as possible, Cisco tried to avoid any sudden movement that may cause an unintentional discharge.

"Give me the money," Tommy mumbled throatily trying to disguise his voice.

"I don't have any money, just my wallet," Cisco coolly replied.

Angrily, Tommy pushed the gun toward Cisco until it touched the skin between his eyes, "The money Sid gave you. I want it!"

Cisco recoiled upon hearing Sid's name. He focused on this thug with an arched eyebrow. Was this a set up?

"Give it!"

Then suddenly, like a page from *Murphy's Law,* a police cruiser turned the corner. Tommy's eye caught the rack of emergency lights on the roof of the cruiser. Panicking he fired the hair-trigger pistol inadvertently. Luckily, Cisco had hit the sidewalk before the bullet ricocheted off the bricks of a nearby house. Working solely on an adrenaline rush, Tommy ducked between two automobiles. His mind, clouded by the natural instinct to survive, was in a vacuous wasteland.

Cisco's mind was just the opposite. Astutely aware of the danger at hand, he ducked into Warnock Street to avoid any additional ricocheting bullets.

The Police exited their vehicle with guns in hand. Taking up defensive postures, one officer radioed for back up. Ignoring Cisco entirely for the moment, they were in hot pursuit of the perpetrator.

Tommy fired his gun once more aiming high, and then ran down Wharton Street aimlessly. Stupidity and fear were the pistons driving him now. Dodging traffic, he approached the intersection with Passyunk Avenue. After turning a corner Tommy slid into the back seat of his GTO unnoticed. Luckily, his car was parked on a street without a street lamp. Covering himself with a blanket, he would remain there for hours. Meanwhile, Police scoured the area in frustration.

Repentantly, he silently prayed the rosary over and over again. His prayers were interspersed with the mental image of a craggy-faced nun hovering over him screaming in his ear that hell and damnation awaited him. His only salvation tonight was sheer luck. Tonight was a night of frustration for all of the parties involved except one.

Cisco was relieved. So was Jimmy the Wop. The shadow that Cisco sought as protection proved to be his undoing. As he breathed a deep sigh of relief a new threat presented itself unexpectedly. He found himself looking down the barrel of a .38 caliber revolver. Its owner was cool, calm and collected someone not to be taken lightly. A black ski mask concealed his identity. His voice was unrecognizable. Cisco was facing a professional. Understanding all this and more, Cisco mentally sought a quick explanation. There was none. His focus now, he realized, was to stay alive. He would sort out all the dizzying implications of this evening's events later.

"Hands against the wall. Two steps back," Jimmy said firmly.

This terse command confirmed Cisco's first assessment and he immediately complied.

"Unbuckle your belt with your left hand."

Slowly Cisco unbuckled his belt buckle returning his hand to the wall.

Jimmy patted Cisco's pockets removing his wallet. Finding nothing except a few dollars he threw the wallet down the alley.

"Kick your shoes off," Jimmy ordered.

Again Cisco complied.

Yanking Cisco's pants down below his knees Jimmy patted Cisco's midriff and found the money belt.

"Unbuckle it."

Cisco hesitated momentarily then acquiesced when he heard the click of the gun's hammer.

"Throw it to your left. Now!"

Searching the money belt, Jimmy smiled broadly behind the ski mask. Bingo!

"Step out of your pants. One leg at a time." His words hung in the cool air like puffs of white smoke then dissipated.

Again Cisco obeyed knowing now that he would survive this episode. As that thought crossed his mind there was a dull thump across the back of his head and he fell to his knees in a stupor.

Jimmy slid his blackjack into his back pocket then kicked Cisco in his rib cage with a sharp blow. Cisco fell on his right side. Assuming the fetal position he flickered in and out of consciousness. Cisco writhed in pain. Jimmy gathered Cisco's shoes and pants then melted into the shadows disappearing into the brisk coldness of the night.

On Eleventh Street across from the police station Jimmy found a trash can and disposed of Cisco's apparel. Taking the money from the money belt he watched some policemen rushing in and out of the station in response to the shooting. He noticed a distinct rhythm within their peripatetic strides up and down the steps. The chaos it depicted, reminded him of the unfolding events of the evening. Jimmy chuckled aloud. Fanning the stack of one-hundred dollar bills, he stepped lively heading west down Wharton Street. "I loved it when a plan comes together," he snickered nearly bursting into laughter.

34

Good Friday, March 31, 1972

Good Friday is an oxymoron unique in the Christian lexicography. Christ's death as commemorated on this day was not a joyous event by any means. It was downright disheartening unless one interpreted it as a day of hope instead of a day of tragedy.

There was little hope or goodness this Friday in South Philadelphia.

Cisco lied still in bed with his head slightly elevated by the underlying ice pack. The dull aches of the previous evening were amplified this morning. His ribs were sore, but not broken. The only thing broken on Cisco was his spirit.

By chance, Cisco was able to avoid Rose the previous evening. Scantily clad, he stumbled into the back of the bar on his way to his room. Ralph noticed, but instinctively knew not to trouble Rose. There was nothing she could do to help him at this juncture anyway. Instead, Ralph quietly brought an ice pack to Cisco, knowing that he undoubtedly was in need of one from Cisco's wobbling stride. No questions. No explanations needed. It came with the territory.

Cisco was tempted to light up a cigarette as he lie prone on the bed licking his wounds, but that would bring unwanted attention to his predicament. He needed time to sort through this mess without any emotional interference. His life depended on it, maybe even Rose's.

There was no question in his mind that the previous evening's event was a set up. Discounting any motivation on Sid's part was easy. He had nothing to gain. And he certainly wouldn't have used an idiot like the one in the Halloween mask. Cisco laughed at that thought, but laughing hurt his abdomen bringing him back to the grim reality at hand. On the other hand, no one outside of Rose knew that Sid had given him the money. Perhaps Rose slipped up he surmised.

That was the only possible explanation for the first attempt Cisco decided. The second one was hazier. This guy was a pro. He had done this sort of work in the past. Cisco knew the drill. Baring the lower extremities minimized the chance of any stupidity on the part of the victim. It was also embarrassing. This guy must've figured that he wouldn't have been embarrassed. Deciding not to chance it, he probably used a blackjack or something blunt, Cisco deduced. Different avenues of possibilities flashed through his mind. They all led back to the same doorstep—the Gimp. With that thought Cisco stopped ruminating. This was getting far too complicated, he sulked. His familiar cynicism kicked into gear and a morose feeling engulfed him. Sid was right, he said to himself. I've got to get out of town and soon. Otherwise, the next stop was the cemetery.

Craving a cigarette, Cisco painfully tried looking on the nearby nightstand. A half-empty glass of water was the only visible object. Taking a deep breath, Cisco forced himself to continue thinking. The logistics for his escape would need to be cautiously approached he concluded. Flying to Las Vegas was out of the question. Cisco didn't want to show his hold card that quickly. Driving was preferable. It gave him precious time to think. Since his driver license sat in a North Carolina sheriff's office drawer, driving cross-country alone was definitely undesirable. A partner and money were basic necessities for this trip, he finally decided. He could beg borrow or steal the money. They wouldn't need much if they slept in the car. A partner was another story. It would have to be someone with a car that he trusted.

Mentally, Cisco drew a wearisome blank. His pulsating head swayed from side to side from exhaustion. The dull pain slowly softened to the siren call of sleep. Finally, he nodded off hoping that an answer would come to him when he awoke.

Tucci emerged from the shower humming a Frank Sinatra tune. His sculpted physique, the result of regular workouts in a gym, glistened under the droplets of water dripping from his body. With a dog-like shake of his wet curly black hair he decided impulsively that the idiom *playing it safe* no longer applied to him. The day of his redemption was here.

Love surged uncontrollably through his veins like a rampaging river leaving destruction in its wake. As he dried himself with a towel, he imagined Anna doing the same, fanning the fire of his desire to a fever pitch. Quelling this eruption temporarily, Tucci began to carefully preen himself in front of a mirror, occasionally glimpsing the photos of Anna tacked on the adjacent wall. Impetuously, he considered surprising Anna. Like a man with a devil and an angel on opposite shoulders debating good versus evil, he vacillated. With his head spinning out of control, he made a decision.

Anna drifted in and out of sleep throughout the night. The morning sunlight peeking through the Venetian blinds forced her to squint her eyes. Sitting up on the edge of her bed, her jumbled thoughts found focus when the passion of the previous night materialized anew. At this moment her parents' wishes no longer mattered. It was like finding a missing part of her life that she never knew existed. She would not allow her feelings to be compromised. Somehow, she would find a way to circumvent her parents' opposition.

As her sleepy eyes regained their focus Anna's curiosity was piqued by a white box wrapped with a flowery bowed ribbon resting on the chair by her bedroom door. Her head cocked quizzically trying to remember if it was there when she came home the previous evening. Confounded by its presence, she got up and gently picked up the box looking for a clue to its contents. Finding no clue and totally intrigued she shook it near her ear. Finally untying the bow and opening it, she discovered a beautiful white dress with a disturbing note from her father, *A pre-engagement present, Love, Dad.*

Consternation overcame her. It was unlike her father to accept a pronouncement like marriage so readily, she silently grumbled. Concern registered an alarm bell in her mind as she modeled the dress whimsically in front of a full-length mirror. She liked the dress. She didn't like her father's speedy acceptance of Johnny. Sighing deeply, she realized that she would have to act quickly to nip this development in the bud. Mulling it over as she undressed to take a shower she braced herself for the coming battle of wills. As she turned on the water trying to regulate the temperature, her personal phone began to ring. Wondering who would be calling her this time of the morning she vacillated between answering it or letting the call go to her newly purchased phone message recorder.

Johnny sat nervously in his cubicle in the basement of the Alumni Building grimly holding the phone to his ear. The office was sparsely populated today due to the Good Friday observance. Coming to work early Johnny finished up a project that was due the previous night. He begged, pleaded, and then bribed the computer operator to slip it into his schedule. Finally succeeding at his groveling, Johnny was free for the rest of the day. When the phone call went to Anna's recorder, he hesitated leaving a message knowing that giving Anna a heads up could be devastating. Hanging up the phone slowly while deep in thought, Johnny decided to take the chance and visit Anna at home. It was unlike her to be out and about this early. Hopefully, her father wouldn't be there and he would be able to get what he had to say off his chest uninterrupted, he thought anxiously. Otherwise, the entire exercise would turn into a fiasco. Looking at the clock Johnny hoped that his luck was changing and returned to finishing the few loose ends that remained in his in-box. Then he would venture into uncharted waters and tell Anna how he really felt.

The Gimp was in an extraordinary mood this morning. He had actually slept the night before without hearing any voices and decided to have breakfast. This was unusual for him since he usually malingered around the house until noon. Entering The Luncheonette on Tenth Street, he decided to have a hearty breakfast of fresh sweet Italian sausage with sautéed broccoli rabe and eggs over easy accompanied by fresh hot Perricone's bread right out of the oven. It was his favorite breakfast combination served up by the proprietor himself. The normal customers were enthralled by the Gimp's presence and the atmosphere was lively. This was due partly because of the Gimp's unassuming demeanor on this glorious morning. Even the uninitiated, who did not understand the implications of the Gimp's good nature, reveled in the camaraderie of the moment.

All was not well in the City of Brotherly Love this Good Friday. Tucci exited his apartment across the street. Crossing the street he initially queried the revelry in The Luncheonette. Discounting it as friendly bantering, he passed the front window unnoticed.

35

Girard Estate was a quiet enclave in the hustle and bustle of South Philadelphia. Originally, the Passyunk Township colonial farm of French born financier, Stephen Girard, it was developed in the early part of the Twentieth Century to meet the growing demand for housing. The semi-detached homes had extra thick walls that kept normal family shouting matches confidential. Today, that theory would be tested.

The Gimp's home, his personal sanctuary, was empty except for Anna. Marie was off to her parents' shop on Ninth Street and the Gimp was enjoying himself in The Luncheonette on Tenth Street. Anna had donned the dress that her father had given her as an engagement present. It was plain but elegant. Delineating the curvature of her anatomy in a sensuously appealing manner, she decided to wear it.

Her father never thought of such things. The Gimp just liked the plainness of its design hoping it would mute any sexual connotation. He was wrong.

Anna was fawning over her eye makeup when the doorbell rang for the first time. She ignored it in her usual detached manner. Instead, she chose to admire herself in the mirror. The persistence of the doorbell ringer, however, quickly became irritating. Angrily, she stormed down the steps ready to dress down the persistent uncouth person who dared to interrupt her normal routine.

Opening the door in a huff she was totally disarmed upon seeing Tucci. Their eyes connected alluringly. Anna was instantly captivated by the unbridled passion in his eyes. The fleeting thought of treading on prohibited ground heightened her desire.

"Cosmo! What are you doing here?" The flesh twitched between her legs. An instantaneous flash of desire snaked its way through her body. In a test of wills she would succumb.

"I couldn't wait." The fire in his loins energized like the sound of a native beating the ceremonial drums. Looking at her with rapt desire he embraced her in one sweeping motion. The pungent taste of tobacco didn't dissuade her from returning the passion emanating from Tucci's lips. Grabbing his hand, she pulled him inside the house locking the door behind her to continue her devolution into the realm of unfettered passion. Bursting with raw uncontrollable desire, Tucci unconsciously pulled her new white dress from her shoulders tearing the straps then letting it fall to the floor.

Anna stopped him momentarily to position herself erotically on the living room sofa. Spreading her legs she beckoned him seductively to continue. Writhing in sexual pleasure, she moaned incessantly. Finally, Anna screamed feverishly, then slowly heaved a sigh of exhaustion. Wantonly naked and more desirous than ever, Anna grabbed Tucci's hand leading him up to her bedroom.

Johnny hurriedly exited from a side door of the Alumni Building and took the steps in increments of two toward Sansom Street. Most days he parked his car here avoiding the daily parking fees of an adjacent lot.

At the top of the steps he stopped a minute to rehearse a prepared monologue to deliver to Anna. With flailing hands he spoke in a low pleading voice, "Anna, this just isn't going to work." Unhappy with the projection of his voice he tried again. He practiced projecting firmness and decisiveness before continuing with the rest of the soliloquy. This action drew the amused attention of passing law students on their way to class at the nearby law school. Self-conscious and somewhat embarrassed, he decided to take a spin in his car up the East River Drive before confronting Anna.

The Gimp was happier than he had been in a long time. Swaggering like a proud rooster, he relished the short walk down Tenth Street toward Annin where he left his car. Carlucci had phoned him the previous night relating the success of their little ploy. His daughter was going to marry someone who had a future outside the mean streets where he grew up. The only way things could be better at this moment, he chuckled internally, was if the Old Man croaked. All in good time he thought chortling in a low voice tinged with excitement, all in good time.

As he walked, the Gimp's thoughts drifted. He wondered if his daughter found the present he left for her. They really hadn't talk at any length about the engagement. There wasn't even a ring yet. However, the Gimp decided that today was a perfect day to discuss her plans. After attending to some small business details, he would surprise her at home he thought with childish glee. Things were going his way just like he always knew they would.

Anna and Tucci were making passionate love. The unbelievable pleasure she was experiencing had her continually gasping for breath. Her body quivered until she dug her nails into his taunt skin and screamed in sheer ecstasy. With heavy measured breath her legs relaxed. Likewise, Tucci breathing heavily fell to her side and gasped for air. Giggling like a schoolgirl, Anna twined her body around his and gently stroked his hair. She was a virgin, but no one ever would have thought so. Her emotions and physical lust were ripe and Tucci had plucked her at a propitious moment. He was now in total control of every facet of her being and she gratefully submitted to his will.

Tucci, however, was somberly reflective. Lying back with his arms outstretched and his hands nestled behind his head Anna caressed his body. "What are we gonna do?" he quizzed unassumingly.

"About what?" Anna replied obliviously.

"About us," Tucci said seriously. Looking intensely at Anna he spoke tenderly, "I love you."

Anna passionately kissed him. Her hard nipples pressing against Tucci's chest responded to his avowal. Time no longer existed for them as they hungrily groped at each other.

Johnny pulled up in front of the Giampietro house, quickly jerking the MGB to a sudden stop. Leaving the car double-parked, he resolutely marched up the steps to the house. Sprightly poking his finger on the bell, he mustered the last semblance of his intestinal fortitude to end the farce once and for all.

Anna and Tucci were about to get dressed when the ominous sound of the doorbell shattered their ephemeral tryst. Anna darted to the front bedroom and spied Johnny's MGB from the window. Tucci was right behind her. "Shit! It's Johnny," Anna snapped in a surprised tone.

"Let me handle this," Tucci said spontaneously.

"You can't. Trust me you just can't. I have to handle this," Anna responded firmly.

"No."

"Yes!"

Tucci saw the dogged determination in Anna's eyes and relented. Meanwhile, Anna frantically slipped into an outfit as the doorbell rang again. "Go down the back steps and out the back door. Don't let him see you."

Tucci quickly buttoned his trousers and accepted a passionate kiss from Anna as he slipped away toward the back of the house.

Frustrated, Johnny was about to leave when Anna partly opens the front door. "What are you doing here?" Anna asked insolently.

Taking a deep breath Johnny replied, "I need to talk to you. Can I come in?"

Playing for time, Anna reluctantly opened the door wider allowing Johnny to enter.

After entering Johnny noticed the tattered dress on the floor and shot Anna a bewildered glance.

Ignoring Johnny's curiosity Anna immediately changed his focus with a straightforward interjection, "Well, talk!"

Momentarily disoriented by the tattered white dress, Johnny belched out his lines in rote fashion, "This marriage business, it, it isn't going to work. It just isn't."

Anna's face exhibited bewilderment as she tried to decipher the implications of Johnny's exclamation. Her ego immediately engaged displacing any rational line of thought. Not fully realizing that Johnny had just solved a portion of her problem, Anna lashed out in a mocking tone, "What do you mean it isn't going to work?"

"I don't think I love you," Johnny murmured unassertively. Trying to soften the blow further he continued, "I mean you're hot, in a sexy sort of way. But what have we got after that?"

Not use to being rejected Anna shot back in a probing tone tinged with derision, "What are you telling' me? You're dumping me?"

"Whatever," Johnny replied in frustration.

"Whatever!" Anna repeated in an elevated tone signaling her rising ire.

"No. Wait. Your father is a scary guy. Okay. I can't live like that," Johnny confided honestly.

"Half of South Philly is scared of my dad. The other half doesn't know any better."

Sighing deeply, Johnny's head bobbed slightly to and fro in a visually incredulous response to Anna. "Can't you see, we're just not right for each other. That's all. Nothin' personal," Johnny pleaded while shrugging his shoulders expressively.

Infuriated at the candid rebuke of their relationship, Anna trembled trying to subdue the anger swelling throughout her body. She was the dumper not the dumpee, she thought angrily. Teetering on the boiling point of rage, she no longer could contain her innate desire to lash out physically. Anna slapped Johnny across the face with all the strength she could muster. Staggering from her unexpected blow, Johnny recoiled. Then, still reeling from her strong blow, he quickly regained his composure.

Staring intently at each other like two survivors of a duel, still seeking retribution but out of ammunition, Anna broke eye contact first. Unaware of Anna's hand imprint on his face, Johnny inadvertently decided to leave when she finally burst into tears scurrying up the steps weeping loudly.

Just as Johnny opened the door to exit the house, the Gimp was about to ascend the front steps. Normally, Johnny would have been taken aback by the sudden appearance of the Gimp. For now, he simply wanted to get away from these dysfunctional people, far away. Johnny pursed his lips tightly as he continued past the bewildered Gimp without any sign of acknowledgement.

The Gimp was dumbfounded. As Johnny passed him, he noticed the red mark on Johnny's face. His hands started trembling. A state of escalating apprehension oozed from the dark chasms of his soul. Gurgling snippets of cynicism began erupting in the Gimp's mind. The trembling in his hands snaked its way up his spine until he felt a nervous prickly sensation on the back of his neck. Momentarily incapacitated by Johnny's boldness, the Gimp watched Johnny drive away with eyes widened in astonishment. The sinister darkness of his eyes registered a vacuous disconnect in his mind. Desperately, he sought to connect the unsavory possibilities.

Entering the house still bewildered, the tattered white dress immediately caught the corner of the Gimp's eye. Picking it up gingerly, he ran the dress through his thick hands noticing the torn straps. Upstairs the sobs of his daughter echoed throughout the house.

A whirlwind of anger abruptly spun about in his mind accompanied by a thunderous voice from within moaning in demonic delight. His left eye began twitching. The voice silently spawned images in his mind sucking him back in time to the bane of his existence. Visions of his mother with another man pierced his heart. It was the moment that his life changed forever. He had suppressed this thought from the very beginning, but it suddenly returned with the force of a tornado.

In the vortex of his mind's eye he was being forced to recognize the man on top of his mother. The vitriolic voice in his head began screaming like a banshee entrapping his very soul. He resisted vehemently. Clenching his teeth within tightly pursed lips, the Gimp rent the already tattered white dress with his thick hands in violent strokes until it was nothing more than a heap of ragged strips of cloth. Exhaling in spurts of heavy breaths like a locomotive letting off steam, he finally crumbled into a nearby chair with his head hung low. The image that he suppressed from his childhood was as vivid in his mind's eye as if it were yesterday. Anger and hatred had long ago replaced his shame and fear. Swearing acrimoniously under his breath to rid the world of its licentious scum, he raised his leonine head releasing a prolonged shrill, agonizing moan. He could no longer resist identifying the man on top of his mother. The man was Salvatore Teti.

36

Hearing the chilling howl from the Gimp's house his next-door neighbor, Vince Ricci, skulked by the breezeway window to see what was afoot. Ricci was on disability from the city where he had worked in traffic court. Surprisingly, he had noticed Tucci stroll nonchalantly beneath his window.

Tucci's name eluded Ricci although his face was familiar. Thinking about calling the Gimp, he decided against it. He knew the Gimp's volatility and didn't want to incur his wrath. Nor did he want to give him the impression that he was nosey, especially if what he saw turned out to be incriminating. That would be personally disastrous, Ricci thought. Swallowing hard, his mind quickly clicked through possible fatal scenarios. Following Tucci to the front, Ricci noticed him getting into a black '65 Chevrolet Impala convertible. He looked at his watch making a mental note—just in case.

Incisively, Tucci glanced toward the Gimp's house. Starting his car after a quiet moment he pulled away from the curb slowly hoping to be as inconspicuous as possible. Impetuous but not arrogant, Tucci needed time. His passion still elevated, he needed some quiet time to think through all of the implications surrounding his fervid behavior. He wanted Anna more than he wanted anything else in his entire life. Smiling inwardly, he knew that she would be his forever. It was a secure feeling deep within the pit of his stomach.

In the last twenty-four hours his inner being was transformed from an angry young man to a young lover. No longer was he thinking about the Gimp and his father or even the perverted teacher. All of that was a long time ago and the circumstances were filled with ambiguity, he rationalized. His love for Anna was strong enough to conquer his lingering vengeance. That was then, Anna was now, he thought.

Turning right onto Passyunk Avenue and heading for the eastside of Broad Street, Tucci decided to seek sanctuary in a place not frequented by any of the Gimp's living associates—the church of the Annunciation.

Unlike Tucci's inconspicuous exit from the Gimp's house, Johnny sped away noisily. He wasn't angry at Anna's physical response. Though it was unexpected, he actually welcomed it as a cathartic conclusion to their relationship. No, Johnny was angry with himself for having gotten involved with her in the first place. "Stupid, Stupid, Stupid," he shouted loudly in a recriminating tone. This self-recrimination continued as he aimlessly sped through the nearly empty streets of South Philadelphia.

Stopping for a red light Johnny finally noticed the lack of street activity. Looking at the time it dawned on him. It was two fifteen on Good Friday afternoon. The businesses were closed and the repentant were in church. Johnny thought for a moment that he belonged in church also, but dismissed that idea. The only thing he was repentant about was that he let the relationship get so out of control. Since the genie was back in the bottle, he mused, I just have to lay low for a while. Then it's back to normal, he kept silently reassuring himself until he convinced himself of the veracity of the statement. Normal for Johnny was soon to take on an entirely new meaning.

The Downtown Bar & Grill was closed. Cisco was sitting at the end of the bar on a stool with a half dozen bottles of Schmidt's beer in front of him. A dozen different schemes brewed in his mind over the last several hours. The dull ache from the welt on the back of his head kept him from focusing insightfully. So, he decided to anesthetize his brain with beer. It had a short-lived effect. At that moment he was contemplating ratcheting up his self-prescribed medication to rum and coke. Perhaps if he became totally soused an idea would come to him, he brooded.

Going behind the bar Cisco poured a half a glass of Morgan's Rum and topped it off with cola. Gulping half the contents of the glass, he refilled the glass with rum and a dash of cola for good measure. If he was going to go down he wasn't going to go down alone. He'd take out the two scumbags with him, he decided.

That way Rose and the boy could live in peace. Returning to his barstool he tried to concentrate on how he would go about it. It would be tricky he silently concluded, very tricky.

Rose was at church. She had become more religious of late. It gave her solace in uncertain times. Ralph had finally informed her of Cisco's condition as far as he could tell. Not wanting to know the details, but fully understanding the implications served to further induce her to attend church on this Good Friday.

Saint Rita's pews were full. Rose noticed Marie Giampietro with her parents several aisles ahead of her on the right. As the service proceeded, Rose wondered about Marie's relationship with the Gimp. However, Rose's thoughts kept returning to Cisco. When the priest recounted Christ's suffering on the cross, she decided that she would suffer no more. This cat and mouse game with Cisco would end now. They loved each other. Maybe they didn't say it, but it was there. She would tell him so. No longer would they be at arms length. It was time to talk about their feelings, she mused, before it was too late.

The Gimp stared aimlessly out the front window of his house to the park beyond. He was emotionally drained and incapable of thinking rationally. In the last hour his entire life had flashed before his eyes in a chaotic sequence of events that disoriented him. Killing everything that made him feel this way was his only logical solution. It was instinctual. However, the voice had counseled him otherwise.

Still, something had to be done to atone for this egregious act. Of that he was certain. Deciding exactly how to go about it would take thought and planning. He would deal with that later. Holding a piece of the tattered white dress in his hand, he brought it to his nose and inhaled. Originally, he hoped the dress represented the cleansing of his demons. In the last hour he had anathematized it. It turned against him and enslaved him in ways that he could no longer resist. His eyes flickered momentarily to the staircase and the sound of rustling sheets from upstairs.

Anna was curled up in bed with a wad of crumpled sheets near her nose. Sniffing Tucci's scent on the sheets, she knew that she was powerlessly in his grasp. Her parents would object, but she could resist no longer. Nothing mattered any longer except being with him. Knowing that she would have to go downstairs and answer to her father, she prepared herself for the inevitable confrontation.

37

Johnny trudged up the steps to the poolroom just as the faithful poured from the churches throughout the city. He was oblivious to the potential havoc swirling around him. His untimely decision and subsequent appearance at the Gimp's house would change the course of his life in ways he could not fathom.

Everyone looked at Johnny suspiciously upon entering the poolroom. A hearts game was underway on a makeshift felt covered table near the counter. Smoke billowed from several hearts players' smoldering cigarettes dangling from their lips. Joe Bags faced the door. His hard brown eyes glared at Johnny bitterly then returned to the game at hand. On a nearby pool table, a few other up and coming attitudinal rascals attempted to act like pool hustlers.

The hustler from two nights ago that had befriended him had piqued Johnny's curiosity. Not seeing Cisco around, he retired to a nearby window thoughtfully peering down on the streets below. He felt a strange connection with Cisco that he could not explain. The cynical crowd would call it naïveté. Johnny merely considered it bonding.

Tommy Dee was a friend. Still, Johnny was reticent to let him know anything personal. Cisco was different somehow. Johnny was unable to put his finger on why he would trust him. Maybe, he was merely seeking a judicious impartial third party to comment on his course of action—blessing it or condemning it. Then, he concluded, he would have a baseline moving forward.

One of the hearts players stood up feigning an obscure appointment. In truth he was broke. Dizzy was a skilled card player. His luck was just bad—very bad. A likeable fellow, the other players went along with his ruse not wanting to cause him embarrassment.

Joe Bags' left leg was shaking nervously under the table. On a winning streak he wanted to keep playing, but was diffident about asking Johnny.

Another player, Freddy the Mooch, wasn't so reticent. Motioning with his head he called out to Johnny, "Hey Cuzz, seat open."

The ninety-five dollars that Johnny won two nights ago was burning a whole in his pocket. He vacillated between paying off the bookie or tempting fate. Although the odds were against him, he decided to take a chance. "Deal me in," he said matter-of-factly even though his eagerness was apparent.

A wicked smile crossed Joe Bags' dourly blemished face. Fresh meat for the grinder he thought indulgently.

Slowly descending the steps toward the angled base of the staircase, Anna observed her father with his left hand covering his mouth deep in thought. It was unlike her father to contemplate anything, so the pose alerted her to be doubly cautious.

Acknowledging her presence, the Gimp disgustedly held up the shredded piece of white dress without looking directly at her. As if on cue, he then sluggishly turned to face Anna still holding the dress in his outstretched hands. "What's this?"

"It's not what you think."

"You don't know what I think."

"It was an accident," Anna pleaded.

A cold eerie silence encompassed the house. Frozen in position both remained silent. Somewhere in the house a clock ticked off the seconds. Approaching him guardedly, she asked in an intimate way that only a daughter could ask, "Please just stop and listen?" Her words fell on deaf ears.

"You let that scum, that no account scumbag into my house. My house! You know the rules," his voice got louder until it reached a fever pitch.

"He just showed up. I'm sorry," Anna implored in a crackling voice.

"You're lying through yer teeth," the Gimp replied in an elevated tone of voice. His washed out haggard look turned menacing.

"Daddy…"

"Daddy nothing. You know my rules. No one in the house." Thrusting the piece of dress toward her face he screamed in a low threatening voice, "This, this bullshit! I don't like it. I won't tolerate it." The Gimp rose from his chair like a volcano about to erupt. "Don't protect this little animal. He couldn't wait 'til you were married? You couldn't wait?"

Anna was confused. Partially regaining her composure she grasped the thrust of her father's infuriation. He was speaking about Johnny while she was focused on Cosmo. "I'm not trying to protect him. Nothing happened. Nothing. Really," she sputtered in a pleading voice.

Thrusting his finger at her in the air, he screamed in a voice parched by his incessant anger, "Bullshit. Bullshit. And more bullshit!" Turning away from her he licked his dry lips swallowing quickly then continued, "I actually liked that little asshole. Then he goes and does this!" The Gimp threw the pieces of dress cloth toward the fireplace.

Anna remained silent. Knowing her father, there was no other recourse. Once he made up his mind it would take an act of God to change it, she brooded. Then, the thought of Johnny dumping her crept into her mind. She balanced the thought of Cosmo and Johnny like the blindfolded woman holding the scales of justice. If she had to choose between the two, the choice was simple. Johnny meant nothing to her anymore, she thought. Actually he never did. Tucci meant everything. She would simply let her father's thought processes continue as they may. It was not her fault or her responsibility to change that process. Johnny had made his bed, now let him lie in it, she crowed inwardly. In her father's mind it was a *fait accompli*, she rationalized. Nothing would change it. Yet, she still had a modicum of decency lurking within her. Making a half-hearted attempt to mitigate her father's outrage, she said, "Really Daddy, it's not what it appears to be."

Pointing at the rest of the white dress strewn about the floor the Gimp replied with finality, "This is what I know. This is what I see. End of discussion." Staring into his daughter's puffy eyes swelled from her sobbing outburst the Gimp asked pointedly, "Besides, why you tryin' to protect this little animal? Why?"

Holding back an emotional outburst swelling in her bosom, Anna said firmly, "I'm not tryin' to protect anyone."

"I talked to this kid like he was my son and this is how he treats me. Does he really think he was goin' to get away with this shit? Is he a total idiot?" The Gimp paused a moment to reflect, thinking only of his daughter as a victim and not a perpetrator.

Exasperated, his mind was etched in stone. "Clean this mess up before your mother gets home. I don't want to hear her mouth. And neither do you. Trust me.

I'll take care of this my own way," the Gimp pronounced in a strange detached voice.

Tucci exited the church of the Annunciation a new man. Heading north on Tenth Street he had a bounce to his step. His morning lovemaking had left him ravenously hungry. When he reached Passyunk Avenue he headed north toward Ninth Street. Even though it was Good Friday and Catholics were suppose to fast from eating meat, nothing short of a cheese steak would quench his hunger.

Sitting in church he had reflected on his life thus far. It was in a sorry state of affairs until today. This morning marked a milestone in his life, he silently acknowledged. He didn't *make his bones* yet so there was still time to pull back from the downward spiral of his present life style.

As he walked up Passyunk Avenue, he fantasized possible scenarios of reconciliation with the Gimp. He was not naïve. He was just in love. His entire attitude about life had changed in the blink of an eye. An arcane metamorphosis had occurred. Dealing with the Gimp was another matter. His first priority was distancing himself from the criminal subculture that permeated his life.

After ordering his steak Tucci looked north up Ninth Street. All the small businesses lining the sidewalks inspired him. A business would do just fine, he thought hopefully. Getting the money wouldn't be much of a problem. Then his thoughts reverted to sports gambling and it hit him. A sporting goods store was just the ticket. He liked the idea. It was doable. Promising himself to look into it further he picked up a cheese steak and coke and began devouring it.

Teti spent Good Friday afternoon in a different milieu. Walking from his apartment in Queens Village he arrived at Nate's Hot Dogs on Seventh Street. He still was a traditionalist as far as the Good Friday observance was concerned. So, he ordered two fish cake sandwiches and loaded them with mustard and onions. Satisfied with his meal he continued his trek to Fourth and Chestnut Street—Independence Hall.

He preferred not to take the tour since he liked to linger at the threshold to the assembly area and tried to observe something new from that sole vantage point. The signers of the Declaration of Independence sat in this very room almost two hundred years before yet it felt like the room was waiting for their return. It was at moments like this that he reflected on his own independence or lack thereof. There was no way out for him. He had already sworn the blood oath of La Cosa Nostra. The Gimp also swore an oath to be his mentor. The Gimp vouched for him. So, there it stood. There was no going back. He had to make it work. In effect, he was an indentured servant.

After his brief tour, Teti liked to sit in the park behind Independence Hall. Sometimes families would pass him. During those moments he wondered if his father were more involved in his life would things be different. He knew in his heart that Cisco was his father though no one ever broached the topic, least of all his mother. The patriarchal dominance of his grandfather was the root of his family's dysfunction. There was no denying that, he conceded. Maybe being in little league or football might have led him down a different path. All those ruminations were conjecture, he realized. Reality dictated his behavior now. And the reality of his life was that he had no life. It was an oxymoron. That word described him to a tee. Enjoying the quiet solitude of a beautiful spring afternoon, Teti had no way of knowing that his world would be thrust into a turmoil that would test his mettle as a man.

38

Carlucci was sitting with his feet up on the desk rocking back and forth on the hind legs of a battered wooden chair in the Downtown Social Club. He had received a curt call from the Gimp and was waiting for him to arrive. By the timbre of the Gimp's voice he knew that something was brewing, something requiring his unique abilities.

The Gimp stormed into the club in an unusually blustering manner even by the Gimp's standards. Normally, he would have chided Carlucci for putting his feet on the desk. That minor annoyance couldn't compare to his roiling emotions at the moment. Snapping his head sharply, the Gimp silently motioned for Carlucci to take a ride with him. Carlucci responded quickly. His anticipation quickened. This was serious he thought.

Driving through the streets of South Philadelphia, the Gimp squealed his tires at every opportunity. Electricity filled the atmosphere in the car. Following a circuitous route, he eventually made his way to Delaware Avenue coming to an abrupt stop on one of the empty piers lining the Delaware River. "Let's take a walk," the Gimp said firmly to Carlucci.

Getting out of the car they headed for the end of the pier. "I want someone to disappear. Car everything no trace."

"Anybody I know?" Carlucci replied casually like it was not a problem.

"That little shit who was suppose to marry my daughter."

Carlucci let out a low whistle. "Didn't work out, huh?"

Raising his voice a decibel on each word the Gimp explained, "I want him dead. Then I want him dead some more! I want his balls in my hand so I can bronze them and roll them around in the palm of my hand!" The Gimp's demeanor was demonic. Apocalyptic retribution emanated from every pour in his body as he made his pronouncement. He was a man possessed.

Momentarily stunned, Carlucci witnessed a new black hole in the soul of the man whom he served. Its magnetic force was hypnotic. Recovering quickly, he looked askance. Afraid to ask the motivation for this decree he asked a simple question. "What's this scumbag's name?"

"His name is Johnny Cerone. He drives a puke-colored English sports car. Shouldn't be hard to find."

"What about the hustler?"

"Kill 'em all! Kill anybody that get's in the way!"

Carlucci let out a slight chortle. The Gimp was not in a laughing mood and shot him a fearsome look. "Just get it done. If you can't handle this yerself I'll get someone who can."

Carlucci flinched at the rebuke, not wanting to be denied the pleasure of personally dispatching Cisco. Still, the Gimp was notoriously cheap in these matters. With a mug on his face he faced the Gimp silently. He had something else on his mind.

Noticing Carlucci's facial expression, the Gimp gruffly asked, "If you got somethin to say, spit it out."

"What you want can't be done pro bono."

The Gimp shot Carlucci a look of amazement. "Antny, you're startin' to sound like a fuckin' lawyer. You got a bug up your ass for that hustler yerself. I'm jus givin' ya cover. When ya do the kid then we'll talk money. Capisce?"

"And the Old Man?"

"What is this a fuckin' quiz show? Fuck the Old Man! This is a matter of honor. Personal honor!" Snorting then stabbing the air with his finger to drive home a point, "It's time that old fart and I had a sit down anyways. I'll handle the Old Man you just take care of those two assholes. The sooner the better."

Carlucci acknowledged the Gimp with a forced nod. He had no qualms about disposing of the kid and Cisco—especially Cisco. The irreverence toward the Old Man was another matter. The Gimp was playing with fire, Carlucci thought. He didn't like it.

Rose entered the back door to the bar and caught Cisco puffing away on a cigarette. The nicotinic-laced smoke made her gag and cough. Any other day she would have read him the riot act. Today, however, she put her personal sentiments aside.

Cisco immediately knew she had entered and stubbed out the cigarette. Finishing the last gulp of rum and coke he turned to face her. "Ready to meet your maker now?" After a pause he continued, "I am." Still holding the glass he sucked on a piece of ice.

Sitting next to him at the bar, she pushed away the disgusting ashtray. Old habits died hard no matter how she tried to contain them. "I prayed. You partied. We make a fine pair," she said stolidly.

"Only pair that beats a full house," Cisco agreed in an alcoholic induced mocking tone.

"The banks are closed today or I'd get you the money."

"You ain't got the money," Cisco replied uninhibitedly, "I saw your books. Unless you got something stashed. You're mortgaged up to your eyeballs. What'd your old man do with all the money?"

"Pissed it away on the ponies and whores," she explained casually.

"Died with a smile on his face. There are worse ways to go," Cisco picked up the pack of cigarettes. Rose held down his hand. He relented.

"Cancer is definitely one of them," Rose warned with a familiar enough face to get her point across.

Cisco gave a quick derisive snort then stood up. The alcohol removed his inhibitions dulling his heavy eyes. Yet, a youthful twinkle transmitted enough sparks to ignite the dormant passion that Rose suppressed for so long.

An alluring smile gently rolled across Rose's face accentuating her mahogany eyes. Her breathing accelerated to the quickening beat of her heart. Shaking her long brown hair loose, she sent Cisco the message that tonight she was his for the asking.

Cisco hesitated.

Rose would have none of that this evening. Sensually, she flung herself forward kissing him with the fury of all the misspent years of fantasizing alone in her room.

Arousing his long dormant carnal desires, Cisco responded in kind subjugating himself to Rose's unfettered passion. Running his fingers through her sweet smelling hair, he slowly caressed her body finally unzipping her dress letting it fall to the floor. Gently kissing her face, he began licking her neck slowly moving toward her shoulder while unsnapping her bra. Burying his face in her supple breasts, he slowly licked every part of her exposed body. Then with an uncharacteristic gentleness, he carried her to a nearby table. Rose tightly wrapped her thighs around him leaning back on her arms to allow the proper angle for Cisco to continue his passionate designs.

At first Rose's hips twitched then her thighs pulsated until she released a powerful scream. Lurching forward she dug her nails into Cisco arms until she begged him to stop. Finally, Rose entwined her legs around Cisco while hungrily kissing him. Pulling away from him, her eyes were ablaze with requiting desire. Tugging at Cisco's belt, she led him upstairs determined to have her full of him this night.

39

Joe Bags clenched a cigarette in the furthest corner of his tightly pursed lips. The smoke from his cigarette spiraled toward yellow-crusted ceiling tiles above the card table as he idly stared at his cards. He was down almost a hundred bucks to this pisser, he thought reproachfully. Eyeing Johnny out of the corner of his left eye, he felt the urge to slap the toothy grin off of his face.

At the same moment Joe Bags was focusing a reproving eye on him, Johnny was recounting his recent luck and the overall change in his fortune. Not counting his winnings, though he knew them to be substantial, he was just delighted to be on a winning streak. It was a positive sign he mused.

The clock on the wall behind Freddy the Mooch read 8 P.M. Like the other players, he was grappling with the frustration of Johnny's newfound luck. His loses weren't as large as Joe Bags' losses. Actually, he was almost even, he concluded. Cranking his head around to view the clock, he feigned the lateness of the hour. Truthfully, he just decided to stop tempting fate. "I'm out," he said with stoic finality.

"Where ya goin," Joe Bags protested.

"I got a family, Joe. My wife's gonna be pissed if I don't show up soon. See ya tomorrow," Freddy patronizingly replied. Scooping up his money, he didn't need to count it. He had already performed that function mentally before deciding to leave. With a tacit nod of his head signaling his goodbye, Freddy exited.

The other player left as Joe Bags counted his money. He didn't need to count it either since he kept a running count in his head too. As he malingered, he sized Johnny up concluding that he could take him in a physical confrontation. Standing up to exit, he felt compelled to vent his reprehension toward Johnny. "Stay lucky, asshole, cause you suck big time at cards." he grumbled in an emphatically repulsive tone tinged with challenge.

Pops looked up from the sports section of the newspaper over the top of his glasses. He knew the attitudinal tendencies of all the cretins who cycled through his doors. Some he liked. Some he didn't. Joe Bags fell in the latter category.

Sore loser, vindictive and all around bad mouth, Pops tolerated the guy because he was good action. He was hoping that this new kid would keep his mouth shut and let Joe Bags run off at the mouth. Otherwise, he would have to step in and stop it. He was getting too old for this shit, he thought uneasily.

Johnny looked at Joe Bags incredulously. No one was going to sidetrack his budding streak of good luck. Not even a jerk like this guy, he thought. His naiveté in matters like this one had been brought up to speed on several previous occasions. Johnny knew from those experiences that guys like Joe Bags were itching for a fight. It served to allay their personal inadequacies in the eyes of others. Opting to keep quiet, he just shrugged impassively.

Joe Bags saw Pops icy stare and backed off. Storming off, he slammed the poolroom door as he exited.

Cisco sat upright in bed. Rose laid beside him in blissful sleep. Previously forlorn, they held nothing back this night making rapacious love for hours until they both fell asleep into each other's arms. Looking at a nearby alarm clock, Cisco noted the time—8 P.M. His mind spun like a computer reading the inputs of a punched card processing all of the available information on his predicament. Its final output predetermined by events out of his control. Flipping Sid's business card between his fingers like some card trick, Cisco knew he would have to take his chances and head west alone.

Lovingly watching Rose sleep, he decided not to wake her. Slipping out of bed quietly, he got dressed and packed a traveling bag. Slowly thumbing through his meager bankroll, he realized that he just barely had enough to buy a bus ticket. Drawing his lips inward and sucking them anxiously, he made a fateful decision. With little money and no other transportation, he decided to remain one more night to see if he could raise additional funds. Rifling though Rose's finances that afternoon depressed him. That little exercise made it hard for him to take what little she had in the till. He considered taking Rose's car, but it was old and in poor working condition. The damn thing would probably break down in some Podunk town, he thought. When the image of the Southern Sheriff crossed his mind, he decided against it. Instead, he decided to gamble on one more night of hustling downtown. Cisco scooped up Rose's car keys from the nightstand. Quietly, he stole down the stairs and out the side door for one last go-round in this City of Brotherly Love.

Bursting out of the exterior poolroom door onto Snyder Avenue Joes Bags was furious. Not daring to face the fact that he was the real loser, his anger escalated. He could've beaten someone to death at that moment and his ire would not have been satisfied. Stopping to watch the ebb and flow of the traffic, he shook the last cigarette from its pack into his mouth. Crumbling up the empty pack he tossed it far into the street. After turning away from the wind to light the cigarette, he chugged on it defiantly. "Asshole," he croaked in a low rasping voice then headed west toward Bancroft Street.

As he crossed the narrow street someone lurking in the shadows of a nearby doorway took a match to a cigarette illuminating his face like a *film noir* scene from a classic movie. The darkness returned instantly leaving a smoldering dot of light as the only clue to the shrouded individual. Looking forward Joe Bags recognized the face. Trying not to stare, he picked up the pace of his stride. It was the face of Mad Dog Anthony.

Upstairs in the poolroom, Johnny was turning over the game's cut cup to Pops. Pops looked at Johnny knowing full well that he was cut from a different bolt of cloth than the rest of his surly patrons. In an affable tone of voice he grinned amiably and winked, "Did good tonight, eh kid."

Johnny tacitly bobbed his head. "Has that pool hustler Cisco been around?" he probed vaguely with feign indifference.

"Not today," Pops responded nonchalantly while flipping the pages of the newspaper sprawled across the counter. Sensing Johnny's intrigue with Cisco, Pops looked up, "What's your name kid?"

"Johnny. Johnny Cerone."

Looking around the room to see if anyone was lurking in the nearby darkness, he peered over the top of his glasses speaking in a low straightforward manner. "Well Johnny Cerone I'm gonna give you a piece of free advice. Cisco is a snake in the grass, double-dealing son-of-a-bitch. He'll leave you dick in hand and scoot off with your dough. So, be careful."

Pops stopped to make sure his words were sinking into this naïve young man's brain. Maybe seeing a little bit of himself in the young man, he liked Johnny. Still bright eyed and full of potential, the insidious strain of cynicism had not yet infected him. The misbegotten detours along the path of Pops' life flashed before his eyes then quickly dissipated. Pops' cloudy eyes registered no signs of subtlety as he continued, "Right now, he's nothing but trouble—in spades. So, if you want adventure go to fuckin' Africa."

With incredulous eyes, Johnny halfheartedly responded, "I'll keep my eyes open."

"Good. Not that it matters any since I can tell you're shinin' me on. So, if you see him tell him his horse came in."

"Really?" Johnny asked excitedly.

"I told you guys to bet the bricks. Twenty to one shot."

Johnny whistled low and long. "I'll bet he'll be ecstatic. Two grand goes a long way."

Waving his right index finger like a metronome, Pops corrected Johnny. "I was in for half, nine hundred and twenty-five to be exact. A mighty fine return for an unbeliever," Pops interjected in a guttural cocky tone.

40

Traffic was light heading south on Broad Street. The wailing sound of an emergency vehicle piercing the ominous quietness of the surrounding streets reminded Cisco of a funeral dirge. Nearly despondent over his dwindling options, he considered turning around and returning to the warmth of Rose's bed. At the intersection of Passyunk Avenue, Cisco turned right heading toward Chickie's Poolroom. He was gambling on eluding the Gimp and his crew this one last time in the hope of fattening his bankroll for the trip ahead. Passing the sparsely populated parking lot of the Diner only reaffirmed his suspicions that tonight's outing was an exercise in futility.

At Sixteenth Street he decided to turn right and park away from the poolroom. Cisco liked to hug the walls of the row homes as a buffer from the predators roaming the streets at this time of night. Ingrained in him from his youth, it was one less angle that he had to protect. Like a bat probing the night skies, Cisco walked down Sixteenth Street after luckily finding a parking space on Emily Street off Sixteenth Street. Rounding the corner at Sixteenth and Passyunk Avenue, he quietly slid into the unmarked door leading up the steps to Chickie's poolroom.

If he had bothered to look across the street he would have noticed the faint dot of a cigarette glowing from a doorway across the street.

Carlucci had relocated himself after being spotted by Joe Bags so as not to draw any further unwanted attention. Like a hunter stalking his prey, he immediately zeroed in on Cisco entering the poolroom over the low top of Johnny's mustard colored sports car. A hideously satisfying smirk animated his craggy face. Bingo, he thought wickedly at first. I have them both. But instinct kicked into gear and his mind began clicking like the leather strap on a spinning carnival game wheel. Finally, he decided to take care of Cisco first. It was a long time coming and he didn't want him slipping out of his grasp. The kid would be easy enough he decided. Johnny Cerone could wait.

Cisco was immediately disappointed when he entered the empty poolroom. He pensively rolled the cigarette dangling from his lips as his eyes wandered the empty tables hoping for some hidden action not readily seen. None materialized. His hopes stymied, Cisco looked at the clock on the wall and figured that he could just about make the last bus out of town before morning.

Johnny twisted his head upon hearing the door swing open. A mischievous grin spread across his lips. He wanted to blurt out the good news. Nixing that impulse, he decided to let Pops do the honors since it was his horse pick.

"Cisco! Front and center," Pops intoned in a terse military style.

His cigarette protruding from puckered lips Cisco slowly made his way to the counter. Grasping Johnny's neck with his strong right hand, he began massaging it as a sign of friendship. "What's up?"

Pops gently tossed a wadded roll of money at an unsuspecting Cisco. "Next time bet the bricks!"

Cisco looked at the roll of money like manna from heaven. His entire demeanor changed instantly. A taunt grin stretched across his lips. It eventually spread into a broad smile as his eyes caught twenty-dollar bills flicking across his fingers.

"Twenty to one. Half plus tip," Pops chortled.

Cisco had forgotten entirely about the bet. Sometimes there was honor among thieves he thought. Pops could have kept the entire sum and he wouldn't have been the wiser. It was a cause for celebration. Cisco's understated style and placid façade, however, didn't register the jubilation in his heart.

Johnny on the other hand was ecstatic for Cisco, even though he didn't know the particulars of his predicament.

Pops looked up at the clock on the wall. It read 9 P.M. "I'm outta here. This place is like a morgue. No action tonight. Get a move on it guys. I'm lockin' up."

Cisco's stomach growled from hunger. His drinking and lovemaking had made him ravenous. "Come on kid. Let's go get somethin' to eat at the Diner."

"Hang on I gotta take a piss," Johnny said uncomfortably.

"I'll meet you over there," Cisco said as he lit another cigarette from the stub of the one he just finished. "Come on Pops, I'm buyin'."

"I'll take a rain check. I'm tired."

Cisco practically danced down the steps. His thoughts were two thousand miles away.

Carlucci stood in a doorway around the corner with a ski cap rolled up around his head. The position that he chose was around the corner from the poolroom on the west side of Sixteenth Street. All the necessary preparation to carry out his assignment had been made long before Cisco arrived. He knew from experience that Cisco would choose the obscurity of Sixteenth Street rather than the openness of the triangular intersection. It was his life's task to know the man and his habits. He wondered for an instant if he would find closure tonight with the culmination of this consuming obsession. Soon, he would find out. Any moment now Cisco should be turning the corner at Sixteenth Street hugging the inside wall on his left. Carlucci was counting on it.

Nearby was a stolen car, black with no observable features and plastic carefully covering the floor of the car's trunk. The trunk was slightly ajar so that Carlucci didn't have to fumble with keys. His plan was to get the drop on Cisco and force him into the trunk of the car where he would fire two specially prepared bullets from an untraceable .38 revolver into his head and abdomen. With luck this should take less than 30 seconds. Then, he would make the short drive down Passyunk Avenue just past Sixty-Third Street to one of the many salvage yards dotting the landscape by the refineries. After disposing of Cisco in a vat of sulfuric acid he would crush the car to a square box of metal ready for shipping to the smelting plant. Proven for its efficiency on several previous occasions, it was a tried and true method he had devised. The salvage yard owner gave him the keys to the facility in order to claim deniable culpability. Besides, Carlucci was on his payroll. So, he was covered.

For this particular contract Carlucci wished that he had more time to slowly torture his long time nemesis. Sadism evoked a strange satisfaction in him. It was delicious in a psychological sort of way. Unfortunately, expediency was required for this job since Cisco had always been a formidable foe from their youth.

Predictable to a fault, a preoccupied Cisco turned the corner slowly almost like he was dancing. Carlucci smiled maliciously. There would be no resurrection in this lifetime for Cisco, he wickedly thought.

Johnny bolted down the steps of the poolroom trying to catch up with Cisco. Storming out the door onto Snyder Avenue, he scanned the streets to no avail. As he stopped to cross Sixteenth Street his left eye caught an erratic movement down the street. Turning slightly, he noticed the glint of a gun to Cisco's head and instinctively reacted.

Rushing up Sixteenth Street unnoticed, Johnny tackled the unsuspecting assailant like a linebacker just as he was about to push Cisco into the trunk of a car. The gun jarred loose from Carlucci's hand. It slid under the automobile as Carlucci's face scraped the sidewalk. Recovering quickly, Carlucci was about to stomp on Johnny. Instinctively, Cisco grasped his two hands together in a ball and stretched them out like a bat. Swinging with all of his might, he caught Carlucci across the bridge of his nose sending him reeling backwards against the car.

Again recovering quickly, Carlucci charged Cisco insanely. Johnny, still on the sidewalk, inadvertently tried to get out of the way and accidentally tripped Carlucci. Losing his balance Carlucci fell forward onto Cisco's raised knee.

With a bleeding nose Carlucci partially regained his footing, but Cisco kneed him to the groin pushing him backwards toward the trunk of the car. Carlucci doubled over as Cisco let loose with a virulent left hook to his face. This sent Carlucci ass first into the trunk of the car. Johnny quickly assisted Cisco. Together they pushed Carlucci all the way into the trunk and slammed it closed.

"Where's yer car?" Cisco asked Johnny hurriedly.

"In front of the poolroom."

"Let's go."

A disoriented Johnny hesitated. "Go where?"

Cisco's mind was crystal clear. He thrived on dire situations like this one. Consequently, his thinking was logical and concise. "Anywhere but here!"

Carlucci's banging from inside the trunk of the car snapped Johnny into the ominous reality of their situation.

"That's Mad Dog Anthony in the trunk. Do you think he's gonna take kindly to us putting him there? Now let's go," Cisco ordered urgently.

Johnny and Cisco rounded the corner of Sixteenth and Snyder Avenue. In the distance Cisco caught a fleeting glimpse of a Police *Meat Wagon* heading west toward them on East Passyunk Avenue.

"Settle down. Get in the car slowly and just drive away. Nothing fancy," Cisco cautioned in a whisper.

They entered Johnny's car unnoticed and waited for the Police Van to turn right on Sixteenth Street. Slowly pulling away from in front of the poolroom, Johnny drove east on Passyunk Avenue. "Where to?"

"Downtown Bar & Grill. I gotta get my stuff then we blow town tonight."

"What do ya mean we?"

"You're in it now kid. The guy you tackled ain't gonna take kindly to having his plans disrupted," Cisco warned.

Slowly the implications of the event that had just transpired began sinking into Johnny's head. He had thwarted a contract and physically accosted a made man. Inwardly shuddering at the consequences, he outwardly tried to remain calm. Silently, he drove along Passyunk Avenue. Grappling desperately with his future, he was unaware that by saving Cisco he had saved himself from a similar fate. Less than an hour ago, he thought, my luck seemed like a rocket heading for the moon. That all ended in the blink of an eye. On some level of his being though Johnny felt good about what he did. It was a manly act—the right act. And he knew it.

Cisco too was in a soberly reflective mood. Grateful to be alive, he had just eluded the man in the black robe and scythe from an untimely appointment with destiny. Though he wouldn't readily admit it, he was also grateful to Johnny. It seemed that destiny had dealt him the cards that he requested—money and a ride. Squirming in the uncomfortable bucket seat of the MGB, Cisco didn't delude himself about what lay ahead. He steeled himself instead to deal with one crisis at a time. And the next one was just moments away.

The Downtown Bar & Grill was closed. It was a Good Friday tradition dating back to Sal Teti's proprietorship. His wife, a religious woman, insisted on it and Rose continued it in her memory. Besides, Rose felt that it was good for the soul to reflect on one's life at least once a year.

Inside Rose was hovering over a jukebox dressed only in a silk robe and slippers. She was dropping coins into the slot and pushing buttons by rote. Once she finished selecting her songs, she sat on a bar stool with her bare leg crossed over the other one. Sipping on a snifter of Chivas Regal Scotch, the music mixed with the liquor to put her in a melancholic mood. Inclined to sentimental fiddle-faddle occasionally, she concealed it well under the brusqueness required by a proprietress of a bar. Reminiscing about what might have been, she stared aimlessly at the suitcase sitting on a chair by the door. She found it tucked away in the corner of her closet and carried it down the stairs. It was a stark reminder that this afternoon's exaltation was to be short lived.

Looking up she noticed Cisco standing in the doorway framed by the outside light of a street lamp. Startled momentarily, she didn't know how long he had been standing there. His taciturn eyes exuded a warm glow that registered more than mere concern.

Cisco noticed her maudlin glance and smiled reassuringly. There would be no slipping away into the shroud of night for him this evening. It was better this way he thought.

Finally, noticing Cisco's new facial abrasions she recoiled with concern. The recrimination of the moment was suddenly supplanted by the beckoning sound of *Moonlight Serenade*. Almost magically the bar was transformed into a previous time and place. A slow dance beckoned as the music enshrouded them. Slowly, they circled the floor. Cisco held Rose tightly against his body while she nestled her head tenderly on his shoulder.

Johnny entered the side door of the bar and stopped dead in his tracks upon seeing this intimate scene. Unnoticed, he stepped back into the shadow of the dark doorway and observed inquisitively. The tender warmth Cisco and Rose emanated was infectious. Its succorable effect pacified Johnny's anxiety over the dire implications of his interference in this evening's pernicious affair. He was totally mesmerized by this display of affection dismissing Pops' advice. This man was no snake. Snakes were cold-blooded creatures.

The song ended. Cisco and Rose just stood there in the middle of the barroom tightly embraced. Johnny revisited Cisco's previous urgency. Not more than fifteen minutes had passed and the entire world had changed for these newfound friends. Interrupting the moment Johnny muffled a cough.

Cisco pulled back with the prowess of a cat sensing danger. Then with suspicious eyes, he rotated his head searching the numerous dark crevices of the barroom until they connected with Johnny standing in the doorway. Allaying his fears, he gently stroked Rose's arm. "Step out of the shadows kid," Cisco intoned kindly.

Johnny stepped forward sheepishly.

"Johnny...What's yer last name kid?"

"Cerone. Johnny Cerone."

"Right. Meet Rose Teti."

Rose held out her right hand, slightly chapped from washing glasses and dishes over the years. "Nice meeting you," she said pleasantly.

Johnny grasped her hand delicately and smiled. "Same here."

Cisco spied his suitcase on the chair by the door. Time was now his enemy also. "Kid. Give me a minute. I'll meet ya outside," Cisco said winking his eye at Johnny.

"Sure. I got the car right outside the door," Johnny responded awkwardly nearly tripping over himself as he exited. "Nice meeting you Rose Teti."

Rose smiled sanguinely while slightly nodding her head in response. Turning to Cisco, Rose looked into his muddy brown eyes. "Just go. No goodbyes."

Cisco picked up his suitcase and looked around the bar then back at Rose. "I want you to think about sellin' this place and movin' to Vegas with me," Cisco seriously proposed.

"Is that before or after your funeral?"

He noticed her glance and smiled disparagingly. "There ain't gonna be a funeral. At least not mine."

She sighed lovingly and put those thoughts out of her head. "You take care Armand. Keep that kid out of it."

Cisco turned his head toward the door and back to Rose. "He's in it more than he knows. I'll be seein' ya." He approached her and gave her a long hard kiss while holding his suitcase. "Remember what I said. Sell the bricks." Suddenly remembering Rose's car, he handed her the keys. "Sixteenth and Emily." Then with an apologetic shrug, "Sorry. We had to leave in a hurry."

She smiled. "Get out of here."

Cisco exited and Rose immediately peeked out the window distraughtly watching him disappear around the corner in Johnny's MGB.

41

The radio call came across the airwaves at 9:15 P.M. while the local Police Precinct Watch Officer, Lieutenant Dominic Pelosi, was making his rounds. Instructing his driver to head for the scene of the crime, Lieutenant Pelosi winced when the second call identified the man being held as Anthony Carlucci. Great. Some wise guy scum he thought sardonically. Their kind gives Italians a bad name.

Upon arriving at the scene, Lieutenant Pelosi surveyed the area. A Sergeant produced a .38 revolver dangling from the end of a pen. "We found it under the car," he said seriously. "It's got dum-dum bullets in the first and second chamber."

Rubbing his forehead apprehensively with two fingers Lieutenant Pelosi responded, "Bag it," he said swiftly and then after a moment, "Anything else?"

"You ought to see the trunk Lieutenant," the Sergeant suggested using his head to point the way.

Casually walking toward the open trunk of an automobile, the Lieutenant immediately noticed the sheet of crumbled plastic sheeting. Sighing heavily, he tightened his lips into a seam of anger. The entire crime scene screamed a botched hit, he thought onerously. This was going to be a long night. "Who owns the car?"

"We're checking it now, sir. Also the first officers on the scene noticed a mustard colored sports car pulling away just as they were arriving." the Sergeant replied.

"That shouldn't be too hard to find downtown. Check it out. Where's Carlucci?"

"Back of the van."

"Cuffed?"

"Yep."

"Good." Pelosi decided to let the miscreant cool his heels while he thought through the implications surrounding this affair. Spying his driver he waved him over and handed him a ten-dollar bill. "Ask the other officers what they want and bring me a cup of coffee from the Diner," the Lieutenant asked politely. He always considered the men under his command first as a matter of respect. It was a habit he carried over from his tour of duty in Vietnam.

Second Lieutenant Dominic Pelosi served in the 101st Airborne Division as a Platoon Leader during the spring of 1968. He graduated from a local college in Philadelphia as part of the Reserve Officer Training Program (ROTC). After training as a Green Beret, he asked to be assigned to the 506th Airborne Infantry Regiment. The reason for his change of heart was unclear.

As Second Platoon Leader of Company A, his men respected him. This respect had nothing to do with his imposing six-foot muscular presence. Beneath his icy cold chiseled features, a warm compassionate heart was beating. Always looking out for his men first, he never commanded them to do anything that he wouldn't do himself. Leadership by example was his motto.

His style of leadership was put to the ultimate test one night when his platoon was on patrol in some god-forsaken part of the Vietnamese jungle called Bien Hoa. A squad of eight men probed the perimeter of their camp when they came under attack. Outflanked, the squad was encircled and under heavy fire. There were several wounded. Appraising the situation on the fly, Pelosi coolly jumped into action. Tactically positioning his remaining troops to counterattack, he personally led the charge to rescue the embattled soldiers. Once engaged, savage fighting ensued until it eventually degenerated into hand-to-hand combat. Every soldier that night sustained wounds, some serious. One died—Private Michael Cerone Jr. Pelosi's coolheaded ferocity in combat that night inspired the men under his command to persevere. He didn't fight for Duty, Honor or Country that dark night in that Godforsaken jungle. Pelosi fought for his men. For his fearlessness and courage in this regard, he was awarded the Distinguished Service Cross.

While at base camp before that gruesome engagement at Bien Hoa, he made the acquaintance of Private Michael Cerone Jr. An enlisted man in his platoon, Private Cerone was considered a good soldier. Both from South Philadelphia, the two developed a true friendship. They traded names back and forth as men from the same neighborhoods always do in these circumstances and found some mutual friends. Lieutenant Pelosi liked Private Cerone. They were drawn together by their strength of character. Nevertheless, Pelosi understood his responsibility. He had to lead his men and sometimes make difficult decisions. Friendship with the men under his command was a heavy burden for an officer. Michael Cerone also understood. So, each promised to look the other one up when they got home. Both would eventually make it home—one to be spat upon, the other to be buried.

When Cerone was killed in action while under his command, Pelosi took it personal—very personal. After brooding for several days he took stock of his own life. Finally, he decided that the less he knew about the men under his command the more capable he would be of leading them.

Regardless of outward appearances, Cerone's death gnawed at him. They shared the same beliefs and had common interests. Their casual acquaintance was destined to blossom into a hard and fast friendship after their military service. On some level Pelosi felt that he had let Cerone down due to his own negligence. That feeling occasionally surfaced even though he mentally knew it to be ridiculous. War does strange things to men's psyches.

So, he became a loner. There was plenty of time for socializing after *the 'Nam,* he would tell himself. It was the one chink in his armor. Pacifying his conscience, he promised himself that he would visit Cerone's parents on his return home. That was several years ago and every time he passed the house on Ritner Street he found one excuse or another to avoid keeping that promise. It became his personal demon.

Completing his service in 1970 with the rank of Captain, his family connections in local politics fast tracked him to his present rank. It was an unprecedented rise in rank, unchallenged because of Pelosi's war record. A Distinguished Service Cross, a Bronze Star with an Oak Leaf Cluster and a Purple Heart with an Oak Leaf Cluster elevated him to bona fide war hero status in some circles.

In other circles he was labeled a baby killer even though he personally disregarded an order to assault a suspected village without receiving proper intelligence. Nothing ever came of the incident, but he knew that his career in the military was over. This also didn't stop the Students Against Wars from insinuating the opposite.

Courageous in the face of disparaging innuendos of all types, he still could never bring himself to visit Cerone's parents.

Tonight, however, Pelosi, the Philadelphia Police Lieutenant, faced a dilemma. Retiring to his police cruiser to drink his coffee and ponder an uncompromising course of action, he closed his eyes momentarily and swore without opening his mouth. Unwilling to kowtow to an unconscionable killer, he evaluated his alternatives.

If his Commanding Officer caught wind of this incident, he would stop whatever he was doing and take personal command of the situation. Carlucci would be afforded every possible courtesy. Then more than likely, he'd be released on the spot. Although Pelosi had never personally been approached, he strongly suspected the generosity of the downtown mob in these matters. In some ways, he thought cynically, it was like Vietnam all over—an abuse of power.

Tapping on the window, the Sergeant made an unintelligible gesture to Pelosi. Rolling down the window, he inquired, "Is something wrong?"

"He wants to talk to you," the Sergeant responded in an anxious voice.

"Who wants to talk to me?" inquired Lieutenant Pelosi.

The Sergeant lowered his eyes and mumbled, "Carlucci."

"I'll talk to him at the station. Any word yet on the car?"

"No sir. Sir…" the Sergeant said in a respectfully pleading tone.

"Yes?"

"Perhaps you should talk to him now."

Lieutenant Pelosi's icy stare froze the Sergeant instantly. The Sergeant fidgeted nervously, lowering his head a second time to break eye contact. The mere presence of the man made him feel ignominious. Being the *bagman* for the precinct, he knew that he would be held accountable for this *inconvenience*. He tried to reason with Carlucci explaining Lieutenant Pelosi's reputation. That only frothed Mad Dog Anthony's ire more. With some luck, he had settled down by now. Otherwise, there would be hell to pay tonight.

After a cold moment Lieutenant Pelosi exited the police cruiser. Throwing his shoulders back, he straightened his leather jacket pushing his hand down slowly toward his sidearm reminiscent of a gunslinger from a lawless time in the past. Looking long and hard at the Sergeant, he icily spoke in accentuated clips. "Alright, Sergeant. I'll speak to the man."

Carlucci sat hunched over in the dark cavernous hulk of a police van. Coldness shrouded him reminding him of why it was called a *Meat Wagon*. His misplaced indignation was seething with contempt for all living creatures this night. Kicking the bench across from him furiously, his anger increased from a simmer to a low boil when he thought of how he had been thwarted. He kicked the bench again as violent as he could in the cramped space. He had eaten enough shit for one night. Nervously, he pumped his leg up and down on the ball of his left foot as if to pump up his fragilely deflated ego. He wasn't about to take any more shit from some self-righteous two-bit asshole that played soldier he told himself.

On that note the back door of the police van opened illuminating the disheveled troll like image of Mad Dog Anthony.

"Do you know who I am?" Carlucci venomously screamed. His breath shrouded Lieutenant Pelosi in a malodorous cloud of contempt.

Unflinchingly, Lieutenant Pelosi countered by whispering in a deadly serious voice. "No. And I don't give a damn!"

Struggling to find a response to the nearly imperceptible utterance of Pelosi, Carlucci squinted his blood-caked eyes warily at the statuesque man silhouetted by the street lamp behind him. The lieutenant's bearing demanded respect.

Pelosi slid his jaw from side to side in a saw tooth motion. His sense of proper decorum was being put to the test. This disheveled hulk of putridity sitting in front of him caused his baser instincts to respond. "But I'll tell you who I am. I'm your worst fucking nightmare."

Defensively, Carlucci blurted, "You can't talk to me like that!"

"I'll talk to you any way I damn well please," Pelosi spoke in a commanding tone then hesitated to let the words sink in to the thick skull of Carlucci. His voice got louder and the pitch higher as he continued enunciating his words slowly, "I've killed better men than you with my bare hands. I've licked their blood off my lips. So, don't make me mad. Because if I sink to your level, I might just enjoy taking you apart. Piece. By piece."

Carlucci looked uneasy as his eyes quickly scanned the street behind Pelosi to see if anyone was present. The man before him had confronted death first hand. He wasn't the kind to meet it out surreptitiously in the night then slink off into the shadows. Afraid to back down but equally afraid to confront this undauntable human being, Carlucci knew that he had met his match.

To the side of the police van, out of direct view stood the Sergeant frozen in awe. He had heard every word of the conversation and didn't know whether to fear or respect his lieutenant. At this moment Lieutenant Pelosi exuded an aura of intestinal fortitude the likes of which the Sergeant had never previously witnessed in a man. This man commanded respect not fear, the sergeant decided.

In the battle of intimidation Pelosi had won forcing Carlucci to lower his eyes in deference. Pelosi could have become his new master at that moment if he had chosen to do so. His moral compass, however, was still true and he merely swung the doors to the police van shut leaving the man to silently whimper in the dark and brood over his moral turpitude.

Turning to his left after closing the police van doors, Lieutenant Pelosi spied the Sergeant watching him intently. A sense of pride swelled in the Sergeant as he gave the lieutenant a proper salute. Pelosi responded. "Take him back to the station. The scenic tour."

42

Johnny's mustard colored MGB was doubled parked in front of the family home on Ritner Street. Cisco waited patiently in the car while Johnny quickly packed a bag.

As Johnny descended the oak and wrought iron staircase his parents were seated anxiously watching his slow descent. Stopping three-quarters of the way down on the staircase with his suitcase in hand, Johnny forced a tight smile before speaking. "This has nothing to do with last night," he said unconvincingly.

"Where are you going," his mother said with a restrained almost cautious probing in her voice.

Descending the remaining four steps of the staircase Johnny put down his suitcase. "I'm heading for Las Vegas. Try my luck out there. Things don't seem to be working out for me here," he said evasively. He didn't want to lie. Above all, he didn't want his parents worrying about him either. They were already in enough pain.

Johnny's father snorted derisively then turned to look out the window. Noticing Cisco in the car, he asked sarcastically, "Is that your traveling companion out there?"

"Yeah. We're gonna share the drivin' and the gas."

"What about your job," his mother asked in a crackling tone that dangled on the precipice of an emotional outburst.

Hesitantly, he realized that he had not thought everything through. Recovering quickly he lied, "It's all taken care."

Beckoning his mother for an embrace, she stood there sobbing. "First Michael. Now you," Assunta said in an almost ominous tone of voice.

Cringing at the implication of her unthinking invocation, Johnny considered his own mortality for a fleeting moment. He had made a fine mess of his short life thus far. Perhaps going to Las Vegas would be good for him. Clear the cobwebs from his skewed thinking he pondered hastily.

His father's weathered face was downturn. Looking at Johnny he pinched his left eye tightly. In his mind and heart he tried to take a measure of this boy, his son, who was now becoming a man. Sensing a newfound strength in Johnny's character, his father acknowledged him with a simple nod. Still seated, Michael Senior turned and stared out the window. He was unwilling to say goodbye.

In a manly act of affection Johnny merely squeezed his father's shoulder firmly and invoked sincerely a vague farewell, "Take care."

Lieutenant Pelosi also decided to take the scenic route back to the Precinct Station House. Slowly heading north on Twentieth Street, he methodically recounted anything that would justify holding Carlucci overnight. Showing a personal resolve to take this man off the street was his personal way of championing the idea that all Italian-Americans were not born criminals.

Carlucci was wearing gloves so there was probably no chance of his prints being found on the gun. Holding him as a material witness was a long shot although Carlucci hadn't explained how he ended up in the trunk yet. He was waiting for his lawyer. Of course he could say that he threatened an officer, Pelosi thought distastefully. In reality it was he who threatened Carlucci. He would need more personal justification to perpetrate a lie, he concluded as his driver stopped at a light on Twentieth and Ritner Street.

Up shifting just after Opal Street heading west on Ritner, Johnny didn't notice the police cruiser until it was too late. Rolling through a yellow light he thought he was legal. He was entirely forgetting the reason for his hurry.

Lieutenant Pelosi's head swiveled as the mustard colored MGB rolled past his direct line of sight. "Go," he ordered his driver who quickly switched on the red light on the dashboard.

Johnny's heart sank when he saw the flashing red light in his rear view mirror. Cisco took it in stride. Better the police than Mad Dog Anthony he thought to himself.

The police cruiser pulled up behind the mustard colored MGB in front of the Edgar Allen Poe Elementary School at Twenty-Second and Ritner Streets. The driver was about to call it in when Lieutenant Pelosi casually motioned with a single outstretched finger for him to stop. "Wait here. I'll handle this," Pelosi said calmly. Before exiting the car Pelosi noticed the driver unsnap the safety strap on his revolver. Nodding his approval, he slid out of the police cruiser.

Stopping a moment to gather his thoughts, Lieutenant Pelosi donned his police cap. Slowly, he strolled over to the driver's side of the car just behind the driver. "License and registration please," he commanded firmly.

"Did I do something wrong officer?" Johnny queried handing Lieutenant Pelosi the identification he requested.

Pelosi's eyes widened upon viewing Johnny's driver license. He always felt that someday he would run into someone from Cerone's family, but never dreamed it would be under these circumstances. "Would the both of you step out of the car slowly please?" he intoned in a non-threatening voice stepping away from the vehicle.

Johnny and Cisco complied. Cisco knew better than to make any sudden moves. Johnny was not as wise.

Pelosi cautioned Johnny immediately, "Stop right there." Looking at Cisco first then at Johnny, Pelosi firmly prodded, "Where are you off to in such a hurry?"

Cisco spoke up quickly. "Over rambunctious kid."

Pelosi shot Cisco a stolid look then countered, "Just like his brother?"

Johnny's eyes piqued curiosity. "You knew my brother?"

"Michael Cerone. Right?"

"How'd you know my brother?" Johnny eagerly asked.

After letting the driver know that everything was okay with a hand gesture, Lieutenant Pelosi vaguely answered, "We served together." Before Johnny had a chance to shoot off another question Pelosi eyed Cisco and commented, "I know you from somewhere." Remembering, he pointed an unsteady silent finger at Cisco then continued politely, "It doesn't matter. Why don't you just wait for your friend here in the car?"

Cisco nodded benignly and complied with Pelosi's request. Pelosi had arrested him for gambling a year ago. He probably read his voluminous police file, Cisco concluded.

Gesturing Johnny away from both vehicles, Pelosi explained himself to Johnny. "I knew your brother in *'Nam*. I was his platoon leader the night he died. I'm sorry for your loss."

"Thank you," Johnny replied humbly.

"He died honorably. He was a hero. All the men that died there were heroes. Don't let anybody tell you otherwise."

Johnny's body tingled with pride. It was the first time anyone had ever mentioned his brother that way. He wished his father and mother could hear the words of this man.

Poking the thumb of his clenched hand toward Johnny's car without looking, Pelosi continued, "You're in unsavory company at best. Be careful. Now I don't want you to say a word. Any word. I'm going to give you a piece of advice and I want you to follow it. Understand?" he prompted for a sign of comprehension from Johnny.

Johnny nodded dubiously not knowing what to expect from this mysterious policeman.

"Your car was reported leaving Sixteenth and Snyder Avenue around the time that one of our police vans was arriving on the scene of a suspected crime. But I suspect if none was committed, one soon will be. We have someone in custody that will be released very shortly. There's very little that I can do about that. But you can." Looking at his watch Lieutenant Pelosi continued. "It's now ten thirty. I can promise you a two maybe three hour head start." Lieutenant Pelosi extended his hand in friendship. "Straighten this mess out. Whatever it is."

Johnny grasped the strong hand and nodded affirmatively.

Pelosi watched the MGB drive away. Seeing Cisco with Michael Cerone's brother filled in a missing piece of tonight's little circus. He could only imagine the discombobulation of what went down. Returning to his police cruiser, he was fully prepared to keep his promise no matter who was waiting for him at the station house.

Considering the unique circumstances of this chance encounter, it was the least that he could do.

43

An hour later Johnny and Cisco finished eating a hearty breakfast of sausage and eggs at a diner on Packer Avenue. Taking the police lieutenant at his word, they decided to eat now since they were in for a hard night of driving.

Johnny was putting the finishing touches on a letter then sealed it in an envelope. Cisco found it intriguing that Johnny would take the time to clean up loose ends. Personally, he could care less as long as the kid didn't let on where they were heading, he thought. Opening a well-worn map on the table Cisco examined it. He had never been west of the Mississippi River. A lot of new ground lie ahead he thought. As he ran his finger up the Schuylkill Expressway and across the Pennsylvania Turnpike, a bold captioned city caught his eye. Tapping his index finger on it, he considered it at length. There was always good pool action there, he thought enticingly. And it was only a stone's throw off of the turnpike.

Breaking Cisco's train of thought, the waitress abruptly arrived at their booth with the checks and a pot of coffee. Cisco coyly looked over the top of his reading glasses at Johnny to see if he was going to reach for the check. He didn't. Oblivious to the checks Johnny simply got up and headed for the Men's Room. Cisco massaged his eyeballs with his fingertips. This was not going to be your run of the mill road trip, he brooded. Cisco picked up the check. Folding the map he peeled off a single one-dollar bill and tossed in onto the table as he rose. Conserving money was the first rule of all road trips.

The commander of the local Police Precinct, Captain Aloysius Mallory, looked at his watched pensively. It was 11:30 P.M. Where in the hell was Pelosi he thought irritably. Dressed fastidiously in a pair of wool slacks, white shirt and tweed blazer, he paced his office like a caged tiger. He was two years away from retirement and this sort of nonsense wasn't supposed to happen in his precinct. It was part of a package deal supposedly. The Gimp kept a lid on crime in the neighborhood. He paid his tithe and the police looked the other way. Everyone prospered was the mantra of those up the chain of command. Tonight's shenanigans, however, pushed the envelope. And it had to happen on Pelosi's watch, Mallory moaned internally.

For the better part of his career Mallory was a good cop. He had several commendations to his credit and rose steadily in the ranks under the tutelage of the various Police Commissioners. As their *bagman* he collected the tribute paid by the local criminals for special consideration in the event that their paths crossed. For their part the criminal lords kept the unruly hooligans under thumb. Everyone prospered.

Lately, the control of the police bureaucracy was waning. A new generation of cops was assuming the reigns of power. This changing of the guard was a natural evolution in most large cities. Mallory saw the handwriting on the wall and called in a big favor before it was too late. As a reward for his faithful years of service Mallory was awarded this plum precinct. Ah, and a plum it was until tonight, he thought.

Pelosi had heard tales of Mallory's connections. No one wanted to disrupt the apple cart. Subtly, Pelosi let it be known before he was approached that he wanted no part of it. Many of the old timers, nevertheless, had come to depend on the payments and rationalized their participation. They went to great length to keep their little secret off of Pelosi's radar screen, but the man was not dumb. New cars and expensive clothing were hard items to hide or explain away. Although personally disappointed with these men, Pelosi was also a realist. Normally allowing them some discretionary leeway, tonight Pelosi drew the line.

When Pelosi finally arrived at Mallory's office the two men circled the small room like boxers squaring off. Mallory felt Pelosi's dark eyes delving into the crevices of his brain. It was unnerving and forced Mallory to speak first. In a careful probing voice he queried Pelosi. "What happened tonight?"

"It's in the preliminary report," Pelosi said matter-of-factly.

"That's not what I mean."

"What do you mean?"

"Why's Carlucci still in the lock up? For chrissakes the man was found in the trunk," Mallory snapped.

"I'm waiting for the report on the car," Pelosi retorted weakly.

Mallory made a gesture of incredulity as he turned away exasperated. "Let him out."

Pelosi looked at the clock on the wall. It read Midnight. He promised Johnny Cerone two hours at least. Taking a deep breath he spoke firmly. "I failed to mention in the report that he threatened me."

Turning to face Pelosi with a cautionary glance Mallory asked, "Your word against his?"

"You can say that."

Shaking his head Mallory chuckled. He measured Pelosi from head to foot then he went to the door and closed it. With pursed lips he gave Pelosi a sidelong glance. "What's this really about?"

"Off the record?" Pelosi quizzed.

"Go on."

The index finger of his outstretched arm pointed like an arrow ready to be released at some unseen object outside the office door. "Let's not kid ourselves. Somebody's alive tonight because they got the best of that smelly asshole sitting in there. And I mean to give them a few more hours of life at the very least. If that means pressing charges, I will. Let the chips fall wherever. It's either that or he sits there for another two hours."

Mallory noted mentally the determination in Pelosi's steely eyes. His entire demeanor bespoke of a man willing to go to extremes to make his point. Mallory had seen his kind before—self righteously stubborn. Deflating his tense posture, he knew that this battle was lost. Pelosi would meet his Waterloo one day, he thought as a wicked smile crept over his face. Still, he was reticent to let Pelosi have his way. After all, Mallory thought proudly, I'm still in command.

Looking back and forth at Pelosi, Mallory weighed his response. He decided to go Pelosi one better. No one could question his action and he may even gain a little respect. Besides, Mallory concluded, the Gimp didn't pay for this kind of service. That was a premium package and a high premium at that. "Let the smelly beast sleep on it. Release him in the morning," Mallory conceded making an expressive gesture mimicking magnanimity. "You satisfied?"

Poised to take a stand, Pelosi was taken aback by Mallory's concurrence. Suddenly, it occurred to him that Mallory was going to use this incident, as leverage for God knows what. Not wanting to look a gift horse in the mouth, Pelosi cracked a coy smile and nodded his agreement. "Yes sir. I'll see to it personally."

Pulling up in front of homes converted into apartments near the intersection of Thirty-Ninth and Baltimore Avenue in West Philadelphia, Johnny hurriedly exited the car. Leaving the motor running, Cisco was contemplatively smoking a cigarette blowing little rings of smoke out of the passenger window.

"It'll only take a minute," Johnny said as he bolted up the stoop and into the entryway. After ringing a buzzer he stood by a glass door and waved a curt greeting. A longish buzz at the door signaled Johnny to enter.

Climbing the stairs to the third floor, Pops' words to Johnny came to mind. He stopped midway up the stairs realizing that he should have taken the keys with him. Wondering if he should go back and get his keys, he decided against it. If Cisco were going to leave him hanging, the car would be long gone by now, he concluded. So, he continued the climb to Karen Bridges' apartment.

Karen was comfortably dressed in a dark blue terrycloth robe. It was apparent from her groggy eyes and pallid mien that Johnny had awoken her from sleep.

"It's after midnight," she stated incredulously.

"I'm sorry. This couldn't wait," Johnny responded hurriedly still trying to catch his breath from the steep climb to the third floor.

"What couldn't wait?"

Handing her the envelope Johnny explained. "This. I'm leaving town as soon as I get back to the car. That's my resignation. Would you give it to Steve for me?"

Still half asleep she shook her head in one jarring incredulous motion. "Come again?"

"Listen I don't have time to go into it. I need to leave Philly for a while. I just didn't want to not show up and have Steve calling my parents. You know what I mean," he said evasively.

"This is so, so sudden. Do you want to come in for a minute?" Karen offered politely.

"No. I just wanted to tell you that I was sorry for hurting your feelings the other day," Johnny said humbly. Handing her some money Johnny continued, "Here's the money I owe you."

Standing in her apartment doorway with the money in her hand Karen was bemused.

Johnny was about to start down the steps, but took a step up and gave Karen a passionate kiss on the lips before she could respond. Then he was gone, dancing down the steps and out of her life.

Apprehensive about exiting the building's front door, Johnny braced himself against what he might discover outside. His heart sank to near despair. Simultaneously, a look of abject disappointment crossed his face when he found the MGB missing. Initially befuddled, he stood inert on the building's front stoop trying to elucidate a potential alternative in his mind. Sighing deeply, he was about to turn back into the building when he thought he heard the familiar sound of his MGB's Stebro muffler. Searching the street, a relieved smile crossed his face. So far Pops was wrong.

44

Louie the Snake collected a disheveled Carlucci at the ungodly hour of 7 A.M. from the local Police Precinct lock up. Relishing Carlucci's screw up, Louie stifled the titillating urge to exhibit a broad sardonic smile. Instead, he presented a stoic appearance as they both slid into Louie's 1967 Silver Buick Riviera. Disregarding Carlucci's incoherent grumbling, Louie drove away slowly.

Carlucci could have been released earlier. He nixed that idea since the Gimp would have been contacted. At the time Carlucci didn't feel like hearing the man's big scurrilous mouth. Regaining a modicum of self-control, Carlucci had taken the extra time in the lock up to buttress himself against the Gimp's inevitable sarcastic tirade.

As they drove along, Carlucci's nose flared in anger. That Irish pig of a commander was going to make them all pay. He was a mother-fucking monetary mercenary, Carlucci invectively thought. Taking a deep breath, he continued. What the hell, that's the price of doing business, he shrugged. Right now, he needed time to think exactly how to correct this mess. If he tried to bullshit the Gimp and he found out, he would never live it down Carlucci assumed. Rolling the palm of his hand across his face, he tried to envision how he got blindsided by that two-bit kid. Only he knew about Johnny's involvement he surmised. One of the cops had mentioned the mustard colored car leaving the vicinity, but that was all he had heard. So, it was probably safe. No, wise, he shrewdly thought, not to even mention the kid at all to the Gimp. It would only send him off into a temperamental snit. Having decided that point, Carlucci tried to put a story together. But the pangs of hunger kept distracting him. "Let's get somethin' to eat Lou," he proposed.

Louie looked at him sideways while driving the Riviera down Oregon Avenue. "Like that?"

"Like what, asshole?"

"Like you smell."

"Like fuck you!"

"Not with your dick smelling like that," Louie replied facetiously. A smug smile floated across Louie's face as he turned south on Twenty-First Street and headed for a diner off the beaten path. He loved taunting the irascible Mad Dog Anthony. It was one of the few enjoyments in his life these days.

When the Gimp first heard of the previous night's fiasco, he thought that it was a cruel *April Fools Day* joke. The voice in his head told him otherwise.

Frantically pacing the floor of the Downtown Social Club, the Gimp kept looking at his watch for no particular reason. With the flick of his wrist he kept rolling the cue ball around the pool table cushions progressively harder. The Gimp hated to be out of the loop, out of control. Realizing his anxious behavior, the Gimp sat down at his desk and dealt a game of Solitaire. His anxiety waned momentarily until he flipped the Queen of Hearts over. Staring vacantly at the card, the Gimp's mind returned to the previous morning and the white dress. That thought furiously roiled the bile in his stomach. Angrily, he swept the cards from the desk sending them fluttering about the room.

Watching with wraithlike rigidity from the front door, Carlucci approached the Gimp at a cautionary pace.

"Where you been?" the Gimp intoned in a callous voice.

"Getting breakfast. There's no room service at that fuckin' lockup."

Taking a deep breath the Gimp regained his composure. "So what happened hot shot?" he asked sarcastically repressing the urge to scream the words at the top of his lungs.

"I underestimated the hustler," Carlucci responded evasively.

"Ain't it the story of yer life?" the Gimp said sarcastically.

Carlucci's nose widened angrily at the inference. He had prepared himself for such sarcastic barbs. Still, hearing it was an abrasion to his ego. Luckily, he was of a mind to let it go.

Louie entered the front door and distracted the both of them for a moment. Retreating to a dark corner, he straddled a chair leaning his folded arms across the back rail. He didn't want to miss the Gimp dress down Carlucci.

"What about the kid?" the Gimp prodded.

Carlucci immediately stopped to think. Was he being tested or did someone witness what went down he quickly asked himself?

"Well? What about the fuckin' kid?" the Gimp continued prodding.

"One at a time," Carlucci again evaded an outright lie. "I ain't a fuckin' octopus."

Breathing hard, the voice in his head fed him his words. "Forget the hustler for now. I want that little shit dead. Dead! Dead," the Gimp said his voice modulating on each word for emphasis. "Burying him in that pukey sports car of his. I don't care. Just do it!" Taking a deep breath to regain his composure once again, he added in a mocking tone, "And don't underestimate that little punk, will ya."

"I'll need help," Carlucci pleaded.

"Take Teti," the Gimp replied smiling deviously. The web of his psychosis expanded in his mind. Eventually the grandson of the fornicator would have to be sacrificed also. Better to keep him close at hand, the Gimp thought fiendishly. "If you need Snake take him too. Take whoever the fuck you want. Just get it done," the Gimp said with finality.

Anna stopped to visit her mother and grandparents at their store on Ninth Street below Washington Avenue. They were surprised to see her since she rarely frequented the busy thoroughfare of hucksters, peddlers and shopkeepers. This unannounced appearance made her mother, Marie, suspicious. She sensed something surreptitious afoot. Especially since Anna's normally pretentious behavior was supplanted by a display of love and respect. Her daughter acted like she was madly in love, Marie voicelessly noted. Her probing eyes darted back and forth from the task at hand to her daughter. Maybe there's something to this Johnny what's his name she thought happily.

Tucci for his part was a changed man also. Straightening out his apartment, he assembled two weeks worth of trash in a large plastic bag. He also called a local widow who supplemented her meager Social Security pension by doing laundry to pick his up. Surveying his apartment, he was proud of himself. He even curtailed his cigarette habit, but snuck a smoke while dumping his bag of trash in a nearby dumpster.

Walking north on Ninth Street through the heart of the Italian Market, Anna smiled and politely greeted different vendors and friends of her parents. Then abruptly, she turned onto Hall Street heading toward Tenth Street. Cosmo had left his door unlocked so she wouldn't be seen hovering near his apartment.

As she proceeded down Hall Street, Anna found it exhilarating to walk on the wild side like this under the noses of all these people. However, she was careful not to pretentiously strut for fear of drawing attention. Her temerity was not boundless. She knew this was a one-time deal. Tucci would either have to move away from the prying eyes behind the curtains and blinds or they would have to go to a motel. She was a risk taker, but acutely understood the statistical odds of being noticed in this tight knit neighborhood.

Those thoughts were put aside to be dealt with on another day. Today she craved Cosmo's muscular body against her bare breasts. She could smell the scent of his body and taste the sweetness of his lips. Just the thought of Cosmo hardened the tips of her nipples.

Arriving at the side door, she entered unobtrusively. Once inside, she locked the door behind her and euphorically climbed the stairs to his one room apartment above Perricone's Bakery.

It was a dangerous game she was playing.

45

Two hundred miles west of Philadelphia, Cisco and Johnny slept in the MGB in the farthest corner of a diner's parking lot just off U.S. Route 219 outside Johnstown, Pennsylvania. Arriving around 4 A.M., they decided to stop for a nap.

Johnny was slightly coiled in the partially reclined passenger seat. The driver's seat was empty. Suddenly, a passing eighteen-wheel truck engaged its air horn jarring him from a fitful sleep. Weary-eyed, Johnny yawned while attempting to stretch the kinks out of his neck. Turning slightly to his left, his jaw dropped when he realized Cisco was gone along with the keys.

Unfamiliar with his surroundings, Johnny groggily stumbled out of the car and into the diner. Once inside, he found it necessary to use the restroom, but first scanned the booths and counter for any sign of Cisco. Mindlessly, he spun around quickly looking for the restroom. Bumping into a waitress carrying water for a nearby table, a glass careened from her tray spilling the clear liquid down the front of his pants. Unfriendly and angry, the waitress stomped away leaving Johnny to examine the spillage. Standing in the aisle with a look of pathos on his pasty face, he could have been mistaken for a character in a Charlie Chaplin movie.

A giggle emanated from a nearby booth. Snapping his head in the direction of the laughter, Johnny met the bewitching hazel eyes of Sandra "Sandy" Edelman. The reflections in the mirror of the morning sunlight enveloped her in a soft ethereal aura accentuating the light robust features of her Germanic heritage. Her alluring smile immediately disarmed Johnny and captivated him.

"You look like you need a restroom," she said in a silky tone. Pointing with a delicate finger she continued, "It's over there."

Staring at her bow-shaped mouth and determined chin, he felt himself blush. Johnny stood dead in his tracks blocking the aisle while gawking at this beautiful woman. Licking his parched-dried lips ever so lightly, he was at a loss for words. Aggravated by his awkward behavior, the waitress returned taking a wide berth around him and placed a glass of water in front of Sandra.

"The restroom is right this way honey," the waitress irritably croaked ushering him toward its entrance.

With his hand on the doorknob Johnny looked behind him and caught Sandra watching him intently. Exchanging uninhibited smiles, Johnny entered the restroom.

Cisco looked at Johnny through the mirror while shaving. "What happened to you?"

"Water. It'll dry," he said still preoccupied with his encounter with the mysterious woman in the booth. The cadence of his heartbeat picked up prompting him to action. "I'll be right back." Rushing out of the restroom, Johnny nearly knocked over the same waitress forcing her to dance gingerly around this love stricken man.

Bursting forth from the diner, Johnny futilely searched the parking lot for Sandra. Catching a glimpse of a blond haired woman in a light green '67 Ford Mustang, he realized it was his mystery woman. "Yo! Yo," was all that he could shout since he didn't know her name. Rushing to the end of the driveway he stopped and watched her get on the ramp for U.S. Route 219 south toward the Pennsylvania Turnpike and disappear from view.

Carlucci mechanically circled the pool table in the Downtown Social Club. Occasionally, he would take a shot. Pool was not his game. It was Cisco's, he brooded.

Alone, he was still pensive. Thinking further, he surmised the Gimp's intention by pairing him up with Teti. This concerned him. Carlucci didn't have a qualm about popping Teti. Actually, he didn't have a qualm about killing anybody. He just didn't understand the Gimp's motives. Teti was a made man and this too bothered Carlucci. It was unproductive and unprofitable. To compound matters, the Gimp made no mention of any kind of payments for his blustering directives. This really bothered Carlucci because he didn't like to think of himself as a serial killer or someone who just does people in for the hell of it. His rationalization centered on payment for services rendered. Plumbers, carpenters even street cleaners got paid. Why not him, he reasoned.

All of this, however, was a mental diversion from what was really bothering Carlucci. Cisco had bested him since they were street toughs. It was now a matter of self-respect. Finishing the job had now become more than an obsession. It was a necessity. No matter what the Gimp wanted, killing Cisco was still his primary objective.

Imperceptibly, a well-dressed figure stood in the darkness of the doorway observing Carlucci ruminate. Stepping into the dimmed yellow light, the Old Man forced an esoteric smile. "Bank the seven ball. Corner pocket," the Old Man interjected like a pin bursting a balloon in a taciturn environment.

Carlucci looked up startled and was about to speak.

The Old Man raised a finger to silence him. "Let's take a short walk," he said motioning toward the door.

Uneasy at first, Carlucci's wide eyes now squinted questioningly. Casually, he laid the pool stick on the table. Taking a long deep breath, he followed the Old Man out of the front door.

Walking abreast of each other up Tenth Street toward Washington Avenue, they presented a contrasting image of the old and new worlds. The Old Man was dressed fastidiously in a suit and tie while Anthony appeared rumpled in his casual clothes.

"I heard about the unfortunate turn of events last evening," the Old Man murmured.

Cringing, Carlucci cast a cautionary glance in the Old Man's direction. "A minor problem. I'll take care of it," Carlucci explained emphatically in a hushed tone of voice.

"I'm sure you will. You're a persistent fellow," the Old Man commented leisurely. "But that's not why I'm here. I need you to do me a personal favor," the Old Man quizzed.

"Of course," Carlucci eagerly replied.

"Don't be so quick to jump over the cliff. Listen to me first," the Old Man instructed like a grade school teacher.

Carlucci nodded his understanding of what the Old Man counseled.

"My old friend Tony Manfredi has a delicate matter that needs attending to by someone with your, your persistence."

"I'm flattered," Carlucci said with a broad smile.

"Are you interested?"

"Of course," Carlucci eagerly responded.

"I need you to meet with him on Monday at 7 A.M. at Java Joe's, a small coffee shop, on Broome Street in New York. Can you do it?"

"Broome Street?"

"It's in Little Italy. Intersects with Mulberry. The shop is two blocks down the street from Umberto's Clam House between Mulberry and Mott Streets."

"I'll find it," Carlucci agreed.

"Good. I'll let Tony know to expect you. He's a very generous man."

Anthony smiled broadly. He knew Tony the Man's reputation well. A jovial but ferocious no nonsense type of guy, he was purported to be an original member of Murder Inc. These days he ran the biggest crime family in New York. The Old Man and Tony were rumored to be blood brothers from the wild heydays of the twenties, Carlucci recounted speechlessly.

"It should only take you a week maybe less."

Carlucci nodded agreeably. No further words needed to be spoken. Excited by this new development, he decided to take the long way back to the social club. He had a lot to think about and prepare for by Monday.

The game was afoot the Old Man thought reflectively. A hint of a smile curled upward at the corners of his tightly pursed lips as he watched Carlucci scurry toward Ninth Street. Only one more player needed to be engaged.

46

Two hundred miles away another type of game would soon be afoot—pool.

Johnstown was one of those out of the way places that pool hustlers sometimes gravitate to. Small bars dotted the landscape catering to the workers from the local steel mills trying to unwind after a hot shift in a cavernous smelter or forge. These were tough men doing a tough job and they didn't like to lose.

In the past Cisco had always made small scores in this town from pool hustlers passing through on their way to Philadelphia, New York or Boston. He preferred these neophyte gambler types to the locals. They were looking to make a reputation in the murky world of pool hustling and had a fundamental understanding of what was at stake. Some even considered it a learning experience or rite of passage. Often coming from small Midwestern towns, they stopped here trying to hone their games in preparation for the final journey eastward. Some were whizzes at straight pool. Others were more comfortable with eight-ball. The seasoned money players liked nine-ball. Many never made it farther than Johnstown.

The Furnace Bar & Grill was a seedy little bar off the Johnstown Expressway near Bedford Street. At the bar sat Roberto Hernandez, a swarthy looking fellow with a shiny robust head of tight curly black hair nursing a gin and tonic. He was dressed in a bright polyester shirt and black pants. The two-inch high heels of his beige slip on shoes gave him a lanky appearance rounding out his Spanish Harlem uniform.

The game room was adjacent to the bar and offered a direct line of vision. Strings of colored plastic beads hung from the ceiling separating the bar from the game room. A jukebox playing country western music illuminated a corner while a quarter per rack pool table occupied the strategic center. Some of the crew from the first shift of the nearby steel mill mulled about watching one of their own, Jimbo Clinton run a rack of balls. These craggy faced middle-aged men resembled overheated thermometers. Tonight they were knocking back bottles of Budweiser beer at a regular clip trying to lower their body temperatures. Unfortunately, the beer didn't help take the edge off their attitudinal demeanors. Their fiery eyes were like flares warning Roberto of impending trouble. Jimbo, a muscular man sporting a permanent scowl on his face, stared with enticing eyes daring Roberto to try his hand at sinking the ivories. Roberto resisted. He got bad vibes from that insidious bunch.

Gulping down the rest of his drink, Roberto turned to exit just as Cisco and Johnny entered the door. "Qué paso, amigo?" Cisco facetiously intoned. Cisco and Roberto had met here previously. Contemporaries of pool hustling, they were cordial, casual acquaintances. Definitely not close friends.

"Nada, cabròn," Roberto responded in a New York accent tinged with a Hispanic inflection.

Cisco grasped Roberto's extended hand sitting down next to him. Roberto returned to his seat and gestured for another drink reluctantly offering to buy a round for Cisco and Johnny. Actually, he was happy to see a friendly face.

Bemusedly, Johnny remained quiet looking askance at this puzzling exchange.

"Any action tonight?" Cisco prodded while subtly scanning the adjacent game room.

"Nah. This gang doesn't cotton to spics."

"I think it's the shirt amigo," Cisco chided. The crease in his forehead signaled his apprehension. "Maybe they don't like dagos either," Cisco whispered in a barely audible tone moving his mouth close to Roberto's ear. Unobtrusively, he felt for the small .25 caliber automatic tucked away on his person. Feeling the small gun gave Cisco a small degree of security. In reality it was a showpiece for tight situations. After taking a swig of beer, he continued, "So where ya headed after this?"

"Vegas." Roberto handed Cisco a well-worn brochure announcing a nine-ball tournament two weeks away at the Cibola Casino.

Cisco let's out a low whistle then commented, "Twenty-five hundred dollar stakes. Mucho dinero."

"Separates the men from the boys. No?"

Cisco handed back the brochure to Roberto, but he motioned for Cisco to keep it. "Keep it cabròn. Maybe I see you there and get even for the last time," he said in a burlesque tone. Looking over his shoulder at the men in the game room, he continued, "maybe not."

Coyly, Cisco responded, "Why wait. You can get even right now."

Smiling broadly Roberto waved his finger like a measured metronome. "No, No. I like the climate in Vegas better," he chortled gutturally.

Cisco understood his comment and replied, "But I ain't got twenty-five hundred."

Roberto stood shrugging his shoulders expressively while simultaneously tightening the corner of his mouth upward. "Do what you got to do. Good luck cabròn," he said benignly before exiting.

Anna and Tucci made love all afternoon and into the evening occasionally taking short naps in between. They couldn't get enough of each other.

Tucci slid out of bed as Anna slept. Peeking between the blinds reflectively, he was mesmerized by the changing late afternoon light falling across the tops of the row homes. He wondered melancholically if some unseen event would cast shadows across his life like the unseen sun hovering above the western horizon.

Anna stirred behind him. Turning around, her sculpturesque form overwhelmed his pensive reflection. Beckoning him back to bed, she laid her head on his chest listening to his heartbeat.

"What are we going to do?" he asked.

"About what?"

"Your father hates me. Your mother thinks you're marrying that Johnny guy. That's what," he said deadly serious.

"Do we have to talk about it right now?" she asked slightly irritated.

"No. But what about this guy? You just gonna dump him. Ain't your parents gonna wonder why?" Tucci said with a sensitive almost cautious probing in his voice.

Anna sat up uneasily. Hugging her legs for security she spoke with a strange detachment, "My father thinks Johnny ripped off my white dress. He flipped out." She looked knowingly at Tucci.

Tucci's demeanor changed instantly. No longer did he feel loathing toward anyone. Love had found its way into his heart. Pursing his lips tightly, he commented, "That takes care of that." Contemplating Johnny's inimical fate for a moment, Tucci stoically queried, "What about your mother?"

"She's clueless at this point."

"You gonna tell this Johnny?"

"Tell him what? That my father's angry as hell and will probably have him killed?"

Feeling a tinge of remorse, he announced, "I'll talk to him."

"And tell him what?" Anna emotionally quizzed.

"The truth."

47

Jimbo Clinton remembered Cisco from the last time he passed through town. Unlike the steel workers mulling around the perimeter of the pool table, Jimbo made his living from loan sharking, card playing and pool shooting. His clientele were these very men now watching Cisco finesse the ivories to Jimbo's disappointment. Even though Jimbo was a parasite on these men, they rooted for him because he was still one of them.

Over the years Jimbo had hustled a few *city slickers,* but was not presumptuous enough to take his game on the road. So, here he stayed weaving his spidery web of backward naiveté. Masking his true intentions of separating the prideful from their money, his little game sometimes backfired.

Tonight he baited Cisco into giving him the seven ball as a handicap against Cisco's supposed superior skill in the game of nine-ball. It was a fair handicap. Cisco knew it and he was in the process of making Jimbo acutely aware of it.

Playing for fifty dollars a game, Cisco was up by ten games. Running five consecutive racks of nine-ball Cisco was in top form. The prize money that Roberto had failed to mention—fifty thousand dollars for first place in the Cibola Casino tournament also motivated him. Thus, he was single-mindedly driven to raise the stake money.

Meanwhile, Jimbo seethed in contempt. He was driven by an entirely different motivational imperative—embarrassment. On a previous occasion Cisco had only given Jimbo the eight ball. He had lost a few dollars to Cisco, but still maintained a respectful reputation among his clientele. The rout tonight might tag him as fair game among the upstarts of this small community looking to take over his action, he thought fretfully. This he could not abide. Searching the dull tired eyes of the surrounding onlookers, Jimbo sought support for an act of duplicity should it become necessary. The subtle nods he received as he hopscotched from one familiar face to the next emboldened him. However, when Cisco got a bad roll of the cue ball, Jimbo smiled smugly thinking that perhaps drastic measures wouldn't be needed.

Circling the pool table, Cisco chalked his cue stick while mentally triangulating the trajectory of his next shot. From the placement of the cue ball and nine ball he would have to make a double bank shot off both side rails into the side pocket. There was a fifty-fifty chance of making it at best. It didn't matter. Cisco felt lucky. Tapping the side pocket to indicate the nine ball's destination, Cisco called his shot. "Nine ball side pocket," he said definitively. Then, assuming the proper stance for fluidity of motion, Cisco took aim. Silence overwhelmed the stagnant air in the smoke-filled game room. With *Zen-like* clarity of mind, Cisco smoothly followed through hitting the cue ball precisely at the point he had practiced many times before at Chickie's Pool Room. The cue ball clacked the nine ball sending it caroming between the rails and dropping into the called side pocket.

In a show of acute frustration Jimbo flitted his last fifty dollars at Cisco indignantly. "New rules mister hot shot. One game. Seven to luck. Flip for the break. Five-hundred dollars. You in?" Jimbo asked with clipped words in a taunting tone of voice.

It was Cisco's turn to hopscotch between the craggy pockmarked faces wraithlike in their gauntness that seemed to encircle him. Their message was an ominous one. There was no alternative but to play. He needed to play for time in order to make a smooth exit. With his tongue forced against the inside of his upper front teeth Cisco made a strange sucking sound as he divined his situation. "Who holds the money?" he asked pointedly.

Jimbo smiled nastily. "Don't you trust me?" he countered with eyes ablaze.

Cisco puckered his lips and emphatically repeated, "Whose gonna hold the money?"

Jimbo walked between his supportive peers collecting money. Counting out five hundred dollars he placed it under a piece of blue chalk on the edge of the pool table. Crossing his arms Jimbo stared defiantly at Cisco.

Turning his whole body to face Johnny, Cisco took out his bankroll and counted out five hundred dollars slowly as he whispered to Johnny in a hushed deadly serious tone. "Get your car kid. Keep the motor running. And make sure the door faces the front exit. Unlocked!" Taking the extra money, he stuffed it into Johnny's top pocket. "Wait until I put the money down and slowly back out. Be cool!" Cisco turned and strode to the edge of the pool table putting the money on top of Jimbo's pile.

Jimbo flipped a quarter in the air above the pool table. "Call it!"

"Heads," Cisco intoned.

The quarter landed on the pool table simultaneously. Jimbo smirked. "Tails. My break."

With a renewed feeling of confidence Jimbo eyed the diamond shaped rack of balls from table level as he slid the cue stick to and fro trying to gain momentum to break the rack and sink a ball, any ball. With a powerful thrust the balls clattered about in every direction loudly. Rolling slowly, the two ball barely dropped into the corner pocket. Relieved, Jimbo smiled nervously then triangulated on the one ball.

As everyone in the game room watched Jimbo's every move with rapt focus, Johnny furtively backed away into the barroom unnoticed. His heart pounded as the thought of imminent danger shrouded his exit.

Once outside he took a deep breath. His hands shook nervously as he hunted for the keys in his pocket. Regaining a measure of composure, he proceeded to his car.

Inside, Jimbo had easily sunk five additional balls and was now about to take the money shot on the seven ball. His hand sweated slightly. A wizened old man wearing a Pirates baseball cap threw him a towel.

Cisco's manner was oddly relaxed watching Jimbo stretch his neck trying to relax and regain his focus.

Jimbo gritted his teeth and stroked the cue ball gingerly toward the seven ball. Slowly rolling toward the corner pocket, the seven ball nipped the corner of the cushion and diverted away from the pocket. Jimbo grimaced as a low moan emanated from the onlookers.

Johnny waited outside in the car impatiently tapping his index finger against his lips. Suddenly, he grimaced stretching his right arm over to the door and unlocked it. Taking a deep breath he quickly reviewed Cisco's instructions again trying to mouth the words speechlessly from memory.

Inside, Cisco quickly sank the seven and eight balls. He now zeroed in on his money shot. Making sure that no one would contradict his call, he spelled it out exactly. "Nine ball straight into the left corner pocket," he called out touching the pocket with the tip of his cue stick. With one confident stroke Cisco sank the nine ball. A groan rolled through the room like a wooden ship battered by a series of waves.

Jimbo stared vacantly at the pool table as he held his breath angrily. Looking into the dark corner of the game room, he nodded with insidious intent to a large lurking figure.

Cautiously, Cisco slid his hand over the money as a large calloused hand encompassed his grip on it. The man standing nearly a head over Cisco was broad of chest with thick oaken like limbs for arms. Cisco was no match for the hulking figure.

With feline agility he produced his small .25 caliber automatic from his pocket pushing the toy like gun into the soft skin under the neck of the hovering giant. "Be cool. Everyone. Stay cool."

At first the menacing man grasped Cisco's hand tighter. Cisco quickly countered by pushing the gun harder into the man's neck.

Temporarily accepting defeat, the man released his grip and slowly backed away.

Cisco pocketed the money quickly then gave a diffident almost arrogant shake of his head stomping away hurriedly.

Outside, Johnny was totally focused on the door. When he saw Cisco exit, he leaned over and opened the door from inside. Before the door closed Johnny let out the clutch and sped away. "What happened?"

"I won," Cisco said tersely. Taking out a cigarette, he lit it blowing smoke out of the window like steam releasing from a boiler. Cisco looked at Johnny with a satisfying grin and ordered, "Take the turnpike west and pick up Interstate 70 just below Greensburg. And don't stop."

48

Easter Sunday, April 2, 1972

Cisco and Johnny drove throughout the night sharing turns at the wheel in order to put plenty of distance between themselves and their troubles back in Pennsylvania. South Philadelphia was over eight hundred miles behind them now and Cisco felt secure. He also felt dog-tired.

Feeling relieved, Cisco drove cautiously along Interstate 70 through Illinois oblivious to the early morning haze that preceded sunrise. We should have stopped in Effingham over a half an hour ago, he silently brooded. Groggily, he realized that Saint Louis loomed ahead.

Awakening from an uncomfortable slumber in the passenger seat, Johnny looked at Cisco blankly. "Where we at?" he asked groggily.

"We just passed Vandalia ten miles back. I guess we're about fifty miles from Saint Louis," Cisco answered in a weary voice accompanied by a growling sound from his stomach. Cisco didn't mind his hunger pangs. He was still reliving the close call in the Johnstown's bar. There were too many close calls lately, he thought. Being hustled was perfectly legit. Being robbed was an entirely different matter. It was no longer an acceptable price for doing business, he declared mentally. Right now, however, he was tired and hungry. Spotting a sign for a roadside diner ahead, he quickly turned off the ramp nearly missing the exit due to his exhaustion.

Once inside the diner, Cisco poured himself into a booth. Closing his eyes, he rested the back of his head against the window. Johnny sat down attentively perusing the menu unsure if he wanted to eat on not.

Recounting the previous evening's hair-raising episode, he was momentarily regretting his interference in Cisco's business. That feeling quickly dissipated because there was a part of him that found the ordeal exhilarating. And then there was the enchanting mystery girl in the diner at Johnstown.

Scanning the diner, he was hoping to meet her again. There were few customers and Johnny quickly reverted to fantasizing about meeting her again. Wondering how he would approach her, he hoped that it wouldn't be preceded by any buffoonery like their last encounter. Dispelling that thought, he evocatively reviewed the images swirling around that encounter.

Her light green '67 Mustang was etched in his mind almost matching her hazel eyes. Her soft countenance accented by golden hair gently twirled into a bun glowed with an aura of beauty. Although he didn't remember the exact number on her license plate, he did remember that it was from Pennsylvania. This disheartened him. Pennsylvania was two states back. Johnstown was over six hundred miles away. Plus, he was *persona non grata* there. All of these negative thoughts still did not dissuade him from thinking about her. His boyish daydreaming, however, was abruptly interrupted by the appearance of the waitress.

"What'll you boys have?" the waitress asked in a displaced Southern accent tinged with fatigue. Her eight-hour graveyard shift was soon over, so her normal exuberance was waning.

With closed eyes Cisco muttered tersely, "Coffee. Western omelet with rye toast and potatoes."

"Two eggs poached very lightly. I like the yoke liquid, whole-wheat toast and link sausage. It's not a patty is it?" Johnny inquired finicky.

"No sweetheart. It's not," she responded through lips that were barely slit open. "Coffee?"

"Decaf."

"Grits or potatoes cowboy?"

"What are grits?" Johnny asked questioningly with a confused glanced.

"Give 'em potatoes," Cisco interceded quickly hoping to end any further discourse. "This kid ain't ready for the regional cuisine."

The waitress gladly agreed and scooted away.

Cisco arched one eye open focusing it on Johnny. Pinning back his lips tightly and shaking his head in disbelief, he shut his eye again. "Where'd you learn to be so picky kid?"

"That's how I like my eggs. Is that a crime?"

"Hope you ain't disappointed," Cisco chided knowing that at a diner like this one you were lucky to get your eggs over easy without cooking the yoke.

"Speaking of crime, are we going to any more places along the way like the one last night?" Johnny inquired in a mocking tone.

"Your guess is as good as mine. This is all virgin territory from now on." Cisco sat up unexpectedly. Fluttering his eyes open, he leaned his elbows on the table while lurching forward. "Ya did good last night kid. And the night before that too. Thanks," Cisco enunciated in fragmented phrases for emphasis. It was his way of showing sincerity.

"You're welcome." After a long pause Johnny continued, "So what's the plan now?"

"The nine-ball tournament at the Cibola Casino."

"That's it?"

"That's it," Cisco repeated emphatically as the waitress delivered their food.

Effingham, Illinois was a town of forty thousand people situated on the east west bound Interstate 70. The motel that Sandy selected the previous night was clean and cheap, perfectly fitting into her meager traveling budget.

This Easter Sunday morning Sandy rose early to attend eight o'clock Mass. Searching the yellow pages the previous evening, she found a nearby Catholic Church, Saint Mary of Help just off Interstate 70. Before embarking on her journey west, she promised her mother that she would at least attend Easter Services. Wearing a dark blue silk dress with matching shoes and complimenting jewelry, Sandy gave the suave appearance of a respectable middle class professional waiting for the elevator to the top floor. Truthfully, however, Sandy would have to wait for the next elevator.

Graduating Penn State University in December of the past year, Sandy was running out of time. To the consternation of her religious parents, she couldn't wait to formally receive her degree and walk down the aisle dressed in a cap and gown. That was still a good two months away. Sandy couldn't wait that long. Although deeply disappointed, they begrudgingly accepted the fact that she was twenty-one and could make her own decisions. In an effort to mitigate this disappointment, she alluded to a job offer on the West Coast. The details she kept vague. When they tried pinning her down, she would sidestep their inquiries and pitch the *perfect opportunity* angle. However, the true story of her westward trek was kept secret from everyone including her confessor. Better to do what one had to do and ask for forgiveness later, she decided heavy-heartedly.

As she ascended the steps of the church with other believers, the steadfastness of her decision began to waver. Kneeling silently among these worshippers, she prayed for her redemption before the end of her journey.

49

Redemption was also the theme of the day in the Giampietro household for everyone except the Gimp.

Regally descending the stairs, Marie and Anna wore elegant silk dresses of varying understated flowery designs. A radiance of beauty enveloped them. Even the Gimp, dressed in his silk robe and slippers, rose in awe to admire them. Walking toward Marie to kiss her, she turned her face to allow him to kiss her on the cheek. "Don't forget Joseph my parents like to eat early," Marie said like a mother reminding a child of an appointment.

"I'll be there around one," he countered cordially repressing his uneasiness surrounding the events of the past twenty-four hours. Pained and awkward, he turned to give Anna a kiss. Her fidgetiness instinctively set off neurotic alarm bells in his head. Pulling away he tried to decipher the alarm's message to no avail. His gut feeling was that his daughter was hiding something from him.

Following her mother out the front door, Anna turned and gave her father a furtive smile.

The Gimp again sensed something amiss as he rubbed his hands back and forth in intemperate contemplation. Shrugging his shoulders in frustration, he ascended the stairs to the bathroom and started to assemble his toiletries. His gut instincts kept gnawing at him until he decided to enter Anna's room. Hunting around, the Gimp searched for something to catalyze his intuitive feelings. Slowly, he began going through Anna's drawers and closets. He smelled her clothes not knowing exactly what he expected to find. Returning to the bathroom, he stared vacantly into the mirror. Small beads of sweat began forming on his forehead. A storm raged inside his head. The voice returned, "*Joey! What you're looking for isn't in mommy's closet. It's right under your nose.*" Every second that it mesmerized him seemed like an hour.

Turning away from the mirror, he was afraid to face himself in the mirror, afraid to gaze upon the face of his departed mother. Her message was simple. His daughter was concealing something from him, something that he could not abide. He placed his hands facedown on the counter trying to get his footing in order to regain control. It worked. Breathing deeply, he again looked into the mirror and began grooming himself.

Preoccupied with his enigmatic thoughts the Gimp was exiting his house an hour later. At the same time his neighbor, Vince Ricci, was exiting his house next door.

Ricci's storm door slamming shut disrupted the Gimp's concentration. "Hey, what's going on Vince," the Gimp shouted his greeting in a cordial tone of voice across the breezeway.

"Not much. Happy Easter," Vince said trying to keep the conversation light.

Again the Gimp's natural instinct picked up something in Ricci's voice. Stopping a moment, he called to his neighbor in a friendly but commanding voice, "Vince! Could I talk to you a minute?"

Unable to evade such a request, Ricci complied laconically, "Sure."

Standing there between their houses the Gimp asked pointedly, "Have you seen anything unusual around here lately?"

"I don't know what you mean by unusual?" Ricci asked with trepidation.

"You know, anybody hanging around or anything while I'm not around."

Ricci hesitated. He religiously tried to avoid getting involved with any of the Gimp's business. It was a fine line that he walked. The Gimp had always been good to him. He never refused a favor. It was his turn to repay him Ricci rationalized. "As a matter a fact, I did notice something odd the other day," he said with a dry mouth.

"And?" the Gimp asked in a prompting tone.

Ricci licked his lips slightly with the tip of his tongue. "One of your guys exited the back of your house. I saw him before with you. Young guy, black curly hair, dressed in black. I think it was Thursday. It was none of my business. I heard some shouting so I looked out the breezeway window. This guy got into a black Chevy convertible and pulled away quietly," Ricci said in a mousy demeanor.

The Gimp's eyes narrowed with the tick above his left eye fluttering. The voice in his head chuckled in delight at being proven right once again. The Gimp mentally acknowledged the voice's oracle like ability. Returning to Ricci he continued probing, "Anything else?"

"That's it. Well, I did copy the license plate number in case you needed it," Ricci said without knowing why. After he blurted out the words, he suddenly realized their possible implication. "Don't take it the wrong way. It was only meant for your eyes. Nobody else. Just you. Know what I mean? I'll get it if you want?" Ricci offered anxiously.

The Gimp understood implicitly. His neighbors were his first line of defense for his home. He needed their loyalty. Drolly smiling, he tried to defuse Ricci's nervousness. Slapping Ricci on the shoulder in a feigned gesture of friendliness, he forced a smile and explained, "Not a problem Vince. I know who it is. Thanks."

Ricci nodded reflexively and began walking away.

The Gimp called out, "Vince."

Ricci turned warily.

"You did good. Happy Easter."

Ricci smiled and quickly strode away leaving the Gimp stewing over this newfound information.

By noontime Johnny and Cisco were rolling across a section of Interstate 70 spanning the Mississippi River with the Gateway Arch visible to the north. It was Johnny's turn to drive while Cisco rested.

On the Missouri side of the river, Johnny decided to take the interchange leading to Interstate 44 west picking up Interstate 40 at Oklahoma City. By taking this route Johnny was hoping to visit the Grand Canyon before turning north toward Las Vegas. Johnny always believed that everyone had a *Checklist of Life* enumerated with his or her hopes and dreams. His list included seeing the Grand Canyon and he wasn't going to miss this opportunity.

Rumbling along, Johnny caught glimpses of the placid countryside as the MGB emerged from the urban areas surrounding Saint Louis into a more rural setting. Suddenly, he realized Interstate 44 followed the old Route 66 of song. In an act of spontaneity, he began humming the words without opening his mouth. With South Philadelphia and Johnstown behind them, the thought of an exploratory road trip was his way of putting a pleasant spin on an unpleasant situation.

Johnny's low humming woke Cisco. Looking at him sleepily, Cisco queried, "What ya thinking about kid?"

"How more peaceful life is out here than in the city," he replied promptly.

Cisco shifted awkwardly in the passenger seat until he found a comfortable position. Continuing the conversation, he commented cynically, "I've been through hundreds of little burgs and towns kid. People ain't no different than us. They cheat and steal. They're just as jealous. Hold grudges and fight. And screw each other's wives. The men all put their pants on and wipe their asses the same way. Ain't nothin' different except the location."

A loud humming noise gradually permeated the interior of the MGB like the prelude to a chorus of a Civil War song. Johnny's ears strained to pinpoint the source of the noise while Cisco shot a cautionary glance toward Johnny. "What's that?"

"I don't know," Johnny replied in a tone of escalating concern.

Their uneasiness surged when a constant thumping developed beneath the floor of the car. Suddenly, the MGB decelerated its forward movement forcing Johnny to quickly pull to the side of the road.

"Shit," Johnny shouted invectively.

The light green '67 Ford Mustang cruised along Interstate 70 quickly approaching East Saint Louis on the Illinois side of the Mississippi River. Sandy was vacillating between stopping to visit an old school friend living in Florissant just north of Saint Louis or continuing her trek. Promising herself to visit her friend at some later time, she opted for the latter taking the interchange leading to Interstate 44 west.

Attending Easter Mass had lifted her spirits. A thin smile spreading across her angelic face gave the false impression of peacefulness. Inside of her head, however, a storm brewed. The purpose of her trip was anathema to everything that she had been taught since childhood. Her future hung in the balance, she thought convincingly. In truth, it really gnawed at her conscience.

Forcing herself to think pleasant thoughts, she idly wondered about the fellow she encountered in the Johnstown diner. Her thin smile arched upward at the ends of her lips. He was cute and intriguing in a tactless sort of way, she admitted. The twinkle in his eyes telegraphed his interest in her, she thought cheerfully. Acknowledging the reality of her fantasy, her cheerfulness subsided. It was this very type of girlish curiosity that precipitated her present predicament. "Gad," she screamed loudly banging on the steering wheel trying to dispel the ubiquitous guilt she felt lurking within every thought.

Three miles northeast of Saint Clair Missouri, Johnny and Cisco took turns examining the undercarriage of the MGB. The cause of the thumping was painfully obvious. The drive shaft was disconnected and slightly bent. Facing eastward toward the on coming traffic, Johnny leaned on the trunk of the MGB. A look of dejection was smeared across his face. With arms tightly intertwined, Johnny hung his head low. Cisco leaned on the fender of the passenger side of the car with a cigarette dangling from his lips contemplating their options. Sighing deeply, Johnny slowly looked up at the on coming traffic.

Approaching Saint Clair Missouri, Sandy was placidly viewing the quickly changing landscape. Out of the blue, she caught Johnny's eyes brighten in hope as he recognized her Mustang. Spontaneously, she pulled off onto the shoulder of the highway in a trail of dust and came to a stop a short distance ahead of the MGB. Sandy hesitated reflectively noting the strangeness of this coincidental meeting. Normally, she would not stop to assist someone on the highway. She had heard of ploys like this one. They usually ended badly. This situation was different. Maybe there was something to this chance encounter, she contemplated while quickly fluffing her hair. Satisfied with her appearance, she got out of her Mustang and strode slowly toward the disabled MGB. Dressed in jeans, sneakers and an oversized knit sweater, Sandy was the picture of wholesomeness especially with her angelic countenance.

Johnny smiled broadly. "There must be a God cause he just sent us an angel," Johnny croaked in a burlesque tone of voice. A tangible wave of excitement was apparent in his inflection.

Chugging on a cigarette irritably, Cisco rolled his eyes then gave an incredulous almost caustic shake of his head at Johnny's corny drivel.

"If it wasn't for bad luck you wouldn't have any luck at all," Sandy laughed dryly. Continuing with concern she asked, "Need a ride to a service station?"

"Yea, preferably one with a tow truck," Johnny replied dolefully.

"This is Bible Belt country. You'll be lucky to find one open today," Sandy explained informatively.

Johnny shrugged cavalierly and said, "Oh well." His exuberance at possibly spending time with this beautiful woman made his flesh tingle. He was smitten by her in every way. It didn't go unnoticed.

"By the way my name is Johnny. Johnny Cerone," he said cordially. "And this is, well this is Cisco," Johnny said enigmatically. At that moment realizing that the man traveling with him across the country was almost as mysterious as the woman standing before him.

"Hi. I'm Sandy Edelman. Now that we're done with the formalities let's get off the highway," she suggested strongly.

Cisco's hesitation at her command caused a quiver of trepidation in Sandy. She lowered her eyes and began walking back to her car.

Stamping out his cigarette in the roadside gravel Cisco wondered how this detour was going to play out.

50

In Philadelphia, churchgoers dressed in their Easter fineries were streaming out of Saint Monica's Church. Anna and her mother emerged amid the crowd. Walking down Seventeenth Street toward her car, Marie sensed a strange detachment in Anna's mien.

"Is something troubling you sweetheart?" Marie asked with a dutiful and cautious probing in her voice.

Anna pondered a moment then nodded with distraught eyes. "Johnny and I aren't going to get married," she uttered in a hush tone.

"Oh," Marie blurted. After the initial surprise wore off she inquired uneasily, "Why not?"

"It's complicated," Anna said evasively.

Stopping to look at her daughter quizzically Marie prompted, "Go on let's hear it."

A group of straggling churchgoers streamed around both sides of Marie and Anna on their way home to enjoy Easter dinner. A few gave a quick puckered smile without any ado and continued down the street. Marie returned a forced smile. Anna remained solemn.

"Mom, you don't understand," Anna pleaded. The expression on Anna's face was familiar enough.

"Do we need to go home and talk about this?" Marie asked demandingly. Marie's eyes delved pensively to the back of Anna's head. "Do we?"

Anna sighed deeply. Her whole body exuded sincerity driving home the deep feelings of her next utterance. "I'm in love with Cosmo Tucci," she said truthfully. A sense of relief burst forth from every crevice of her body.

In stark contrast to her daughter's relief, Marie languished in the throes of a dreadful stupor. Her daughter's words roiled the acid in the pit of her stomach. Unthinkingly, she uttered loudly, "Impossible!"

Gesturing incomprehensibly with her hands, Anna argued, "Why is it so impossible?"

"Because it is," was Marie's banal reply.

"That answer just won't do," Anna shot back caustically.

Marie and only Marie could give the definitive answer to Anna. No one else could speak her thoughts. Grasping for some credible reason, she made a feeble effort, but her voice was mute. In a last ditch effort to fend off the truth, Marie played the Gimp card. "Ask your father why," she said acidly.

Anna's jaws tightened. She was hoping to get her mother's approval before confronting her father. Reverting to her *little girl lost* persona, she flashed a benign smile. "Cosmo isn't like his father," Anna argued.

No he's not, thought Marie smiling deprecatingly. "Can't you talk to him?" Anna pleaded.

"No I can't," Marie said adamantly.

"He would understand if you talk to him," Anna beseeched.

"Get over this boy Anna. He's not right for you. Trust me on this."

"I can't. I love him too much," Anna declared in a sobbing singsong manner.

Empathizing with her daughter, but unable to tell her the truth, Marie embraced her daughter warmly in the middle of the street. Closing her eyes, she envisioned Cosmo's father embracing her just before he stepped into the street twenty-two years ago and out of her life forever. He left her with a part of him. It was a story she absolutely could not tell. Embracing their daughter now was like embracing him. It sustained her all of these years. Stroking her daughter's dark silky hair gently with the tips of her fingers, Marie Giampietro whispered softly, "I know sweetheart. I know."

That same afternoon a thousand miles away at the junction of Missouri State Route 47 and Interstate 44, Johnny's MGB was unhitched from a tow truck at the Saint Clair Gas Station. Luckily, the gas station was open. However, the repair bay was closed until Monday. Easter Sunday was held in special reverence in this neck of the woods.

Johnny paid the tow driver cash, and then shuffled over to Sandy and Cisco waiting nearby in the Mustang. "No mechanic around until tomorrow," Johnny said curtly.

Lyle, the gas station attendant, finished pumping gas for an out of state straggler heading west. Intrigued by the fast-talking East Coast accented duo of Johnny and Cisco, he sauntered over to quell his boredom and learn something of the world outside of rural America. "Howdy," he drawled with a friendly smile.

"Ditto," Johnny replied impassively.

"Something I can do for you fellas?" Lyle asked.

"Is there somewhere to eat?" Sandy queried.

"Only place open is down the road apiece," Lyle replied.

"Whadaya do for fun in this burg?" Cisco asked in a voice tinged with a mixture of sarcasm and skepticism.

"Poker," Lyle responded proudly.

This piqued Cisco's interest immediately. His eyes brightened with anticipation. With the barest hint of a grin, he prodded, "What kinda stakes?"

"One and two. It's a friendly game," Lyle was excited by the attention. "Care to join us? We're playin back of Jed's place tonight. Probably could use an extra hand."

Acting complacent, Cisco shrugged his shoulders while inwardly suppressing his interest. "Sure. If my partner don't mind," he mumbled staring intently at Johnny.

"Why should I mind," Johnny answered. Then struck with an idea he turned to Sandy and smiled invitingly. Hoping that she wouldn't take what he was about to say the wrong way Johnny proposed, "That is if Sandy here keeps me company. Whadaya say? Is it a date?"

Sandy's uneasiness swelled. The word date was on her list of anathemas. Yet, she did like Johnny. He made her feel special while distracting her troublesome state of mind. Besides, it was too late to get back on the road. What the hell, a diversion was in order, she silently proclaimed. "We can hang out if that's what you mean?" she asked questioningly in a trepid voice.

"That's exactly what I meant. Let's get something to eat. We don't want Cisco to miss the game," Johnny stated drolly.

Circling the Mustang to open the car door for Sandy, Johnny made a promise to be a gentleman. On that count he didn't need to worry.

51

Monday, April 3, 1972

It was 6:30 A.M. when Carlucci's car emerged from the Holland Tunnel dumping him onto Canal Street in New York's Little Italy. Making a left turn onto the Bowery and another left at Hester Street, he luckily found a parking spot right away. Carlucci didn't bother to check the conglomeration of signs on a nearby pole to see if it was legal to park there. Instead, he hastened up Elizabeth Street for two blocks slowing his gait as he turned south onto Broome Street.

He was early. That's the way he liked it. Feeling redeemed for his Friday night fiasco, he was determined to execute this request with professional expedience. This was his chance to make his reputation outside the small criminal subculture in South Philadelphia, he thought shrewdly. It was especially important with gambling on the immediate horizon for Atlantic City.

Arriving at Java Joe's ten minutes early, Carlucci found the coffee shop closed and dark inside. No one had even begun to brew the coffee. Suspiciously, he looked at his watch then slowly walked away. His alert eyes darted around hyperactively for a potential duplicitous set up.

Turning west onto Mulberry Street he swore a barrage of expletory invectives without opening his mouth for not carrying a *piece* to this meeting. Wondering why the Old Man would set him up, Carlucci unthinkingly hurried past a balding man. Built like an oak tree, dressed in a dark blue corduroy suit jacket and beige khaki pants, he was the same man who previously spied the Gimp and Bellino nearly two months ago in Atlantic City.

"Anthony Carlucci?" the balding man called out in a firm questioning New York accented voice.

Carlucci stopped dead in his tracks.

"Keep walkin' and don't turn around."

Carlucci moved forward in a normal gait. His uneasiness swelled to tsunami proportions. "Tony?" he quizzed nervously.

"Just keep walkin' and listen. I'll do the talkin'," the bald man said in a calm controlled tone. "Turn right on Spring Street. There's a pastry shop right past Mott. Go in an order a cappuccino," the bald man commanded, then disappeared down an alleyway.

Carlucci did as he was told. The virulent uneasiness coursing through his veins ebbed to mild anxiety then suddenly spiked to admiration upon realizing the necessity for such forethought. Manfredi ran a tight ship he thought impressively.

Inside the pastry shop Carlucci ordered his cappuccino. While waiting for the drink to be prepared, the bald man appeared in the shadows of the entry to a back room behind the counter. He beckoned Carlucci to the back room with his dark incisive eyes and a lopsided head motion. Carlucci gathered his drink and unobtrusively obeyed.

Navigating a rickety set of stairs to the basement, Carlucci was ushered into a bomb shelter like room. Actually, the room was built to specifications used for Department of Defense Special Access Programs. The room's design acronym *SCIF* stood for Sensitive Compartment Information Facility. It had lead-lined walls and doors impervious to the most sophisticated listening devices. The fastidiously dressed hook nosed, silver-haired man sitting behind an unpretentious desk controlled the door lock electronically.

Tony "The Man" Manfredi was purportedly the head of La Cosa Nostra. Giuseppe Vecchio and Tony Manfredi became fast friends and partners in crime during the Castellamarese War over forty years ago. Theirs was one of the few remaining friendships that survived throughout years of duplicity among the Mafia families. Each man knew his own limitations and strength. In this way they prospered and survived. The expression on the bespectacled unsmiling face of this cold-hearted killer was one of curiosity. No doubt that this slovenly man before him was of the same ilk in matters of business, Manfredi mused. This one even had the same crazy eyes like the man he was here to dispatch. Instinctively, he questioned his allegiance evaluating his every word and movement for suspicious signs. It was a paranoia that came with the territory.

In comparison Carlucci looked like a beggar in his rumpled pants and his mid-length leather jacket that was worn at the elbows. His ill-kempt mien would serve him well on this assignment. Even though he was out of his league on this particular assignment, he was genuinely excited.

Manfredi motioned with an extended hand for Carlucci to take a seat. Carlucci obligingly sat down with his cappuccino and took a sip. The bald man brought a steamy cup of the espresso drink for Manfredi. "You like your cappuccino with foam?" Manfredi said conversationally.

"I don't know. I don't usually drink it. Your man here told me to buy one so I did," Carlucci said honestly.

Manfredi smiled thinly at Carlucci's honest response. He also liked the fact that he listened and obeyed. This was a good sign.

Arching his eyes and motioning with his head for the bald man to leave, Manfredi locked the door with a push of a button sealing the room like an Egyptian Pharaoh's tomb. "You know why you are here?" he stoically asked.

"I know why. I don't know who," Carlucci respectfully replied.

"Good. Because only I should know who," Manfredi responded. Rubbing his hands over his eyes, he continued, "When you leave here shortly there will be a pastry box neatly tied with everything that you need inside of it, plus a down payment. Do not open it until you are somewhere that you cannot be observed. Do you understand?"

"Absolutely."

Producing a full-faced mug shot of the prospective victim Manfredi slid the photo gingerly toward Carlucci who was now seated. "Recognize this man?"

"Yea," Carlucci affirmed in a respectful whisper while nodding gamely.

"Good. You have one week. Contact Don Vecchio in person when you are through. One week is that clear?"

"Clear as crystal."

After a quiet moment Manfredi buzzed the door open staring intently at Carlucci.

Taking this as a dismissal Carlucci gulped the rest of his drink. Bowing respectfully, he turned and exited.

Manfredi sipped the foam from his cappuccino with a smug look on his face. Carlucci and the one that he was just sanctioned to eliminate were a disgrace to their Italian heritage, he thought. No matter, one would soon become a legendary martyr while the other probably just an obscure John Doe in some makeshift Potter's Field.

The Old Man looked at his watch as he sat patiently in the lobby of the Hotel on Eighteenth and Rittenhouse Square. Standing up in a regal manner, he straightened his black woolen topcoat and exited the hotel for the park across the street.

Rittenhouse Square is situated between Eighteenth and Nineteenth Streets facing Walnut. Conceived in 1682, it was one of the original four public squares established by William Penn's surveyor General Thomas Holmes when he laid out the city grid. In 1825 it was named for astronomer David Rittenhouse, the first director of the United States Mint. Since its inception, the benches in this small urban park were the gathering places for many informal business meetings. Fortunes were made and lost here. Life and death decided. Today was no exception.

Sid Greenberg sat patiently feeding the pigeons when the Old Man walked up and sat down on the end of the bench.

"Good morning Mister Vecchio," Sid said formally with overtones of affability.

"Good day Mister Greenberg," the Old Man responded in kind.

This little exchange was a sign of respect that each man afforded the other for close to forty-five years. Over the years, however, their business interests diverged. Meetings became less frequent. Still, they maintained the tradition of this little salutatory repartee. Each hesitated to be the first to speak. Words became like chess pieces between these two old masters. However, expediency led Sid to speak first.

"What's on your mind Mister Vecchio?"

"Business my friend, business," the Old Man replied cryptically.

"Mine or yours?" Sid retorted.

"Ours," the Old Man replied tilting his head slightly toward Sid to note his response.

Sid arched his lips tightly and sat back against the bench. "Atlantic City?"

"Partially."

Turning their upper bodies to face each other Sid tersely stated, "The Gimp."

"Bingo," the Old Man commended.

Returning to feeding the pigeons, Sid asked with special emphasis on one word, "I warned you about him from day one. So why is he *our* problem?"

"Do I need to spell it out?" the Old Man countered implying Sid's relationship with Rose Teti and her family.

"What are you proposing?"

"Las Vegas touches your sphere of influence. If he or any of his henchmen show up there, you're free to do whatever you like," the Old Man offered up hoping for some confirmation of his theory. "Manfredi concurred," he said upping the ante.

"Like Pontius Pilate I suppose?"

"That was last week's moral conundrum. This week's problem is more easily solved."

"By me of course?"

"Or your associates," the Old Man responded generically not wanting to mention Sid's son by name.

Sid chuckled sarcastically. "You're a real piece of work, Mister Vecchio. You've managed to lay your problems on my shoulders," he lamented while shrugging his head incredulously.

"Not entirely. They may not show up," the Old Man baited.

"Someone will. You can make odds on it," Sid said unthinkingly.

The barest hint of a smile creased the Old Man lips. He had his answer.

"And if by some miraculous chance this is all taken care of properly, what do I gain?"

"My undying appreciation."

Sid shot the Old Man an incredulous glance.

"And a chance to invest in some prime Atlantic City real estate transactions. Just like Monopoly," the Old Man proffered.

Sid chuckled then bobbed his head agreeably. Continuing to feed the pigeons, he commented, "We're too old for this kind of business."

"Hopefully it will be the last."

52

In a different time zone a thousand miles away Johnny, Cisco and Sandy were attending a different type of meeting. The gas station mechanic had been on the telephone for more than an hour trying to locate a new drive shaft and universal joints for the MGB. Finally locating the parts in Saint Louis, the dealership said that the parts would arrive late the next afternoon. Cisco and Johnny begrudgingly nodded their approval. It was a moot point since the only other dealership was in Chicago three hundred miles away.

Looking over the mangled parts in the repair bay, Johnny looked up at the mechanic and asked, "How much?"

The mechanic made several different obtuse facial gestures as he calculated the price then muttered, "What the heck, make it an even three hundred."

Johnny noticed Cisco shrugging apathetically then asked, "When will it be ready?"

"Afternoon day after tomorrow if everything goes okay," the mechanic responded in a placative tone. "Best I can promise."

Quietly, Sandy observed the proceedings with ambivalence by the roll up door. Even though they slept in separate rooms, she and Johnny spent most of the evening enjoying each other's company. Sitting on a swinging creaky bench in a nearby decrepit gazebo, they talked about their similar college experiences, irritating relatives and a host of other inane topics. Situated on a greenbelt surrounded by native green hawthorn and paw paw trees away from the motel proper, they interspersed their conversation by teasing one another, giggling and laughing. They were oblivious to the bench's squeaking noises and the abundant rural sounds encompassing them. Once during a quiet interlude, they came close to the spontaneous spark of a kiss. Sandy's inhibitions flared up and she immediately dampened the moment. Physical attraction was no longer the centerpiece of a relationship. She desired more. She needed more. Immediate sexual gratification was becoming commonplace. Common interests, common goals, respect and thoughtfulness had fallen by the wayside in the past, she brooded. Discontented with mere sexual gratification, she meant to resurrect those qualities necessary to sustain longevity in a relationship. So far, she detected these qualities superficially in Johnny. She needed more time to be sure. Her schedule was flexible she thought. At least for a few days she could transgress from her estimated timeline. Teetering on how to approach it, she decided to wait Johnny out.

A gentleman to a fault Johnny innately sensed Sandy's discomfort with any physical contact and proceeded accordingly. Totally captivated by this mysterious woman, Johnny busily searched the crevices of his mind for a tangible excuse to spend more time with her. Cisco's indifference to their delay gave him pause to explore this option further.

Cisco was no slouch in matters of the heart either. Of course he would never admit to it. Still realizing the warmth generated from the chemistry of his two young companions, he too teetered on a course of action. His agenda differed from Johnny's at the moment. Romantic dalliances were time consuming. For the time being, however, this new situation left some room for him to play cupid. Impishly, he decided to interject himself into the arena. After all, he thought, what was he going to do for the next two days since he broke the local gambling cartel the previous evening?

Returning to the motel room with two huge sacks of pennies on Sunday evening, he chastised himself for assuming that betting one and two meant dollars not cents. Still, every penny counted he thought watching his two lovelorn companion's eyes dance with anticipation. Manipulating a cigarette with his index and middle finger into his mouth, he lit it and took a long drag of its potent gaseous mixture.

The three stepped outside on this sunny morning. Each reflected on their situations separately. Finally, Cisco croaked in his hoarse bass like voice, "Let's go get something to eat and talk about all of this. Mind drivin' Sandy?"

Without a hint of trepidation she blurted, "Sure. Let's go. "

Johnny could hardly contain his excitement. His demeanor assumed a mellifluous quality of motion as he literally danced toward her light green Mustang. Her unfettered response was like music to his ears.

That afternoon in South Philadelphia at the Downtown Social Club, the Gimp sat alone in the dark mulling over his neighbor's observance and its possible implications. His gut reaction was to kill the son-of-a-bitch. But the voice in his head counseled patience. All in good time was its soothing message.

Changing subjects he vociferously screamed, "Where the hell is that Antny?" His angry words ricocheted off the walls of the club without finding a target in the room.

Breathing heavily, he paced the room like a caged animal seeking its freedom from some confining cell. That was the state of his mind when Teti entered the front door alone.

"Where's that little son-of-a-bitch you're suppose to be babysitting?"

Taken aback by the Gimp's unexpected vitriolic utterance, Teti noticed the tick above his left eye fluttering wildly. Stopping in his tracks, Teti stood there motionless.

"I better not fuckin' catch him with Anna," the Gimp continued vituperatively.

Aptly sensing the ramifications of the bombastic outburst, Teti sat down as calmly as he could hoping to ebb the bloodthirstiness pumping through the Gimp's veins. "What happened?" Teti whispered questioningly in a soothing tone hoping to further defuse the Gimp's rage.

Remaining speechless, the Gimp frantically stomped around the room a few more times. Out of breath he sat behind his desk and rubbed the heels of his hands in a massaging motion on his forehead above each eye. "My neighbor saw him lurking around my house the other day," the Gimp explained without giving all the gory details. "You know anything about it?"

"Of course not. I can't be with him every minute of every day. Whataya expect me to hold his dick when he pisses?" Teti sarcastically asked. Losing his patience with the Gimp's attitudinal mood swings Teti reacted instinctively.

The Gimp's balding head popped up with eyes like stilettos poised to thrust. "Is that so asshole?" he responded invectively.

"Whataya want me to do?" Teti responded in a subdued tone and expressive hand gesture.

"What I want is for you to find out if he's been fuckin' around with my daughter. That's what I wantyata do," the Gimp said firmly using his pointed finger for emphasis.

"And if he is?"

The Gimp stood up like the crown of a volcano about to explode. Slamming the flat of his hand vehemently on the desk, he forced the phone receiver from it cradle to dangle wildly from its stretched cord. "Leave that part to me," he answered in a controlled ominous tone that was the embodiment of evil incarnate.

That afternoon in a sleazy motel near the docks in Hoboken on the New Jersey side of the river, Carlucci cut the thin white string that was neatly tied around the large white pastry box.

Inside the box he found ten thousand dollars in old bills of varying denominations. Fanning the money under his nose, he smiled wickedly. Doing business in New York definitely had its upside, he thought. Putting the money aside, he also found a 9mm Uzi submachine gun equipped with a folding metal stock and two fully loaded thirty round clips. Whistling lowly, he realized Tony the Man wasn't fucking around. He wanted his man and anyone near him dead. Admiring the weapon, he held it in varying positions under the light with one hand. This was a killing machine extraordinaire, he thought. Perfect for close in and dirty work. Noticing that the serial number had been neatly filed away, he lamented the necessity of discarding such a beautiful weapon. For a moment he considered retaining the gun. He quickly nixed that idea in favor of professionalism. This was an opportunity to redeem himself and he didn't want anything to screw it up. Placing the weapon gently on a pillow like a mother cradling her baby in a crib, Carlucci removed the contents of two other packages lying on the bed.

During the earlier part of the afternoon, he rummaged through the Salvation Army and Goodwill thrift shops in nearby Jersey City. Excited by finding the right clothing to complete his planned disguise, Carlucci now removed the wrappings from a tattered full-length brown overcoat. It was perfect, he thought as he donned it. Examining the inner pocket, he slid the Uzi into it. The overcoat would be the foundation of his disguise as a professional panhandler. It was the ideal accoutrement for his scraggly hair and gritty countenance. Smiling at himself in the mirror, he modeled the overcoat from several different perspectives. The coat's unobtrusive fit and appearance blended well with the community's usual street denizens. Above all, it was unremarkable. This made him feel good about his assignment.

Taking pause he compared the present adrenaline rush that he was experiencing with his experience doing the Gimp's obtuse dirty work. There was little comparison except in the end someone was always dead, he concluded. Not wanting to lose his present momentum, he decided to deal with that issue later. Right now, things were going well.

Marie's parents' business was closed on Mondays like most of the businesses on Ninth Street. She reserved Mondays for the mundane chores associated with every household.

As she went about cleaning the house and doing the laundry her daughter's revelation on the previous day weighed heavy on her heart. Her secret was hers alone. Not even the doctor knew. Of course a blood test might prove that the Gimp wasn't Anna's father. No one else except her, however, knew who the real father was. Now this unfortunate development kindled-anew old animosities. Rather than reveal her daughter's true parentage, Marie would let the relationship take its course if the Gimp was amenable. But she knew he wasn't. She had lived long enough with the man to know that his neurotic behavior had escalated to psychosis. He was capable of anything except murdering his daughter. As long as he believed she was his daughter. If he knew she was the daughter of Carmine Tucci God knows what he would do, Marie fearfully lamented. That would never happen Marie vowed in the sanctity of her heart. She would die first.

Anna descended the staircase with a gentle smile on her face. Luckily, the Gimp and Carmine Tucci had the same physical coloring that sometimes was a dead giveaway regarding the genetics of the parents. It was the subtle traits that Marie cherished the most. The twinkle in her eye compared to the Gimp's vacant stare was the most obvious. There were other traits Marie noted, mere wistful imaginings embellished by time.

Anna noticed her mother's far away stare and wondered for a moment what she was thinking. "Mom," Anna said in a silky tone of daughterly affection.

Jolted from her fanciful mental meanderings she responded, "I'm sorry. There for a minute you reminded me of your father. In better days." Marie said threading the truth through the eye of a double entendre. She smiled enigmatically. It was the closest she could come to telling her daughter the truth.

Anna giggled. "I won't be home for dinner."

Marie pursed her lips as a look of concern spread immediately across her face finding its way into the deepest recesses of her body. "We need to talk about this sweetheart. No good can come of any of this. You know that," she said with deadly seriousness.

"I'm having dinner with Gloria and her husband. Is that okay?" Anna grumbled irritably.

"And her brother? Will he be there?"

"I don't know. It's her brother. She can invite who she likes," Anna responded forcefully.

"This is not a game young lady," Marie warned impassionedly.

"I know that."

"Don't fool yourself. You're playing with fire here," Marie pleaded.

"It's my life."

"No. It's Cosmo's."

Mother and daughter stared at one another in wide-eyed defiance. One was acting on pure emotion while the other emoted from past experience.

Anna was the first to disengage eye contact. "I gotta go," she said with finality and left.

In her heart she felt the stirrings of the unremitting agony that her daughter would soon experience. For over twenty years she was able to suppress the flow of her emotions to a manageable level of agonizing remorse. Today the dam burst. This perpetual ache in her heart exploded into a torrent of pain.

53

Tuesday, April 4, 1972

Fifteen miles down the road from Saint Clair Missouri are the Ozark Caverns. They were opened as a tourist attraction in 1935 along the historic Route 66 before the onslaught of the interstate highway system.

Local Indians over the centuries took refuge in the caverns as shelter. However, one of the most famous uses of the caverns was as a hideout for Jesse James and his gang after their numerous train and bank robberies. Its multi-levels and over twenty-five miles of passages were ideal for bandits needing to escape detection.

That was the gist of the billboard advertising that caught Sandy's attention. Sandy had teased Johnny about his accent. Taking it one-step further, she chided him about being on the lam. Johnny took the teasing in good measure although he was a bit edgy thinking that he may have slipped and mentioned his real reason for heading west. His paranoia dissipated when she turned to him with a coquettish smile.

"Let's go there," Sandy said giggling while pointing to the billboard. "You can get some pointers from a professional."

Unable to say no to this alluring woman, Johnny acceded. Besides, he thought it was the perfect excuse to spend time together in a different environment.

After dinner the previous evening, they again sat in the gazebo swinging to and fro establishing the nuances of a budding romance. That was Johnny's perspective of their time together. Sandy labeled it a pleasant diversion, but was unmistakably enamored with Johnny. It was at best a feeble effort at fooling herself. Today, Johnny was going to up the ante and ask some probing questions. This would be the perfect milieu.

As visitors from all walks of life mulled around waiting for the next scheduled guided tour, the inscription on a bronze plaque engrossed Johnny and Sandy. They finished reading the plaque honoring an outlaw reunion held in 1949 on James' 102nd birthday by a man claiming to be Jesse James.

Looking incredulously at each other and chortling they rejoined the other visitors. Nothing more needed to be said about outlaws on the run.

"This place is different," Sandy said in wonderment. "It's like time doesn't exist."

"Wouldn't it be nice if this was just a spontaneous universe. No constraints. No expectations," Johnny replied with a theatrical flair.

"Maybe it is and we just don't know it. Maybe that's what gets us all into trouble," Sandy said reflectively in a hush tone.

Clutching the perfect opportunity to take his curiosity to its next level Johnny said cautiously, "Is that why you're heading west?"

Tilting her head toward him questioningly, she responded, "Do you think I'm in trouble?"

Shrugging his shoulders, Johnny defensively replied, "I guess it depends on your perspective."

Their conversation ended on that note because at that moment the ranger moved through the group of visitors to the front of the line and announced, "Listen up folks. The tour is about to begin. Let's stay close together. We don't want to lose anybody in the caverns." Finished with his spiel he led the group into the caverns.

Inside the caverns, they wound their way along the well-lighted walkways amid stalactites, fossil and limestone deposits. Noticing a roped off path to the side, Johnny beckoned Sandy silently with animated eye movements combined with a rapidly flexing index finger. Sandy instinctively hesitated then gave in to her girlish curiosity.

Like characters out of Mark Twain's *Huckleberry Finn,* they traversed the rope and explored the dimly lit pathway. Speaking in a hushed toned voice, Johnny asked, "Do you think that Jesse James really lived under an assumed name until he was a hundred an' three?"

"Maybe. But I think it's probably a legend," Sandy replied with a puzzling look on her face.

Johnny remained unusually silent. They finally came upon an area of ultraviolet rocks. Sandy arrived after Johnny. The dim lights dancing off the rocks accentuated Sandy's beauty in an exotic way. Johnny immediately noticed. Vulnerable at that moment Sandy and Johnny's eyes embraced. Arching his head forward, Johnny gently kissed Sandy on the lips in such a way as to preserve the moment forever. Extending his arms to wrap them around her, the moment was broken by the echoing voices of the visitors who appeared to be fast approaching.

Reddened with embarrassment, Sandy gently pushed Johnny back, "We better go."

An awkward wall of silence separated Johnny and Sandy as they drove back to the motel in Saint Clair. Johnny's head kept rotating back and forth toward Sandy with varying facial expressions indicative of high anxiety. Enmeshed in some profound state of contemplation, Sandy just kept her eyes on the road.

Pulling into the motel parking lot in front of Johnny and Cisco's room, Sandy kept her motor running. Turning toward him with a stoic face, she stated, "I'm checking out. I've got to get going."

"You know, I'm sorry about back there," Johnny said penitently.

"I'm not."

"Then what's the rush?"

"Listen Johnny, you and me. It's the wrong time and the wrong place," Sandy lamented with forlorn eyes.

"Then let's find the right time and the right place," Johnny pleaded vigorously.

"We had fun. You're a really nice guy. But that's it. Really," Sandy explained firmly.

"I don't believe it. There's more to this story," Johnny said incredulously.

Sandy leaned across the bucket seat and kissed Johnny dearly on the cheek. "Now please. Let me go?"

"But where are you going? I'll come with you. I have no particular place to go. Really," Johnny said knowing that he was grasping at straws.

"We're all running from something Johnny Cerone. You. Me. Your friend. If it's meant to be we'll run into each other again."

"It may be too late."

"Then it wasn't meant to be. Now please let me go?" Sandy pleaded loudly and then smiling archly at him.

His determined eyes imprinted Sandy's countenance on his brain like a cattleman's branding iron. Reluctantly, Johnny exited the car. He banged on the passenger door gently as he stepped back. Standing there like a whimpering puppy dog, he watched Sandy slowly pull the Mustang away.

Inside the motel room, Cisco was practicing dealing seconds from a deck of cards in front of a mirror. Johnny entered dejectedly.

Without missing a beat Cisco looked up with a cigarette dangling from his mouth, "Ended badly, huh?"

"I don't want to talk about it," Johnny said emotionally.

"Listen kid, where we're goin' there's thousands of 'em in all shapes and sizes. I'm sure you'll find one to your liking," he said patronizingly.

"That's the problem. I found one to my liking."

Cisco fell silent as he took a drag on his cigarette. Meanwhile, Johnny began to change his clothes and noticed the bags of pennies. "What have you been robbing, piggy banks?" Johnny asked sarcastically.

"Don't knock those pennies kid. Someday you're gonna be glad we got 'em," Cisco said in a lecturing tone of voice.

"Spare me the *when you're on the road* bullshit. Please," Johnny responded flippantly.

"Maybe you got a better idea. Like sticking up convenience stores?" Cisco shot back.

"I don't need you to survive."

"Good. Then you can pay for your car repair tomorrow, hot shot. I'll take the bus."

Johnny jumped up from the edge of the bed to face Cisco eye to eye without realizing the source of his anger. "If it wasn't for me you'd be dead in the trunk of some car right now," Johnny snapped acidly.

It was Cisco's turn to stand up. They stared each other in the eyes as if they were plumbing the depths of their own souls. Cisco could see that Johnny was hurting inside. He had been there himself. The boy was in love for the first time and didn't know how to deal with the rejection. Handling the situation in his unique way, Cisco said queerly, "And for that I thank you. Now I gotta take a shit, if you're finished." It was Cisco's slinky method of defusing a volatile situation.

"Thanks for sharing that with me," Johnny replied grumpily not knowing whether to laugh or cry.

54

Friday, April 7, 1972

Friday's are particularly busy days on Ninth Street in the Italian Market of South Philadelphia. This is the day that most of the local women do their shopping in order to avoid the hustle and bustle of the casual shoppers and tourists on Saturday. The older women especially liked to haggle over the prices. Occasionally, they managed to squeeze an extra piece of fruit or vegetable from the various hucksters manning the stands along the street. With fifty-five gallon drums ablaze nearby, the scene was a step back in time that gave the neighborhood its unique historic flavor.

Friday was also collection day for the loan sharks, bookmakers and other nefarious types associated with the downtown criminal organization of the Old Man. Usually, the Gimp liked to make the rounds on the first Friday of each month to remind everyone of his ominous presence within the community. Since last Friday was a religious holiday, the usual hustle and bustle had been down to a trickle. Opting to make his rounds today rather than appear sacrilegious, the Gimp always wore his gold cornicelli on a gold chain around his neck. Since it was a gift from the Old Man, the Gimp felt that it had a special meaning. To those who still believed, it was an amulet protecting him from the evil eye. In

– 244 –

private he pooh-poohed such beliefs. However, on some subconscious level he adhered to the old traditional mores and would not entirely discount them.

Heading north on the west side of Ninth Street on his daily pilgrimage to The Pasticceria, he noticed Teti heading south across the street. Stopping to greet one of the street vendors just below Christian Street, the Gimp looked down the street further and noticed his daughter Anna having coffee with Tucci. His blood began to boil, but the voice in his head quelled his roiling blood by counseling patience, *"Joey, don't let people know what you're thinking."* Verify was the mitigating message, the silky voice whispered in a soothing tone.

Tightening his lips while still focusing on his daughter's tête-à-tête with Tucci, the Gimp lightly patted the vendor's back and said distantly, "Nice seeing ya again Ralphy."

Then inconspicuously, he stepped back into the abundant shadows along the busy byway to coyly observe the couple.

With a coquettish tilt of her head, Anna puckered her lips blowing a kiss aimed at a skittish Tucci. Moments later, he stood up throwing some money down onto the table. Walking away briskly, he looked south at the oncoming traffic heading up Ninth Street then sprinted across the street turning down Hall Street.

The Gimp returned his focus to his daughter. Was this some childish teasing from their youth he thought, trying to make some sense of what he was observing? His heart pounded with the force of a sledgehammer when Anna followed Tucci's lead almost skipping childlike down Hall Street.

Following his love-struck daughter from across the street, the Gimp unobtrusively followed her movement then stopped some distance away to watch Tucci turn into a side door followed by his daughter seconds later. He clenched his teeth with the force of a steam turbine in an effort to retain some semblance of self-control. The voice in his head helped in this effort as a mellifluous nursery rhyme that his mother hummed to him as a youth began playing inside his head.

Circling the block to view the love nest from a different angle, the Gimp decided to have a bite to eat at The Luncheonette directly across the street from Tucci's apartment. Finding a seat in the window with a view of the apartment he could watch their coming or goings. The waitress noticed his somber reflection and brought him his usual cup of coffee. She hovered nearby waiting for him to order. With his eyes focused above the bakery across the street, the Gimp vacantly gestured for her to leave. He had lost his appetite.

Teti sat at the bar of his mother's establishment eating a plate of calamari in tomato sauce and considering his options. He didn't need to follow Tucci or Anna anymore today. Observing them outside having coffee together was enough proof for him. It wasn't a stretch to make the connection since he knew beforehand about Tucci's obsession.

Breaking a piece of Italian bread and dabbing it in the tomato sauce he was toying with ways to get around breaking the news to the Gimp. It didn't take a genius to know what the outcome would be, he brooded. Tucci either was a total idiot or blindly in love. Teti sighed deeply knowing that it didn't matter.

Teti chewed the tomato sauce-drenched piece of bread slowly while he searched his mind for a redeeming solution. He toyed with the idea of lying, but knew that was not an option. The idiot was right there on Ninth Street with the Gimp's daughter. Did he think it would go unnoticed, Teti asked himself knowing the answer beforehand. Poking several ringlets of calamari with his fork he held them before his eyes and decided at that moment it was every man for himself. Biting into the chewy delicacy he thought mockingly that Tucci would have to reap what he sowed. Hope she was worth it.

Driving into the setting sun along Interstate 40 just west of Clines Corner, New Mexico, Cisco noticed an old weathered Route 66 sign. They had driven straight through after the MGB was repaired two days ago stopping at intervals for short breaks and food. Johnny was fast asleep in the passenger seat. Cisco was glad. He didn't want to make small talk with this lovelorn kid, he thought grumpily. Silence was like a healing balm to him. It cleared the extraneous baggage that cluttered the mind. His main concern right now was raising the stake money for the nine-ball tournament at the Cibola Casino. This thought consumed his attention for the next twenty-five miles.

Approaching Moriarty, New Mexico, a light green '67 Mustang rolled slowly onto the highway. Automatically changing to the passing lane Cisco didn't recognize Sandy's car at first. As he drove closer, his eyes widened. Quickly, he glanced over to make sure Johnny was still asleep. Hoping to put some distance between them, Cisco took his foot off the gas pedal. It worked. Cisco was relieved. They were getting close to their final destination and he didn't want to deal with any more complications especially those that could not easily be resolved. Further down the road the sun was setting just above the horizon. As Cisco passed Albuquerque on the right, the setting sun danced off the reddish landscape onto the colorful hot air balloons adrift to the north.

Awaking from his slumber, Johnny immediately noticed the beauty of the moment. Staring wide-eyed in awe he exclaimed, "Wow!" Continuing to watch the plethora of balloons as they passed, Johnny idly wondered out loud, "I wonder where Sandy is right now?"

Cisco kept his eyes straight ahead and lit a cigarette using the car's cigarette lighter. His silence was deafening.

It was 9 P.M. in New York City. On the corner of Mulberry and Spring Streets in the heart of New York's Little Italy section a man in a tattered brown overcoat wearing cracked sunglasses and a sign asking for help stood staunchly against a street post. Carlucci had been there only an hour and had already been gifted over ten dollars by well-heeled passers by on their way to dinner at the multitude of restaurants and bistros that populated this infamous section of the city.

As the bald man from three days ago approached him in a long black cashmere topcoat, Carlucci slowly pushed his hands down to his side in an unthreatening motion just like he had practiced all week in front of a mirror. He was in the big leagues now where duplicity was commonplace.

Handing Carlucci a five-dollar bill the bald man stoically said, "Your man will be here shortly. He'll be having dinner across the street." Smiling broadly he strode away and blended into a nearby crowd of people out on the town for the night.

Heeding the bald man's instructions, Carlucci casually crossed the street and took up position in front of the appropriate restaurant. Once again practicing his unthreatening movement, he felt an adrenaline rush like an actor performing in a title role on Broadway for the first time.

55

As it happened, Carlucci did not have to wait long for his man to arrive.

Johnny Bellino's appetite to become head of the Manfredi Crime family was long suspected. Unsatisfied and impatient with the progress of his ascent in the family, he began to disregard the normal chain of command. Discretion was not one of Bellino's defining characteristics. Hubris was.

Manfredi gave Bellino enough leeway to hang himself. Meeting Joey Giampietro from South Philadelphia in Atlantic City in February alerted Manfredi to imminent danger ahead. Immediately, he contacted his long time associate and friend Giuseppe Vecchio, the head of the Philadelphia Family.

Atlantic City was traditionally Philadelphia turf as defined by the loose arrangement initiated when the Commission was established by Lucky Luciano and the other high lords of crime after the Castellamarese War over forty years ago. With Atlantic City gambling certain to come to fruition in New Jersey due to the backroom intersession of Manfredi and Vecchio, the two old friends felt that they deserved the lion's share of the bounty. The Gaming Commission hopefully would miss the obvious and focus heavily on regulating the gaming tables. However, the wily Vecchio and Manfredi came up with a plan to make their money the old fashion way—earn it legitimately.

Blatantly flamboyant and arrogant, Johnny Bellino and Joey Giampietro's pushed the envelope of sanity to its limits. Caution and reasonableness never factored into either man's thought processes. Their ambitions only served to complicate matters. Perhaps even derail the impending measures in the New Jersey Assembly.

Using Carlucci was a masterstroke of planning. Gambling that he wasn't in the Gimp's confidence yet, the two old friends had won the bet. Once the snare was set, they could sit back with clean hands. Their deadly triangulation to eradicate the conspiracy was assured. All that was needed now was patience.

Carlucci knew nothing of the machinations swirling about him. With veritable horse blinders on his head, Carlucci's vision of the future was limited to the black Lincoln Continental pulling up to the curb a few feet away.

At a moment like this the synapses of any other man's mind would have been helter-skelter. Carlucci was not like any other man. He craved moments like this one. The Cisco fiasco was an aberration. It happened. There would be no repeat tonight, he assured himself. He had enough firepower to take out the entire entourage if necessary.

Behind the cracked sunglasses, Carlucci's unseen eyes were riveted on the rear window of the black Lincoln Continental. The craggy face in the picture Manfredi had shown him turned to confront him with a dubious look. Bellino's eyes were red and glassy as a result of consuming a full bottle of Ruffino Classico Chianti at a previous rendezvous.

Carlucci recognized his man. Callously frozen in place, he lowered the makeshift cardboard sign slightly to cut his hands travel distance to the concealed submachine gun. Timing was everything. A single second could make the difference between success and failure. He knew that.

The wine deadened Bellino's natural instincts and he impetuously swung open the heavy rear door of the black Lincoln Continental extending his leg to exit.

Carlucci slowly pushed his hands down to his side unnoticed and in one supple movement was at the car door. Kicking Bellino back inside with the heel of his foot Carlucci fired the Uzi with a relentless detachment painting the windows of the vehicle in crimson red splotches.

Quickly striding away, Carlucci slipped the Uzi back into the inside pocket of his soon to be discarded tattered overcoat and disappeared into the shadows of Spring Street.

Thirty minutes later, Carlucci paid the toll on the New Jersey side of the Lincoln Tunnel. Proceeding south through Union City he headed for the outskirts of Bayonne Park on Newark Bay. Cautiously, he exited the car and threw the Uzi and the second unused clip into the murky waters of the bay. Changing into newly purchased clothing in the darkness of a grove of tall bushes, he bagged up the panhandler disguise dumping it in a nearby trash receptacle. Back tracking to Interstate 78, he picked up the New Jersey Turnpike South heading back to Philadelphia. He shook his head in disbelief when he realized that it was only a little after 10 P.M. With a deep prideful sigh, Carlucci settled into the driver seat maintaining the speed limit while ruminating over the events of the night. Tonight, he thought dutifully, he had graduated from the Gimp's bowl washer to a man of respect. Settling the score with Cisco would come next. His body tingled at the satisfaction of eliminating Cisco. After that, the Gimp could go to hell for all that he cared. Smiling imperiously, he smugly thought, who needed that lunatic.

While Carlucci was congratulating himself on the night's accomplishment and the rewards he might garner from its success, the Gimp had something more troubling on his mind—Cosmo Tucci. With his feet kicked up on the desk, the Gimp impassively shot darts at the nearby dartboard. A half-empty bottle of Jack Daniel's was near his feet. He rarely drank hard liquor. Tonight, however, he needed something to steady his roiling anger lest he do something impetuous. Drinking half the bottle over the last several hours, it had the dual effect of muting the voice in his head and stemming the anger in his veins. It was the calm before the storm.

Teti strolled through the front door deciding that nothing he could say or do would forestall the inevitable. He felt like his soul was spiraling around a toilet bowl about to be vacuumed into oblivion. Cautioning Tucci had solved nothing. There was no other recourse. He came here tonight intending to give up his partner.

"You seen Antny?" the Gimp inquired throwing his last dart.

"Nope. Maybe he's sleeping with the fishes," Teti coyly retorted with a tinge of flippancy.

"Don't be a wise ass. That movie shit is a lotta wistful crap," the Gimp said gruffly. Noticing Teti's uneasy demeanor he continued, "So, what are you just standing there for? Whataya got?"

"Ya asked me to follow Tucci."

"So what?"

"So, I thought you wanted to know."

"I already know."

Snapping his feet off the desk, he nearly knocked the bottle of Jack Daniel's to the floor. The booze had loosened his lips as he rambled on barely coherent.

"That frickin' Antny is probably hiding in some shithole embarrassed about his screw up last Friday."

"That don't sound like Anthony," Teti added conversationally.

The Gimp stretched his torso from side to side while seated. "Damn right it don't. But that hustler got the best of him."

This piqued Teti's interest immediately. "How?"

"You can ask Antny when you see 'em," the Gimp suggested sarcastically. Feeling the buzz of the alcohol receding he took a swig of Jack Daniel's. As he removed the bottle from his lips, the Gimp's nose widened in anger. Standing before him, he envisioned Teti's grandfather smirking at him. Looking contemptuously at Teti for a long moment that seemed like an hour, the Gimp's face contorted like an ogre on the parapets hovering above Notre Dame Cathedral in Paris.

The Gimp's contemptuous stare chilled Teti's bones. The extent of the man's malevolence surfaced in his ominously hollow eyes. At that moment Teti was glad that the Gimp was in an alcoholic stupor.

Falling back into his chair he took another swill from the bottle trying to suppress his hateful memory from rearing its ugly head. Instead, the faces blurred then slowly transformed as Anna and Tucci.

Teti exited unnoticed. He had witnessed enough. As the door quietly closed, the Gimp lowered the bottle from his lips and threw it wildly at the door. Slumping forward in the chair, his head fell into his crossed arms. After a deep sigh he began sobbing woefully.

56

It was 2 A.M. and the Downtown Bar & Grill had just closed. Rose was counting the evening's receipts when her son let himself into the bar with his key. Glancing at him, she immediately noticed his morose demeanor. His eyes formed a conduit to a maelstrom of questions churning inside his head. Concerned, she stopped counting the night's receipts and asked with motherly concern, "Is everything all right?"

Teti shrugged negatively. Without uttering a word he just slipped onto a bar stool and faced his mother. "I think it's time you and I had a long talk."

"About what?"

"Everything," Teti replied in a voice packed with emotion.

"That'll be a very long conversation," Rose advised trying to forestall him.

"Cut the crap Mom. I want the truth. Now!" Teti demanded, and then after a moment, "You owe me the truth."

Rose flushed lightly. The questioning glare in his eyes was now mirrored in his face. She gave him a sour look suspecting the questions that were on his mind. Still, Rose hesitated. It wasn't in her nature to be an iconoclast.

"Well?" Teti asked calmly.

Sighing deeply, Rose jiggled her slightly clenched teeth nervously. "This is a story I've told no one. Many know fragments of it, but no one knows how they connect together." Looking him squarely in the eye she said somberly, "You may not like what you are about to hear."

"It can't be worse than what I saw tonight."

Rose looked at her son quizzically for a long moment then continued. "First off Armand Francesco is your father."

"I figured that much out myself," Teti replied with a tinge of arrogance in his voice. "Why didn't you two get married? What's the big secret?"

"There was bad blood between your grandfather and Armand's father. Your grandfather wasn't exactly the man you thought he was. He was a lecherous one without a shred of decency." Rose exhaled heavily. Although she was painfully aware of her father's shortcomings, Rose was uncomfortable speaking of him this way preferring to remember him as a kind and doting father. "He was a cad, cheating on your grandmother every chance he got. Armand's Aunt Cara had a raucous affair with him and got pregnant. Your grandfather told her it was her problem. It got ugly. He gave her some money to get an abortion. There were complications and she died. By then your father and I were in love. Do I need to go on?"

"Does the Gimp know I'm Cisco's son?" Teti asked poignantly.

"I don't think so. The Old Man helped keep it a secret. He even fixed the records for my father's sake. He was afraid of trouble with Armand's father. Besides, I was seeing other men at the time. But I only made love to one." Rose tilted her head slightly looking deep into her son's questioning eyes.

Teti's sullen demeanor brightened a little. Curiosity now animated his face. "What about the Gimp? Why does he hate our family?" Teti quizzed.

"It's quite possible that Joey Giampietro is your uncle, my half brother," Rose replied deceptively.

Teti's mouth was agape in shock.

"My father denied it up to his dying day, but he wasn't the kind of man to adopt an orphan from the kindness of his heart," Rose added misleadingly. It wasn't the whole truth.

"Crap," Teti exclaimed.

"You wanted the truth. Should I stop?"

Teti shook his head negatively. "Might as well get it all on the table."

Rose turned and grabbed a bottle of eighteen-year-old blend Chivas Regal from the top shelf above the bar. After pouring two large iced-filled glasses of the scotch she drained one of the glasses then quickly refilled it. Sliding the other glass across to her son, Rose then leaned against the bar on her elbows gazing into the refilled glass of scotch with her one hand as if looking into a crystal ball.

Teti took a gulp of the mixture and stared at his mother in astonishment. "Go on."

"I use to feel sorry for Joey. His mom was a first class whore. The Leonetti's gunned down his dad along with Lou Arena, the mob boss back in the thirties. After his father died she abandoned him. Out of respect for Joey's dad, the Old Man asked your grandfather to take care of the boy. So, when he ended up at our house people began to talk. Somehow, my father convinced my mother. She accepted the situation. There was no other choice. Joey was clueless. Probably still is. You grandfather always treated him rotten. But when my father found out he had a crush on me well, he beat him so bad that he limped. That's when he got his nickname. It goes hand-in-glove with his last name."

"How'd grandpa find out he had a crush on you?"

Rose rotated her tightly pursed lips around her face uneasily before replying. "Your grandfather caught me laughing at him standing in front of me with an erection."

"That don't mean he had a crush on you."

"You would've had to been there. Besides, there were other things. If I could take that one moment back I would. In a way I kinda feel sorry for 'em. The rest you can put together yourself. I'm tired," Rose said exhaustively.

Teti drank the rest of the scotch in one gulp. "Uncle Joey," Teti mumbled incoherently. A spasm of ironic laughter surged through his being. What a fucked up family, he thought. Putting the glass on the bar he leaned over and kissed his mother on the head.

Rose smiled sweetly. She told the truth to her son except for her father's deathbed confession. Knowing that piece of truth about the South Philadelphia gangland mosaic could be dangerous if not deadly. It was an item better saved for some future date.

Baring his soul as he laid dying, Sal Teti confessed to Rose the truth—Joseph Giampietro was really the Old Man's illegitimate son.

Shortly after 2 A.M. Carlucci entered the side door to his apartment off of Annin Street. Noticing a light under the adjoining door to the social club struck him as peculiar. The room was rarely used this late at night except for a monthly poker game. Listening for voices through the door, he heard none. He debated whether to go upstairs and retrieve his gun or just walk in on whoever was there.

Feeling invincible this night, Carlucci casually entered the door to the club. Sprawled out on the couch in the far side of the room was the Gimp, a disheveled mass in an alcoholic state of slumber. With quietly measured steps, Carlucci strode over to view him close up. In the middle of the floor was an empty bottle of Jack Daniel's. Nearly falling off the couch while rolling onto his side, the Gimp mumbled incoherently. Now hovering over him, Carlucci glared down at the Gimp. How easy it would be to dispose of him at this moment. Vulnerable and asleep, it would be tantamount to a mercy killing he thought, dastardly giving it a second consideration. The timing wasn't right, however. Plus, it would have to be sanctioned. Pushing that thought to the back of his mind, he earmarked it for another day and time. Oh, yes, Carlucci silently crowed, the Gimp's day was coming. Oh yeah, it was coming he continued in silent observance. On that note, he reminded himself that he needed him right in order to settle a personal score—a festering malignancy on his reputation. Cisco had bested him. The demeaning affair was not easily forgiven. His reputation was on the line at least as far as his own self-respect was measured. No, he needed to wipe the plate clean with Cisco. The pathetic lunatic lying below him could take care of that snot-nosed kid.

Walking back toward the side door, Carlucci flipped off the light locking the door behind him. As he slowly climbed the steps the titillating specifics of the evening's event replayed in his mind over and over again.

57

After driving for nearly thirty hours straight Johnny picked up U.S. Highway 180 in Flagstaff Arizona heading north toward the Grand Canyon.

Driving through the San Francisco Mountains, the first light of dawn outlined the ridges and peaks. A chill gave rise to goose bumps on Johnny's arms then worked its way around the rest of his lightly clad torso. If they were lucky, he thought they might get to see Sunrise paint its unique introduction to this day on the walls of the Grand Canyon.

Semi-consciously awake in the passenger seat, Cisco stirred. Huddling his body tighter, he sought to ward off the same morning chill that overcame Johnny. Personally, he was ambivalent about seeing one of the natural wonders of the world. This feeling derived from the fact that time was running out to raise the stake money for the nine-ball tournament at the Cibola Casino. The thought of the stake money electrified Cisco's mind automatically opening his eyes. That was his main priority at the moment not sightseeing. Knowing that it was important to Johnny, however, Cisco relented.

"How much farther?" Cisco inquired groggily.

"Less than an hour. We may get to see Sunrise over the canyon," Johnny replied enthusiastically.

"I'll make special note of it," Cisco said sarcastically while squirming around still trying to get warm.

An hour later, Sandy Edelman was making special note of the imminent Sunrise. Perched on a rock ledge shrouded in a warm multicolored short coat wearing dungarees and hiking boots, she embraced her folded knees. Although she had left Saint Clair two days ahead of Johnny, she did not have the energy or stamina to drive for long stretches. Therefore, she planned her stops with sightseeing in mind. The Grand Canyon at Sunrise was on the top of her list.

Sitting there waiting for the Sunrise, Sandy recounted her encounter with Johnny. She lamented not telling him where she was heading. Unfortunately, that would've led to the circumstances of her plight she melancholically thought. She wasn't willing to do that just yet.

Her mood changed immediately when the glowing amber ball broke the jagged surface above the horizon with glowing brilliance. It warmed the hearts and bodies of all who were watching. Etched in her mind's eye, she hoped the brilliance of the moment would help sustain her during her coming ordeal. More cheerful and confident, she stood up and breathed deeply the clean crisp air surrounding her.

Johnny and Cisco experienced the same Sunrise. Unlike Sandy, its sustenance was nothing they deemed necessary in the ensuing days. Instead, they gazed at it with a sense of awe. Cisco wouldn't admit it, yet he was glad that he gave into Johnny's whim for this unique experience. Thinking longingly about Rose, he wished she could see this with him. Life was quickly passing them by he mused. He promised himself to enjoy what was left once his situation was resolved.

Like Cisco, Johnny felt a longing in his heart. He reprimanded himself for letting Sandy leave without some way of contacting her. Watching the rising sun spread its light across the vastness of the Grand Canyon, Johnny felt depressed when he realized that trying to find her was like trying to find a needle in the gorge below. Striding back toward his car he perked up. In the distance he thought he saw Sandy's Mustang approaching the road to the exit.

"Johnny," Cisco called out from a distance.

Reflexively, Johnny turned away. By the time he turned back there was nothing there. In a frenzied state he scanned the horizon in a one hundred eighty degree arc, but came up empty handed. Shrugging it off to wishful thinking, Johnny returned to where he had left Cisco.

While heading south on Arizona State Route 64 to pick up Interstate 40 west, Sandy looked at the clock on the dashboard of her car and figured that she could make her final destination in around four or five hours. Releasing a sigh of relief, the tension of travel slowly dissipated from her body. Soon, a decision-laden burden would replace it. Her moment of truth was fast approaching. Las Vegas was only a little over two hundred miles away.

Dragging himself to his feet and stumbling around the room, the Gimp felt like he had been run over by a Mack truck. The room reeked of stale tobacco and whiskey causing a slight nauseating turbulence in the center of his head just above his nose.

This was immediately trumped by a dry cottony taste in his mouth. Thirsty, he searched a nearby refrigerator for water. He found a one-gallon water jug. Gulping down the remaining contents, the cold liquid splashed sloppily from his gurgling mouth onto his shirt. Finished, he shook his head like a wet dog after a bath. Feeling better, the Gimp wiped his mouth across the sleeve of his rumpled white shirt.

Taking two paces toward his desk, dizziness again engulfed him. Then his ears buzzed with modulating intensity. Rubbing the tips of his fingers up and down and all around his face, the Gimp tried to regain a measure of self-control. After a few seconds that felt like a few hours, he succeeded. Hazily, the events of the previous day that precipitated his present condition filtered into his consciousness.

Stumbling to the chair next to the desk the Gimp plopped into it. His descrying eyes turned introspective. Without fanfare, he decided to settle all his old scores, vendettas or whatever in one fell sweep. Gruffly banging the phone in front of him, the Gimp dialed a number with his stubby index finger. After several rings someone answered. "Where you been Antny?" the Gimp demanded.

"I left until the Good Friday thing blew over," came Carlucci's reply through the telephone. "Where you at?" he probed knowing that the Gimp was most likely downstairs.

"In the club but I'm going home to clean up. I'll be back in an hour or two. Don't go no where," the Gimp commanded firmly pressing the receiver button to abruptly end the phone call. Holding the button while contemplating what he was going to say, the Gimp regained enough clarity to be dangerous. Dialing another number, an iniquitous grin crossed his oily unshaven face. "Teti?"

"Yeah. What's up?" Teti sleepily replied.

"Meet me at the warehouse on Mifflin Street in an hour or so. Bring your side-kick," the Gimp ordered nonchalantly then added, "I got a special assignment for you two."

"Gotcha," Teti numbly replied and hung up. Still half asleep, Teti never gave the request a second thought.

On a reflective note the Gimp slowly hung up the phone. Contemplating the execution of his scheme, he nodded approvingly. His hard brown eyes exhibited the rampant insidiousness in his soul. His wicked grin expanded into a raucous belly laugh causing the Gimp to stand straight up in an attempt to contain it. Supremely self-confident, the Gimp had just decided to humiliate one and kill the other. How appropriate, the Gimp thought vengefully. Poetic justice was going to be rendered at last. The voice in his head concurred, *"Good boy Joey. That's the way to do it."*

58

Situated between two small side streets, the Gimp's warehouse occupied more than half a city block. Originally constructed during the Prohibition Era to house trucks, fixtures and other assets necessary to operate speakeasies, it was now used as a storage area for a local string band club that paraded up Broad Street in the Mummer's Parade on New Year's Day. But today the facility was being used for another, more pernicious purpose.

Unbolting a weather worn lock on a side door, Teti and Tucci entered the cavernous structure unnoticed. After relocking the door, Teti noticed a dim light in the back corner of the warehouse. Unthinkingly, he continued toward the lighted area with Tucci several paces behind. Their steps echoed ominously off the brick walls and cement floors.

Without warning the menacing figure of Mad Dog Anthony Carlucci appeared from the shadows of a pile of boxes. Fiercely swinging a baseball bat across the small of Tucci's back, Carlucci caught him off guard. Tucci immediately fell to his knees. Carlucci swung again, this time sending the battered Tucci careening to the floor. Swinging the bat like a sledgehammer, Carlucci finally bashed Tucci's legs simultaneously with one swift blow.

Teti's eyes went instantly wide, stunned by the pure savagery of the attack. Unable and unwilling to intercede for Tucci, the bile from his stomach rose in his throat. Blatantly underestimating the Gimp, he should have sensed the warning signs of a set up. Teti knew that this day was inevitable. But he didn't have to enjoy its consequences. Feeling numbed and isolated, he barely managed to glare in disapproval at the panting monolithic Carlucci hovering over Tucci like a caveman vanquishing his enemy.

Misinterpreting the glare as a sign of approval, Carlucci smiled triumphantly at Teti through crooked yellow teeth. "Get some rope we'll tie this bastard up in the corner. The Gimp will be around soon," he directed between gasps of breath.

Teti regained control of his temporarily defunct thought processes. Swiftly realizing the lack of options, he readily complied with Carlucci's request. After all, he warned the kid that he was playing with fire. It was out of his hands now. Love and self-respect were honorable notions for the truly brave of heart or psychotic criminal mind. Everyone in between was a survivalist in the wilderness of criminality. Teti fell into that category.

Wriggling in abhorrent agony, Tucci made one last attempt to fight back. Clutching Carlucci's ankle, he unsuccessfully attempted to topple his unsuspecting assailant.

Angered by this flippant attempt to strike back, Carlucci smashed both of Tucci's hands extricating a deep bellowing moan from the bloody hulk sprawled on the floor. Grabbing Tucci by the scruff of his neck, Carlucci dragged him across the floor to the lighted area near some empty fifty-five gallon drums.

Binding and gagging Tucci on a chair, Teti made the mistake of looking into his swollen eyes. A wave of sympathy swelled within Teti. Tucci's sullen eyes spoke and Teti loosened the gag.

"You do it," were the words Tucci's bloody swollen lips barely whispered.

Teti paused unable to reply. Unsure of the meaning of what he thought Tucci was requesting, he reattached the gag. At that moment the motor of the roll up door engaged. Squeezing Tucci's shoulder in a sign of empathy, Teti moved away to sulk in a nearby shadow.

The Gimp wheeled his nondescript car into the bowels of the warehouse as the roll up door closed behind him. Exiting the car, the Gimp's shoes clicked like a ticking time bomb as he approached the lighted area. Looking wickedly at Carlucci, the Gimp's normally vacuous eyes were not his own. Their glint reflected the presence of some other pernicious creature seeking vengeance. "Where's Teti?" he wanted to know.

Teti emerged from a nearby shadow. "Right here," he replied with a caustic edge.

Crimping his lips into a smile against his teeth the Gimp jabbed an acknowledging finger at Teti and said misleadingly, "Thanks!"

Teti's eyes leveled in outrage at the Gimp. Shaking his head negatively he turned to face Tucci whose eyes relayed understanding of the Gimp's cruel game.

Meanwhile, the Gimp pulled over a nearby chair to face Tucci. Straddling it, he rested his arms on its back. The tick above his left eye fluttered uncontrollably. Closing his eyes, he fought to control the anger seething to the surface. "So you've been boffing my daughter," he gutturally grunted through clenched teeth. Opening his eyes, he stabbed his finger accusingly and shouted invectively, "You little fuckin' scumbag. A chip off the old block, I should've buried your little fuck-ing ass with your father!"

His breathing accelerated like a bull about to charge. Expressing himself wildly with his pointed finger, he continued, "It was you who fuckin' ripped off her new white dress. The dress I just bought her." Looking down at his hands like they were still holding the dress, the vehemence in the Gimp's voice accelerated, "A white dress, a sign of purity, an engagement present. And you raped her!"

At this point the Gimp shot up like a rocket and kicked the chair. "I blamed that dumbshit working stiff. But it was you!" The Gimp leaped at Tucci. Unleashing a furious backhand across his face sent Tucci and the chair careening off of the empty drums onto the floor. Losing any semblance of personal control, the Gimp stomped and kicked Tucci repeatedly while screaming, "You violated my daughter! You made my life a living fuck-ing hell! This is how you show me respect?" Beads of sweat formed on the Gimp's forehead. Removing his hat and coat he wiped his forehead with a clean linen handkerchief. His rapid breathing became shallower. Slowly, he regained his composure. "Teti. Get this bastard back up," he ordered in a raspy inimical voice.

Teti required Carlucci's assistance to upright the inert body of Cosmo Tucci. Miraculously, almost brazenly, a flicker of life showed through one of Tucci's blood-encrusted eyes. The other was swollen shut.

Flicking his lips reflectively with his index finger, the Gimp then motioned with it for Teti to approach him. "Teti." Imperceptibly, Teti approached the Gimp just as he pulled a gun out of his pocket. Shoving the gun into Teti's hand, the Gimp prodded mockingly, "Go ahead. He was your fuckin' responsibility."

Teti looked at the .38 revolver in his hand with tightened lips. His nose flared as he tried to contain his anger. With a slight turn of his head he met the furtive eyes of the Gimp with a calculated stare. The realization struck him like Carlucci's baseball bat. If he hesitated slightly, he would be sitting in that chair next. For a split second he thought about using the weapon on the Gimp, but his back was exposed to Carlucci who was behind him. Raising the .38 revolver he took aim at Tucci.

With his last bit of energy Tucci smiled approvingly through cracked lips while nodding affirmatively.

Teti realized what Tucci was trying to say before. He would rather have Teti kill him than give the Gimp his final due. Accepting Tucci's silent pronouncement, Teti squeezed the trigger. It clicked empty. Angrily, Teti continued squeezing the trigger as if by the sheer force of his hand he could get a bullet to fire from its chamber. It repeatedly clicked empty. Disgustedly, Teti flung the handgun against the wall shattering the pistol grips. Quickly turning to face the Gimp, Teti instead was looking down the barrel of a Beretta 9mm automatic pistol in the Gimp's beefy hand.

With a trenchant belly laugh the Gimp explained sarcastically, "Sorry to spoil your fun, sport." Without the slightest hint of recrimination the Gimp blithely turned toward Tucci immediately emptying the Beretta into him in one continuous explosion.

Tucci's body jerked back, and then forward teetering on the back legs of his chair at times. Blood and bone fragments expelled from his body and head like a starburst during a fireworks exhibition. Moments later his limp, lifeless body slumped forward, dead.

Embittered by this sordid affair, Teti stood by helplessly with a sour face and distressful eyes. Wondering if he would meet a similar fate, he hung his head low when it was over.

A sense of satisfaction overcame the Gimp. All the pent up anger drained from his body. With a hellish look in his eyes the Gimp stuck the Beretta into the waistband of his pants. Stretching his chest forward while pushing his thick shoulders back, he looked like a rooster about to crow. Satisfied with his handiwork, he donned his brown leather coat and fedora. Readjusting the fedora on his head, he noticed Teti's look of askance. "Hey, I felt it was my parental responsibility. Ya know," the Gimp explained with a tauntingly hideous smile.

Carlucci surveyed the mess on the floor then scrutinized Tucci's inanimate body. "How we gonna handle this?" he asked callously as if Tucci's corpse was some spoiled commodity that needed special handling.

Momentarily irritated by the question, the Gimp responded like the abattoir foreman that he was. "Disinfect the floor. We don't want the scumbag's blood infecting anyone else. Then put that little pile of shit in the can and dump it. But do it later. Right now, I'm hungry," he exclaimed with an indulgent chuckle. Then after a thoughtful moment he repeatedly snapped his fingers and asked, "Say, isn't there a new place over on Seventh Street. I can't think of the name of the place."

"Momma Rosa's," Carlucci tersely replied.

"Yeah, that's it. They got the best sweet meat gravy," the Gimp commented nonchalantly. Holding the tips of his fingers together on his right hand, the Gimp brought them to his mouth and made a kissing sound as he pushed them straight away.

Teti watched the interaction incredulously as the Gimp and Carlucci shuffled toward the side exit. The Gimp suddenly stopped and turned toward the hesitant Teti.

"Come on, you're driving," the Gimp ordered. Then continuing with a wide toothy devious smile, "Besides, I'm gonna make today up to you. You can team up with Antny here and get those other two scumbags."

"Not a problem," Teti lied with a smirk on his face as he strode past the Gimp who followed his movement with a suspicious look on his face.

59

Sandy wheeled her light green Mustang down Fremont Street, a bustling thoroughfare cutting through the heart of downtown Las Vegas. Gawking at the Horseshoe and Golden Nugget Casinos, she seemed happy to be at the end of her trek. Later in the evening, she would return to this street then drive down the Las Vegas Strip marveling at the glittering plethora of lights that mesmerized first time visitors.

"All that glitters is not gold" is the often-quoted aphorism from Cervantes *Don Quixote* that aptly applied to Las Vegas' beginnings. Founded on May 15, 1905 as a water stop for wagon trains and railroads between Los Angeles and points east, it was merely a dusty little town in the middle of the desert. Gambling was legalized in 1931. The nearby Hoover Dam was constructed during the thirties. However, it wasn't until organized crime took an interest in 1941 that Las Vegas started to really be noticed.

That year it gained the attention of Benjamin *"Bugsy"* Siegel who enlisted his good friend Meyer Lansky to begin development of the first Las Vegas casino. Siegel with his girl friend Virginia Hill had a flare for the luxurious. The Flamingo, Siegel's pet name for Hill, went way over budget and eventually led to Siegel's untimely demise. Even so, his idea took root and a modern day Sodom & Gomorrah was born.

Las Vegas or *Sin City* as it inevitably became known was an oasis of legalized gambling, adult entertainment, legalized prostitution and an endless river of booze. The foibles of human nature were serviced and nurtured here. Whatever the rest of the country found vile or disgraceful, this city embraced with open arms. That was the reason that Sandy Edelman chose this town to have her abortion.

Sandy could not have known or cared that *Roe vs. Wade* would be decided in her favor ten months in the future. By then she would have born the child and her future would be heading for uncharted waters. When the father was confronted with the same prospect, he graciously offered to pay the cost of an abortion within reason. Thirty days at a swank hotel in Las Vegas was out of the question. More modest accommodations would have to suffice. Agreeing on an appropriate amount, he wrote the check never to see Sandy again.

At first Sandy lauded her decision encasing it in the feministic framework being touted across the country. However, during her trip across the country the first inklings of misgiving started to surface. This actually began at the outset when she encountered Johnny Cerone for the first time. Their subsequent encounter, however, reinforced her original decision and she steeled herself against any emotional involvement with him. No man wanted another man's baby, she convinced herself. Maybe someday I'll meet someone like him and begin a new chapter of my life, she idly speculated. Afraid that Johnny would try to dissuade her, she did not want to take a chance on telling him her secret.

Passing a motel on the outskirts of town just off of East Charleston Boulevard, Sandy noticed its signage advertising monthly rates. Hoping to save a little extra money, she pulled into the parking lot.

Nighttime on Las Vegas Boulevard South better known as *The Strip* is an inveigled orgy of excess. Lights, limos and lascivious ladies abound. High priced entertainers performed then tried their hands at private gaming tables cordoned off to the average player. The stakes can be high. The odds are always in the houses' favor. If you are on a budget, play the slots. Card counters and card sharks keep out. Welcome to Las Vegas!

Motoring up the main drag from their motel just off the Boulder Highway north of Henderson, the razzle-dazzle atmosphere had Johnny spellbound. A wide-eyed expression of wonderment cast an imprint on Johnny's face. Cisco appeared indifferent. Nevertheless, with the top down on his MGB, Johnny and Cisco enjoyed the aroma of unlimited expectations that the gentle breeze off the desert enticingly delivered to their senses. This town was more intoxicating than booze or drugs.

Like two ships in the night passing each other unnoticed, Sandy's light green Mustang and Johnny's mustard colored MGB crossed each other's path at the Sahara Avenue intersection. Preoccupied by the heightened sensory perceptions surrounding them, neither noticed the other as they drove in opposite directions.

Jabbing his finger toward the Cibola Casino, Cisco immediately noticed the large marquee touting the Nine-Ball Tournament underneath the larger font of the headliner's name.

Inside the glistening casino the two road warriors split up. Still overwhelmed by the trademark glittering façade of the Las Vegas casinos, Johnny meandered through the gaming tables like a child in a toy store at Christmas. With anticipatory fervor Cisco single-mindedly sought the requirements for entrance into the tournament.

Finding the information posted near the cashier's cage, Cisco's eyes darkened in disappointment. To his dismay he noticed the precipitous change in the amount of the stake money needed to enter the tournament. Instead of twenty five hundred dollars, he now needed five thousand.

Coming up behind Cisco, Johnny sensed something out of kilter. With questioning eyes he looked at Cisco who responded with an unsmiling jerk of his head toward the posted information.

"I guess that's it," Johnny exclaimed after reading the requirements.

Cisco pursed his lips outwardly in frantic contemplation.

"You know we can both get jobs and wait it out for the next one," Johnny suggested halfheartedly attempting to soothe Cisco's obvious pangs of disappointment. Continuing in a dispirited tone, "After all, we ain't going anywhere."

Desperation emoted from Cisco's dark crestfallen eyes. He wasn't yet ready to give up. It was now or never. The money meant keeping his promise to Rose. That was important to him at this very moment. During the cross-country trek to this refuge in the desert, he had reached an epiphany. Tired of pussyfooting around, Cisco innately sensed that he and Rose could have a life here and be happy. His oft-touted wanderlust was only a self-serving excuse to avoid any type of commitment he realized. Time to step up to the plate he decided.

Running his tongue across his top lip, Cisco impetuously yanked the roll of his remaining money from his pocket. Peeling off a one-hundred dollar bill he folded the bill in half then stuffed it into his back pocket. Scanning the gaming tables, he focused on a blackjack table with only one player. "Come on kid. Let's try our luck," Cisco said in a sober tone trying to bolster his resolve. He was breaking all of his tried and true rules learned in the school of hard knocks over the years. Unthinkingly, they strode into the lion's den of legalized gambling.

Food in Las Vegas was plentiful and cheap. Buffets abounded. Great food reasonably priced was another matter.

Sandy found a quiet little Italian restaurant off of Convention Center Drive that came highly recommended for several diverse reasons. The food was great and reasonable, the atmosphere was campy red Italian and the clientele were working class locals.

Lately however, another class of people discovered this diamond in the rough restaurant—tourists on a budget. This included male predators of naïve young women looking for a little cheap *action*.

Sandy fit into one category but not the other. Some men, however, didn't know the difference because their brains hadn't evolved above their groin area. One such hairy degenerate noticed Sandy sitting alone deep in thought. A masochist at heart, this ill-mannered cretin became excited when women played hard to get then later abused him. Seeing her review her check, *the John* decided to approach her.

"Mind if I sit down?" he boldly asked.

Taken aback at first, Sandy assumed the man was just hitting on her. "Yes I do," she responded irritably.

It was music to *the John's* ears. "You up for a little action?" he prodded with a smirk. "I like your style."

"I don't like yours. Do you mind," she said nastily.

"I know. I'm a bad boy. I need to be punished," *the John* said with heightened excitement.

"You're drunk. Leave me alone before I call the cops," Sandy threatened.

"No need for that I have handcuffs."

Sandy finally comprehended the implication. In a no man's land of emotional disgust between tears and abject anger, she grabbed a nearby glass of water and flung the contents into *the John's* face. His eyes alight in desire as Sandy screamed in his face, "Go to Hell!" Storming out the door, she threw some money at the nearby waiter who looked on flabbergasted.

60

The cameras in the Cibola Casino surveillance room usually were focused on the turning of cards on the table watching for any duplicity on the part of a dealer or player. Occasionally, they scanned the faces of those playing. Tonight Ben Greenberg was personally monitoring the cameras. His focus was a Cibola Blackjack Pit Boss, Jack Down, and his shift of dealers.

Jack Down was a roommate of another Pit Boss, Danny DeWitt, from Cleopatra's Palace who was also suspected of *knocking down the house*. Unfortunately, DeWitt was found with a bullet behind his ear at the base of his head, face down in a gutter. The case was still under investigation and would probably remain that way for some time to come.

Hopefully, Jack Down got the message. Otherwise, his penance would not be as swift and as painless as his cohort's. Instead, he would be exported to an obscure corner of the scorpion-infested desert just north of Las Vegas where men had been buried in the sand up to their necks—Indian style—for lesser offenses.

Hank "The Tank" Thani quietly, sat in the back of the room reading a wrestling magazine while Ben watched the multitude of television screens. A six foot, two hundred seventy five pound bull-necked, thick-shouldered specimen, he was Ben Greenberg's retribution specialist.

Hank hailed from the campy days of professional wrestling in the late nineteen fifties. In those days Hank butted heads with the likes of Killer Klusinski and Gorilla Santilla. Although quite the showman in his fiery red leotards his cranky and contentious disposition worked against him among his fellow wrestlers. There was an ugly side to Hank's performances. He played for keeps.

This personality trait in the ring wasn't Hank's total undoing. What finally pinned Hank to the mat was his attitude toward a member of the audience one fateful night. It made Sid Greenberg, an avid wrestling fan take note.

Sid enjoyed watching the huffy bravado of these burly human bulwarks in capes and tight pants. Describing it to his son once as a great way to relieve anxiety, it was a great diversion. Watching it actually gave him a laugh. Once he attended a match being taped for television. He witnessed something that turned his lighthearted amusement into one of personal opportunity.

A taunting member of the audience began calling Hank a faggot. Hank took it in stride trying to play the part of an angry wrestler. Stabbing a stubby finger at the man, he warned him vehemently. It was all great theater, but Sid sensed something else afoot during this exchange and began paying closer attention. The heckler continued ribbing Hank regarding his manhood and any other invective inferences that came to mind. Eyeing the man bitterly, Hank became increasingly agitated. It showed in the wrestler's twitching invidious eyes. Finally, unable to maintain his self-control Hank leaped over the ropes. Physically pummeling the heckler, Hank managed to get a hammerlock on the man. Without further fanfare, he meant to twist the man's head around in a full 360-degree circle and would have if Sid didn't intervene.

Speaking in a silky voice, Sid lulled this steamroller of a man back from the dark precipice of his inner anger onto the road of rationality. With veins still throbbing on the side of his neck, Hank released the unrepentant heckler. Not comprehending his near death experience, the heckler was about to continue his bombast. Sid smacked the heckler forcefully with the back of his hand. Glaring at the man with frigid foreboding eyes, Sid froze the stunned man in place.

The heckler pressed assault charges and Hank's career as a professional wrestler was over. Again, Sid intervened. Posting bail for the down and out behemoth, Sid eventually got the charges dropped.

Hank was confused. No one had ever taken an interest in his well-being in the past. Born of a Jewish mother and Muslim father, Hank was an outcast from birth. Fending off this mantle of disdain, he claimed to be of Jewish and Italian parentage. That didn't work either. The toughs from the neighborhood started calling him *Jewop*. In his inimitable way Sid understood this man. Given the right guidance, he could be a force of nature unto himself. So, Sid took the man under his wing. In the process Sid acquired a loyal servant willing to do his biding.

The year was 1959 and Sid's son, Ben, was managing a casino in Havana, Cuba. Concerned for his son's safety during these turbulent years in Cuba, Sid sent Hank as a quasi bodyguard for his petulant son. A loyalty developed between the two akin to a squire to his knight during the Middle Ages. Ben was the knight. Hank was his squire. Enemies were vanquished. New conflicts were always just over the horizon. Escaping Cuba one-step ahead of Castro's Revolutionary Guard, the two displaced men eventually made Las Vegas their home.

Sid Greenberg's cabal of criminal associates read like a who's who in the criminal world. Together they owned controlling interests in four Las Vegas casinos through various shell corporations. Since his son Ben had no criminal record plus hands on experience as a casino manager in Cuba, he was their odd on favorite to manage the day-to-day operations of their gambling establishments in Las Vegas.

It was a good choice. Ben Greenberg, like his father, had a suave demeanor with a silky voice that masked his ironfisted principles of business conduct. These were all solidly based on his guiding principle of *Don't fuck with me or else.* No one usually did or was alive to tell about it.

This night no one was screwing with Ben Greenberg. Jack Down had gotten the message. Still, in a few hours the entire shift would be escorted out of the casino and barred from ever entering the premises again. Ben was a reasonable man, but not a forgiving one. Happy that he didn't need Hank to close the loop on this particular chapter of business, he decided to take one last look around his casino. Recalibrating the cameras to see the players, he scanned the tables once more before retiring.

Ben's happiness quickly dissipated when the camera caught a familiar face in its probing sweep. Zooming in on the face, Ben recognized Cisco's dour look. He could tell by the look that he was losing. "Damn! Another charity case," hissed through his teeth.

Sliding back into his chair he brushed his index finger across his lips in an unconscious act of contemplation. He had totally forgotten about the talk he and his father had almost ten days ago. This presented him with a whole new set of problems. Complicated problems. Delicate problems. No matter how far one traveled the past always caught up with you, he thought pensively. Lurching forward he mumbled incoherently, "That's tomorrow's problem."

Hank looked up questioningly. "What?"

"Nothing. Let's go get something to eat," Ben said in a toneless voice. Standing up and stretching out his back, he regained a lighter mood. Without looking back, Ben and Hank left the room leaving the camera focused on Cisco.

Gamblers as a whole are a superstitious lot of individuals. Each one subscribed to a personal idiosyncratic ritual. Some wore charms or amulets to ward off bad luck. Others looked for omens. A few engaged in obsessive courses of action. A few worked, most didn't.

Cisco nixed this ritualistic behavior. Instead, he subscribed to the theory of creative visualization. Simply translated it amounted to positive and negative attitudes. Giving this belief lip service was not enough. One had to feel the attitudinal force coursing through their veins. If it was positive you gambled. If not you passed. Tonight, Cisco disregarded his better judgment and was paying the price.

Hanging on every turn of the card at the blackjack table, the dealer beat Cisco's two consecutive pat hands of twenty with two blackjacks. Cisco's normally placid composure began to deteriorate. It was as if his life was on the line. His normal calculating mental processes were now anxiety driven. His demeanor transformed into a surrealistic composition. Slipping the one-hundred dollar bill out of his back pocket, Cisco noticed Johnny's panicky stare. Nervously lighting a cigarette, he sucked a long drag of the toxic fumes. Exhaling the smoke through his nose, Cisco curtly ordered, "Take a walk, will ya kid."

"Why?"

"Cause I can't win a hand with you breathing down my neck every minute like some dog in heat," Cisco inveighed. After an uneasy moment, he added sarcastically, "Go take a piss or something. Humor me."

Shrugging his shoulders in exasperation Johnny turned to watch the card action on the next table.

Cisco bet the entire hundred dollars on the next hand. He lost. A tingling sensation crept across his skin in conjunction with a quickening pulse. Cisco turned abruptly.

"Hey Johnny," Cisco called out with a quiver in his voice. "You got any money on ya?"

"A few bucks," Johnny replied guardedly.

Waving his fingers in an oscillating manner Cisco commanded firmly, "Give it here."

Ire rose from the pit of Johnny's stomach like bile, leaving a sour taste in his mouth. This transformed into disquietude quickly. He turned to walk away from the erratically behaving Cisco. Something was different, he thought. Something was drastically different. Thank God they paid in advance for the motel room, Johnny silently intoned.

Grasping Johnny's arm Cisco pleaded, "Wait a minute kid?"

Johnny hesitated then turned around with noticeable irritation etched on his face searching for some explanation in Cisco's eyes for his sudden transformation. What he found was unbridled fear.

Cisco was exposed. Unable to conceal his fear any longer it seeped out of its tomb and overwhelmed him. Afraid of his past, uncertain of his future, Cisco had been in a downward spiral since his encounter with the North Carolina sheriff. His spirit had been broken by that episode. Realizing for the first time that his wily ways were nothing more than a house of cards, Cisco's impregnable confidence was breached. In Philadelphia he had put up a good front for Rose rallying his teetering self-esteem in the face of Carlucci and the Gimp. He also knew that his cool bravado was an unsustainable façade. The years of duplicitous behavior reached a crescendo purloining the essence of his being. Tonight, this naïve kid standing in front of him pulled him back from the edge. It wasn't enough.

Finally hitting bottom, Cisco was a candidate for a nervous breakdown if Johnny would have uttered a single word. Imperceptibly clinging to a hope for a future, Cisco saw an inner strength in Johnny Cerone's eyes. It was like a strong elixir healing Cisco's troubled soul. All these words coalesced into a simple unintelligible feeling for Cisco. Salvation was attainable.

Johnny's strong silent stare bolstered Cisco in this way. Lifting him out of his funk, it prompted Cisco to sincerely utter a single word without consciously knowing why, "Thanks."

Lying couchant on the metal-framed bed in her sanitized motel room clutching a tattered hand sewn doll, Sandy felt overwhelmed by the *anything goes* atmosphere of Las Vegas. She had always considered herself cosmopolitan in nature. But this town put an entirely different perspective on the term. It seemed to be an uncontainable amoral virus infecting the country as a whole. Considering herself infected, she prayed for guidance for what she was here to do.

After her silent prayer, Sandy looked at her hand-sewn doll, a link to a happier time and place, and idly thought about her family. Her devout Catholic parents preached abstinence rather than condone the temptation that the birth control pill afforded. Sandy had become painfully aware of the shortcomings of that school of thought. If she had flaunted her human failing in that area to her parents face, they would have insisted on her having the baby. Afterwards, they would insist that she give the child up for adoption.

That solution might be logical in a perfect world, but the emotions of motherhood were a fluctuating variable. Such a solution would therefore be unpredictable. In any case it would stigmatize her in the community and be a point of contention in her family for the foreseeable future Sandy wisely noted.

This rationalization lowered Sandy's anxiety level considerably, but the Las Vegas lifestyle gnawed at her conscience as she teetered on the edge of slumber. Afraid of falling into its dark grip, her sleep was uneasy that night. Nightmares of dressing in lewd costumes and selling her body to the devil plagued Sandy. Each outlandish guilt driven dream would awaken her in a frenzy. The emotions of motherhood were slowly seeping into her consciousness. Her years of parochial education stood guard in the night against the encroaching exigencies of the outer world. If anyone were there to hear her cry out in a pleading voice, "I want my baby," they would have known the agonizing turmoil raging inside her soul. However, no one was there to pay witness. Dissipating into the ethers of the night, her pleading was forgotten like so many other noble aspirations.

61

Nestled in Willings Alley near Fourth & Walnut Streets in the Society Hill section of Philadelphia, Old Saint Joseph's Church has the distinction of being the first Catholic parish in Philadelphia. Today, the faint intonation of Gregorian Chants could be heard as Carlucci approached the church along the cobble stoned Willings Alley from Fourth Street.

Even though Carlucci was educated in a parochial school for his elementary education, he was obviously not a religious person. Although his peers professed a belief in the hereafter, he was focused on the here and now. Besides, his mind was not capable of understanding abstract ideas such as God or love. Not wanting to conspicuously enter the small church after the mass had begun, Carlucci decided to walk around the neighborhood on this beautiful spring morning.

Inside the church the Old Man sat solemnly listening to the liturgical music. It made him feel peaceful, even forgiven at times. Since his first name, Giuseppe, meant Joseph in Italian, he had a personal preference for this Pre-Revolutionary War house of worship. He loved the music, the sermons and anonymity of the congregation. If he had his druthers, he would attend mass here every Sunday. However, establishing a regular routine could prove fatal in his profession. So, he randomly attended services in different churches throughout South Philadelphia. After mass he always lit a candle for Grace Giampietro's soul. It was the one routine that he allowed himself.

Her death would have been unnecessary if he hadn't faltered and dishonored her. As he lit the candle the Old Man would make a loosely clenched fist and gently beat his breast in repentance while repeating in a hushed voice, *"Mea culpa, mea culpa, mea maxima culpa."* He confessed this litany once a week as he lit the candle and made his offering at a simple shrine that was off to the side of the main altar. Today, this silent profession of guilt gave the Old Man no solace. He must do the unthinkable. Though he enjoyed his work as a criminal chess master countermanding his opponents' potential moves, he did not enjoy engineering the death of his own flesh and blood. Unfortunately, he was left with no other choice, he brooded. There was just no other choice. His lips formed the words silently, but his mind was somewhere else.

The continuation of his life's work was tantamount. Both his legitimate family and the brotherhood that he swore to uphold must prosper and grow. Otherwise, his life had no meaning. Joseph Giampietro had become the antithesis to his life's work and thus must be eliminated, the Old Man sadly concluded. Others would do the pernicious work for him this time. Nevertheless, the blood of the Gimp would still stain his hands, he thought while lingering in front of the statue of Saint Joseph. Desperately trying to avoid comparing and contrasting himself to the exalted earthly father of Christ, he knelt, closed his eyes and quietly mumbled the Act of Contrition.

Before he finished this repentant intonation a chill swept over the Old Man like a wraithlike evil presence passing him in the night. Looking over his shoulder, he saw the foreboding figure of Anthony Carlucci hovering in and out of the shadows of the vestibule in the rear of the church. Acknowledging him with a slight nod, he rose to his feet, shuffled to the center aisle then genuflected in front of the tabernacle while making the sign of the cross. Standing erect, his penitent mien changed immediately. Remorse had no place outside the walls of a church where men were measured by their intestinal fortitude and wily manners. Like the man he was approaching, the new generation was miserably lacking in both areas. Mired in hopelessness, the Old Man saw more brawn than brain. Shuddering at that thought, he consoled himself with the notion that at least he was going to do something to stop its propagation.

The Old Man strode authoritatively up the aisle toward Carlucci. He exuded old world charm and grace. Sizing up the Old Man, Carlucci fell under his spell. There was an air of reasonableness swirling around the Old Man. It paled in comparison to the devilish dervish of emotions that enshrouded the Gimp like a human tornado. In time the Old Man's influence might have changed the course of Carlucci's life. But Carlucci had run out of time.

At the same time the Old Man was seeking penance the Gimp was seeking answers. Hanging up the phone in his house, he had just learned about Johnny Bellino's fate on Friday evening. Preoccupied with his own business all day Saturday, the Gimp missed the newspaper account of the high profiled hit. The Gimp was just about to contact Bellino about their conversation two months previous. Thank God I put him off, he thought with a measure of relief. Inarguably on his own now, he wondered in reflective silence if he was also suspected of treachery. Making a mental note to be extra cautious about his safety, the voice in his head lulled him back to the issue at hand—retribution.

Eliminating Tucci was totally justifiable. Even the Old Man would agree. Putting the hustler down would take some fancy finagling, he quietly conceded in his captivated mind. Then it struck him like a lightning bolt. Blame Carlucci. Thinking like a prosecuting attorney, the Gimp could argue that Carlucci had motive and means. The man was like a rogue elephant stampeding out of control. The Gimp's duplicity surged through his body manifesting itself as a wicked smile in sync with his insidious eyes. He liked the analogy and loved when a hideous plan came together. That would be his story and he would stick to it. Teti, however, was another matter.

As these thoughts and other mundane issues of his everyday world ricocheted in his brain, Anna descended the staircase on her way out. Unaware of her lover's fate, she was perturbed that she could not get in touch with him.

"Hi daddy," Anna mumbled melancholically.

"Hi sweetheart," the Gimp replied sheepishly avoiding eye contact with her. After an eerily silent moment, he continued, "Going out?"

"Yeah. Gloria and I are going to lunch then to the mall." Anna lied. She was on a mission to find Tucci and the reason that he stood her up the previous night.

"Have a good time," the Gimp said guiltily with a doting nod. Suspecting for the first time that his daughter may have had feelings for Tucci, the Gimp offered her the only solace that he knew, "Need any money?"

"No. I'm okay," Anna responded curtly as she exited the front door.

The voice in his head was silent as a tinge of remorse passed through his mind with the speed of electricity through a wire then dissipated. Returning to the matters at hand, he didn't give his bloodthirsty act a second thought.

Heading north on Fourth Street toward Walnut, the Old Man slipped an envelope from his inside pocket and smoothly handed it to Carlucci who was walking abreast with him.

"My friend sends his thanks for a job well done. I'm sure you'll be satisfied with his show of appreciation," the Old Man said in a clever way.

Carlucci pocketed the envelope reflexively then commented, "I'm sure I will."

They walked silently a little further until the Old Man spoke again. "The cause of your Good Friday distress has surfaced amid the bright lights of the gambling Mecca out west," he offered with circumlocutory accuracy.

"I figured as much."

"No one will think the lesser of you if you let this affair go," the Old Man said baiting Carlucci.

Stopping for a moment when they reached Walnut Street, Carlucci pursed his lips. "I will. It's who I am," he said firmly.

The Old Man looked into Carlucci's eyes and smiled tightly. "Then do what you have to do," the Old Man coyly suggested.

"I will," Carlucci said adamantly.

The Old Man was counting on such an emotional response. It fit in nicely with his game plan. Breaking eye contact, the Old Man graciously offered, "Well then, would you like me to put your money to work for you in the meantime?"

Greed sprang into Carlucci's mind displacing any thought of duplicity or failure. Handing the envelope back to the Old Man, he said agreeably, "Yeah. Sure. I'd like that." Carlucci mistook the Old Man's offer as a tacit sign of approval for his intended vengeance. It was not.

Smiling in a patronizing manner, the Old Man nodded slightly. Outwitting the witless amused him.

62

Sitting with legs akimbo on their bed in a motel just off the Boulder Highway north of Henderson Nevada, Johnny and Cisco were busy counting and wrapping the pennies from Cisco's erstwhile poker triumph in Saint Clair, Missouri.

Johnny tried to ignore Cisco's silly smirk as he counted the wrapped tubes of pennies. "Twenty-five bucks. You took those kids for a week's salary," Johnny chided Cisco playfully.

"They would've taken my money just the same. But look at it this way kid, now they got a story to tell their kids someday," Cisco chuckled lightheartedly. If he was uncomfortable about being down and out he didn't show it. Coming to terms with his fears the previous night seemed to take a load off his shoulders while buoying his spirits.

Johnny pulled his remaining money from his pocket and turned the pockets inside out in a comic gesture. "I'm all in, as you professional gamblers like to say," he said emphasizing the word *professional* in a facetiously modulating voice.

Cisco counted the scattered money neatly organizing the bills. "With the twenty-five in pennies we got a grand total of fifty-six dollars and thirty-two cents." Peeling off six dollars he handed it to Johnny. "Gas money."

Standing up to stretch his legs, Johnny sighed deeply. "Okay. Where to?"

"Cleopatra's Palace. This time let's roll the bones."

The institutional version of Craps can be traced to returning Crusaders where it was referred to as Hazard from the Arabic word for dice, al zahr. However, various renditions of the game have been traced as far back as 3500 B.C. to the game of astragalus, or knucklebone. Hence, the term *roll the bones* is derived.

Throughout history famous people have also been associated with this form of gambling. At the crucifixion of Christ Roman soldiers were purported to have cast *lots* for the robe of Christ. Marcus Aurelius, a Roman Emperor, had a personal croupier. George Washington hosted regular games in his tent during the American Revolution. Even Egyptian tombs have been found with paintings of young men *rolling the bones* into a circle.

Therefore, this evening Cisco found himself in good company when he decided to take a chance and cast his lot with his remaining money. After losing all of his bankroll the previous evening, fifty dollars didn't seem like a lot of money. Like the parable of the loaves and fishes in the New Testament it all hinged on faith. This time faith won out. Without any psychological encumbrances, Cisco approached an idle crap table in order to be assured that he and he alone would roll the dice. Starting off with three consecutive sevens before establishing a number, his confidence began escalating. Spreading his money across the board to take advantage of the odds he continuously made his number, rolling the dice for nearly twenty minutes before crapping out. By that time he had won close to seven thousand dollars, more than enough to enter the nine-ball tournament at the Cibola Casino. No longer afraid of losing it all, he had made a miraculous comeback from the throes of shiftless losers shuffling along the miles of casino aisles in Las Vegas. All of them were near or at the end of their rope. Cisco had hit bottom and survived. His confidence was back. He was ready.

This evening Carlucci was ready also. His mindset, his whole purpose was now directed to settle an old score. It seemed that his entire life was a preparation for what was about to come. Sometimes, he even felt that it gave his life meaning. On some level he believed self-redemption would be a byproduct of his action. A week ago his vengeance was so close to being satisfied that he could taste it. Discouragingly, it was snatched away like an owner teasing his dog with a bone. Carlucci girded himself against a disappointing repeat of that night.

Catching a redeye to Las Vegas with Teti, he silently recounted the embarrassment that Cisco had heaped upon him in his youth. To some it may have seemed petty, at best trivial, but to a man whose only self worth was shrouded in pride it was momentous. It was all that he had. Their strong competitiveness and the constant bickering that often led to fights were all rooted in this one incident that Carlucci could not shake off. Growing to mythical proportions over the years it was his well-concealed personal demon. Cisco's narrow escape from his retributive clutches on Good Friday only accentuated it.

Carlucci wanted to nail him to a cross that night like they did to Christ nearly two millennia ago. Strip the son-of-a-bitch naked making him feel shamefully inadequate before killing him, he thought vengefully.

Then the motherfucker would've known how I felt over thirty years ago running up Passyunk Avenue naked with all the girls laughing at me. Laughing at my "little thingy." Cool and sly, Cisco. He thought it would be funny to steal my clothes while I showered in the local boy's club. Ha! Ha! Ha! We'll see who laughs last!

An annoying murmuring sound caused Teti to shoot a side-glance at Carlucci. The man was grinding his teeth while muttering incoherently in hateful unearthly contemplation at thirty thousand feet. Teti had no way of knowing that the vehemence Carlucci was exhibiting was the real engine driving this showdown with the man that was his father.

63

Since its introduction in England as Methaqualone in 1963, Quaalude had cata-
pulted to the sixth best selling sedative on the market by 1972. This was in no
small part attributed to the *drug culture* of the sixties. When mixed with alcohol,
ludingout produced a euphoric state with aphrodisiacal benefits. It was the date
rape drug of choice for unethically licentious men. Anna Giampietro could attest
to that this morning. At this point she didn't care.

After spending Sunday afternoon desperately searching for her lover, Cosmo
Tucci, at all of Tucci's known haunts, she decided to go to his apartment.

He had given her a key in case the door was locked during one of her indis-
creet arrivals at his apartment door. As she approached the door with key in hand,
the thought crossed her mind that she may catch him in bed with another
woman. She dismissed that thought outright. They were like one. She could sense
it. Climbing the stairs to Tucci's second floor apartment, the other more obvious
alternative came to mind. Fear sent a pulsating spike to her heart. The wrath of
her father knew no bounds. Accepting her father for the man that he was ever
since she could remember, Anna knew his potential for violence. She let him
think that Johnny ravished her. If he found out otherwise, his anger would break

new ground. A cold chill suddenly ran up her spine at that thought. So, she suppressed it.

Reaching his apartment door she unlocked it. Slowly, cautiously she entered without knocking. The room felt eerily cold. His perpetually rumpled bed linens gave no clue if he had slept there the previous evening. Picking up one of his shirts from the floor, she breathed in his aroma as if she could magically exhale him into her presence. She could not.

Continuing her exploration the smile on her face broadened successively as she noted her pictures pinned to the walls all around. Somehow, she missed these displays of affection during her previous visits. At those times her focus was elsewhere. It was at that moment, she stopped deluding herself. Something was terribly wrong with this picture. It was abundantly obvious that he cared for her deeply. He would have never stood her up, she thought. Nervously, she searched her mind for a third less scary alternative. Her mind was blank. There was none.

Not wanting to scare Gloria, Anna decided not to call her. First, she would try to find Teti. If that failed, she would track down that gossipy trafficker of hearsay, Tommy DiRenzo.

Unable to locate Teti, Anna spent two frustrating hours before finally locating Tommy. She found him by chance on her way home idly standing alone on a corner at Nineteenth and Ritner Streets. The bars were closed. The poolroom was empty. So, Tommy was in limbo. Pulling up to the corner in her Camaro, Anna leaned over the passenger seat and rolled down her window. "Tommy," she called in her most enchanting tone.

"Yo, Anna," Tommy responded matter-of-factly.

"Take a ride with me," she said in a polite but commanding way.

A hesitant moment ensued. Tommy made a cross-sawing motion with his jaw. Unable to conjure up an excuse, Tommy reluctantly slipped into her car and they drove off. Suspicious of Anna's sudden interest in him, he was a bit cagey and decided to let her talk. This was unlike him. He had heard about her split with Johnny. Then there were rumblings about her and Tucci. Ah, Tucci he thought only if she knew. Dumb sap, this broad was bad news. Even he knew it. It made him nervous just sitting in a car with her. Now, she was going to pump him for information. Well, she could kiss my ass, he thought assertively. Although deep in his heart, he wanted to spill his guts.

"I hear Johnny left town," Anna said trying to jump-start the conversation.

"That's what they say," Tommy replied tersely.

Coyly giving Tommy a side-glance, she sweetly prodded, "Have you seen Cosmo Tucci around?"

"You mean Cuzz. Nah. Haven't seen him."

Making a right hand turn onto Passyunk Avenue, Anna decided to backtrack to Tucci's neighborhood searching for a sign of his black Impala Super-Sport. "Have you seen his car around?"

"Nope."

Tired of playing her little game, Anna was becoming irritable. Her nerves were razor thin like her patience. "I want to know what's going on. I know that you know something." She lied. Her bluntness surprised Tommy.

Tommy quickly thrust his lips forward in little puffing motions like a fish sucking oxygen from the water. "I don't like to perpetuate a rumor, you know," he said evasively in an anxious voice.

"That never stopped you before," Anna shot back flippantly.

Flinching then squirming in his seat, Tommy motioned for her to pull over as they crossed Broad Street. "Listen, you ain't gonna like what I heard."

"Let me be the judge of that." Anna knew he was right. Still, she wanted to know. One way or the other she had to know. How she would deal with the news was one of those unknown variables in the equation of life.

"You play with fire you get burned." Then flicking his fingers in an expandable manner while moving away from his pursed lips, he said only one word, "Poof." After letting his little allegory take root, he lowered his head toward her without moving his impish eyes and continued, "Get my drift?"

Coming to climatic terms with her innermost fear, Anna screamed at the horrific image of her dead lover racing through her mind. "Get out of my car! Get out of my fucking car now!"

Giving an *I told you so* shrug of the shoulders, Tommy quickly exited the car. Frantically, Anna raced away before Tommy had a chance to close the door. "Bitch," he shouted irascibly almost certain that she could not hear him. "Spoiled fucking bitch," he said angrily lowering the decibels of his vocal volume. Sighing deeply, he turned to walk back home. Walking down Passyunk Avenue, Tommy suddenly laughed indulgently. Serves the bitch right for dumping Johnny, he thought amusedly.

An hour later after combing the immediate vicinity of Tucci's apartment, Anna headed to South Jersey with tears streaming down her eyes. She was seeking consolation in one of the few nightclubs open on a Sunday night. Not having the heart to tell Gloria, she decided to get drunk alone in unfamiliar surroundings. Closing her eyes to hold back the tears, she swore a string of vicious invectives without opening her mouth.

The rest of Sunday night was a grayish blur of drug induced euphoric self-destructive behavior. It dampened the fire in her eyes and the anger in her heart.

And the rest of the world could go to hell, she giddily thought after the alcohol and Quaaludes assumed total control.

Waking up on this Monday morning naked with a cute, but unknown man sleeping beside her was like jumping into a cold dark lake in the middle of winter. The throbbing temples of her head inhibited the functioning of her mental processes. Not knowing or caring where she was at the moment, she could only feel the dull pain in her heart begin to grow anew. Gathering up her clothes, she quietly got dressed leaving this anonymous person to his own design.

In the master bathroom of the Giampietro house, the Gimp was standing before the mirror loading two untraceable .38 snub nose revolvers. Strictly precautionary measures, he kept silently repeating to himself hoping that the rote repetition would somehow make it so.

Putting one in the top drawer of the cabinet where he kept his grooming tools and lotions, he stuffed the other in the waistband of his pants for the time being. The news of Bellino had unnerved him to the point of heightening the paranoiac variable of his ingrained schizophrenic behavior. Well aware of the consequences of treacherous liaisons, the Gimp decided to go down fighting rather than be led to the slaughterhouse like a lamb. Taking out the Old Man was no longer a viable option as long as Manfredi was still alive, he thought while preening himself in the mirror. Lurching into the mirror searching for strands of wild nasal hairs, a sinister apparition appeared to him in the mirror.

The voice in his head had taken form as a dark-eyed vamp enshrouded in black. It was the face of his mother incarnate. Her black lips formed words, but uttered no sounds. Still, the Gimp understood the context of the warning. Stepping back from the mirror involuntarily the apparition disappeared instantly. Leaving him immobile, the ominous warning reverberated cacophonously against the inner walls of his mind. Someone close to him would do him harm soon was the approximate interpretation. With eyes wild with frenzy he shouted out one word to no one in particular, "Who?"

Hearing this frantic noise, Marie appeared from the bedroom and tapped on the door gently. "Joseph? You alright in there?" She spoke with unusual concern.

"Fine. I'm fine," the Gimp replied from behind the door with the words interspersed between erratic gasps of breath.

With her ear to the door quietly listening for any unusual sounds, Marie shrugged it off to the Gimp's normally erratic behavior. "I'm going out to run some errands," Marie said in a detached manner and quickly descended the stairs.

Entering the front door with her clothes disheveled, Anna encountered her mother at the bottom of the staircase. Marie was aghast.

No words needed to be spoken. Anna saw the reprehension in her mother's eyes. Right now her emotions were well beyond accepting any type of parental rebuke. And her demeanor projected it angrily.

Instinctually, a nauseating dread overcame Marie. At once she felt her daughter's pain and knew its source. He was descending the stairs at that very moment.

Anna shifted her glaring rage from Marie to her father. Recoiling from his daughter's glaring eyes, his mind replayed his mother's warning. Cautiously, he proceeded to the bottom of the steps.

"Murderer," Anna shouted at the Gimp with epithetical implications.

The Gimp's eyes narrowed simultaneously as his nose widened. The answer to his beseeching outcry was apparent. Somehow, his daughter sensed his pernicious deed and misconstrued his actions. Deception was his first course of action. He knew he wasn't capable of the second. It was his child, his own flesh and blood. Self-preservation was not an option in this case. "What are you talking about?" he asked evasively.

"Where's Cosmo Tucci?"

"Home sleeping I guess," the Gimp offered with a questionable expression on his face and an upright palm. He lied.

"He's not home. He's not anywhere downtown. I looked. His car is missing. Why did you do it," she screamed on the brink of tears. "How could you do it? I loved him. He loved me!" Leaping at him like a tigress she beat at him, but he stood there impassively accepting the blows as some perverse form of penance.

Unable to explain the necessity of his action, the Gimp remained eerily silent. How could he tell his daughter it was for her own good, he brooded? Men like that use women for a time then discarded them, the voice in his head recounted on several occasions. The Gimp knew that he could tell no one of his personal oracle, not even his family.

Marie wrapped her arm around Anna consolingly when she finally stopped beating incessantly at the Gimp. Retiring to the nearby couch, Anna laid her head in her mother's lap. On some level Marie too was guilty, but for entirely different reasons than the Gimp.

Marie was adamant that the two should never be more than just friends. It was one of the few areas of common agreement that she knew the Gimp and her were in sync on. The Gimp hated Tucci's father, whereas, Marie loved him. It was a secret she kept for her entire life. A story she told to no one.

Anna Giampietro was not the Gimp's daughter. She was the daughter of an illicit union between Carmine Tucci and Marie. Genetically, Anna was Cosmo Tucci's half sister, making any marriage between the two an unholy affair.

Unlike her daughter, Marie acquiesced to her parents' wishes and married the Gimp at the urging of her mother's first cousin, Giuseppe Vecchio, the Old Man. At first Marie resisted the union until she found out she was pregnant with Anna. Confused and anxious, Marie spent days in her room trying to conceive alternatives. Since she witnessed the shootout from the upstairs' apartment, she considered going to the police, however, realized that such an action would benefit the Gimp who could honestly claim self-defense. Desperate and depressed, at one point she considered suicide. After making a novena at Saint Rita di Cascia, another alternative presented itself to her while deep in prayer. She would immediately marry the Gimp and claim the child sprang from his loins. This way she could keep a part of Carmine Tucci, her lover, forever close to her and slowly torture Joseph Giampietro over their lifetime together. It was the most ironic form of punishment she could imagine.

However, this was not an easy conspiracy to maintain. The Gimp treated her like a queen and Anna like a princess. He denied them nothing. His reputed anger was somehow left at the door when he entered the portal to their home. It was as if he were two different people. Her ploy corroded her soul while giving strength to the Gimp. He rarely demanded his marital rights as a husband. This Marie could never understand especially from a man with such strong emotional energy. Instead, he held her on a pedestal meekly succumbing to her slightest wish. At first Marie tested the limits of his patience. She hoped for an emotional outburst that would condone her hatred of the man. Roiling when he submitted to the most inane request, she finally gave up trying to incite him. Over the years she settled into marital limbo. It was a workable arrangement and Anna's younger years were pleasant and joyful. The only two exceptions were his obsession about the house and Anna's infatuation with Tucci.

Anesthetized to her original hatred of the man, it came back with a vengeance this morning. She realized that her daughter was suffering the same fate that she had been dealt over twenty years ago. Suddenly, Marie's ambivalence toward her relationship with the Gimp unraveled. Her dormant emotions aroused. She promised herself that her daughter would not end up like she had, an empty shell of a human.

64

Johnny lay couchant on a small double bed in a dingy motel room in a subconscious zone of delight. Sandy Edelman had managed to bewitch him like no other woman he had ever known. Speechlessly berating himself for not probing deeper into her life, he was at a loss to begin a search to find her. Fantasizing about finding her and sweeping her off her feet, Johnny seriously considered hiring a private investigator to find this mystifying woman. He quickly pooh-poohed that option.

Sitting up on the side of his bed, he watched Cisco sleeping in silent repose. Johnny thought about how Cisco's success at the craps table the previous night had invigorated the man. He was happy for him. Maybe there was still hope for him and the woman at the bar in South Philly, he happily ruminated. Although Cisco never mentioned her during the entire trip across the country, Johnny sensed that was the underlying motivation for their trek to this glitzy oasis in the desert. Otherwise, Cisco would be nothing more than a nilhist.

After quietly dressing, Johnny slipped out of the over sanitized room and decided to take a spin around Las Vegas before the heat became stifling. Let Cisco sleep, he thought considerately. He earned it.

At McCarran International Airport a different scenario was unfolding. Teti wandered off to the Men's Room leaving Carlucci to wait for their luggage at the baggage claim area. Impatient, Carlucci aimlessly paced around the empty luggage carousel. Tired and grumpy, his disoriented mind continued drawing blanks in his search for the wily Cisco. Inadvertently, he bumped into a free-standing advertisement sign. Reaching out to keep the sign from tipping over, something registered in his heavy eyes. The sign was advertising a nine-ball tournament at the Cibola Casino on Saturday April 8th. The prize money was large, fifty thousand dollars large. Carlucci's heavy eyes lightened. His face reflected all the guile of a bobcat stalking its prey in the nearby mountains circling Las Vegas.

A motor whirred nearby and the luggage carousel crepitated to life. Seconds later, Teti suddenly appeared. Noticing Carlucci's mood change, Teti became acutely suspicious. Making a mental note to be extra alert for treacherous behavior, he didn't want to be caught off guard like the Tucci incident.

After a short wait, they gathered their luggage. Exiting the terminal a sudden blast of hot air stimulated them temporarily. Carlucci hesitated a moment— undecided about renting a car. The airline tickets were purchased under aliases. A car, however, would require a driver's license. Not wanting to leave any type of paper trail Carlucci hailed a cab.

"Where are we heading?" Teti asked wearily with an unsmiling face.

"Cibola Casino," Carlucci replied confidently with his chest puffed out like a strutting rooster.

Wearing newly purchased sunglasses, Johnny drove north toward Las Vegas along Boulder Highway with the top down on his MGB. It was a grand spring morning, one of the most pleasant times of year in Las Vegas. The temperature was bearable and a soft breeze blew in from the desert. Wheeling his way down the road, he idly thought that life could be good here.

Turning left onto Flamingo Road, he stopped at Las Vegas Boulevard for a red light. Johnny's mind had shifted from enjoying his surroundings to fantasizing about Sandy Edelman. This was a common occurrence that distracted him quite a bit these last few days. Consequently, he didn't notice the taxicab crossing his path with Carlucci's awe struck angular face framed in the back window. Turning right onto Las Vegas Boulevard, Johnny subconsciously gravitated toward the familiar, capriciously deciding to pull into the Cibola Casino. Stopping behind a cab discharging passengers, his heart sank.

Spying Carlucci and Teti exiting the taxicab, Johnny was frantic. Thinking quickly, he decided to pass the taxicab. There was just enough space to allow the small sports car to roll past the cab. Now on the alert for potential treachery, Teti caught Johnny's eye for a second even though he tried to avoid any visual contact. Johnny's heart was pounding. Luckily, Carlucci was exhausted from the overnight flight and his visual acuity was diminished. Without any fanfare or obvious reason, Teti quietly turned away allowing Johnny to adroitly slip past them without being noticed.

Knowing that Carlucci was on the scent, Teti didn't want to be sent after the small fish. It also served as a warning to Cisco. For the moment Teti wanted to stick close to Carlucci. It was his only hope of interceding on his father's behalf.

Johnny was confounded. His utter anxiety was mirrored in his face. The joyful mental meanderings of a few moments ago drained from his body changing his facial complexion to a shade of ashen white. Pulling into an empty parking spot, he speculated on the implications of this new development. It wasn't pleasant. These ruthless *goombas* were relentless, he moaned internally. A morose sense of doom overcame him like a cloud suddenly blocking the warming rays of the morning sun.

As Johnny fought to control the fear that was gurgling in his stomach, a ray of hope seeped into his distressed mind. Teti had definitely seen him drive past. Yet, he acted as if he didn't recognize him. This thought perplexed Johnny. After all, Teti extended the Gimp's invitation to lunch. He had to remember. Besides, Johnny concluded, the mustard colored MGB with Pennsylvania plates was a dead give away. Something else was going on here, he surmised. "Teti, Teti, Teti," he repeated in a hushed cadence. The name rang a bell in his addled mind. Slowly driving the car forward between two parked cars, Johnny couldn't quite put his finger on it. Guardedly, he continued his train of thought. Hoping for the best, he decided to prepare for the worst. He automatically shifted his car into second gear wheeling the MGB onto Las Vegas Boulevard heading north. Needing time to think about what had just transpired, he decided to take the long way back to the motel.

Cisco looked at the alarm clock next to his bed. It was almost 11 A.M. and he was hungry. He was also anxious to enter the nine-ball tournament. Abhorring the polyester look, he dressed in khaki pants and a light cotton shirt. Before stepping outside of the motel room to smoke a cigarette, he searched his belongings for his .25 automatic. After checking the ammunition clip, he slid the weapon into his pocket as insurance. It was the only policy that he could trust these days. So far, it hadn't failed him. Shaking a lonely Marlboro cigarette from the pack on the dresser, he stepped outside to light it.

Old habits die hard, he thought leaning against a post enjoying the warm morning air. In another hour or two the temperature would heat up and he would either have to stay inside or go swimming. Regaining a lighter mood, he laughed quietly to himself with anticipatory delight. *Fifty G's* would be his largest score, he indulgently thought. The previous night's score had made him more cheerful and confident.

After lighting the cigarette he took a long drag on its toxic blend of tobacco. Gently blowing the cigarette smoke through lips formed like a circle, he playfully formed a series of rings in the air. Finished amusing himself, he let the cigarette dangle from his lips. His thoughts drifted to Rose wondering what she was doing at the moment. Probably cleaning up after the lunchtime crowd, he idly speculated. Thinking about the last time they had made love, he took a deep drag on his cigarette then put it out. Another practice Rose had coerced him into performing. Cheerfully, Cisco reminisced with a distant look in his yearning eyes.

Just before reentering his room a taxicab pulled up to the motel and discharged its inebriated passenger. Cisco was chafing at the bit to get a head start. Impetuously, he hailed the cabbie.

"Where to buddy?" the cabbie asked. The question was second nature to him.

"Cibola Casino," Cisco answered not bothering to leave Johnny a note. After all, the kid didn't leave him one, he rationalized. Besides, the kid was starting to get on his nerves, he thought. They both needed a break.

Sandy brushed her hair with contemplative strokes of the brush in a slow methodical fashion. Vacillation kept gnawing at her resolve. Peering long and hard into the mirror, she was looking for a supportive sign. Any indication that she was making a sound decision would do just fine. None appeared.

Putting the brush down, she put a spattering of make up on her face hoping to change her mood. That didn't work either. Finally, she slipped her college graduation ring on her finger. Nervously turning the ring around her finger, she calculated the amount of time and effort it took to graduate. Working part-time while attending school, she paid her own tuition and keep. Her parents helped where they could, but the bulk of the money she had earned. Then in one night of bacchanalian revelry, it had all changed. "How stupid. How utterly stupid," she kept repeating to herself in a barely audible voice. If this was the price she had to pay, so be it, she thought. Hoping those words would wash away her recrimination and in the process restore her to that fresh and clean ivory soap girl image that everyone said she possessed. They didn't. Still, she convinced herself they did. Tired of thinking about it she just wanted to get it over with, soon, now, this minute. Blanking her mind she got into her light green Mustang and drove off to meet with a counselor.

Sandy chose Las Vegas because she was less likely to meet anyone she knew here. New York State offered legal abortions, but that was too close to home. Besides, she wanted to see the west coast and planned on looking for a job in Los Angeles after she recuperated from the procedure. She had heard there were plenty of jobs there and the weather was gorgeous. This also helped mitigate the lie she told her parents. New surroundings, new people all equated to a new life. The allure was overpowering. Interspersed among these thoughts drifting in and out of her mind as she drove west on E. Charleston Boulevard was her encounter with Johnny. For some strange reason she kept recounting her short time with the sincere city slicker. Just the thought of him brought a quirky smile to her face. All these thoughts consumed her as she crossed Las Vegas Boulevard searching for an address on W. Charleston Boulevard without noticing Johnny's mustard MGB stopped at the red light.

Although Johnny was thinking of how to break the news to Cisco, he watched in amazement as a light green Mustang crossed his path. Slightly cocking his head to follow the vehicle, he was leery about darting after this one. He had followed other light green Mustangs only to be disappointed. This one looked like it had Pennsylvania plates. Deciding that Cisco wasn't going anywhere since he had the car, he made a dangerously illegal turn. His luck held out. Hearing no sirens, he concentrated on looking for Sandy's Mustang. Weaving in and out of traffic, Johnny caught a glimpse of the light green Mustang turning into a two story parking structure across from the Desert Mall. Suddenly, the light on Rancho Road turned red and the car in front of him stopped abruptly. Unable to get around the lumbering Thunderbird in front of him, Johnny slid down into the MGB seat and pouted until the light turned green.

Turning into the parking structure, Johnny slowly cruised through the facility until he found the light green Mustang. Bingo, he thought exuberantly as a broad expectant smile crossed his ruddy face. Pennsylvania plates and plenty of road grime was enough confirmation for him.

Parking nearby, he exited his car and reviewed the office listing posted near an elevator. It was a medical center with at least two dozen various types of medical services offered. Postulating in his mind several different scenarios to find her, he decided to sit still and wait. After all, her car was right here. And doctors never take more than an hour, he deduced.

Finding a closer spot to view Sandy's car, Johnny adjusted the mirrors. Cisco could wait; the world could wait, he thought sternly. He wasn't about to lose track of Sandy Edelman again. Delicately dancing around the reason that he felt that way, he waited.

65

Cisco slid out of the backseat of the taxicab in front of the Cibola Casino after paying his fare. Looking around nervously for no particular reason, uneasiness enshrouded him. Involuntarily, patting his pockets for a cigarette he realized that he left them on the dresser back at the motel. Stifling a frown, his hand lingered offhandedly on the .25 automatic in his pocket. On the lookout for anything suspicious, a cagey Cisco entered the casino with radar-like eye movements scanning the immediate horizon.

The labyrinthine aisles lined with gaming tables reminded Cisco of the House of Mirrors from the traveling carnival shows that visited the small towns of South Jersey during the summers of his youth. Although these aisles seemed to lead to nowhere, Cisco was sure that there was a method to their convolution.

After several wrong turns, Cisco finally arrived at the Special Events Office. The woman sitting at the desk was cookie-cutter beautiful like most of the women employed by the casinos in Vegas. Once he gave her the obligatory once over look, Cisco immediately sat down in a chair facing her without being asked.

"Hello sir. What can the Cibola Casino do for you?" the beautiful dark haired woman asked in a singsong modulating voice that masked a hidden sensuality noticeable only when looking directly into her hazel eyes.

"I'd like to sign up for the nine-ball tournament," Cisco said casually.

The woman's facial expression changed like a chameleon into one of discouragement. The somber look indicated that Cisco's request was to be met with resistance. After a drawn out moment, she replied in an oddly forced sad tone, "I'm sorry sir, but the roster is full."

Cisco's eyes narrowed caustically with an intense focus as he prodded, "As in no openings. No way. No how?"

"Yes. That pretty much covers it."

Cisco had not taken this possibility into account. His dark face hardened. His lips pursed. Unaccustomed to begging, he pleaded, "But miss, you have to understand, I came a long way for the opportunity to play here."

"Most people who come to this town do. I'm sorry. It's Mister Greenberg's policy."

The name elicited a response from his mental queue. Snapping his fingers, Cisco remembered the business card. Anxiously, he searched his wallet. Upon finding it, a smile cracked his swarthy papier-mâché face. Immediately, he presented it to the woman with a relieved look. "Would ya give this to Mister Greenberg, please?" he asked repressing the anxiety in his voice.

Eyeing the business card skeptically, she stood up pointing to Cisco with the business card scissored between her index and middle fingers. "Wait right here. Okay?"

Carlucci hoisted his suitcase onto his bed and immediately zipped it open. Removing a toiletry case, he opened it eagerly and removed two meticulously wrapped .38 revolvers from their packing material. With a flickering finger, he gestured to Teti. His eyes bored into him trying to measure the man's resolve. The Gimp wanted Teti dead too. Carlucci would have much rather taken care of the Gimp. That matter, however, required a bit more finesse and careful execution like the Bellino affair. Instead, Carlucci evasively sidestepped a direct commitment. Teti was milquetoast, he concluded. As long as he didn't get in the way, Carlucci could care less. Even that stupid kid and his misplaced heroics didn't matter any longer. Let the Gimp dispose of his own dirty laundry, like he was about to do, Carlucci thought defiantly. Soon. Very soon. It would all be a moot point, Carlucci chuckled to himself. Like two gunslingers from the Wild West, Carlucci and Cisco would finally have their showdown.

In contemplative preoccupation Carlucci was caught off guard when Teti tossed a box of bullets to him. Contorting his body while juggling the box of bullets, Carlucci finally grasped the elusive package. After loading both weapons, Carlucci tossed Teti one of the guns. "This one's loaded. So don't shoot yourself, will ya," he said smiling through his yellow teeth intending the remark as a snide innuendo.

Teti was indifferent to the remark. These past couple of weeks convinced him that he could never be a killer like this man next to him. Self-preservation was an entirely different matter, Teti thought. Still he wasn't certain he could do that either.

Watching Carlucci load the guns then toss one to him actually lowered the threshold of his trepidation. Still, it could be a ploy to gain his confidence. He made a mental note to check the bullets in case, well just in case. The thought didn't need to be finished. It was painfully obvious.

A mangy looking Carlucci paced the room like a tiger in a cage. Anxious and nervous, he had trouble focusing on his next move. "Let's go down to the casino and see what's shaking," he asked in a manner that was more like a command.

Cisco waited impatiently for the elevator just off of the casino's main lobby. Apparently, the business card that Sid Greenberg had given him was his ticket to the top floor of this establishment, he shrewdly thought. What this little jaunt to the top of this gambling micro world would buy him, he could not fathom. Maybe, it was just an obligatory courtesy to simply tell him—sorry, better luck next time. Cisco pressed hard on the up button on the elevator indicator panel for a second time in the hope that it would speed the elevator's arrival. It did not.

Finally, several elevators arrived simultaneously. Cisco entered one, a step ahead of Carlucci and Teti exiting the other. Timing was everything and for this particular moment it was in Cisco's favor.

Ben Greenberg's office had a one hundred and eighty degree panoramic view looking out over Las Vegas toward Lake Mead and a range of snow capped mountains resembling the parapets of a castle. The décor was contemporary chic. No chi chi glitz, a Las Vegas' trademark, was anywhere to be found except in the casino fifteen floors below.

Looking down on the Las Vegas Strip, Ben Greenberg was the master of his world and several others within his line of sight. Dressed in a dark sharkskin suit with blue shirt and light yellow tie, he was not the image of a stodgy businessman who crunched numbers. His business decisions were more strategic, sometimes unorthodox, but always profitable. Grimly mulling over the decisions about to confront him, he remained peering out the window. When Cisco entered his office, Ben Greenberg held up the business card without looking at it. "Did you read the inscription on the back of this card?" he drolly asked.

"I did."

"One get out of jail free," Ben Greenberg chuckled. Turning to face Cisco, he smiled lightly. "When I was a boy my father loved to play Monopoly with me. I think he still does. If things work out next year, he may get to play it for real in Atlantic City."

"I wouldn't want to play against him."

Ben Greenberg nodded in proud agreement. "Nor would I." With an amiable outstretching of his hand, he gestured for Cisco to have a seat. "Let's get right to the point. I'm not interested in anything but the trouble that you're laying at my feet."

"I'm just here for the tournament," Cisco said.

"And you brought a trail of trouble. So, save me the excuses," Ben Greenberg said expressively lurching forward in his chair using his finger for emphasis. He pulled no punches. Sliding back into his chair making a loose fist, he patted the lower portion of his index finger against his lips in nervous contemplation. "So, what did you do to this Gimp lunatic to get him so pissed?"

"I don't know, but it's a package deal. Maybe he doesn't like my face?"

Sighing deeply, Ben Greenberg made a steeple of his fingers holding them in thought near his face. "Okay. Okay. He's a nut case. So, here's how it's going to come down. I'm going to let you in the tournament to play for the house." Holding up the palm of his hand as a signal to be quiet he continued, "Keep your seed money. You're going to need it. Second. I want you to leave this casino now. Stay away until the tournament begins on Friday morning. Maybe by then I'll have a better handle on this situation. In the meantime, we keep any unpleasantness out of my casino. I won't stand for this kind of bullshit coming down within these walls. You understand?"

"Perfectly."

"Good."

"Leave a phone number and address where I can reach you with my secretary."

"What kinda split we talkin' about?" Cisco said offhandedly.

"You're worried about a split? That's ballsy, real ballsy," Ben Greenberg commented, surprised at Cisco's hubris. "Forget the money. Worry about your ass my friend." and then after a hesitant moment, "I tell you what, if you survive the week I guarantee it will be worth your while if, and only if, you win the tournament. Deal?"

With an unsmiling face Cisco asked flippantly, "Do I have a choice?"

"Yeah. Oh yeah. You can leave Vegas right now and save me some heavy aggravation. I'm doing this only because I respect my father's judgment. If it were up to me I'd hang you out to dry. So you see, you do have a choice."

His bluntness surprised Cisco. "Since you put it to me in such a nice way, I guess I'll accept."

Standing up straight, Ben Greenberg offered Cisco his hand, "I'm not the bastard that you think I'm just a simple businessman with demanding clients. I'll see you Friday morning. And remember, stay out of the Strip casinos. These *goombas* looking for you don't understand proper protocol. Apparently, Joey Bellino didn't understand it either."

Cisco clenched his teeth and nodded affirmatively. Bellino's name was all over the newspapers. Dragging himself to his feet, he shook Ben Greenberg's hand with a firm grip that was reciprocated by the edgy casino overlord. It was a positive indication that he was sincere about keeping his word. "Thanks," Cisco intoned with vocal sincerity.

"Thank my father," Ben Greenberg said in a dismissive tone of voice signaling the end of the meeting.

Turning to exit, Cisco shuffled toward the door unsure if what he had just heard at this informal meeting was really good news or the prelude to a death sentence.

66

A somber mood hovered low over Sandy's head like a dark rain cloud about to burst. Slowly, she redressed after being examined. Trying to keep from thinking about what was sure to transpire in the coming week, she interposed fantasies about her future in California. This helped to allay the nauseating dread that she felt on the examining table during the pelvic examination.

Sitting in a waiting area thoughtlessly paging through a magazine, Sandy waited to speak with a counselor. Restless, she stood up to stretch, walking to the window to watch people's comings and goings in an effort to derive some justification for humanity's banal existence on this planet. Such profound ruminations eluded her today. The barest hint of a smile managed to crack her solemn countenance when she thought about Johnny Cerone. Thoughts of him wheedled their way into her melancholic musings like a burst of omniscient light to save her from spiraling into the black hole of perpetual self-recrimination for her predicament.

However, her greatest fear, even greater than what she was about to authorize, was that Johnny was all smoke and mirrors like so many other men she had met on her way to this sterile institution. It was as if sex was a genetic byproduct of the male brain's synaptic function, Sandy thought irascibly. Although she had sensed that he was different, she couldn't afford to take the chance especially at this particular moment in her life. That was in the past she said to herself. At least the thought of him kept her from being mired in hopelessness of ever finding a man like him. Sighing deeply, Sandy turned and was startled to find a woman in a white coat staring benignly at her.

"Sandy Edelman?"

"Yes."

"Hi, I'm Joan Metzger, your counselor," she said directing Sandy with a gentle swoop of her arm into her brightly lit office.

Almost directly under the counselor's office in the parking structure, Johnny sat slouched in his car. He looked at the clock intermittently. Committed to keeping Sandy in his life, Johnny rehearsed several different spiels to argue his case. Unsatisfied with all of them, he decided to simply be spontaneous no matter what he blurted out. This decision made his stomach flutter in an exhilarating sort of way. Thinking back to his mental anguish just before Easter he realized that one of the questions he posed to himself may have been answered right now. Never having experienced this feeling for a woman before, he assumed that this was how one felt when they were in love. Hitting the steering wheel of the MGB with the palms of both hands in a self-congratulatory gesture, a disturbing thought seeped into his ebullient consciousness. The broad upwardly curved smile on his face flat lined into one of concern. What if Sandy didn't feel the same way about him?

Sliding into the rolling armchair behind her desk, Joan Metzger smiled warmly trying to put Sandy at ease. She glanced at Sandy's file quickly then looked at her making sure to maintain eye contact. "You certainly have come a long way. New York would've been much closer."

"Too close."

"I see. After a reflective pause, Joan Metzger continued in a soothing tone, "This is not an easy decision. It never is. Societal pressures, parental disdain and personal feelings mix together to form an emotional imbalance that sways to and fro constantly. One day you're prepared. The next day you're not so sure. Have you considered all of this?"

"I've had a lot of time to consider every aspect. Driving across country for me uncorked my inhibitions. I've had a lot of time to think this week or so. So I'm here to tell you I'm sure," Sandy said in a slightly quivering voice that cracked occasionally.

"You're still in your first trimester, so you still have time to reconsider," the counselor reminded Sandy.

"Reconsider what? My parent's are devout Catholics who know nothing of my circumstances. The father gave me the money for it. So I can't go back to him can I? This is my life. It is my choice," Sandy explained firmly. "I'll get over it. So let's just finalize the paperwork and make the appointment, please."

Flipping through her appointment book, Joan Metzger calmly ran her finger down the page. "This Friday morning at nine?"

"That's fine."

As Joan Metzger prepared the paperwork she instructed Sandy, "Have someone drive you to and from the center. Otherwise take a taxi. It would be much better if you have someone with you."

"I guess it'll be a taxi. There's no one here for me."

With the back of his seat in the MGB tilted at almost a forty-five degree angle, Johnny's head was barely visible above the car door. Sulking over the uncertainty of what he was about to do, he perked up at the sound of approaching footsteps.

Sandy approached her car with a large manila envelope under her arm. Searching for her car keys in her purse, she was oblivious of the man standing in front of her.

"Hello Sandy," Johnny said.

Startled for the second time this morning, Sandy's eyes ignited like a brushfire, fast and furious then settled down to a mere flicker when the reality of the moment struck home. "How did you find me?" she asked as her facial muscles contorted her eyebrows into a questioning arch.

"You crossed my path on The Strip and I followed you here. Is something wrong?"

"Just asking. I thought that you might be some kind of weirdo stalker. This town is full of them."

"I see." Tongue-tied, Johnny gestured incomprehensibly with his hands until the words came out in a crisp staccato fashion, "Would you like to have lunch?"

"You just won't give up, will you?" Sandy asked incredulously.

"Nope. Never will."

Sandy sighed. Seeing him here in this place and at this time only complicated an already complicated scenario she thought. Then again, maybe not, she thought wistfully. "Then I guess we'll just have to have lunch." Still she wanted to keep some distance between them. So, she added, "Just lunch."

67

Teti sat at a blackjack table in the Cibola Casino nervously counting the two stacks of green twenty-five dollar chips in front of him. Even though he was winning, counting the money lessened his anxiety about the purpose of the trip. Hopefully, that Johnny kid would warn Cisco, he kept praying. Somehow, he knew that Cisco wouldn't back off. Must be in the blood he thought wistfully.

People with zombie-like eyes hovered nearby watching the game in progress. Most were looking for a vicarious infusion of hope into their shallow lives. Carlucci was among them, but his eyes were scanning the gaming tables for another reason—Cisco. Nervously cranking his neck from side to side, Carlucci's innermost feelings were mirrored in his striated belligerent face. Then while scanning the outer edges of the casino area his hyperactive eyes caught a sign for the Special Events Office. A light bulb went off in his low wattage brain. In unison his one eye arched his bushy eyebrow forming a hideous portrait.

Meanwhile Teti, bored with the slow pace of the blackjack table, wagered his two stacks of chips, all five-hundred dollars worth on one hand. With a subtle nod from the pit boss, the dealer adroitly slid the cards from the card shoe. The dealer showing a face card caused the two players ahead of Teti to go bust rather than standing pat. Teti had a five showing and a ten in the hole. Throwing caution to the wind, he decided to go against the odds to test his luck. With a lowered head he viewed his hold card. He rolled his eyes to the top of his head looking at the dealer with a calculating smirk. Taking a deep breath through wide nostrils, he held his breath and called, "Hit me."

The dealer drew an ace and placed it next to the five on the table in front of Teti.

Releasing his pent up breath Teti idly wondered if he would be so cavalier if his life was on the line. After a moment's hesitation, Teti smiled recklessly. With a flickering index finger, he signaled for another card. "Again."

This time Teti drew a five. His smile reconfigured instantly to one of subdued satisfaction, he flipped over his hold card for a total of twenty-one.

Emotionlessly, the dealer flipped over his hold card. It was the king of spades. Teti won.

Reflexively, Carlucci patted him in congratulatory fashion on his back then whispered into his ear. "Stay here. I'll be right back."

Carlucci flounced through the aisles of the casino to an office off to the side of the cashier's booth. Teti backed down his bet to twenty-five dollars. Meanwhile, he kept a suspicious eye on Carlucci's movements.

Arriving at the Special Events Office post haste, Carlucci approached the same woman sitting at the desk that Cisco had encountered.

"Hello sir. What can the Cibola Casino do for you," the beautiful dark haired, hazel-eyed woman asked in the same singsong modulating voice that became rote after hundreds of continuous greetings.

"I'm here about the nine-ball tournament," Carlucci said brusquely.

"I'm sorry sir, but the roster is full," the woman responded with a bland look on her face. She didn't want to waste a smile on such a scruffy character.

"That's okay. Can I see it?"

"It'll be posted the day after tomorrow," she said caustically.

"Now would be better," Carlucci stated in a forceful manner accompanied by a threatening stare.

Reluctantly handing him the sheet with the names, she had not yet added Armand Francesco's name to the list.

Disappointed, Carlucci handed the sheet back to the woman then turned to walk away. "Who are you looking for?" she queried in a mater-of-fact tone.

Turning back, Carlucci said, "Armand Francesco."

With bright eyes the woman replied, "Oh him. He went up to see Mister Greenberg ten minutes ago."

"Which floor?" he asked hastily.

"Why the top floor," she replied snobbishly expecting Carlucci to know her boss.

Without saying thanks, Carlucci abruptly rushed out of the office toward the elevators.

Noticing Carlucci's dash to the elevators, Teti sensed imminent danger. He scooped up his chips and stuffed them into his pocket quickly. Automatically, he triangulated the shortest distance to the elevator and proceeded to intercept the fiery-eyed Carlucci.

Someone else also had noticed Carlucci's desperate dash toward the elevators. Ben Greenberg played his cards close to his chest. Never letting on that he observed Cisco's pathetic performance at the blackjack table, he instructed his security detail to alert him immediately if any unusual situations developed. When the camera showed Carlucci rushing for the elevators, the security guard monitoring the cameras vacillated for a moment. Deciding that it was better to get chewed out for nothing than getting blackballed for something, he made the call.

Cisco watched the descending numbers on the panel above the elevator door. It was the only distraction he could find at the moment to keep him from going into a pessimistic funk. Leaning his shoulder solidly against the wall of the elevator, he closed his eyes momentarily trying to conger up his most recent memories of Rose and him together.

Appreciating the guard's diligence, Ben Greenberg instructed the guard to follow the man that he just described as long as he was in the casino. After thanking him, he immediately summoned Hank. He was taking no chances. If Carlucci were so arrogant as to compromise the only unwritten rule in Las Vegas then he would take matters into his own hands.

Cursing himself for not heeding his father's warning, Ben Greenberg never thought that personal vendettas would trump good business sense. What was that idiot thinking? Greenberg asked himself over and over again as he removed a .357 Magnum from the top drawer of his desk stuffing it into the waistband of his expensive suit.

Standing back from the elevators Carlucci's eyes danced erratically from one elevator to the next watching the panoply of ascending and descending numbers. Two were headed down, the rest of the elevators were headed up. If he could catch Cisco on the top floor, it would be perfect he thought hopefully. He imagined forcing Cisco to the roof and pushing him off. The entire affair would look like a suicide. It happened all the time in Vegas, Carlucci rationalized. A little suffering on the way down would mitigate his bloodlust. Easily explainable to the authorities, it was a foolproof plan. The thought of it brought a satisfying smile to his craggy face.

Carlucci focused on the two descending elevators assuming that Cisco could be on his way down. He would take the second elevator up if Cisco were on neither of them. As the first elevator approached the first floor he slowly pushed his hands down to his side. Unnoticed like he had practiced for the Bellino hit, this technique was becoming second nature to him now. It gave him the split second edge that men in his line of work needed. Suddenly realizing that he would have to improvise this time, Carlucci's satisfying smile turned to one of escalating concern.

Awkwardly grasping the gun in his pocket with one hand, Carlucci let it remain on the gun for the time being. There were too many people mulling around for him to position it properly. This made him self conscious and nervous. It showed in his sweaty face.

Arriving at the elevators Teti noticed Carlucci's uneasiness also. "What's going on," he asked with a demure almost cautious probing in his voice.

"Cisco's upstairs," Carlucci replied tersely.

Teti's mind whirled into action. But like a hamster on a treadmill, his thoughts went nowhere. Knowing that men like Carlucci could sense treachery, he changed the focus of his thought patterns. By sheer determination he prodded his mind into inane territory. Still, his manner seemed awkward and his smile unnaturally stilted.

Carlucci looked suspiciously at him, and then broke away when he heard the ding of the elevator bell. The arrival of the first elevator was disappointing. Carlucci reminded himself that he needed to get Cisco to the roof for his impromptu plan to succeed. Teti continued forcing a smile. Carlucci redirected his attention to him temporarily. "What's with you?" he asked narrowing his eyebrows quizzically.

I've got a pocketful of chips. It's kinda awkward," Teti shot back thinking quickly on his feet.

"You let me handle this cowboy," Carlucci warned with a jabbing finger directed toward Teti.

Pursing his lips, Teti nodded apprehensively.

Carlucci faced the elevator like a gunslinger ready to draw. If Cisco was on this elevator, he wasn't going to get off Carlucci promised himself resolutely.

With his eyes still closed, the elevator Cisco was riding reached the casino level. Unaware of impending danger, Cisco was caught off guard when the elevator doors slid open and Carlucci quickly plowed inside.

"Well, well, what do we have here," Carlucci chortled with delight removing his gun quickly from his pocket before Cisco had a chance to react.

Teti stepped into the elevator moments later giving Cisco a sullen stare.

Pushing the up button quickly before anyone had a chance to enter behind them, Carlucci returned his insidious gaze to the doleful looking Cisco. "I guess the gangs all here," he said mockingly. Emboldened by the lucky break of events, Carlucci pushed the barrel of the .38 deep into the soft skin of Cisco's neck. Putting his face close to Cisco's, Carlucci whispered sarcastically, "Feeling a bit naked asshole?" The stench of his breath temporarily repulsed Cisco, but he was determined not to give him even that satisfaction.

Resolved to the fact he was going to die, Cisco decided not to quiver and shake in the face of it. Perhaps he would spit in Carlucci's face before taking it like a man. Hopefully, an opportunity to strike back at this pathetic excuse for a human being would develop. With a lucid mind he tried to determine how he was going to get the .25 automatic out of his pocket. There was also another variable in his death defying equation, his son.

Teti stood straight back against the rear wall of the elevator facing the doors impassively. He too was seeking an opportunity to end this madness. A son could not stand by and watch his father die like a dog, he recited like a mantra over and over again. Even if he never really knew the man, he sensed the man's presence on occasion. Besides, they still had the same blood. Wondering if Carlucci had the slightest inkling about his relationship to Cisco, Teti decided to remain still until he sensed imminent danger.

Then a queer event occurred, disconcerting at the least. Instead of ascending, the elevator began to descend into the bowels of the Cibola Casino.

Carlucci's face flushed bright red as he angrily banged at the floor numbers. Noticing no numbers lower than the ground floor, he clenched his jaw so tight that his cheeks twitched spasmodically. With flared nostrils he teetered on killing Cisco. Sensing Carlucci's volcanic anger about to explode, Teti interceded.

"Anthony! Settle down. Let's wait to see where we're going," Teti pleaded knowing that he had no other recourse. Otherwise, if he pulled his gun out, the elevator car would become a communal coffin. Teti didn't relish the thought of spending eternity with this vulgar madman.

Cisco's eyes swiveled back and forth between Carlucci and Teti with icy calmness. He understood the boy's logic. Even if he couldn't show it, he was proud of him.

"As long as he's alive, we're alive," Teti said emphatically. "I don't know about you but I want to cash my chips in upstairs and not in some dingy basement." It was a ploy to add a little levity to the situation. It worked for the moment.

Then without warning the elevator stopped. The doors opened slowly.

Ben Greenberg had taken personal control of the security room ordering the usual guard to take an early lunch break. The guard was astute enough to know the importance of the request and left without uttering a word.

All of the elevators leading to the casino lobby had the ability of descending to the lower levels of the building in case of emergency. However, they could only do so remotely from the security room that Ben Greenberg now commanded. Focusing on a stairwell camera, Hank was just passing the eighth floor. His arrival in the lower level would still be minutes away. Without further vacillation, Ben Greenberg decided to take matters into his own hands. In a highly unusual course of action, he switched off all the cameras throughout the casino. Quickly, he exited the room to take personal control of this insane situation. Damage control was always his first order of business. It was what he did best. But death was suddenly on the agenda today. Ben Greenberg would be its Grim Reaper.

With a silent jerk of his head, Carlucci commanded Teti to exit the elevator in front of him. Grabbing the back of Cisco's collar tightly, Carlucci held his gun firmly against his skull just below the ear. Forcing Cisco out of the elevator car, Carlucci inadvertently exposed his back to Teti.

Suddenly, plastic chips clattered on the concrete floor. The sound startled Carlucci. Pirouetting like an awkward danseur, he found himself looking down the barrel of Teti's .38 as the hammer of the gun clicked back ready to fire instantly.

"Surprise," Teti intoned sarcastically. "Now drop the gun," he commanded.

With one eye squinting Carlucci quickly calculated Teti's mettle. The hubris drained from his face as the veins on the side of his neck throbbed. He wasn't about to let this milquetoast son-of-a-bitch interfere. Still clutching his weapon, he slowly allowed his arms to fall to his side.

Maintaining almost hypnotic eye contact, Teti knew exactly what Carlucci was thinking as a villainous smile expanded across his face. "Be my guest," Teti said with a tinge of delight in his voice.

In a flash Carlucci's somber face returned to one of arrogant belligerence as he looked past Teti and chortled.

The sound of another gun's hammer clicking back flipped Teti's cocky mien to one of anxious surprise like a cue card during a theatrical performance.

"Put your finger on the hammer and slowly release it," the voice of Ben Greenberg instructed with crisp clarity.

Cisco meanwhile unobtrusively slid his .25 automatic from his pocket instinctively crouching in slow measured increments.

Teti complied reluctantly. Meanwhile, Carlucci was focused solely on Cisco. Unable to comprehend the duplicitous crapshoot unfolding around him, he constantly misread people's intent. This included the man holding the .357 magnum handgun. With an itchy finger and a pounding heart Carlucci wrongly assumed that Ben Greenberg was there to back him up. Pivoting on his heels, he instinctively crouched while raising his .38 to finish what he set out to do.

Anticipating Carlucci's movement, Cisco was positioned to gain a slight advantage and fired the .25 automatic twice before a surprised Carlucci was able to complete his turn. Stumbling to the concrete floor, Carlucci's gun fell from his hand.

Hank arrived with gun in hand. Ben Greenberg restrained him momentarily with an outstretched arm. Walking around Carlucci, Ben Greenberg heard a low moan from the disheveled mass on the cement floor. Angrily kicking Carlucci's gun away, he motioned expressively for Hank to cover Carlucci with his gun.

Carlucci suddenly reached out to grab Ben Greenberg's ankle, but the beefy Hank viciously stomped on Carlucci's wrist with the heel of his heavy black cowboy boots. The snapping sound of breaking bones accompanied Hank's sadistically satisfying kick to Carlucci's rib cage.

Taking this entire affair personally, Ben Greenberg pointed his handgun while cocking the hammer back at Carlucci's head with blazing eyes and oscillating nostrils. He had dispatched better men than this disheveled disrespecting slug for lesser offenses. They were strictly business deals gone sour. This one was different. Then, the appropriate solution occurred to him like a gentle breeze cooling his flushed red face. Sliding the hammer back on the handgun, a droll smile crossed his face. Turning around abruptly, Ben Greenberg waved the cannon in his hand around haphazardly at Teti. "Who the fuck are you?" he asked in a demanding tone of voice.

"Americo Teti."

His narrowing eyes accented the astonished look on his face. Swinging around Ben Greenberg faced Cisco.

"He's my son," Cisco answered without being asked.

"Teti, huh," Ben Greenberg said to no one in particular. Stuffing the .357 into the waistband of his suit, he began massaging his forehead with two of his fingers. Quickly improvising on his previous solution, he pointed a stern finger at Teti. "Okay. Awright, Teti. Help Hank here get rid of this pile of shit," looking at Hank, "Indian style."

Hank nodded approvingly.

Teti held his .38 out handle first toward Ben Greenberg with a questioning lopsided look.

"Keep it my young friend." Spinning his finger around, Ben Greenberg pointed at Carlucci lying on the floor, "This little tap dance ain't over yet. You got one more chorus to perform."

68

By early evening Johnny and Sandy were still together. Seeing Johnny again peeled away a layer of the pessimism enveloping Sandy. Mesmerized by the water from the Colorado River cascading down the spillway of the Hoover Dam, they were enjoying the moment.

The concrete gravity-arch dam was named for Herbert Hoover, the thirty-first President of the United States. Located on the border between Arizona and Nevada, just thirty miles southeast of Las Vegas, it was built in the nineteen thirties to tame the unpredictable rampaging waters of the Colorado River by creating a reservoir called Lake Mead. It is a testament to man's ability to overcome adverse conditions.

Dancing around the relationship topic all afternoon Johnny hoped that tonight this unique place would serve as an allegory for his pursuit of Sandy. "Over a hundred men lost their lives building this behemoth," Johnny said working his way subtly into a thematic conversation with Sandy.

Looking around in awe at the sheer magnitude of the surrounding canyon walls, she replied, "I guess I can see why."

"The people who built this all took a chance to build a better life. It was a grueling gamble. So why won't you take a chance on me?"

"You think you know a lot about me Johnny, but you don't," Sandy explained evasively trying to stay away from specifics.

"Then I want to find out."

"You may not like what you find."

"Try me," Johnny said in a slightly challenging tone of voice.

Sandy looked searchingly into Johnny's endearing eyes wanting to bare her soul. Was this man the real thing or just another patronizing heartbreaker, she asked herself? Quickly, she weighed the pro and cons of what she already knew about him. Although the mental list came out in Johnny's favor, Sandy was still leery, afraid of making another mistake. Turning to look far downstream, she shaded her eyes from the quickly setting sun with her hand. "I'd love to try white-water rafting sometime," she said totally avoiding the train of thought their conversation had just taken.

In frustration Johnny blurted out, "What are you running from?"

Sandy quickly snapped her head around to face Johnny and retorted like an echo, "What are *you* running from?" emphasizing the *you* of his blatant question.

Johnny said one word, "Gangsters."

Taken aback by his directness, Sandy's jaw dropped as her eyes arched in amazement.

"Your turn," he said righteously.

Sandy tersely replied after a long moment, "I'm pregnant." It was a half-truth.

"What a fine pair we make," Johnny said with a judgmental timbre to the statement.

"See!"

"See what?" Johnny asked with confusion spreading across his face.

"You already think less of me," Sandy stated in a voice that quivered and cracked. Trying to forestall any further discussion, she emotionally demanded, "Take me back to my car, please."

Insensitive to the stigmatization that he was perpetuating, Johnny became defensive, "Fine."

The ride back to the parking lot where Sandy's car was parked gave both of them time to reassess their feelings. With the top down on the MGB the star-studded sky enveloping them was like a *Van Gogh* painting. Unfortunately, their impression of one another was a bit tarnished. They had fallen off of their idealistic pedestal and were now face to face with the drama of the reality called life.

At the same time in a different time zone, Anna Giampietro was also coming face to face with the reality called life. Dismayingly, she found herself unable to deal with it.

The grim reality that she would never see the love of her life again was beginning to settle in. The mere thought of it was like a dagger to her heart. She did not like the feeling. Therefore, when it surfaced, she dispelled it with whatever means was available.

In her heart she knew that his disappearance was her father's handiwork. Unaware of the true reasons for his action, she could not totally bring herself to hate the man. After all, she thought, he was her father. Below the surface, however, she secretly feared that making a stand now would seriously impact her lifestyle. Being the center of attention buoyed her existence. Anything less was unacceptable. Eventually, she would find more devious ways of making him pay for her pain, she quietly swore. So, instead of confronting the reality of the situation, she chose the escapist route for the time being. It was more in line with the person that she really was.

It was hard to find any nightclubs open on a Monday night. Improvising, Anna decided to hold court at a local bar. She chose one that was below her father's radar. She wanted to let her hair down and forget the pain that struck at her heart like a sledgehammer.

To ease her pain she ingested a Quaalude from the supply she had purchased the previous day. The drug eased her troubled mind and took the edge off of her high-strung attitude that was wearing thin on her usual acquaintances and casual friends.

As the music got louder, the drug's effect began its sedation of her senses. Men who slithered past her would find an anonymous hand caressing their derriere. One particularly lustful man under the same pharmaceutical influence began massaging her neck with his lips amid the swelling crowd of partying sycophants seeking favor with this princess of the dark side.

Recoiling from his amorous advances, tears trickled down Anna's cheeks unnoticed by this maddening crowd. Her sorrow ran so deep that one pill could not quell its pain.

69

Tuesday, April 11, 1972

Just off of Nevada State Route 375 in Lincoln County amid the Timpahute Range, the sun began to peek its large saffron-colored eye behind a range of mountains in the distance. Carlucci struggled to open his eyes to the glowing morning light. A smile cracked Carlucci's blistered lips. He had survived the night to see the light of day. A parade of dancing variegated colors greeted him. Dying alone in the darkness would have been an ignominious end, he thought drifting in and out of a semiconscious state. He could ask for no more. Today would most certainly be the last day of his miserable life.

Hank and Teti had buried him naked in the sandy bronze-colored desert with only his head above ground facing east the previous afternoon. If he survived the night, they reasoned, the sun would most certainly finish him the following day.

Regaining momentary consciousness, he found a small but significant pleasure in the fact that at least his nakedness would be covered. Suddenly, he began blinking erratically as a light breeze off the desert blew sand in his eyes and mouth. Carlucci found it hard to cough with the heavy sand compressing his body nearly choking him. A rattlesnake slithered nearby, but diverted its direction for some reason when it approached the raunchy choking mass in its path. Even the scorpions were wary.

Regretting nothing in his life, the ultraviolet rays of the ascending sun began to burn the cornea of Carlucci's eyes. In one last act of defiance he cranked his head back trying to curse. Nothing came out. His leathery tongue fell limp as he descended into the unconscious unforgiving abyss of his black-hearted soul.

Hank would retrieve Carlucci's head the next day and dispose of it in the smelter of a metal cleaning operation in North Las Vegas.

Carlucci would have approved.

Cisco slept peacefully for the first time in his recent memory. His trusty .25 automatic along with his wallet and cigarettes lay asunder on the table between his bed and Johnny's.

Johnny, on the other hand, had a deep but fitful sleep and was muttering incoherently when Cisco arrived at their room earlier that morning.

Waking refreshed, Cisco exhaled a sigh of relief. He had done that often the previous night while having dinner with his son, Teti. So much so, that it became a moment of levity every time it occurred.

Ben Greenberg had given them carte blanche for the evening and they had taken full advantage of it. The usually reticent Cisco held nothing back including his sincere avowal of his deep love for Rose. The evening was a festive occasion even with the dark cloud of the Gimp hovering overhead. Neither brought it up. It was another story for another day and the father and son had a lot of catching up to do.

A knock at the door disgorged Cisco from his pleasant recounting of the previous evening and he leaped to his feet. Old habits die hard he realized, knowing that Teti was doing the knocking. He offered to pick Cisco up so that he could practice before Friday's tournament.

As Teti entered the motel room, his face stiffened, his eyes went cold. Cisco sensed the change and spun around.

"Get out of the way Cisco," Johnny ordered while pointing the .25 automatic at Teti.

"What are ya doing?" Cisco asked with a confused look on his face.

"Him and that ugly guy, what's his face, Carlucci, were at the casino yesterday. The Gimp, remember?"

"A lot's changed since yesterday," Cisco said in an assuring tone. Turning his torso toward Teti, he proudly said, "This is my son, Americo Teti." He then swiveled back toward Johnny, "Meet Johnny Cerone."

Johnny lowered the gun reflexively with a look of astonishment. "What about Carlucci?"

"He's out of the picture," Teti said evasively.

"What do you mean out of the picture?" Johnny asked with confused filled eyes.

"Gone on to better things."

"How?" Johnny pressed for a definitive answer. Was Carlucci dead or lurking in the shadows like their first encounter just waiting to vengefully pounce on him? He wanted to know. He needed to know. Otherwise, he thought, he would be looking over his shoulder the rest of his life.

"You figure it out," Teti responded frustratingly. Then turning on the ball of his foot he left the motel room, "I'll be outside."

Cisco shrugged his shoulders disbelievingly. Slowly removing his .25 automatic from Johnny's grasp, he silently followed Teti.

Johnny figured out the implication of their conversation later that evening. That wasn't the only thing he figured out.

Marie Giampietro didn't go to the store this Tuesday. There was more important work to be done at home. Waiting for Anna to awaken, Marie kept herself busy straightening up the bathroom that she shared with her husband. Opening his top drawer to put the toothpaste away, she noticed the .38 revolver. She quickly closed the drawer and tried not to think about why the gun was there. It could only mean trouble, she thought. This thought was reinforced by the media coverage of the Bellino hit the previous Friday. A truly independent woman in every respect, she told herself that the Gimp's business did not concern her. Repeating that mantra, she returned to the task at hand.

Doing this busy work kept her mind off of what was really troubling her. Unable to sleep lately, she sensed a paradigmatic shift in Anna's normally cheerful mood to one of melancholy. Her daughter did not have the strength of will that she had, Marie brooded. This was confirmed when she overheard the acrimonious exchange between Anna and the Gimp earlier that morning. Father and daughter were escalating their rhetorical exchanges rapidly. Their intemperate language sent off alarm bells in Marie's head. Afraid for her daughter's mental health, Marie toyed with the idea of confessing her ruse and telling Anna the identity of her real father. Truly wanting to reveal this information to her, Marie instinctively knew it would be counterproductive. She concluded that this would only ignite a bombastic interchange with possible dire consequences for everyone. Instead, Marie decided to just have a serious chat with her daughter. Hopefully, this would suffice.

Today was perfect, she thought. The Gimp had left early on god knows what business. This allowed her an opportunity to have a private conversation with her daughter without the chance of being overheard. She didn't have to wait long.

Hearing the stirrings of Anna in her sequestered room, Marie had no way of knowing that she had misjudged the depth of her daughter's despair. It was as if Anna was bearing her mother's pain along with her own.

Tapping lightly on the closed door, Marie spoke a cappella in a mellifluous voice, "Anna, Anna, are you awake?"

"What," screeched the voice from behind the door.

"I want to speak with you."

"There's nothing to talk about," Anna said modulating between firmness and anger. "Go away!"

Marie tried the door, but found it locked. "You come out here right now young lady," Marie demanded without knowing what she would do or say if Anna did not comply.

"What are you going to do if I don't? Have daddy kill me?" Anna said sitting on her bed in a voice holding back the floodgate of tears swelling up in her eyes.

Marie leaned her forehead against the door and sighed heavily. Then replied with a contrite timbre in her voice, "Of course not."

Inside the room a black river of tears ran down Anna's cheeks carrying away the previous evening's smeared mascara. Unable to control her emotional surges without drugs, Anna succumbed to their euphoric allure and digested a Quaalude quickly. It was the only way she knew how to mask her pain and face her mother.

The Gimp was a man who dealt with emotional pain differently. He suppressed it by sheer will, whereas, Anna sought a chemically induced euphoria. One was becoming addicted; the other had devolved into the psychotic abyss of voices and paranoia depending on the circumstances of the day.

For the Gimp today's circumstances dictated the paranoia route. The Old Man wanted to meet him.

The Old Man indulged in his own type of paranoia that he aptly described as *good sense*. This usually meant meeting in a public place. Then a casually stroll down different streets. In this manner business would be discussed in vague terms. Any government agency trying to record the conversation would find it difficult due to the random pattern of the participants' meanderings. Even though the organization had the head G-Man compromised, the various fiascos of the sixties had made such precautions necessary.

Today's meeting was to start at the corner of Eleventh and Chestnut Streets on the southwest corner. A chilly breeze blew down the half-shaded street between the tall buildings in a tunnel-like effect. The Gimp anxiously waited with his one hand in the pocket of his leather coat gently caressing his .38 revolver. Standing with his back to the wall next to a pay telephone, his eyes scanned the passing pedestrians for signs of potential danger. Occasionally, his eyes would dart upward toward the endless rows of windows of the building across the street, but the glare on the widows from the sun gave any observers anonymity. Momentarily shifting his eyes to his wristwatch, he realized that the Old Man was unusually late. That was a bad sign. Just as he decided to leave, the phone rang. The Gimp looked at the phone, then casually examined around it for any signs of explosives. Answering the phone on the fourth ring a muffled voice ordered tersely, "Start walking down Eleventh Street." Then the line went dead. Hanging up the telephone slowly, the Gimp turned with a cautionary glance to look over his shoulder. The voice in his head spoke up and told him not to worry. Relieved, he began walking down Eleventh Street hugging the wall just in case.

As the Gimp approached the corner of Eleventh and Sansom Streets the Old Man suddenly turned around from a window he was facing to join him. Casually motioning with his eyes to head west on Sansom Street, the Gimp complied. Sensing the Gimp's uneasiness from his tensely clenched teeth the Old Man spoke in soothing tones to calm this dangerous beast of a man next to him.

"I love walking on a sunny day through these streets," the Old Man said casually. "People seem more cheerful and happy in weather like we have today. Nothing like the weather in New York recently."

"Yeah," the Gimp answered gruffly.

"An unfortunate occurrence that didn't have to happen."

Unsure where the conversation was going the Gimp concurred, "Unfortunate indeed."

After crossing Twelfth Street the Old Man veered north toward Drury Lane. "Gambling is coming to Atlantic City. Maybe not this year, not even next year, but it is coming. Bet on it. And there will be plenty to go around for everyone," the Old Man assured him.

"I see. That's a good thing," the Gimp said with a tinge of notable excitement in his voice. Perhaps there was a residual benefit from Bellino's death after all, the Gimp thought fortuitously.

"Good. I'm glad you understand. You're an important part of the equation. And so will receive your appropriate share as things develop," the Old Man inveigled convincingly.

Easily patronized, the Gimp took the bait. The voice in his head was silent— unable to decipher the Old Man's deceitfulness. "I never doubted your generosity," the Gimp said in an ingratiating voice buoyed by respectful mannerisms.

"Your undying loyalty was the deciding factor," the Old Man replied in a velvety tone of satisfaction that had a facetious element to it.

Stopping in front of Ye Olde Ale House, the Old Man put a friendly hand on the Gimp's shoulder. "Let's have a drink to our future success," the Old Man asked in an uncharacteristically theatrical way. Devoid of any emotion or vacillation surrounding his machinations regarding the Gimp's treacherous intentions, he managed to perform his shtick convincingly for the benefit of the Gimp. He was a master at compartmentalizing future events, pushing them aside to savor the moment.

The Gimp nodded agreeably never suspecting the trap that was being laid by the Old Man. It would be their last drink together in this lifetime.

70

Johnny awakened early. He couldn't sleep. While sharing the revelry of the previous night with Cisco and Teti, he suddenly understood everything that had transpired in the preceding days. The message was crystal clear. Carlucci was dead. He was sure of that. Cisco was like a new man. A great weight was lifted from his shoulders. It was obvious.

Sandy, on the other hand, was still coyly reticent. Instinctively, he surmised that she was telling him only part of the truth. He believed she was pregnant. Her elusive behavior also led him to believe that she was here to have an abortion.

This last assumption troubled him. He needed to think about it at length before he approached her again. Soul searching would best describe it. Johnny was unprepared to deal with the ramifications of this new type of life and death situation, he concluded. Leaping out of bed, he lost his balance momentarily as he stumbled for his clothes.

Cisco rolled over and looked at the alarm clock. "Where the fuck you going this early?" he mumbled half asleep.

"For a ride," Johnny said hurriedly.

"Get back before noon and get your shit together. We're checking out today," Cisco reminded Johnny in a hoarse voice before rolling over and going back to sleep.

"Don't worry about that. I'll be here."

Outside, Johnny unzipped the tonneau cover on the MGB and sped off for an early morning spin in the desert to clear his mind. In less than a month his life had taken an entirely new direction, he thought amazingly. Miraculously, he had been given another chance. This time he decided, he was going to be master of his own destiny, no longer a passenger along for the ride. Before any further decisions were made, he needed to seriously consider the consequences. It was a perplexing dilemma and he needed to make the decision soon.

Waiting to board his flight back to Philadelphia, Teti had encountered similar life changing events this past month. Nevertheless, he knew what transpired in the next day or two would determine whether he lived or died. Predestination had determined his life's course, he readily acknowledged. How it would end was entirely up to him.

Amid the cold seriousness of his musing, his heart was warmed by the reconciliation with Cisco, his father. This bolstered his normally melancholic mien and gave him a reason to survive the coming tribulation. He wondered at length if he had the right stuff to persevere. One way or another, at the end of the flight he would have to know for sure.

The Gimp awoke on the couch this day with a brimming smile on his face. His mental processes whirled like a well-oiled machine without the erratic interruptions of the second-guessing voice in his head. Even his daughter's noisy early morning entrance did not disturb the deep sleep that he enjoyed that evening. Thinking of her asleep upstairs, he convinced himself that she would eventually understand that the elimination of Tucci from her life was altruistically executed on her behalf. Such were the delusions emanating from his misbegotten mind.

The Gimp practically danced up the stairs to the bathroom for a quick shower and shave. Opening the top drawer to retrieve his electric shaver, he paused for a contemplative moment to look at the gun. Deciding to leave it there for the time being, he whistled an obscure song from his youth for no apparent reason.

Unlike her husband's cheerful mood, Marie Giampietro was slipping into an unabated moroseness. Feeling personally responsible for her daughter's unhappiness, she quietly left the store on Ninth Street and proceeded to the Saint Rita di Cascia Church at Broad and Ellsworth Streets.

After lighting a candle at the statue of the Blessed Virgin Mary on the side of the main altar, Marie retreated to a quiet corner of the church and sat with her eyes closed reflecting on her life. Finally coming to the realization that she used her daughter to leverage her suppressed hatred of the Gimp, tears began trickling from the corners of her tightly closed eyes. Unable to forgive herself for her daughter's pain, she prayed the rosary. Slowly, she moved her fingers from one bead to the next seeking solace in each prayer that she silently intoned for every bead. She found none.

Rose Teti returned from the beauty parlor and examined herself in the full-length mirror attached to the back of her bedroom door. She like what she saw. Her hair, her face and her whole demeanor were fresh and vibrant. Her long-sufferance was at an end she hoped.

Going to Las Vegas was an entirely new experience for her. She had heard many stories over the years from many of the bar's regular patrons. Now she would find out who was telling the truth and who was exaggerating.

Gleefully packing an overnight bag, she wondered what traveling in an airplane would be like. The extent of her travels revolved around the East Coast corridor between New York City and Washington, DC and that was always by automobile. Trying to remember her last trip, she could only come up with a summer jaunt in the late sixties to see the Ice Capades at the Atlantic City Convention Center on the Boardwalk. The deterioration of that once proud city was abundantly evident on that trip, she sadly thought in passing. Not wanting to linger on anything depressing at this moment, she quickly rebounded to more joyful thoughts.

Glad to finally be free of the self-imposed emotional bondage, she was looking forward to seeing Cisco and her son. No one had the heart to tell her that her son wouldn't be there.

71

The plane from Las Vegas landed at Philadelphia International Airport by late afternoon. Teti deplaned quickly with his sole piece of luggage in tow. He was in a hurry to see his mother and tell her the good news in person. If he had waited around the airport for another ten minutes, he could have done so. Unaware of her travel plans, the moment passed. It was relegated to the conjectural bin of life where speculation abounded regarding the potential outcome of a chance meeting.

After settling in the back seat of the taxicab and directing the driver to take him to the bar, Teti forced himself to think about his next move. The result was predetermined. The method of arriving at the result was not. Simply put, it was either him or the Gimp. Ben Greenberg was perfectly clear about that point. His father was painfully silent. Sighing heavily, he promised himself that once this contract was completed, he would quietly fade into the obscurity of private life. He hoped.

Teti didn't have any compunction about killing the Gimp at least not at the moment. Later, he might not feel that way even though over the past few years he concluded that some men just needed killing. Their elimination from this earthly plane was a necessary societal function. Everyone benefited. No one suffered. The Gimp and Carlucci were prime examples of his theory. One down, one to go, Teti thought wistfully.

As the cab snaked its way over the Penrose Bridge and up Moyamensing Avenue, Teti knew that he would have to accomplish this deadly deed soon. He could buy himself some time, he thought by telling the Gimp that Carlucci accomplished his task and was having his fun in Las Vegas. This story would buy him a few days at least he surmised.

Arriving at the Downtown Bar & Grill, Teti paid his fare and exited the cab. He would spend the night devising a plan of action and report to the Gimp tomorrow. Right now, he was tired from the long flight and late nights. The Gimp wasn't going anywhere anytime soon he thought—except to hell.

Later that evening Anna Giampietro scurried out of her home. Her father was rarely home at this time of the night so her chances of avoiding any type of confrontation were very good. She never thought about her mother.

Appearing from the kitchen, Marie put on a smiling façade speaking in a tone of suppressed irritability, "Where are you going tonight?"

"Out," was Anna's singular response.

"Out where?"

"Just out."

Marie's facial expression was downturn. Her eyes probing and her voice exuded urgency. "We need to talk."

"About what?" Anna replied swiftly and then after a moment, "It's all been said."

"What you are doing won't solve what's bothering you. It'll destroy you in the end."

"Better to go out fast and furious than lead a life of quiet desperation like you're living," Anna shot back sarcastically.

Mother and daughter exchanged pained and awkward stares. Anna, frowning from some inner angst, assumed a defiant stance. Marie assumed a defensive one trying to refrain from blurting out the secret that could explain her actions all these years. Intuitively, she stepped backed from the explanation that she feared would trigger even greater self-destructive behavior from her daughter.

"I chose to live this way because I had few options. You have many. Cosmo Tucci was only one and a poor one at that. Don't do this to yourself. Please. I only wanted better for you. I'm here to help. It's your choice," Marie explained in a pleading tone with matching eyes appearing more desperate and sullen in their highlighted expression.

"I made a choice," Anna said definitively in an unyielding tone of voice accented by a resentful sneer. Abruptly turning away, she exited the house without uttering another word.

Lieutenant Dominic Pelosi preferred the graveyard shift, even volunteering for it to allow his peers more time with their families. It wasn't an entirely altruistic offer. He did it to avoid the petty politics of the Philadelphia Police Department. Patience in these matters was definitely not his forte.

Rotating between the two all night diners in his district for his lunch break, he decided to take an early break tonight. His usual driver had the night off. So, he snaked his way through the metropolitan morass of South Philadelphia on his way to the diner in the heart of his district. Like most nights the radio traffic was light. Consequently, his mind strayed beyond the periphery of his consciousness like an itinerant wanderer.

Women he knew and men he fought beside always drifted in and out of his mental meanderings. Inadvertently passing the Cerone house on Ritner Street, however, was the pinprick that deflated his highflying thoughts. It was the chink in his armor of self-righteousness, an unfulfilled promise to himself that gnawed at his conscience.

As his thoughts lingered in this limbo of the past, the radio suddenly came alive in a crackling fashion. A car had speeded across a red light and careened off a parked vehicle into a telephone pole.

Pelosi's mind leaped into survival mode and he sped off to Sixteenth & Oregon Avenue. His agility of mind in times of crisis was his defining characteristic. It wouldn't fail him tonight.

72

Thursday, April 13, 1972

Teti slept later than he had planned. He awoke to the murmuring coming from the bar area. It was almost lunchtime and he felt the rumblings of hunger starting to erupt in his stomach. A plan of action still eluded him. Silently, he fretted that he might never conceive one. Dragging himself to his feet, he stumbled around the room aimlessly assembling his clothes. This was the room that his father used, he fondly thought. How appropriate for him to be sleeping here now. Grooming himself in the matchbox size bathroom adjacent to the comparatively small room, the clanging plumbing hastened the dissipation of grogginess.

Ralph, the bartender, had heard him puttering around in the back room and ordered up something for him to eat. He knew that he would be famished since he went straight to bed from the airport.

Shuffling into the bar area, Teti plopped onto a barstool at the very end of the bar. He chose this location to avoid being wreathed in a gray cloud of cigarette smoke emanating from the patrons at the other end of the bar. His mother would be proud of him. Ethereally smiling at the thought of his mother, he gleefully mumbled his thoughts out loud.

Ralph slid a hot dish of sweet Italian sausage mixed with mushrooms and fried green peppers smothered with a fresh marinara sauce in front of him. It was a staple of Teti's life since childhood. "Did you say something?" Ralph asked with an inquisitive glance.

Stabbing a piece of sausage with his fork, Teti elaborated, "I was talking to myself. Going over how I won large at the blackjack tables."

"Good for you," Ralph added as he returned with a fresh sliced hot Italian roll in a basket.

After soaking the marinara sauce with a piece of the roll like a sponge, Teti asked matter-of-factly, "Snake been around?"

"Few times," Ralph tersely replied.

"Anybody else?" Teti said a cautious probing in his voice.

"The Old Man, stopped by the other night for a grappa. Otherwise, just the usual stiffs," Ralph poured a glass of Chianti for Teti without asking.

"I guess I didn't miss much," Teti coyly added draining the Chianti in one large gulp.

Lurching over the bar Ralph whispered drolly, "Just the look on your mother's face when Cisco called."

The hint of a smile perked up the ends of Teti's lips. He was happy for his mother.

Refilling Teti's wine glass, Ralph asked, "So what's the plan?"

Teti cringed. His face flushed bewilderingly. The thought that Ralph knew something that he didn't, raced through his mind like a wild fire.

Picking up on Teti's helter-skelter expression, Ralph added, "I mean for this place."

Tilting his head with a far away stare, he paused then replied jokingly, "I don't know. I'll make it up as I go along." Beneath his smiling façade, however, Teti meant something entirely different.

The Gimp and his wife Marie were unexpectedly predisposed this Thursday. Their daughter Anna had wrapped her Camaro around a telephone pole late the previous night and was now in a comatose state in the intensive care unit of a hospital on South Broad Street. Her prognosis was still being evaluated.

Numbly staring out the window, the Gimp was deeply sullen and distraught. Lack of sleep had left him partially incoherent and confused. The voice in his head returned and warned him of the danger ahead without spelling it out. He thought the message pertained to his daughter's condition and fell into a darker funk.

Marie was in a self-flagellating frame of mind. She blamed herself entirely for this event. No voices in her head were needed to forewarn her of this tragic episode. The indications were readily apparent and she did nothing to forestall them.

Both parents were catnapping in their respective seats when the neurologist entered Anna's intensive care unit. Hoping to awaken them gently, the doctor cleared his throat with his mouth-closed making a muted tonal grumbling sound.

Groggily, the Gimp immediately awoke with fluttering dull eyes. Getting his bearing, he gently shook Marie. With an undulating stomach, Marie awoke with sleepy eyes. Staring vacantly at the doctor hovering over her, he appeared like some otherworldly harbinger of ominous news to come.

Unsmiling the doctor gave the unlikely couple the bad news. Speaking in a toneless voice the doctor said. "The alcohol level of your daughter's blood exceeded well beyond the legal limits. I can give you the exact numbers if you like later. We also found a substance called Methaqualone in her blood. The street name is Quaaludes. The combination of these substances precipitated the comatose state she is presently experiencing."

Unsure of what they were hearing from the doctor, Marie spoke first. "I don't understand?"

The doctor pursed his lips then spoke, "We are hopeful, and I say this with guarded optimism, that as the drugs and alcohol wear off, it is highly possible that she will regain consciousness."

Marie breathed a heavy sigh of relief. The Gimp's eye produced a twinkle that expanded into a smile, as he too was relieved.

The doctor continued, "Please understand Anna is in very, very serious condition. She also suffered a dislocated shoulder and a broken leg." Rustling through the medical file on his clipboard, he found what he was seeking, "If it wasn't for a police Lieutenant Pelosi this might have been a very different type of meeting. He resuscitated her on the spot. Still the next twenty-four hours will be crucial. It can still go either way."

The Gimp kept noticeably silent. It was Pelosi who had thwarted Carlucci. Now, he had to thank the bastard, the Gimp begrudgingly thought.

Marie on the other hand just wanted her little girl back. Her daughter's well-being was the only thing that mattered any longer.

73

Sandy Edelman also found herself in the hospital under entirely different circumstances. It began with severe abdominal pain during the night. Sandy thought that she had eaten something that didn't agree with her and went back to sleep. It was a fitful sleep. Slipping in and out of a dreamlike state, she tossed about trying to gain a comfortable position. At one point she dreamt she was in a swimming pool alone. It was so realistic that she actually felt wet. She was.

Awakening in the middle of the night, Sandy found her nightgown covered in blood. Scared and confused, she whipped off the cover and found the sheets drenched in blood with a thick coagulated mass between her legs.

An emergency team responded quickly. Weak from the loss of blood, Sandy rested in a hospital room peacefully in a drug-induced state. Settling the moralistic debate raging in her soul, her body had made the troubling decision for her. It was as if some benevolent power looked down on her sympathetically, evacuating Sandy's uterus in the process to give her another chance at life. In reality her miscarriage was the result of a chromosomal abnormality that produced a blighted ovum. There was no fetus, just an empty sac.

Johnny had thought long and hard all morning about the responsibilities of marriage and parenting. Watching Cisco practice in the empty ballroom of the

Cibola Casino, he kept squirming in his elevated chair. His constant movement distracted Cisco.

"Hey kid! Whataya got ants in yer pants?" Cisco asked in an annoyed voice.

"No a wedgie. Satisfied?" Johnny responded in an annoying tone of voice.

Standing up Johnny paced and fretted until Cisco finally yelled. "Sit down or go see that girl. Willya. Yer drivin' me nuts."

Johnny sat down quietly. Cisco had facilitated Johnny's decision with his belligerent decree. He loved Sandy Edelman. She was his equal intellectually and socially. All of that was just part of the pasticcio of his love song. The piece that made this serenade special could not be so easily described. It came from one's heart, uniquely written and dedicated only for the ears of one's true soul mate. Sandy Edelman was his.

Deciding to support Sandy's decision unequivocally, he tried calling her all morning. There was no answer. He vacillated between showing up at her door and giving her some space. Still, he didn't want to let her disappear into the night without baring his soul. Sliding off the high stool anxiously, Johnny decided to try calling Sandy's motel room one more time.

Cisco was distracted by Johnny's sudden movement and miscued. Looking around the room nervously, he secretly wondered if he wasn't making a big mistake. After a heavy sigh, Cisco nervously rolled the tip of his tongue around the inside of his mouth. Ben Greenberg had given him and Johnny a comp on the room and dinners. The man was expecting great things from him, Cisco thought with some trepidation.

A casino worker assigned to the tournament racked the pool balls into a diamond configuration for Cisco again. Gingerly, he rearranged the balls according to the rules of the game. Chalking his cue stick, Cisco resolved himself to do his best. With a shaky hand he grasped the cue stick focusing on the white cue ball. Knowing that his best included being cool, calm and collected, he would have to wait and see what tomorrow would bring.

74

Teti searched the Gimp's usual haunts to no avail. He was nowhere to be found, not even the social club on Tenth & Annin Streets. The thought of calling on the Gimp at his house crossed Teti's mind. That wasn't his first option. It was his avenue of last resorts. Visiting his home did not sit well with the Gimp. Right now, Teti did not want to upset the man.

Returning to the Downtown Bar & Grill, Teti slid onto his customary seat at the end of the bar after uncapping a bottle of Rolling Rock beer. It was midafternoon. The lunchtime crowd scurried back to their jobs as masons, carpenters, city workers and an occasional office group looking to get away from the humdrum routine of their day-to-day lives.

Ralph crept his way along the bar toward Teti cleaning ashtrays and wiping the bar. Finally, he approached him with a fresh bottle of beer in hand. Removing the empty bottle from in front of Teti, he asked, "Talked to your mom?"

"No. Has she called?"

"No," he responded.

"What's on your mind?" Teti asked pointedly.

"I need Saturday night off. It's my kid's birthday…"

Cutting him off before he went into a winded explanation, Teti quickly said, "Not a problem. I'll take care of the place." Teti, however, attached a silent caveat, *if I'm still alive.*

Ralph nodded his appreciation and returned to the tasks at hand.

Teti pondered the thought of tending bar. It was good enough for his grandfather and mother, what the hell he concluded. His lips formed the silent words. Maybe it's my destiny, he idly wondered. Sipping at his beer, his thoughts danced around haphazardly. With brooding seriousness he tried framing the past week's events in separate windows within his mind.

Louie the Snake slinked into the bar through the side door. He stepped up to the bar at a ninety-degree angle facing the thoughtful Teti. "Good to see you back," Louie said in a sincere but surprised tone of voice. Personally, he never thought that he would see Teti again even though he harbored no ill feelings toward him.

Ralph slid Louie's usual order of Schmidt's draft down the slick bar.

Teti sensed the tinge of surprise to Louie's voice. Distracted by his other ruminations, he couldn't make a connection.

At that moment Tommy DiRienzo entered the front door and sashayed up to the bar between Teti and Louie. Both men looked annoyed at the presence of this oafish gossiper. They put up with him because occasionally he had a bit of good information.

"Hey guys," Tommy casually said.

Ralph bristled when Tommy raised a finger using it as a signal to get a beer.

Taking a large gulp of beer, Tommy ran his tongue around his lips. "So how's Johnny doing out there in Sin City?" Tommy asked looking directly at Teti.

Teti hesitated wondering whether Johnny had called this blabbermouth son-of-a-bitch. "You talk to him?" Teti asked coyly fishing for information.

"No. Not since he skipped town," Tommy said oblivious to Teti's real intent.

Louie the Snake knew what he meant, but kept quiet avoiding any eye contact.

Then Tommy said something that piqued both men's attention. "Hey, did you hear that the Gimp's daughter totaled her car last night on Oregon Avenue?" he blabbed with a voice shrill with excitement.

"No I didn't," answered Teti in a laconic manner.

Shrugging expressively, Tommy continued, "Intensive care right now. Vegged out." He drained the remaining beer in his glass. "Couldn't have happened to a nicer bitch," he chuckled sarcastically. "That hit the spot. Gotta go."

Exiting without paying the tab, Ralph was about to say something, but Teti motioned to forget about it.

Dead silence enshrouded the bar as Louie finished his second beer. Standing to leave he looked Teti dead in the eye speaking in a hushed tone, "Take care." Pursing his lips soberly, he added, "Your grandfather looked out for me. I owed him. Since he's not around anymore, I figure I owe you. You get in a jam call me." Throwing some money onto the bar, Louie nodded his head with a face masked in intensity at Teti. Pointing his finger for emphasis, he reiterated his offer, "I mean it. Call me."

Teti nodded then watched him jauntily saunter out the side door. It suddenly occurred to him that Louie didn't expect to see him return from Las Vegas. Picturing himself buried up to his neck in the hot sandy desert like Carlucci, Teti clenched his teeth in anger. That vivid thought countered his vacillation making what he was about to do a whole lot easier.

Later that evening Marie Giampietro decided to go home and freshen up. She had been at Anna's side for most of the day. Since there was no change in her daughter's condition, she felt the fresh air and a change of clothes would reinvigorate her for the travails of the coming evening.

Totally exhausted, the Gimp had left Anna's bedside earlier. Marie was happy that he did. His presence only added additional tension to an already stressful situation, she thought.

Arriving at her front steps, Marie suddenly realized that the Gimp might be camped out on the couch in the living room. Adroitly, she decided to enter the house through the kitchen rather than chance an unpleasant encounter with the cold-blooded man who she blamed for her daughter's present condition.

Readily accepting her share of the blame, she promised herself a new beginning once Anna recovered. She would leave this god-forsaken house and move her and Anna into her parent's house temporarily she thought hopefully.

Quietly unlocking then relocking the back door, Marie scurried up the narrow back staircase leading to the upstairs from the kitchen like a mouse seeking sanctuary from a hovering predator.

Asleep on the sofa for most of the afternoon, the Gimp's eyes widened in abject fear at what he heard. Voices resonated in his head like a cacophony of squawking birds fearing for their lives after being flushed out by a hunting dog.

Sitting on the edge of the sofa with his head in his hands, the Gimp felt slightly nauseated from the raucous turbulence still reverberating between his ears. It felt like vertigo with sound. A faint intermittent thumping sound became persistent. Grousing at the noise, he suddenly realized that someone was knocking at the front door. Standing up slowly to mitigate any dizziness, the involuntary twitch over his eye became momentarily pronounced then disappeared. An ominous feeling enshrouded him as he shuffled to the front door. He shrugged it off as a residual effect of his daughter's present condition. As he spied out the peephole in the door, Teti's face appeared in a fishbowl effect. There was cautious curiosity in his eyes as he stepped back suspiciously. A voice shouted in his mind to beware. The Gimp shrugged it off with a smirk as a residual effect of his positional vertigo. Thinking back to all of Teti's missteps along the way, he discounted any threat from this *pussy*. Then the thought quickly crossed his mind that Teti was the harbinger of bad news from Carlucci. Slightly panicked at that thought he rushed to open the door. "Where's Antny?" the Gimp asked with the force of an interrogator.

Moving his lips in a saw tooth motion before speaking, Teti lied, "He's taking a little R an R. Sent me back to report."

"Umm, Antny's been disappearing a lot lately," the Gimp stated suspiciously. "Anything I should know?"

Still standing outside, Teti's nervous stomach precluded him from speaking lest he vocalize his anxiety. So, Teti silently motioned with his wide eyes to enter the house.

"Oh, yea. Come in," the Gimp said motioning with an arching unenthusiastic head movement toward the living room. Thoughtlessly turning his back to Teti for a split second, the Gimp realized his vulnerability immediately. As the door clicked shut, he swiveled around to find Teti pointing a gun at his chest. Astonishment mirrored in his face, the Gimp stepped forward as Teti pressed the barrel of the gun into his chest.

"What do you think you're doin?" the Gimp asked in an imperious tone of voice with tightening lips while squinting nastily at Teti through one eye.

"Putting you out of yer misery," Teti answered in a mocking tone.

"You're dead meat! You know that don't ya," the Gimp yelled.

Upstairs the modulating intensity of the conversation caught Marie's attention. Frantic to protect herself in the face of this potentially unknown threat, she remembered the Gimp's gun in the bathroom drawer.

Downstairs Teti's nose flared in anger at the Gimp's presumptuousness. "No deader than you!"

The Gimp pushed his chest forward defiantly against the gun.

"Go ahead, make it easy for me," Teti challenged the Gimp in a tantalizing voice. "Maybe your thinking that I didn't check the gun for bullets," Teti continued tauntingly. "Well, I did asshole. But to show you I'm a *sport*," Teti went on emphasizing the last word, "I only put one bullet in the chamber and its got yer name on it. Then again maybe I didn't."

The Gimp stepped back involuntarily with fear creeping into his eyes. His face lined in worry.

In the upstairs bathroom Marie's hand shook as she removed the gun from the drawer. Clasping the shaking hand with her free hand, she took a deep breath exhaling slowly. Always knowing but never thinking that a day like this would come, she thought of Anna and knew that she had to survive somehow.

"You jus can't kill a made guy," the Gimp argued in a voice buffeted by a sub-conscious pleading undertone.

"You're right. But I got the good housekeeping seal of approval," Teti smugly said as he pulled the trigger clicking on an empty chamber.

The Gimp shuddered.

Teti repeatedly pulled the trigger, but the gun was empty. "Opps! It's empty," Teti said sarcastically while quickly producing another gun and jamming it into the Gimp's corpulent gut. "But this one ain't."

The voice shouted shrill with unfettered anger in the Gimp's mind. Enraged beyond reason, he lunged for the gun.

Marie heard the gunshot. Closing her eyes she steeled herself against the fear swelling in her stomach and headed for the staircase.

The Gimp was slumped over on the floor holding his stomach like a man pro-tecting his life savings. He was still alive. Hovering over him, Teti took aim, but for a second took pity on this shivering mass of misguided amoral turpitude. Thinking back to his youth, he remembered his grandfather's mistreatment of Little Joey and found it ironic that the grandson was asked to finish what his grandfather could not bring himself to do.

"Drop the gun," Marie said with deadly seriousness in her voice.

Keeping his gun aimed at the Gimp, Teti cocked his head toward Marie standing midway down the staircase.

Marie descended the remaining steps pointedly aiming her gun with both hands at Teti. "I will shoot," she said emphasizing each word with a bitter resolve.

Teti relented. Reluctantly he dropped the gun to his side.

"Toss it on the floor," Marie exhorted.

Tossing the gun toward Marie, Teti's mood immediately changed from eager retribution to one of sullen self-recrimination. He had counted on the Gimp's wife being at her daughter's side. Now his life or the swiftness of his death was in her hands.

Taking short breaths and bleeding profusely, the Gimp forced an arrogant smile to his lips through spasms of coughing. Now, personally wanting his pound of flesh, his adrenaline surged giving him a renewed purpose. Languidly stretching for Teti's gun, he began babbling between gasps of breath. "Good Girl. I always knew you had it in you." His fingers danced on the gun's handle unable to take it in his grasp. "Be a good girl and push it here. I want to give this pussy what I gave to Tucci," he said arrogantly through now wheezing breaths.

Marie's embittered eyes darted back and forth between Teti and the Gimp questioningly, her mind weighing the value of each man's life.

The Gimp barely managed to grasp the slippery gun in his bloody hand. His mind buzzed with the modulating intensity of the voice within it as he slithered around on the hardwood floor in a pool of blood trying to position himself to take his revenge.

Looking at Teti she was prepared to protect the sanctity of her home, her life, by killing this interloper standing before her. A split second later, she realized that it was the Gimp who needed killing. With judicious resolve Marie looked into the Gimp's dark soulless eyes and aimed her gun at his head.

Immediately the dynamics of the sordid scene changed. The Gimp's face rippled through several changes of expression. Finally, his eyes widened with a sense of astonishment and misplaced recognition. Pleading loudly, he called out, "Mom! No!"

In tandem to his plea Marie fired the gun pointblank at the Gimp's forehead, sending shards of bone amid splattering blood onto the already sticky floor. It was a responsibility that she could no longer shun. Looking down on the inert body of the man who caused so many so much pain, she felt a warm rush of righteous relief throughout her body. The tension abated. It was over. She and her daughter were finally free of her self-imposed imprisonment. Tilting her head slightly to look at Teti, there was strength in her eyes amid a flickering shadow of satisfaction discernable only to one who knew her pain.

Unable to speak, Teti nodded thankfully. His eyes were full of respect for this woman who did what he was sent to do but could not.

Averting her eyes from Teti, she tossed the gun onto the floor next to her dead husband, the murderer of her hopes and dreams, the fornicator of everything sacred in her life. Pivoting toward the staircase she quietly prayed that her daughter would reawaken from the evil influences that she foisted on her so long ago. Then with profound sincerity she offered up the Gimp's death as a burden that would weigh on her heart for the rest of her natural life. A morose penance to God made for the salvation of her immortal soul.

Teti followed her movements up the staircase as a subject would follow his queen. He would clean this mess up and dispose of the evidence so that no one would ever suspect that the Gimp existed. It was the cruelest of fates. It was what he did best. His job was easy. He knew no one would care.

75

Louie the Snake had quietly arrived at the Gimp's front door an hour later. He had expected a call either from the Gimp or Teti, but not so soon. Nervously running his tongue over his teeth and making a low sucking sound, Louie was personally happy that it was Teti making the call tonight. For the past two months he had tried to distance himself from Carlucci and the Gimp sensing the wild gyration of their mental compasses. Wanting no part of their craziness, he made himself scarce. Consequently, even Teti had to make half-dozen calls to contact him. True to his word earlier that evening, here he was in the flesh, living to tell his story another day he thought wistfully. Congratulating himself for being a survivor, an ironic smile curled from the ends of Snake's mouth. After a hesitant moment he tapped lightly with a bent knuckle on the door.

Teti answered the door immediately. Standing to one side, he did not want his face to be seen by any voyeurs of the night. These past weeks he had become a professional at cleaning up these types of messes. His mind had created a mental checklist of all the details needing attention. Each time he added a new one to the list. Expediting them with a morose élan, he was just happy that it was not his blood splattered across the hardwood floor.

Louie slipped past the partially opened door and was astonished by Teti's attentiveness. The Gimp was neatly trussed like a plumb turkey for a holiday dinner. All of his clothing had been removed and stuffed into a thick heavy-duty plastic bag for later disposal. The gun used in this dastardly deed was also neatly residing inside a smaller plastic bag.

Teti had removed a gold cornicelli on a chain from around the Gimp's neck as a memento. He really didn't have a compelling reason for keeping the good luck charm, yet did it anyway. Using a mild bleach to clean the bloodstains from the furniture and rugs, Teti almost had the room back to normal. That is, as normal as anything could be in the former psychotic world of the Gimp.

As Teti and Louie leveraged the Gimp's limp body into a thick black heavy-duty plastic bag, the telephone rang several times until Marie answered the extension upstairs. Both men became still and stood straight up like an Egyptian obelisk as they tried to listen to the conversation for any warning signs of impending trouble. Marie's garbled voice was incomprehensible. However, her tone was inordinately cheerful. Taking deep breaths, they returned to the odious task at hand.

Marie descended the staircase as if she were walking on a cloud. "It was the hospital. Anna's awake," she said in a mellifluously uplifting tone. It was as if a righteous and benevolent God gave his tacit blessing to this most unholy of deeds requiring no further supplications.

"What about that neighbor next door?" Teti ominously quizzed.

"I called the house. There wasn't any answer," Marie said without looking down at the black bag bearing the forty-three-year-old garbage of misplaced human endeavor that she disposed of this evening.

"We'll need to talk eventually," Teti warned.

Marie drolly approached Teti and kissed him lightly on the cheek to everyone's surprise. "Thank you," she said with profound sincerity.

Speechless as Marie turned toward the door, Teti finally swiveled around toward her, "No. Thank you," he said. It was as if a burden had been lifted from his shoulders.

They smiled understandingly for a long moment at each other then Marie exited her house. Both now free of the mental bondage that entrapped them for all of these years.

Just before midnight the Gimp's car pulled down a weed-infested road in the Tinicum Marshes just south of Philadelphia on the way to Chester. Coming to a slow stop a half a mile down the road near a partial clearing, the car's lights went off.

Louie slid out of the passenger seat and stood rigidly listening for any unusual sounds. He only heard the muted roar of a jetliner taking off from the nearby Philadelphia International Airport. Satisfied that there was no one lurking in the shadows, he motioned with his head to Teti that the coast was clear.

Opening the trunk of the car, they donned gloves and removed shovels. Walking ten feet into the weeds they began digging the final resting place for the Gimp.

Meanwhile, a storm was surreptitiously approaching the Philadelphia Metropolitan Area under the cover of darkness.

As Teti and Louie dug down nearly four feet, Teti's shovel careened off a human femur bone. Momentarily taken aback, they continued to poke around the dirt until they uncovered a skull. Suddenly a cold wind whipped through the tall weeds like the eerie spasms of an unsanctimonious dervish spreading goose bumps throughout each man's torso. Teti steeled himself against any superstitious meanderings and examined the skull with the metal tip of his shovel. It appeared small, perhaps the skull of a woman unfaithful to her jealous husband who exacted a pernicious revenge, he imagined. But that was the ramblings of a creative mind rationalizing murder as a natural occurrence in the course of human events. Not wanting to disturb the remains any further, both men silently agreed to stop here and dispose of their decomposing load.

Struggling to carry the Gimp's inert and naked body wrapped appropriately in black plastic, they finally managed to roll it on top of his eternal partner in anonymity. At that moment Teti felt obliged to silently say a prayer for the tarnished soul of this misbegotten man. Louie too felt the necessity to pray lowering his head in deference to the dead. The wind returned. This time gently caressing the faces of each man as if in appreciation for their kind thought.

Stuffing his hands into his pockets, Teti felt the gold cornicelli and chain. He removed it from his pocket and dangled it in front of his face. A momentary break in the clouds allowed the starlight to illuminate it, but just as quickly enshrouded it again in darkness. Gazing at it like an oracle of old, he finally tossed it into the circular grave as a symbolic offering to God to spare the occupants of this unholy ground from eternal retribution, mindful that he too sought peace of mind.

Louie and Teti began filling the hole as a light rain began to fall, anointing them like a priest administering baptism. By the time they had finished their toiling, the drenching rain soaked them to the bone.

Driving back both men fell into a deep contemplative silence. The rain possessed a redemptive quality that reinvigorated their souls.

76

Johnny Cerone awoke to the bright morning light of a Las Vegas morning, a tell-tale sign for an unseasonably hot day. Arching his head back against the seat of the MGB to stretch it, he wondered if Sandy had slipped past him during his somnolent interlude.

Limping out of his car, he tapped at Sandy's motel room door with a graduated intensity. His mind awash in melancholic possibilities, it began spiraling downward with each unanswered knock. Feeling the fool, he leaned his head against the door hoping that this was all just a bad dream.

In a squeaky, heavily accented tone a concerned voice asked, "Senor! Are you alright?"

Pivoting his head on the door, Johnny turned toward the direction of the voice and beheld a small swarthy looking middle-aged woman pushing a cleaning cart. "I'm fine, really," he said trying to convince himself more than this concerned person next to him. Afraid to ask at first but wanting to know, Johnny hesitantly asked, "Have you seen the lady in this room?"

Unsure if she should answer, the middle-aged woman reverted to her native tongue, "Por qué?"

Johnny sensed her reticence and mindlessly tried to mimic the woman's language. Pointing his index finger at himself then at the door, he said one word, "Amo!"

This brought a giggle to the woman's lips at first that quickly devolved into a frown. Reverting to English, she said with a heavy heart, "Senorita very sick," turning and pointing down the road, she gave a shrug, "She in hospital."

Elation, sadness and confusion mixed convulsively together in Johnny's stomach. Touching the woman's hand thankfully, he rushed to his car and drove away, unsure of where he was going. He only knew that he had to find Sandy.

Rose Teti was preening herself in front of a mirror in the bathroom of the Royal Suite in the Cibola Casino. She had accompanied Sid Greenberg on a non-stop flight from Philadelphia to Las Vegas on the previous day. Together they were going to surprise Cisco.

Unaware of her son's roller coaster plight back in South Philadelphia, Rose had never been happier in her life. Moving from the bathroom to a sitting area, she gazed out the window to the mountains encircling Las Vegas. It was an entirely different world to her. She liked it. Getting use to it would be easy, she whimsically thought.

Sandy was slowly recovering from her drug-induced sleep when Johnny appeared in the doorway of her hospital room. He spent over an hour trying to track her down, calling frantically every hospital in the phone book. He found her and she was going to be fine, just fine he benignly thought.

Mustering up a coquettish smile, Sandy's head fell to the left side as she looked at him lopsidedly. "You just keep showing up, don't you," she chided in a playful way.

"I told you I'd find you no matter where you went," he retorted with a beaming smile.

Kissing her lightly on the lips, he sat down grasping her free hand. Winking at her, he whispered, "We'll save the good stuff for later."

She managed a muted giggle.

A nurse appeared and was both surprised and happy to see someone so obviously caring sitting next to Sandy. "Oh, well, hi," she blurted out before taking Sandy's vital signs and checking her intravenous lines. "I'm glad you showed up. She was getting a little down," the nurse informed him.

"I'm not going anywhere. So don't worry."

"Sandy should be just fine in a few days," the nurse continued while making notations. "The doctor will be around this afternoon." Looking questioningly at Sandy and Johnny, the nurse wanted to know, "So, you two got plans?"

With an impish smile Johnny responded firmly with one word, "California."

Inside the large and lustrous main ballroom of the Cibola Casino, a low murmur filled the air. The room abounded with entrees in the nine-ball tournament. Some exercised their idiosyncratic dalliances such as picking lint off the felt covered pool tables or rolling the cue ball off the cushions. Others stood arms folded with dour looks on their face. All were nervous, especially Cisco.

Scanning the room for familiar faces, Cisco only found Roberto Hernandez sporting a toothy grin of self-confidence. Like poker players, pool hustlers could read the tea leaves of their opponents' mental state by looking in their eyes. Right now, Cisco showed uncertainty, a bad sign for someone playing for high stakes.

Cisco was already formulating excuses for a poor showing, knowing that Ben Greenberg was expecting the exact opposite. But thoughts of Rose tenaciously consumed Cisco skewing his focus.

Around the periphery of the room, observers eagerly awaited the first break of the tournament. Hank the Tank strolled in and assumed a director's chair, positioned strategically in such a way as to keep all the tables under scrutiny.

Magically, the room turned icily quiet. From somewhere in the shadows of the outer reaches of the room a wraithlike announcer ordered, "Would all the players proceed to their assigned tables."

Cisco shuffled over to his table specially positioned for advantageous viewing. Today's game would be a first. It was to be televised.

Taking a deep breath, Cisco chalked his cue stick, but was distracted by a waving hand. With squinted eyes, a smile splashed across his face like an ocean wave. It was Rose. Sid Greenberg ushered her to a front-row seat followed by his son, Ben.

Roberto distraughtly watched the sudden change in Cisco's demeanor. His own confidence now waning, he realized that the odds had changed in favor of the house.

A new game plan was afoot and Cisco had the edge.

77

Saturday, April 15, 1972

Dominic Pelosi found the time this afternoon to finally talk to Michael Cerone's parents. He had spoken to his brother and it was time to speak to the parents. It had occurred to him after that encounter why he found it so difficult to speak to them. In his heart he felt that Michael Cerone's death had been wasted by a government of bean counters who viewed death statistically without regarding the personal sacrifice of the individual. In the end that could be said of all wars.

No longer afraid of spouting simplistic platitudes to a man who had seen war first hand, Pelosi knew what to say. Walking up the steps to the Cerone house, Pelosi shook the rain from his head. Ringing the doorbell, he thought sullenly, the war in Vietnam was wasting good men. Michael Cerone was one of them.

The storm that had begun during the witching hour on Thursday night continued into early Saturday evening. At times torrential, the storm had a cleansing effect on Teti's life. Sequestered in his room for most of Friday, the frantic, sometimes chaotic events of the previous week replayed in Teti's mind like an old classic movie. Emotionally exhausted, he laid couchant on his bed that day trying to gather the intestinal strength to face his final gauntlet. Hoping again for divine intervention, he emerged from his sequestration to work the bar for Ralph like he had promised. Teti found tending bar had a therapeutic effect on his psyche. He enjoyed it, relishing the fact that it was quasi-productive rather than destructive and a service to those in need of a friendly face or a crutch to forget life's troubling moments. No longer able to live the lie that he had perpetrated all these years, Teti faced the ultimate conundrum.

The cook had closed the kitchen and left early. Business was slow. So, as the last patron at the bar left, Teti began the process of cleaning up, ruminating on possible solutions to his dilemma. Lost in thought, he somehow sensed a presence in the bar. Looking up, he saw the silhouette of a man framed by the doorway.

Teti stood erect arching one eyebrow in curiosity. Emerging from the darkness, the Old Man slowly walked up to the bar. "You remind me of your grandfather, back there, with that apron on cleaning up," the Old Man said in a mellifluous sforzando tone.

Teti nodded patronizingly. "Can I get you something to drink?" Teti asked in a deferential voice.

"Do you still keep grappa under the counter?"

Teti quickly produced two slim shot-like glasses and an odd shaped bottle of clear liquor. Pouring both glasses full, he delicately placed one in front of the Old Man fingering the second glass for himself. One did not drink grappa alone. It would have been a sign of disrespect.

The Old Man lifted the glass to eye level and said one word with an emphasis that came from deep within his being, "Salut!"

"Salut!" Teti echoed.

Both men quickly drained the liquor in one gulp.

Sitting on a barstool, the Old Man looked deep into Teti's eyes. An eerie silence ensued for what felt like an hour, but was merely a matter of seconds. "Americo, you are either a very lucky man or wily like a fox," he said with a hint of a smile.

"Neither. I'm just a survivor," Teti answered. Hesitantly, Teti continued, "Actually, I'm a simple man, looking to live a simple life without the complications my grandfather had to endure."

The Old Man's face broke into an understanding smile. "Ah, if life were only so obliging," he retorted with a reflective glint in his eye. Taking Carlucci's envelope from the inside pocket of his overcoat, the Old Man laid it on the bar and slid it gently toward Teti with his long bony index finger. "This belongs to you."

Teti stared at the envelope before replying. "I did nothing to earn this."

"I didn't say you did. Accept it as a gift to the start of a new and simpler life." The Old Man stood up regally and turned to exit. Swiveling around before opening the door, he authoritatively pointed a finger at Teti for emphasis, "It was what your grandfather truly wanted for you." Looking around the bar, he unfolded his hand supinely, "His real legacy to you. You're a lucky man Americo, not everyone gets another chance."

Outside Louie the Snake waited in his car. The Old Man exited the Downtown Bar & Grill breathing in the clean air that the rain had left in its wake. Deciding to walk awhile, he gestured for Louie to follow him.

Peace had come to the Old Man's little world for the time being. Tomorrow at church he would listen to the redemptive music of the Jesuit Mass at Old Saint Joseph's Church and begin lighting a second candle for the soul of Joseph Giampietro. May he finally rest in peace.

978-0-595-40612-8
0-595-40612-2